NEW YORK
UNIVERS

NEW THRILLER

THE ARK

Chosen by the American Booksellers Association as an Indie Next notable pick for May 2010

"Skillfully entwines biblical history, archaeology, and religious fanaticism with high technology to create a riveting adventure of high-stakes terror and international intrigue. Wow. This is one fine heart-stopping thriller."

—Douglas Preston

"Mach-speed mayhem. *The Ark* crackles with tension and imagination from the first page to the last. Just the right blend of menace and normality. Boyd Morrison is a writer to watch."

—Steve Berry

"*The Ark* features the perfect blend of historical mysticism and clever, classic thriller plotting. . . . Boyd Morrison manages that flawlessly in this blisteringly paced tale packed with the best twists and turns the genre has to offer."

—Jon Land

"Lightning paced, chillingly real, here is a novel that will have you holding your breath until the last page is turned. One of the best debuts I've read this year."

—James Rollins

Turn the page for more rave reviews!

"It's been a long time since I've read a novel as technologically satisfying and downright scary as Boyd Morrison's *Rogue Wave*. Morrison's smooth and savory mix of science and suspense brings the absolute best of Michael Crichton to mind. *Rogue Wave* could be this generation's *The Andromeda Strain,* a terrific page-turner tucked neatly inside a cautionary tale of our own fragile place in the ecosystem."

—Jon Land, *New York Times* bestselling author of
Strong Enough to Die

"Boyd Morrison's *Rogue Wave* is a disaster novel stripped straight out of today's headlines. As a mega-tsunami sweeps for Hawaii, readers will be caught in the riptide as Kai Tanaka fights for his family's survival. Not to be missed!"

—James Rollins, *New York Times* bestselling author of
Altar of Eden

"Boyd Morrison delivers the goods. Expertly researched and gripping, *Rogue Wave* is a pulse-pounding tale delivered by a born storyteller."

—John Case, *New York Times* bestselling author of
Ghost Dancer

"*Rogue Wave* is the best thriller I've read this year."

—Chris Kuzneski, *New York Times* bestselling author of
The Lost Throne

Rogue Wave *is also available as an eBook*

Other books by Boyd Morrison

The Ark

ROGUE WAVE

A NOVEL

BOYD MORRISON

POCKET BOOKS
New York   London   Toronto   Sydney

Pocket Books
A Division of Simon & Schuster, Inc.
1230 Avenue of the Americas
New York, NY 10020

This book is a work of fiction. Names, characters, places, and incidents either are products of the author's imagination or are used fictitiously. Any resemblance to actual events or locales or persons, living or dead, is entirely coincidental.

First Pocket Books paperback edition December 2010

POCKET BOOKS and colophon are trademarks
of Simon & Schuster, Inc.

For information about special discounts for bulk purchases, please contact Simon & Schuster Special Sales at 1-866-506-1949 or business@simonandschuster.com.

The Simon & Schuster Speakers Bureau can bring authors to your live event. For more information or to book an event, contact the Simon & Schuster Speakers Bureau at 1-866-248-3049 or visit our website at www.simonspeakers.com.

Cover design and illustration by Tony Mauro

Manufactured in the United States of America

10 9 8 7 6 5 4 3 2 1

ISBN 978-1-4391-8958-0
ISBN 978-1-4391-8960-3 (ebook)

Previously published in different form as *The Palmyra Impact*.

To Frank and Arden. I'm so glad it's you.

ACKNOWLEDGMENTS

I'd like to thank Dr. Chip McCreery and Dr. Stuart Weinstein at the Pacific Tsunami Warning Center for listening to my wild stories and showing me around the facility. Thanks also to Delores Clark of NOAA for assisting in setting up the tour.

Much appreciation to Dr. David Kriebel, professor of ocean engineering at the Naval Academy, for information about the effects of tsunamis on structures.

Thanks to Ray Lovell at Hawaii State Civil Defense for talking to me about HSCD response procedures in emergencies.

Thanks to pilot Doug Skeem for his advice on helicopters.

Thanks to my good friend Dr. Erik Van Eaton for his medical expertise.

It's great to have a brother who was an Air Force pilot, and I'd like to thank him—retired Lt. Col. Martin Westerfield—for his help with all things military and airborne.

Susan Tunis and Frank Moretti provided invaluable input on this book at an early stage, and Machelle Allman and TJ Zecca were readers who gave the book an early boost when I needed it.

This book wouldn't be in your hands if it weren't for the tireless efforts of my agent, Irene Goodman, and my editor, Abby Zidle. I'm grateful for everything they've done.

Finally, thanks to my wife, Randi, for going on this journey with me.

Civilization exists by geologic consent,
subject to change without notice.

—Will Durant

Carpe diem, quam minimum credula postero.
Seize the day, put no trust in tomorrow.

—Horace

CHAPTER 1

CAPTAIN MICHAEL ROBB OPENED his eyes and found himself lying on the cockpit floor. Heat washed over him as if the airliner had been plunged into a blast furnace, and multiple warning horns blared. Blood trickled from his brow, stinging his eye. For a second he lay there, dazed, wondering what had happened. Then he remembered. The impact.

He had just returned to the cockpit, swearing off coffee for the rest of the trip. It had been his third trip to the lavatory, and the flight from Los Angeles to Sydney wasn't even halfway over. His copilot, Wendy Jacobs, a good twenty years younger than he, had smirked at him but said nothing. He had been about to climb back into his seat when a streak of light flashed by the airliner's starboard wing.

Robb thought it was a lightning strike from the storm they were flying above, but then the plane was thrown sideways, as if batted away by a giant hand. A sonic boom blasted the plane, and he smacked into the bulkhead, his head and shoulder taking most of the blow.

He must have been out for only a few seconds. Though his mind was still fuzzy, his vision quickly came back into focus. Robb sat up and wiped the blood from his eye. The instrument panel was intact. Jacobs had disengaged the autopilot and grabbed the yoke, which she now fought for control. Robb pulled himself to his feet. He had no idea how badly he was injured, but he was moving. That was enough.

As Robb clambered into his seat, he glanced at the cabin differential pressure gauge. Its needle was pegged at zero. Explosive decompression.

Reflexively, he reached for the mask hanging to his left, years of training taking over. His shoulder protested the motion, and he winced in pain.

"Oxygen masks on, one hundred percent!" he shouted.

Robb pulled the mask over his head, and Jacobs did the same. The masks in the passenger compartment had already dropped automatically. He mentally raced through the possibilities for the blast. A terrorist bomb? Missile attack? Fuel tank explosion? To depressurize that fast, some of the passenger windows must have blown out, maybe an entire door. The aircraft was still flying though, so that meant the fuselage was intact.

With his attention focused on getting the airliner under control, there was no time for Robb to talk to the passengers. The flight attendants would have to deal with them. The best thing he could do for the passengers was to get the plane down to ten thousand feet, where there was breathable air.

He pushed the yoke forward and silenced the decompression horn, but another one continued to wail. The lights for the starboard engines flashed red, meaning both were on fire.

"Pull number three engine T-handle!" Robb barked out. He suppressed the panic edging into his voice.

Jacobs pulled the handle and pressed the button

beneath it, extinguishing the fire. She glanced out the starboard window to make a visual check.

"Fire's out on number three engine! Number four engine is completely gone!"

"Gone?"

"Sheared off from the pylon."

Robb cursed under his breath. His 747–400 was certified to fly with only three engines, but with just the two port engines they'd be lucky to stay in the air.

He turned to Jacobs. Her face was ashen but otherwise professional.

"Issue the distress call," Robb said.

Jacobs nodded, understanding the implications. Even if someone heard the radio call, it would make little difference. The best they could hope for was to report their position in case they had to ditch. She keyed the radio.

"Mayday! Mayday! Mayday! This is TransPac 823. We are going down. We are going down. We've lost both number three and number four engines. Our position is seventy-five miles bearing two four five from Palmyra VOR."

No answer, just static.

"Activate the emergency transponder," Robb said. He knew activating it was a useless procedure. They were beyond the range of any radar units.

"Setting transponder to 7700 in squawk emergency," Jacobs replied.

As their rapid descent took the plane through thirty thousand feet, an unearthly glow bloomed within the cloud cover ten miles to their right. At first the clouds softened it, but then the light pierced them, shooting toward the stratosphere, for a moment brighter than the sun.

"What the hell?" Jacobs said.

A fireball rolled upward in the distinctive mushroom shape Robb had seen in countless photos. He gaped, mesmerized by the sight. Atomic weapons testing in the Pacific had been outlawed for years, and there were no volcanoes in this region of the ocean. What else could have caused such a massive explosion?

Whatever it was, the explanation didn't matter.

"Roll left!" he yelled. Stabilizing the plane should have been his highest priority, but they had to get away from the blast zone.

"Rolling left," came Jacobs's response after only a second's hesitation.

Robb just had to hope that he could ride out the shock wave and find someplace to land. They had passed over the Palmyra Atoll only ten minutes before, but the runway built during World War II had been abandoned decades earlier. Christmas Island, five hundred miles away, had the closest operational runway. Despite all the damage the plane had sustained, it was still flying. They might make it.

"Come on, you bastard!" Robb grunted as he strained at the controls.

The nose of the enormous plane came around slowly. Too slowly.

The blast wave from the explosion caught up with them and slapped at the plane from behind, heaving its tail up. A colossal crack of thunder hammered the aircraft. The windows shattered and wind howled through the cockpit. The number one engine was wrenched from its mounts, shearing half the port wing from the plane and setting the fuel tanks aflame. The plane plummeted like an elevator cut from its cable.

With two engines gone and another shut down, the airliner was mortally wounded. Thinking of the 373 men, women, and children in the plane—people who were his responsibility—Robb didn't give up, but he had no more hope of flying it than one of the passengers. He battled the controls trying to level the plane, but it was a dead stick. Despite his efforts, the plane spun downward in a death spiral. By the time the airliner plunged through the lowest cloud layer, the altimeter read one thousand feet. For the first time in an hour, Robb could see the blue water of the Pacific.

Realizing that their fate was inevitable, Robb let go of the yoke and sat back. He held out his hand to Jacobs, who grasped it tightly with her own. Never much for religion, Robb nonetheless closed his eyes and found himself reciting the Lord's Prayer. He was up to the words "Thy kingdom come" when the plane slammed into the ocean at over five hundred miles per hour.

CHAPTER 2

THE BROCHURE WAS SLICK and professional, but Kai Tanaka still hated the idea of sending his thirteen-year-old daughter away to a scuba diving camp. He sipped his coffee at the kitchen counter as he scanned the pamphlet and thought about how to let Lani down gently.

She and her best friend, Mia, sat close together at the dinette table, talking over a magazine in low, conspiratorial tones. Then they erupted into shrill screams that dissolved into giggles while they pointed at a glossy photo.

Kai walked over to the table and made as if to get a better look at the magazine. "And what are you guys reading this morning? Is it *Newsweek* or *Car and Driver*?"

Lani quickly flipped the magazine closed. It was *Seventeen*. Mia must have brought it with her. Like most fathers, Kai couldn't help wonder at how fast they were growing up. They were barely teenagers. To him, seventeen was far in the future.

Lani giggled at Mia, and then adopted a mock-serious tone. "We're just doing some research for our trip this morning." Mia nodded in agreement.

"Uh-huh," Kai said dubiously. "*Seventeen* has an article about boogie boarding, does it?"

"Not exactly," Mia said. "But there are some tips about

beachcombing." At this, Lani and Mia erupted into another peal of laughter. Kai assumed it was something having to do with how to meet boys, but he didn't want to know.

"So, what do you think about the camp, Dad?" Lani said. "It looks awesome, doesn't it?"

Bilbo, the family's wheaten terrier, lapped noisily from his bowl, then dribbled water across the floor after he finished. Avoiding Lani's question, Kai busied himself wiping up the drool. While he threw the paper towel away, he glanced at the countertop TV. It was tuned to a Honolulu newscast with a graphic that said Breaking News, but the volume was so low that all Kai could hear was the indistinct mumbling of the anchorwoman.

"Hello? Dad? Can I go?"

"I don't know," he finally said. "When is this?"

"First week in August."

"You two are pretty young to be diving."

"I'll be fourteen next month," Lani said indignantly.

That was true, although Lani didn't look thirteen. She looked sixteen. At five foot eight, she was now taller than her mother by a good two inches, and even more distressingly, she had developed a womanly figure. Her hair was auburn, not the strawberry blond of Rachel's Irish heritage, but she had gotten her mother's delicate facial structure and lean athletic body. From Kai, she inherited the olive complexion and almond-shaped eyes of his Italian-Japanese background. To Kai's chagrin, the effect made her not only beautiful but exotic. He was going to have to plan for dates very soon, and he was terrified.

"And Teresa gave her okay?" Kai said.

Mia nodded. "I think Mom needs some alone time," she said. She was Lani's age but darker, shorter, and more petite. Kai couldn't imagine her lugging an oxygen tank around on her back.

"Where is she?" he said.

"Getting dressed," Mia said.

"So, can I go?" Lani said.

After a pause, Kai said, "I'll have to think about it."

Lani looked at Mia in disgust. "That means no."

Kai waved the brochure. "It means I have to check out this outfit, see what their safety record is. Scuba diving is a dangerous sport."

"You've been diving fifty times," Lani said, pouting.

"So I know what I'm talking about. Plus, I have to talk about it with your mother."

"She already said it was cool. We talked about it with her and Teresa while you were out jogging."

"She was *cool* with it, huh? Maybe I should just confirm that with her."

Usually Rachel's Monday shift didn't begin until ten a.m., but that morning she had to be at the Grand Hawaiian early for the disabled vets' brunch. As the hotel manager, she wanted to make sure everything was perfect, especially because the governor would be addressing the veterans. Kai dialed her cell.

"Hello?" Rachel said above a truck horn honking in the background. She was still on the road. Even on a holiday, the commute from Ewa Beach to Honolulu wasn't fun.

"Traffic?" he said, moving into the family room to get a little privacy.

"As usual."

"You sound tired."

"I didn't get much sleep last night. Teresa and I were up late talking. It's great to have her and Mia in town, but I'm going to be exhausted by the end of the week. Is she there?"

"I think she's getting into her swimsuit."

"Ask her to give me a call on her way to the beach."

"I will. So Lani had a surprise for me this morning."

"About the scuba camp? I think it's a fantastic idea."

"You do?"

"Sure. Why not?"

"Because she's thirteen. You can't even get certified until you're fifteen."

"It sounds like a wonderful program. Master instructors, top-notch facilities, lots of fun activities. One of the mothers in Lani's class raved about it."

Kai didn't bother to ask which mother. He wouldn't know her. Taking the post of assistant director at the Pacific Tsunami Warning Center had been a great career move for him, but he hadn't counted on how demanding it would be. Including Kai, there were only eight geophysicists on staff, and the PTWC had to be monitored by two of them twenty-four hours a day. That meant they regularly had to pull twelve-hour shifts. Kai had been so busy that he'd participated in only one parent-teacher conference.

"Lani has to have something to look forward to," Rachel said. "She's been here nine months now and hasn't made any friends yet."

"What do you mean? She hangs out with her soccer friends all the time."

"Getting pizza after the game with her teammates doesn't count. In the whole time we've been here, she hasn't once brought somebody back home. Now that she's with Mia, I see how she used to be in Seattle. And being in that compound hasn't helped."

"Please don't call it a compound." Kai hated that word.

It was difficult to recruit geophysicists who were willing to spend that many hours on-site, so to sweeten the deal, the National Oceanic and Atmospheric Administration—better known as NOAA, the parent organization of the PTWC—built houses on the Center grounds that some of the staff lived in for free. As assistant director, Kai had been given one of the houses. The biggest perk was that it was only three blocks from the beach, but the run-down neighborhood around the complex wasn't safe enough for Lani to explore on her own.

"She feels isolated there," Rachel said.

"Maybe we can do more family outings, like the luau tonight."

"Kai, your heart's in the right place, but she needs to learn some independence. She isn't going to be your little girl forever."

"Oh, yes she will."

"You know what I mean."

"Yeah," Kai said with a sigh, "I know. But I still think she should wait to do this scuba camp until next year."

"Listen, I'm about to go into the garage, so you're going to lose me. Just think about it, and we'll talk more this evening. All right?"

"Okay. I'll think about it."

With a click, Rachel was gone.

"So you got the spiel, huh?" a voice behind him said.

Kai turned to see Teresa Gomez. Like the girls, she was already dressed in a tank top and sarong over her bikini.

"Oh yeah," Kai said. "The hard sell."

"What's the verdict?"

"Still thinking about it."

"Good luck with that. I lasted about five minutes." She yawned and stretched her arms. "I need to mainline some more coffee."

Kai followed her back into the kitchen. Lani and Mia stopped giggling and looked at him expectantly.

"Still thinking about it," he said, eliciting a groan. He handed the coffeepot to Teresa. "I heard you stayed up late with Rachel to continue our conversation after I went to bed."

"She can't hear enough about my residency program. Sometimes I think she's the one who should have gone to med school." As she filled her mug, Teresa looked at the TV. A TransPac Airlines logo was next to the anchorwoman's shoulder. "I hope to God it's sunny today. If I came all the way from Seattle for more rain, I'll curl up into the fetal position."

"Don't worry. The report earlier said no rain is projected, so you and the girls should have great weather today."

"If it's your day off, grab your towel and come with us."

"Day off? I wish. I'm on call today. I have to give a tour this morning, and there's a paper I'm submitting to the *Science of Tsunami Hazards* next month that I've got to finish."

Teresa appraised Kai's outfit and began to laugh. "I forgot. We're in Hawaii."

He looked down at his clothes and realized why she was laughing. To a Seattleite like Teresa, the flowered shirt, khakis, and tennis shoes he was wearing might seem like weekend wear, but it was perfectly normal office attire for him.

"This is formal wear for me," he said with a laugh. "Where are you guys boarding?"

"Well, *I* wanted to go somewhere quiet, but no, I got vetoed!" She jabbed a finger at the girls. "So it's Waikiki. While they're swimming, I plan to sit my butt down and do absolutely nothing."

Kai winced. Because of the holiday, Waikiki would be packed not only with tourists but with locals as well. May was a big month for travelers, and three-day weekends were always popular with American tourists from the mainland. Almost fifty thousand visitors stayed in Honolulu at any one time, and Waikiki claimed most of them. Teresa would be hard pressed to find any peace on the beach.

"I think they just want to check out the eye candy," she said.

"We do not!" said Lani.

But Mia at the same time said "Yeah!" and Lani turned red.

Kai tried to help Teresa out. "Why don't you go to Kahana Valley? There's a great beach there."

"It's boring," Lani said. "If I finally get to go to a beach, I want to go to a good one."

"What do you mean? We go to our beach all the time."

"Yeah, right. Only when you're with me. What's the use of living three blocks from the beach if I have to wait for you to take me?"

"Here we go," Kai said. To Teresa: "One time, I saw some kids smoking dope down at the little park that leads to the beach. Now she's mad that I won't let her go on her own."

"If I didn't live in this compound, I might have someone to go with."

"Why does everyone call it that?" Kai said.

"I'm sure it's not because of the barbed wire and security gate," Lani said, her sarcasm reaching new heights. "Come on, Mia. Let's get our stuff."

They ran off to Lani's bedroom.

"Good God," Teresa said. "You know the attitudes are only going to get worse as the day goes on. I'll pay you a thousand dollars to switch places with me."

Kai laughed and shook his head. "No way. I like having the easy job." Kai handed her the keys to his Jeep. "When do you think you'll be back?"

"If I can endure it, I'm thinking around five. That way I'll have plenty of time to recover before the luau tonight."

"Perfect," Kai said. "The boogie boards are in the garage."

"We'll get them!" yelled Lani from the other room.

As he and Teresa went outside, Kai paused to turn off the TV. Just before he clicked it off, he noticed a new graphic saying AIRLINER MISSING OVER PACIFIC.

CHAPTER 3

T HE RAIN HAD BEEN falling constantly for two hours now, but that didn't keep Yvonne Dunlap from her duties. In her three weeks on the Palmyra Atoll, she had come to appreciate the damp weather, which gave the island a serene quality. Even with 175 inches of rain per year watering the lush vegetation, she could think of worse places to do scientific research.

She picked her way across the beach looking for her quarry, avoiding the plastic garbage that marred the otherwise pristine habitat. Dark clouds stretched to the horizon, broken only by an occasional flash of lightning in the distance. The breaking surf and soothing patter of rain were her only companions.

None of Yvonne's three colleagues on the island had joined her on this excursion. They were back at base camp, working on their computers out of the rain, compiling figures about the nesting habits of sooty terns or analyzing data about the impact of non-native species on the island's flora.

Yvonne had come hunting much more interesting prey than birds and shrubbery. Her graduate studies in invertebrate biology had brought her to this isolated outpost for one reason. And it didn't take long for her to spot what she was looking for. She took out her digital camera and approached slowly to add more photos to her collection.

An enormous blue coconut crab scurried up a thick palm tree looking for its favorite food. This rare example looked like it measured three feet across and weighed close to ten pounds, a size that would put most Maine lobsters to shame.

The Nature Conservancy had purchased the Palmyra Atoll as a wildlife preserve. To minimize the impact of humans on the ecosystem, they granted only a limited number of permits to researchers. Yvonne was one of the lucky few, and she reveled in exploring the island's natural wonders. Rainy mornings like this were especially good for her outings, giving her time to enjoy nature as it was meant to be, alone and in silence. To her, the experience was spiritual.

Yvonne interrupted her photography to jot some notes in her journal. The crab in front of her was one of the finest specimens she'd ever seen, and she wanted a full record of it. At the top of the tree, the crab grasped a coconut in its claws and ripped it open like a ripe melon, tearing at the meat inside. Yvonne was setting her camera to video mode to capture its eating ritual when a great boom echoed across the island. The sound was so loud that she dropped the camera.

The crab, also startled by the noise, dropped from the tree and scuttled back to the safety of its burrow. Yvonne stooped to pick up the camera, waiting for the thunder to abate. She searched for the source of the noise, but the clouds looked uniformly gray in all directions. Nothing suggested a major storm headed their way.

In a minute the sound dissipated, and Yvonne strode over to the hole the crab had disappeared into. She plopped herself on a fallen log not far from it and waited for the crab to reemerge, aiming her camera in hopes of a close-up.

She continued staring at the burrow until a new noise intruded on the soft drizzle. A rumble from the island's interior. At its widest, the Palmyra Atoll was only a half mile across. For some reason, Yvonne thought the sound was reaching her from the opposite side of the island.

She stood and peered into the thick foliage. The noise grew quickly, coming toward her. It sounded like a thousand elephants stampeding, knocking down every tree as they charged. Yvonne stepped back involuntarily, stopping only when her boots were splashed by the surf.

She spotted movement in the forest. It was indistinct at first, but within seconds it resolved into an image that took Yvonne a moment to comprehend. A churning mass of water raged toward her, uprooting and splintering every tree in its path. She couldn't have been more shocked than if it had actually been elephants.

She froze, paralyzed, her voice choked by fear. The roar was so loud that it seemed to go through her, and the wind pushed before the wall of water blew the hood of her windbreaker backward. Yvonne's eyes locked in terror on the rushing mountain of debris, and she hopelessly wished that she could find some kind of burrow to plunge into as the crab had done.

As the water reached the beach, the closest palm tree—the same one that had seemed so solid when the crab had climbed it—was yanked out of the ground. Just before it crushed Yvonne, she finally screamed.

CHAPTER 4

A S WAS USUAL ON Oahu, the May morning was bright blue, with just a few wisps of mist perched on the mountains northeast of Honolulu. The flowers lining the path contributed their sweet aroma to the ocean breeze that tickled the trees. The forecast was eighty and sunny. Kai sighed contentedly as he soaked in the warmth. Teresa and the kids couldn't have picked better weather for a day at the beach.

They were busy packing the boogie boards into the Jeep when the center's security gate hummed to life. Kai saw a jet black Harley idling on the other side, the distinctive exhaust gurgling.

"Oh no," he said.

"What's with the Hell's Angel?" Teresa said.

"It's Brad."

"The playboy, huh? This ought to be good."

"Don't say I didn't warn you."

"Believe me, I'm immune. Divorce will do that for you. What's he doing here?"

"I have no idea, but I bet I won't like it." Since Kai's move back to Hawaii, Brad stopped by on a regular basis to pester Kai into doing something crazy with him, usually while Kai was supposed to be working.

Brad tore up the drive at a rate that Kai didn't think

possible. He screeched to a stop next to the group, hopped off his bike, and flipped off his mirrored helmet in one move. Kai felt a flare of envy at Brad's effortless grace, which complemented his rugged surfer-dude appeal.

Brad ruffled his fingers through his thick blond hair and clapped Kai on the shoulder.

"Great day for a round of golf, wouldn't you say?" Brad waved to the sky as if it had bestowed this day at his request.

Before Kai could answer, Lani ran up and jumped into Brad's arms.

"Uncle Brad!"

"Hello, my darlin'!" He spun her around and then dropped her and gave her a huge smile. "You are looking as pretty as ever. What? You're heading to the beach and didn't invite me?"

Another voice piped up. It was Mia.

"You can come with us if you want," she said, her eyes wide at the sight of Brad's tight T-shirt, muscular arms, and sky blue eyes. Her mouth was slightly agape, as if she couldn't believe what she was seeing. He usually had that effect on women, even thirteen-year-olds.

"And you must be the lovely Mia I've heard so much about." Brad took her hand and gave it a gentle squeeze. Kai thought Mia would melt into the pavement.

"And I must be her mother, Teresa Gomez," Teresa said. She seemed unaffected by Brad's physical gifts and looked a little disturbed at her daughter's reactions to this thirty-five-year-old smooth talker.

"Brad Hopkins." They shook hands. "So you're the doctor?"

"Third-year resident."

"Well, it's great you got some time off to come visit. I see you're ready to enjoy our fine weather." Brad looked her in the eye, but Kai knew he had already given her tall, tan figure the once-over from behind that mirrored visor.

Teresa rolled her eyes, but Kai could see that she was amused. "Your brother is exactly like you said he was."

Even though the only physical feature Brad and Kai shared was their six-foot height, they were indeed brothers. Half brothers, specifically. When Kai was four, his father died of cancer. Kai's mother remarried within a year. She was wooed by Charles Hopkins, owner of Hopkins Realty, one of the most successful real estate companies in the islands. They immediately produced Kai's little brother, Brad, and Charles adopted Kai. Although Kai kept his birth father's last name, they were a close family. But it was apparent from an early age that Charles was grooming Brad to take over the business. That was fine with Kai. He had no interest in real estate or business. Science was always his passion.

When their parents died in a car crash five years ago, the estate had been split between them, but Brad kept control of the company. Being a consummate playboy, he enjoyed the freedom the business gave him. He could party all night, play golf the next morning, and still have time to close a major hotel deal before the sun set. No wife, no kids, no responsibility for anything but his business. Even though Kai loved his life, sometimes he wished he could trade places with Brad.

Brad flicked his eyes at Kai. "So I hope all you heard was good things about me."

"Don't worry, haole," Kai said. "Your dark secrets are safe with me."

"Haole?" Teresa said to Brad. "That your nickname?"

Brad laughed. "To some people. It's Hawaiian for 'white boy.' At least he didn't call me 'ass-haole.'"

Kai shook his head in mock disgust. "See what I have to deal with? I'm thinking about changing the gate code. Again."

"It is so freakin' boring around here, you need me to come in and liven things up." Brad winked at Teresa. "I swear, this is the most secure nerd farm in the world. I don't know why they need a fence around this place, anyway. Who wants to break in here?"

"That decision was before my time, after the Oklahoma City bombing. I suppose the higher-ups thought some nut would think we were a secret CIA base and try to blow us up."

"Whatever. Come on, Kai. Let's go shoot a round of golf."

"I have work to do this morning. Some of us work most days."

"Today is Memorial Day, you know. A holiday?"

"Not for me. The director is on vacation, so I'm in charge while he's gone."

"So give yourself the day off," Brad said. "Hop on."

"You know there's no way I'm getting on that thing. You drive like a maniac, and I hate donorcycles." Kai had adopted Teresa's nickname for motorcycles, so-called because a disproportionate number of organ donations came from motorcycle crash victims. "You're about as likely to get me on that thing as I am to get you scuba diving."

Brad's smile vanished. "That's not funny."

"Why not?" Teresa said.

"He had a scuba diving accident a long time ago."

"It wasn't an accident," Brad said with a scowl. "It was a near-death experience."

"You've got my attention," Teresa said. "What happened?"

"He's exaggerating," Kai said. "Nobody got hurt. We were diving in a shipwreck off Oahu, and a rusty bulkhead came apart, blocking the door. Brad got locked inside, and his oxygen gauge almost pegged zero before we could get him out."

"Now I know why you were reluctant about the scuba camp," Teresa said.

"I didn't want to scare you."

"He *should* scare you," Brad said. "My Harley is a hundred times safer than scuba diving."

"I'm not coming with you," Kai said.

"Okay," Brad said, and the smile returned bigger than ever. "But you're missing out on some easy money. I'm playing with a couple of guys from Ma'alea Realty. They have no idea you and I are two-handicaps. I've already got them up to twenty bucks per hole. With any luck, I can double it with a little creative playing on the first couple of holes."

"I'm not going to swindle a couple of guys out of their money. If they want to play a fair round . . . Wait a minute. Why am I even talking about this? I'm not going."

"If you want to spend the day inside, it's your loss." Brad turned to Teresa. "I'll buy you a mai tai tonight at the luau and dispel all those lies Kai told you." Brad lowered his voice and spoke into Kai's ear. "Make sure my seat is next to Teresa's." Then he made a slight bow to the girls. "Ciao, ladies!"

In a well-choreographed motion, Brad put his helmet

on, fired up the Harley, and peeled off, much to Lani and Mia's delight. When he was gone, the girls finished putting their supplies in the Jeep.

"He's a good guy," Kai said, "but he can be a little much to take."

"Don't you dare let Rachel try to play matchmaker. I'm very happy being on my own right now."

"I wouldn't dream of it," Kai said. "I'll make sure you don't get stuck with him all night."

"I'll hold you to that," she said, climbing in. She unrolled her window and nodded at the center's main building, a low, squat structure typical of the government cinder-block construction from the 1940s. It was bland but tidy, with a fresh coat of whitewash and neatly manicured hedges. The words "Richard H. Hagemeyer Pacific Tsunami Warning Center" were emblazoned on the front of the building in large letters, honoring a longstanding director of the National Weather Service. It was only a hundred yards from Kai's house.

"Must be nice being a thirty-second walk from the office," Teresa said.

"Not always."

"I get it. The good part is being close to work. The bad part is being close to work."

"Exactly."

Teresa laughed. "All right, you two," she said to the girls. "Seat belts."

"Oh, I almost forgot," Kai said. "Rachel wants you to call her on your way."

"Okay. And I might as well get your number in case I have to reach you." Teresa dug her cell phone from her purse and flipped it open. "Oh, crap!"

"What's the matter?" Kai said.

"I didn't charge my phone last night. The battery is almost dead."

"Now, don't you wish we had *my* cell phone here?" Mia said.

Teresa swiveled in her seat. "What I wish is that I had taken it away from you *before* we got that bill for three hundred dollars' worth of text messages last month." She swung back around to Kai. "What's your number?" Their fingers pecked at the phones as they traded info.

"I'll just talk to Rachel for a minute," Teresa said. "If I don't answer my phone, you'll know why."

"No problem," Kai said.

They gave a wave and were off. Kai patted Bilbo on the head.

"Looks like it's just us boys now," he said, but the dog was already sniffing around the hibiscus bushes and making his mark.

Kai's cell phone rang. He opened it assuming it was Rachel, but the caller ID told him it was the PTWC. He punched the Talk button and heard the voice of Reggie Pona, the only other geophysicist staffing the Center that morning.

"Hey, Kai," Reggie said. "I tried you at home but no answer. Are you around?"

"I'm standing outside. Just saw the family off."

"As you can see, the tour group isn't here yet. But I thought you might want a few minutes to look at something before they get here."

"Why? What's up?"

"I just issued a tsunami bulletin."

CHAPTER 5

THE GRAND HAWAIIAN WAS the newest and swankiest of the luxury hotels lining Waikiki Beach. Constructed over the razed remains of a 1940s apartment building, the 1,065-room hotel was the brainchild of a Las Vegas resort mogul looking for new locations to expand his empire. An airy pedestrian skybridge at the sixth-floor conference facility connected its two twenty-eight-story towers.

Rachel strode onto the skybridge from her offices in the Akamai tower toward the main ballroom in the Moana tower, carefully reviewing the checklist for the disabled veterans brunch while she walked. The governor of Hawaii was scheduled to address the group and then accompany them to a remembrance ceremony at the Hawaii State Veterans Cemetery. It was the biggest event in the young hotel's history, and she was on the hook to make sure everything went off without a hitch.

As she ran through the routine checklist, Rachel couldn't help but think about her late-night conversation with Teresa. As a resident, Teresa was charged with saving patients on a daily basis, making a fundamental difference in their lives and those of their families. Rachel, on the other hand, was responsible for making sure that there were enough servings of mahi mahi at the brunch.

Her job as a hotel manager was comfortable and paid well, but being a doctor had to be infinitely more rewarding. Rachel had thought about going into medicine long ago, but for financial reasons she never seriously considered it. So when she met Teresa, it was Rachel's opportunity to help someone else achieve her dream.

Teresa had been a nurse when she introduced herself to Kai and Rachel during Lamaze class. Teresa and Rachel had hit it off immediately, but the lout Teresa was married to at the time didn't get along as well with Kai. The two women got even closer once Rachel, after years of working on Teresa, finally convinced her to pursue her passion and go to med school. Teresa's husband, who wanted her to give up working altogether and become a stay-at-home mother with five children, filed for divorce. To make things worse, it also turned out that he'd been having serial affairs on his business trips. During that difficult period, Teresa had leaned on Rachel, and Lani and Mia spent every non-school hour together.

When Kai accepted his new job, Lani was devastated about leaving Mia. So as soon as Teresa had a week off from her third year of residency, she planned a trip to Hawaii, and the Tanakas happily agreed to host them.

With Teresa visiting, Rachel was reminded that she had abandoned her dreams for practicality, and she didn't want her daughter to make the same mistake. If Lani wanted to become a scuba diving instructor or a professional soccer player or anything else, Rachel wanted her to have that opportunity.

Halfway across the bridge, Rachel was so deep in thought that she nearly ran into Bob Lateen, the chairman of the veterans conference. His frown told her she was about to have another problem.

She shook off her reverie. "Can I help you, Mr. La-teen?"

"Mrs. Tanaka," Lateen said, keeping up with Rachel in his motorized wheelchair while she walked, "you assured us that we would have sufficient accommodations for our accessibility needs, but there is a serious situation in the ballroom that needs to be taken care of immediately."

Rachel squinted from the sunlight streaming through the floor-to-ceiling windows of the skybridge but still maintained a polite smile.

"Mr. Lateen, I want you to know that we take your concerns very seriously, and we value your patronage. I will do anything I can to help. Now, what's the problem?"

They exited the bridge and came into a lavish foyer. Some of the attendees were already milling about. Rachel and Lateen weaved their way through and entered the Kamehameha Ballroom, the largest in the hotel.

"The problem," Lateen said, "is that we are supposed to start the brunch in less than an hour, and I can't even get onto the dais."

He pointed to the wide raised table at the back of the ballroom. On the right side, a standard staircase led up to the dais. On the left side, a short ramp had been constructed over the staircase. Now Rachel could see the problem.

As instructed, a ramp had been installed, but whoever oversaw the construction either hadn't done it before or hadn't thought about the needs of the person that would be using it. They had essentially laid the ramp directly over the stairs, canting it up at a slope impossible for anyone in a wheelchair to negotiate.

"If I use that ramp," Lateen continued, "I will look like

an idiot because I will have to have three people help me up. They might as well carry me up the stairs on the other side."

"I understand the problem, sir. Let me contact the contractor. We'll have this fixed before the brunch starts." She pulled out her walkie-talkie.

"Max, is the dais contractor still in the hotel?"

Max Walsh, her assistant manager, picked up immediately.

"I'm just signing some papers with him," Max said.

"Put him on the walkie-talkie. Now."

A second of silence elapsed before John Chaver, the contractor, came on the line.

"This is John."

"John, this is Rachel Tanaka. You and your men need to come back up here immediately. The ramp is installed improperly."

"It's built according to my specs."

She edged away from Lateen so that she was out of earshot and explained the problem with the dais. This guy picked the wrong day to mess with her.

"The ramp is useless. Now, if you want to continue to do business at this hotel—a hotel that's scheduled to have over a hundred and fifty conferences this year—you better get back up here and fix that ramp in the next twenty minutes."

"Just a minute."

Another few moments of silence. Then Chaver came back sounding much more contrite.

"I'm sorry, Mrs. Tanaka. I just checked with one of my guys. He installed the wrong ramp. We've got the right one in our truck. I'll be there in a minute."

"Good." Rachel walked back to Lateen. "A Mr. Lateen

will be up here to describe exactly what he needs," she told Chaver. "He is a very important guest, and I expect you to extend him every courtesy."

"Of course. I'm on my way."

She replaced the walkie-talkie on her belt.

"Thank you, Mrs. Tanaka," Lateen said. "I appreciate your help."

"Not at all. I'm sorry for the inconvenience. I hope this won't discourage you from using our hotel in the future."

"If we get this fixed, you can consider me satisfied."

Chaver arrived, and Rachel left him with Lateen to get the ramp changed.

As she walked away, her cell phone rang. It was Teresa.

"Are you still awake?" she said.

"Are you kidding?" Teresa said. "Most nights I'd kill for five hours' sleep."

"Thanks for staying up late. You've got so many good stories about the hospital."

"I just told you the glamorous stuff. Tonight I'll tell you the things I normally deal with, like strung-out junkies, idiotic insurance forms, and every bodily fluid you can imagine. It's not pretty."

"I'm still proud of you."

"Yeah, well, I'm proud of you too."

"For what?"

"For having such a great family. You've got something good going there."

"I know. Thanks."

"Okay, I gotta go. The juice on my cell is running low."

"Wait! The reason I wanted you to call was because I reserved you a spot in the Grand Hawaiian parking garage. Just tell them I sent you."

"You kick ass, Rachel! I'll see you later."

"Bye."

Rachel got only two steps back into the skybridge when her walkie-talkie crackled to life. It was Max.

"Rachel, we have a problem with the Russian tour group."

"What's the problem? Something with their rooms?"

"I don't know. I can't understand them. But they're getting pretty irate."

"There's no interpreter?"

"Nope. And none of them speaks a word of English."

"That may be the problem. Where are they?"

"Second-floor mezzanine."

"I'll be right there."

Rachel stopped and leaned against the skybridge railing. She took a deep breath to gather herself as she watched thousands of carefree people enjoying their holiday on the beach. Then she headed to the elevators, ready to take on the day's next emergency.

CHAPTER 6

Kai WASN'T WORRIED ABOUT the tsunami information bulletin Reggie had issued. It was a standard message issued whenever sensors picked up seismic activity in the Pacific basin that might be powerful enough to generate a tsunami. Since it hadn't been a tsunami *warning,* the event must have been between 6.5 and 7.5 on the moment magnitude scale, fairly common readings that rarely resulted in a tsunami. Below 6.5, they didn't even bother to issue a notification.

The bulletin was sent to all of the other monitoring stations in the Pacific as well as the West Coast/Alaska Tsunami Warning Center in Palmer, Alaska, which served as the warning center for Alaska, British Columbia, and the west coast of the United States. The PTWC covered the rest of the Pacific. All of the emergency and civil defense organizations in the Pacific Rim were notified, including the U.S. military, which had extensive bases in the Pacific.

None of these organizations had to take any action; the message was strictly to inform them of a seismic event and its potential to generate a tsunami. Already that year, the PTWC had issued over forty bulletins. None had actually resulted in a tsunami.

Once the bulletin was issued, the real work started.

They had to analyze the data to determine how likely it was that a destructive tsunami was heading for a populated coastline. If the event happened off the coast of Alaska, the closest tsunamigenic zone to Hawaii, remotely operated buoys called Deep-ocean Assessment and Reporting of Tsunamis buoys—commonly called DART buoys—would be able to tell the size and velocity of a tsunami headed across the Pacific. While much of the work was computer-automated now, it still took a lot of sweat to verify the threat and calculate specific wave arrival times. It only took five hours for a tsunami to reach Hawaii from Alaska, which was barely enough time to mount a coordinated mass evacuation.

The interior of the PTWC was just as neat and functional as the exterior. A reception area greeted visitors, and next to it was a small conference room. The receptionist, Julie, had the day off, as did most of the rest of the staff. Kai picked up a sheet of paper lying on the front desk to look at the specifics of the school group that would be touring the facility that morning. Since the Southeast Asian tsunami disaster, tours had become much more in demand. When Julie had scheduled the tour for Memorial Day, Kai was a bit surprised that a school would want to do anything that day that didn't involve sand and surf. Then she told him the school group was from Japan, one of the countries covered by the PTWC, and it made sense.

He scanned the sheet. Twelve sixth graders from Tokyo for a thirty-minute tour, escorted by a teacher fluent in English. They planned to be done by nine thirty and move on to a full day of sightseeing.

These students might actually be interested in what I have to say, Kai thought. Sometimes he'd get a school group of bored American teenagers who'd be itching to leave as soon as they got there. Kai couldn't get those tours over fast enough.

He dropped the sheet back onto the counter and patted Bilbo.

"Come on. Let's find out what's going on."

Following Bilbo, Kai walked the few steps into the data analysis facility, which was packed with state-of-the-art computers and seismic sensing equipment. Huge maps of the Pacific lined two of the walls. Since the news media often got information faster than the PTWC did, the two TVs on either side of the room were perpetually tuned to CNN. He and Reggie spent most of their time in this room. Still farther back in the building were the individual cubicles and Kai's tiny office.

Normally, George Huntley and Mary Grayson, the two most junior geophysicists, would be manning computers on the other side of the room. It hadn't taken Kai long to realize they had started a relationship, and the last he had heard, they had both taken their day off to go surfing together on the North Shore.

Three of the other scientists were attending a conference that week in San Francisco, while the director, Harry Dupree, was on a three-day holiday to Maui.

Kai found Reggie hunched over a computer monitor, munching on an egg salad sandwich, the empty wrapper of a second sandwich lying next to him. When Reggie heard the dog's claws clicking on the linoleum, he looked up.

"Thanks for joining us this fine morning," Reggie said. "I thought maybe you were gonna play hooky today."

Kai nodded toward Reggie's sandwich, which was already half its previous size. "Is there ever a time of day when you don't eat?"

"Hey, I don't want to get all skinny like you."

There was no danger of that. Reggie Pona, a huge bear of a man who used to be a defensive lineman at Stanford, must have weighed at least three hundred pounds. Reggie was also one of the brightest geophysicists Kai had ever met. A Samoan by birth, he had used his college football scholarship to accomplish his true goal of becoming a scientist.

Reggie took a bite and continued to talk while he chewed. "I thought you might go with your friends to the beach. Teresa is hot, by the way."

"You know, sometimes you almost convince me that you're not a nerd," Kai said. "But then you open your mouth to talk and remind me. Besides, I couldn't leave you alone with all those impressionable sixth graders. You scared the bejesus out of the last group."

"I was just telling it like it is."

"But did you have to show those pictures from Sri Lanka? I think ten-year-olds are a little young to see photos of dead bodies."

"Hey, if it keeps them from running down to the shore during the next tsunami warning, I've done my job."

"Yeah, well, maybe I'll do the next few tours. Where's the bulletin?"

Reggie handed Kai a sheet of paper. On it was the date followed by a standard tsunami information message:

TSUNAMI BULLETIN NUMBER 001
PACIFIC TSUNAMI WARNING CENTER/NOAA/NWS
ISSUED AT 1858Z

THIS BULLETIN IS FOR ALL AREAS OF THE PA-
CIFIC BASIN EXCEPT

ALASKA—BRITISH COLUMBIA—WASHINGTON—
OREGON—CALIFORNIA.

. . . TSUNAMI INFORMATION BULLETIN . . .

THIS MESSAGE IS FOR INFORMATION ONLY.
THERE IS NO TSUNAMI WARNING
OR WATCH IN EFFECT.

AN EARTHQUAKE HAS OCCURRED WITH THESE
PRELIMINARY PARAMETERS

ORIGIN TIME—1858Z
COORDINATES—7.1 NORTH 166.4 WEST
LOCATION—NORTHWEST OF CHRISTMAS IS-
LAND, KIRIBATI ISLANDS
MAGNITUDE—6.6

EVALUATION

A DESTRUCTIVE TSUNAMI WAS NOT GENERATED
BASED ON EARTHQUAKE AND
HISTORICAL TSUNAMI DATA.

THIS WILL BE THE ONLY BULLETIN ISSUED FOR
THIS EVENT UNLESS ADDITIONAL INFORMATION
BECOMES AVAILABLE.

THE WEST COAST/ALASKA TSUNAMI WARNING
CENTER WILL ISSUE BULLETINS
FOR ALASKA—BRITISH COLUMBIA—
WASHINGTON—OREGON—CALIFORNIA.

Kai looked at Reggie. "It doesn't seem like anything to be concerned about."

Normally Kai would consult with Harry, but today Reggie and Kai were on their own. Although Kai was growing more comfortable with his responsibilities, he was still fairly new. This was the first bulletin issued while he was in charge.

The previous assistant director had left for NOAA headquarters in Washington to coordinate the development of a worldwide tsunami warning system. Kai's position at NOAA's Center for Tsunami Research put him on the short list of replacement candidates. From Kai's perspective, the job had seemed perfect. He could move his career forward while still doing interesting research. Rachel had plenty of job opportunities at Honolulu hotels. And Kai could finally get out of Seattle's rainy climate and back to warm, sunny Hawaii.

"No, it shouldn't be anything to worry about," said Reggie. "But it *is* pretty exciting."

"Why?"

"I'll get to that in a minute. But the threat of a tsunami is almost negligible because the event was not tsunamigenic." The statement was made as a fact, not an opinion.

"You seem pretty confident."

Reggie smiled. He always smiled when he was about to explain something that was perfectly obvious to him. "It barely triggered the alarms. The reading was just 6.6. A couple of ticks down, and we wouldn't have even sent the bulletin."

"Remember the Asia tsunami?" Kai said. "The initial readings on that were 8.0. It ended up being a 9.0." Because the moment magnitude scale for earthquakes—a successor to the Richter scale—is nonlinear, the power of an earthquake goes up exponentially the higher it is on the scale: an earthquake measuring 9.0 releases over thirty times more energy than an 8.0 earthquake.

"I'm just checking with NEIC now, but I don't see it going up much." The seismic equipment at the National Earthquake Information Center monitored data readings from stations around the world, allowing them to determine the location of an earthquake to within a hundred meters.

"And," Reggie continued, "the seismic wave patterns suggest a strike-slip event." Strike-slip faults move sideways instead of vertically. Vertical displacements of the ocean floor cause most tsunamis, like the one that had struck South Asia in 2004.

"Besides, it's in an area that has never generated a tsunami. That's actually why I called you," said Reggie. "Look at this." He pointed at the computer monitor.

The screen showed a map of the central Pacific with a blue dot pinpointing a position five hundred miles northwest of Christmas Island, southwest of the Palmyra Atoll. The color blue meant that the quake was located near the earth's surface.

"What's the distance from here?"

"About two thousand kilometers," said Reggie. A little more than twelve hundred miles.

Kai did the quick mental calculation in his head that was second nature to all tsunami scientists. Since all tsunamis traveled at approximately five hundred miles per hour in open ocean—about the speed of a jet airliner—it was easy math. But before Kai could speak, Reggie handed him a printout.

"Already got it."

The printout showed a list of station names and codes of all of the tide gauges in the Pacific Ocean. Next to each station name was its latitude, longitude, and the estimated arrival time for the potential tsunami.

"Looks like that gives us between two and two and a half hours."

"I'm predicting we'll barely see a tide change," said Reggie. "The tide sensor at Christmas Island will tell us for sure."

Kai looked back at the printout. Any wave generated by the event would reach Christmas Island in thirty-five minutes.

He checked the tide gauge schedule. Most of the tide gauges would transmit their readings to a satellite, which then got relayed to the PTWC. Although the gauges were cheap to produce and monitored tide levels twenty-four hours a day, their main drawback was that they sent the tide-level data only once an hour.

Kai scanned the list to find Christmas Island. The next transmission would be only five minutes after the wave was supposed to arrive there.

"Show me the earthquake map."

Reggie clicked on the appropriate icon, and colored dots bloomed on the map around the blue marker. The circles showed the seismic events around the Pacific Rim, with the different colors representing the depths of the events. A few red stars punctuated the map, showing where tsunamis had started. None of the stars was located within five hundred miles of the blue dot.

"That area has never even had an earthquake," Kai said.

"Weird, huh?" Reggie said. "I'd guess one of two things.

First, it could be a fault that we've never detected before."

"Highly unlikely."

"Right. But second—and this is the exciting part—it could be a new seamount. That would explain why it's so shallow."

Now Kai understood Reggie's excitement. A new seamount was a rare phenomenon, essentially the birth of a new island. An underwater volcano erupted over a magma hot spot on the ocean floor, building a mountain around itself and regularly unleashing earthquakes in the process. If the seamount got high enough, it broke through the surface of the water, which is exactly how the Hawaiian Islands were formed and were still forming, as the continual eruption of Kilauea on the Big Island spectacularly demonstrated.

If this event did turn out to be a seamount, Reggie would get the credit for discovering it. For a geophysicist, it was analogous to an astronomer finding a new comet.

"Congratulations," Kai said. "If it turns out to be a new seamount, you'll get journal articles out of it for the next five years."

"Damn straight." Reggie winked. "If you're good to me, I might have room to put you as second author."

"Your generosity is overwhelming." Reggie let out a huge belly laugh at that. "But before we start celebrating," Kai continued, "let's make sure that we're not dealing with a tsunami here. You're doing the usual?"

"Other than figuring out a name for my seamount," Reggie said, "I'm working with the NEIC to pinpoint the quake more precisely. I'm also scanning the ANSS database to check our readings against theirs." They had a direct feed from the Advanced National Seismic System, the data source for the NEIC estimations.

Kai nodded in appreciation for how fast Reggie moved. "Good work. After Christmas Island, our next tide reading won't be until the wave reaches Johnston Island."

Then Kai remembered something.

"Hey, isn't the *Miller Freeman* testing a new DART buoy about a thousand kilometers southeast of here?" The NOAA research vessel was responsible for maintaining all of PTWC's oceangoing equipment.

Reggie tapped on his computer. "Yeah, they started setting it up two days ago. They should be there for another week." He overlaid the ship's location on the earthquake map. Before the Asian tsunami, there were only six operational DART buoys, but now new ones were coming online every few months, one of the few positive outcomes of the Southeast Asian disaster. The buoy they were currently testing was intended for the coastline of Russia.

"Is the buoy active? This might be a good test for them. At their location, they should be getting a wave reading just about the same time Johnston Island does."

"I'll call NOAA and have them radio the ship to be ready."

"What do you need from me?"

The buzzer for the front gate sounded.

"You need to handle the tour group," Reggie said, pointing toward the reception area.

"Looks like it's showtime. Come find me when we get the tide readings from Christmas Island."

Kai pressed the button to open the gate, then quickly assembled his presentation materials. It looked like it was going to be a busy day after all.

CHAPTER 7

Harold Franklin seethed quietly as the catamaran cruised through the water three miles west of Christmas Island. He had been looking forward to this vacation for months, primarily because of the island's world-renowned bonefishing. Standing in the surf, casting a line, and hauling in some bonefish—that was why he was here. Not to sit on some boat with seven other people he didn't know. Besides, he hated snorkeling.

"How long are we going to be out here?" Harold said.

His wife, Gina, who was sunning on the canvas stretched between the catamaran's hulls and nursing a piña colada, narrowed her eyes at him. "Listen, buddy, I let you plan this trip because you said we could spend some time doing things other than fishing. I'm not sitting in the hotel room every day by myself while you're down at the beach. I should have talked you into going to Hawaii. At least there they have shopping and a decent cup of coffee."

"But come on. Snorkeling? Do you really need me here for this?"

"At the hotel, they said this is the best reef in the area. And I don't know anyone else here, so I don't want to hear another word about it. You'll get to fish plenty this week."

"If we're going snorkeling, then I wish we'd get it over with."

"The captain said he got a report of some whales out here. Don't you want to see them?"

"Whales live underwater. We won't see anything." It had taken Harold and Gina six hours to get from Sacramento to Honolulu, then another three hours on the one weekly flight that traveled the thirteen hundred miles due south to Christmas Island. He didn't come all that way to watch a bump in the ocean. Harold looked up at the azure sky.

"At least it's not raining," he said. Just as they had set sail, they had heard a huge boom, like a gigantic thunderclap. But there hadn't been a cloud in the sky, so the cruise left as scheduled.

"Have a drink," Gina said. "Get comfortable like everyone else."

Harold put his hand on her shoulder and stood up, looking back toward Christmas Island.

"What's the matter?" Gina said.

"I don't know. Something's going on with the birds."

The island was small and sparsely populated, its 3,200 residents surviving primarily as subsistence farmers and on whatever tourist dollars they could bring in. But it was so expensive and inconvenient that few tourists—mostly Americans like Harold and Gina— vacationed there. The island, an expanse of crushed coral sand only twelve feet above sea level at its highest point, provided a home for hundreds of bird species and colorful underwater life.

Because Harold was an avid hunter as well as a fisherman, the birds had caught his attention. It seemed like every bird on the island, thousands of them, had suddenly taken flight.

"What do you make of that?" Harold said to no one in particular.

By this time everyone on board was looking at the island, including the dive master and captain. Both of them were Americans who had moved to Christmas Island to start their small dive business. Captain Pete and Dive Master Dave, they called themselves, which Harold had thought a bit corny. Pete cut the motor to a crawl.

"Hey, Pete," Dave said, "you see any smoke?"

"Nope," Pete said. "Looks like they got spooked by something, though."

"What about an earthquake?" Harold said. He knew from his lifetime in California that dogs and other animals could detect natural disasters before people could.

"Nope," Pete said again. "This isn't an earthquake zone. No volcanoes, either."

Harold pulled out the binoculars he kept in his bag.

"We better radio in and see what's going on," Dave said.

As Pete called in to the shop, Harold got a closer look at the island. From this distance, even with the binoculars, the birds looked like a swarm of bees circling the island. But something else grabbed his attention.

"That's weird," he said.

"What?" said Gina.

"The beach is getting bigger."

"What do you mean the beach is getting bigger?" Gina said, her voice rising in volume. Dave must have heard her.

"What about the beach?" Dave said to Harold.

Harold described what he could see. The beach, which had extended about a hundred yards from the ocean to the trees only a minute before, was growing by what seemed like the same amount every few seconds. After another moment he could see exposed reef around the entire island. Several beachgoers ran down to the newly uncovered sand, while others simply stood and watched.

"Oh, no!" said Dave. He ran over to Pete, who had just reached the dive base on the radio and asked what was happening there. Before they could reply, Dave yanked the transmitter out of Pete's hand.

"Get the boat as far away from the island as fast as you can! Right now!" he yelled at Pete. Confused and not used to taking orders on his own boat, Pete nevertheless saw the alarm in Dave's eyes and told everyone to hang on. He gunned the engine until they were doing twenty knots.

Dave clicked on the transmitter. "Base, this is *Seabiscuit,* do you read?"

A woman on the other end answered. Harold remembered her as Tasha, the girl who had checked them in for the dive. Before they'd left on the trip, Dave and Tasha's canoodling in the shop had been practically pornographic.

"I read you, *Seabiscuit,*" she said. "I just looked out the window. The tide is going way out."

"Tasha, that's not the tide! A tsunami is coming! Get out of there!"

"Oh my God! What should I do?"

"Get to the highest point you can."

"What about you?"

"We're okay. We're in deep water. Tsunamis only get big in shallow water."

Tasha's panicked voice came back. "But there's nowhere to go!"

Harold knew she was right. Not only was the highest point on the island only twelve feet above sea level, there was only a smattering of two-story buildings on the island, and none near the dive shop.

"Then climb a tree!"

"It's too late!" Harold said and pointed.

Gina screamed. "Look!"

Even faster than it had rushed out, the water began pouring back toward the beach. The small figures Harold could see with the binoculars ran back toward the island. Some of them were caught by the incoming wave even before they reached the trees.

But the image between him and the island grew more terrifying. The water rose until it completely obscured even the tallest tree. Harold realized it would be only seconds before the mammoth wave covered the island.

A hiss of static issued from the radio. Tasha was gone.

Harold, wide-eyed, could only shake his head and mutter to himself.

"I guess we should have gone to Hawaii."

CHAPTER 8

THE PACIFIC TSUNAMI WARNING Center was tiny, so the walking portion of the Japanese school tour went quickly. Kai took them into the conference room where the children could sit. The sixth graders had been listening quietly, the teacher translating while Kai spoke. Kai knew the Japanese language of his father's ancestry about as well as he knew the Italian language of his mother's, which meant that he could order sushi or rigatoni and that was about it.

Japan had always been particularly susceptible to tsunamis, and the videos from Indonesia, Sri Lanka, and Thailand showing the tsunami carrying away people, buildings, and cars had only added to the students' curiosity. Kai capitalized on their interest by telling stories about tsunamis that had hit Hawaii in the past.

"Do you remember me telling you about the tsunami that struck Hilo in 1946?" he said.

A couple of kids nodded. Kai always started the tour off by telling them how the Pacific Tsunami Warning Center was founded. On April 1, 1946, an earthquake measuring 8.1 on the Richter scale was generated in the Aleutian Islands. No one in Hawaii knew that it had happened, except for a few seismologists. Five hours later, the first of a series of waves hit the northern shore of the Big Island. Hilo, on the northeast side of the island, was the only large city facing that direction. Even when people got word that a tsunami had struck, many thought it was an April Fool's Day prank. But it wasn't a joke. More than 150 Hawaiians perished that day.

Kai went on with the story: "One of the common misconceptions about tsunamis is that they consist of one huge wave. In fact, tsunamis typically come in a series of waves created by the earthquake-displaced water rebounding up and down, with the third or fourth wave in the series usually the biggest. The waves alternate with troughs that are just as low as the waves are high, which is why the water recedes from the beach before every wave. The energy of each wave extends to the bottom of the ocean, accounting for the long periods between waves. Because people aren't aware of these tsunami behaviors, they often put themselves in unnecessary danger.

"There was a school in a town called Laupahoehoe to the northwest of Hilo," he added. "In fact, the kids at the school were just about your age, and they saw an actual tsunami."

That brought a gasp from the kids.

"I'll even show you a couple of pictures from the event." Kai clicked on the conference room projector, which was linked to his laptop. The first photo showed the schoolhouse as it had looked before the tsunami, perched only one hundred feet from the shore on a beautiful beach with swaying palm trees. Several smaller houses surrounded it.

"This is where the kids went to school. Imagine being able to go to the beach for recess!" The children murmured at that thought.

"When the second wave of the tsunami arrived at

nine a.m., the kids were already in class. None of them had even seen the first small wave. A few of them who could see out the window noticed the receding water, and the rest of the children jumped up and ran out to see what was going on, with a schoolteacher following them. Some of them even ran into the bay to look at the exposed seafloor.

"As they were playing around, the water started to come back in. It just seemed like a fast-rising tide at first, so they weren't too worried as they ran back toward the schoolhouse. But the next thing they saw was a massive wave rushing across the bay at forty miles an hour." Kai saw some quizzical looks and realized that he was accustomed to giving tours to Americans. Japan used kilometers. "That's about seventy kilometers per hour." He pointed at a girl sitting near him. "How fast do you think you can run?"

The girl shrugged and spoke unexpectedly good English. "I don't know."

"Do you think you could run seventy kilometers per hour?"

Her face turned crimson. She shook her head.

"You're right," Kai said. "Actually, the fastest man in the world can only run about forty kilometers per hour, and even then he can only keep it up for a hundred meters." He winked at the girl. "Next time you're on the sidewalk, try to outrun a car that's passing next to you on the road. If you can't outrun that car, you can't outrun a tsunami, either. Now, where was I?"

A boy courteously raised his hand. Kai nodded, and the boy spoke in a measured voice. "The wave approached." Apparently their English was much better than Kai's Japanese.

"Right. Well, despite what you may have seen in the movies, a tsunami is seldom a big curling wave like the ones you see on the Banzai Pipeline, the popular surfing spot on the North Shore. Instead, a tsunami is usually a churning mass of white foam that we call a bore." Kai clicked to the next slide. It showed a wave approaching the beach that was the height of the trees. "This is a picture from Phuket, Thailand, during the Asian tsunami. As you can see, it looks a lot like the waves you see in a river rapid. This bore smashes everything in its path and carries the wreckage along with it, so that you have not only the water coming at you but also boats, trees, cars, pieces of buildings, and anything else it has scooped up.

"Now, I've heard some kids come through here and say that if we ever got a real tsunami coming this way, they'd like to try to surf that big mama." Some of the kids laughed and nodded. "Oh, you think you would too? Let me show you video of a relatively small tsunami coming into shore in a bay in Alaska."

Kai clicked on the icon, and the screen showed a cove with several fishing boats and a tiny village perched on the shore to the left. The jittery camera was held by an amateur videographer standing on a cliff. From the right, a white froth about fifteen feet high rushed toward the shore. The man holding the camera yelled something incomprehensible just as the wave smacked into a boat, immediately capsizing it. Other boats got caught in the onslaught as the wave swept the wreckage toward the shore. No one was on the boats, but small figures on the shore could be seen scrambling for higher ground. They all rushed to the peak of a small hill just as the wave crashed along the shore, washing over and through the buildings. One of the buildings collapsed.

"That is the kind of wave the kids at Laupahoehoe Elementary School saw rushing toward them. Except the wave that day was twice the height of the one you just saw. It swept toward them at seventy kilometers per hour, ten meters high, and all they could do was run. Some made it to high ground because they were still in the school when they saw the wave coming in." Kai put on his most serious face. "But sixteen children and five schoolteachers died that day. They never even found three of the children. They died because they didn't understand what was about to happen until it was too late. And that's why most of the 250,000 people in Southeast Asia died. They didn't know the signs of a coming tsunami, and they didn't have any warning."

A boy near Kai raised his hand. "But we have a warning system, don't we?"

"Yes, we do. Where do you live in Japan?"

"Tokyo."

"Well, if an earthquake happens in Alaska, or even as far away as Chile, we would have at least three hours, and usually a lot longer, to warn everyone in Japan about a possible tsunami. But you could have an earthquake right off the coast of Japan, and people would have only a few minutes to get to high ground before the tsunami hit. That's why it's important for you to know the warning signs yourself."

Kai had gone over the warning signs earlier in the tour, but kids often weren't paying attention at that point, so he had come up with a technique to make the warning signs more memorable. He closed the laptop and looked at each of the children in turn.

"Now I have a little quiz for you, and I've got prizes for the person who can yell out the answer first. When you hear the tsunami warning siren at the beach and you can't get to a TV or radio to find out what's going on, what do you do?"

A girl to Kai's right blurted out an answer. "You go to high ground!"

"That's correct," he said. He turned and called out, "Bilbo, bring the prize!"

Bilbo trotted out from the room behind him with a little bag dangling from his mouth. Kai pointed at the girl and the dog walked over and dropped the bag in front of her. The girl squealed with delight and gave Bilbo a pat before he walked back over to Kai. They had practiced that routine all year, and Bilbo was getting good at it.

"Very good," Kai said. "And remember to get an adult to help you whenever you can. Next question: When you feel an earthquake and you're at the beach, what do you do?"

Another girl at the back screamed out before the others, "Get to high ground!"

"Exactly. Bilbo?"

While Bilbo took the next bag to the student, a voice that was definitely not a child's whispered in Kai's ear.

"I can't believe you are still doing that cheesy trick with the dog," Brad said. "You are such a nerd."

"Excuse me," Kai said to the teacher, pushing Brad back into the reception area. "What are you doing here?"

"The guys from Ma'alea chickened out. Since I have the morning free now, I thought I'd come by and see what's up."

"I'm not done yet. Can you just stay out of the way for a little while?"

"No problem."

When Kai returned, the teacher, a pretty, petite

woman in her thirties, raised her hand. "Excuse me, Dr. Tanaka." Out of the corner of his eye, Kai saw Brad still leaning on the door frame, smiling at her.

"Yes, Ms. Yamaguchi."

"How high is 'high ground'?"

"That's a very good question," Kai said. "We develop inundation maps that show us where the water would reach on dry land, usually about thirty feet above sea level. You can find them in all the phone books." Kai held up the tsunami evacuation route sign he kept around for the tour. The blue pictograph depicted a series of small stylized white waves followed by a final large wave. "And you should see this sign all over Hawaii and something very close to it in Japan. It will tell you where to go. Any other questions?"

Nobody raised a hand, so Kai continued. "Now the last question: If you're at the beach and you see the water receding very quickly from the beach, what do you do?"

This time all the kids yelled the answer simultaneously: "Get to high ground!"

"Well, since you all answered, you all deserve a prize." Kai thrust some bags into Brad's hands. "Here, make yourself useful."

As they were handing out the gift bags, Reggie walked into the room. He had an odd look on his face, as if he had uncomfortable news to deliver.

"You done?" he said.

"Yes. In fact, I've probably already kept them longer than they planned." Kai said his good-byes to the teacher and kids. "Brad, would you show Ms. Yamaguchi the way out?"

"My pleasure," Brad said, leading her to the door.

Kai turned to Reggie. "What's going on? You look like you just swallowed a bug."

"It's Christmas Island. We were expecting a telemetry report from the tide gauge five minutes ago. It never came."

"That's funny. Didn't we just get a reading from it an hour ago?"

"Sure did. Everything was fine."

"Did you check the equipment on our end?" Kai asked, a sudden chill creeping up his spine. He didn't like where this was going.

"Just finished. It's not us. That leaves two possibilities. Either the tide gauge is malfunctioning . . ."

Kai completed Reggie's sentence. "Or it's not there anymore."

CHAPTER 9

As the Japanese students filed out to their van, Kai followed Reggie back into the warning center's telemetry room. Reggie's calm was now replaced by an edginess Kai had only seen a few times.

"Kind of an odd fluke," Reggie said. "Don't you think?"

"What's happening?" said Brad, entering the room. He saw the tension, and his eyes lit up. "Is it a tsunami?"

"Look, Brad," Kai said, "I don't mind if you want to hang around, but we could get very busy. If you're going to get in the way, you'll have to leave."

Brad put up his hands in a gesture of appeasement. "No problem. I just want to watch. This is fun. Usually, your job is so dull." He retreated to the other side of the room and took a seat.

Kai leaned over Reggie as he typed into his computer.

"You think the busted tide gauge is too coincidental?" Kai asked.

"I don't know," Reggie said. "We detect a seismic disturbance in the general vicinity, and that's the exact time for the tide gauge to go on the fritz?"

"It hasn't failed since I've been here, but you said it has in the past?"

"Well, it has broken down two times in the past three

years: once from a short circuit and once from a storm that knocked over the satellite uplink antenna."

"Is there a storm in the area?"

"I just checked. There is one, but the storm is north-west of Christmas Island. Shouldn't be affecting it."

"How big would the tsunami have to be to take out that tide gauge? Is it a mark seven?"

"Yeah. The wave would have to be at least eight meters high to take out a mark seven gauge."

Over twenty feet high. High enough to cover the entire island.

"Who's our contact on Christmas Island? Steve something?"

"Steve Bryant. He does a little maintenance on the gauge from time to time. No answer, either at his home or his office. In fact, I can't even get his voice mail. It won't ring through. All I get is a fast busy signal."

"Let's try again. The phones down there aren't very reliable. You keep trying to get Steve, and I'll call the operator."

The operator didn't have any better luck getting through, so Kai had her attempt several different numbers they had in the Rolodex for Christmas Island. None of them went through.

"Can you get the main island operator for me?" Kai asked.

She tried without success. Just that fast busy signal again.

"All I'm getting is an out-of-order tone, sir," she said.

"Is that unusual?"

"The power goes out down there on a regular basis. It always shuts everything down, including communications. Comms also failed once when there was a fire at the switching station on the island, but we haven't had any problems lately. It's probably just a power outage. Would you like me to continue trying?"

"Yes, please." Kai told her who he was and asked her to call him back when she got through. Their inability to get through to anyone was troubling, and Kai couldn't help feel like there was pattern to all of this that he was missing. Still, he didn't have the hard data to show that it was anything other than a coincidence.

Reggie didn't have any more luck contacting someone than Kai did.

"Any signal from the tide gauge?" Kai asked, hopeful that it was just a temporary glitch.

"Not a blip," Reggie said.

Kai told Reggie the operator's theory about a power outage.

"That's a fine idea," Reggie said, "but the tide gauge has a battery backup."

Kai had forgotten about that. "It has enough juice for twenty-four hours, right?"

"Up to twenty-four hours at full capacity. Of course, that's if the battery is charged. Steve has been known to put off tide gauge maintenance in the past. It's possible the battery is dead. Then a power outage would definitely take the gauge offline."

"So we were expecting a wave to reach Christmas Island at 9:25 a.m.," Kai said, summing up the series of coincidences. "The tide gauge was supposed to send a signal at 9:30 a.m. But there was a power outage on the island that started sometime between when we received the last tide gauge reading at 8:30 and when we were supposed to receive the 9:30 signal. And because the battery backup was not charged, the power outage knocked out the comm equipment on the tide gauge." Despite the skepticism in his voice, the scenario was possible. Kai would have felt better if the 8:30 signal had also failed to come in, but there it was on the log sheet, right on time.

Reggie opened his mouth to speak, then hesitated.

"What?" Kai said.

"Well, I just thought I should bring it up. Do you want me to send out a warning?"

"A warning?" Brad said. "Oh, this'll be good."

"Brad, please," Kai said, putting up his hand to show that he wasn't in the mood for Brad's giddy enthusiasm. He needed to concentrate.

Sending out a tsunami warning would be a bold step. The situation didn't fit any established scenarios. Kai would simply be going on gut.

Issuing a tsunami warning was not a responsibility that he took lightly, particularly because he'd been on the job for less than a year. Doing so would cause a massive disruption to businesses and tourists in Hawaii, not to mention the enormous cost associated with an evacuation.

In 1994 a huge earthquake near the Kurile Islands in Russia measuring a magnitude of 8.1 prompted the PTWC to issue a tsunami warning for the Pacific region. Despite getting tide measurements at Midway and Wake islands that indicated a surge could be expected in Hawaii, they couldn't predict how big the waves would be. In fact, a tsunami did arrive, but it never rose above three feet. The tsunami warning had cost the state an estimated $30 million.

More recently, the PTWC had issued a warning based on a magnitude 7.6 quake off the coast of Alaska, but when tide data showed that no destructive waves were expected, the warning was called off forty-five minutes later. The financial cost had been minimal, but it didn't help the public trust the system. Many news programs had repeatedly shown videos of frightened residents evacuating the city, even after the warning had been rescinded. The false alarm was implicated as just another failure of federal disaster readiness, even though they had followed procedure to the letter.

If Kai issued a warning based on just his hunch and it turned out to be another false alarm, not only would he be criticized by everyone from the governor to the NOAA administrator, but the public would get so frustrated by the repeated false alarms that they might start to ignore subsequent warnings. A repeat of the full 1994 warning now would be even more expensive than it had been then, at least $50 million.

"So you think we should issue the warning?" Kai asked Reggie.

"No, not at all. I just wanted to throw it out there. But you're the one who gets the big bucks to make the call."

Kai paused. The signal loss was a strange coincidence, yes, and he couldn't help thinking that there was some small nugget of information that he wasn't seeing that would offer an explanation for what was happening. But the raw data didn't justify a tsunami warning. Historically, the earthquake just wasn't strong enough. Even with a stronger earthquake, a tsunami was unlikely.

"Kai?" Reggie said. "What should we do?"

Kai sighed. Despite his misgivings, he just couldn't issue a warning. Not yet. Not without knowing more.

"We're going to wait," Kai said. "Let's hope the power comes back on soon and we can get on with our day."

Reggie nodded and got back on the phone while Kai tried to ignore the nagging little voice in his head that said he was making the wrong decision.

CHAPTER 10

As Teresa now saw, the Memorial Day holiday's beautiful weather brought out not only the travelers from the mainland but what seemed like every local on the island. Waikiki was packed. By the time they pulled into the Grand Hawaiian's parking lot, it was nearly full.

"But Aunt Rachel let Lani get her ears pierced," Mia said as they got out of the Jeep. "And my friend Monica got a tattoo on her ankle."

Teresa popped open the hatch. "If you think I'm going to let you get a navel piercing, you're dreaming."

"Mom, please!"

"You're too young. And don't even start with the tattoos." Mia had been bringing up the subject of belly button piercing for over a month.

"What is the difference between getting my belly button pierced and my ears pierced?" Mia's voice was headed into whine country.

"One is harmless decoration, and the other is an advertisement for sex. You're not mature enough for it. We can talk about it again when you turn eighteen."

Mia pulled a boogie board out and slammed it to the ground.

"Be careful with that!" Teresa said. "Are you trying to prove my point?"

"Mom, I'm almost fourteen. I know a lot of girls my age that have them. And it's not sexual."

"Sure it isn't." Teresa locked the car and headed toward the sunlight beckoning from the garage exit. "Come on."

Mia reluctantly picked up her board and followed her mother.

"Lani," Mia said, "don't you think Mom should let me get my navel pierced?"

"I don't know," Lani said. She obviously didn't want to get involved.

Teresa stopped at the exit. "Mia, while I'm in charge, you are not lifting up your shirt to show some boy your navel ring, which is about the only thing it's good for. And yes, I realize you are about to be prancing around the beach in a bikini in a few minutes anyway, but that's the way it is. Got it?"

Mia ground her teeth, but said nothing.

"Good," Teresa said. "Let's go find some beach and have fun."

They emerged from the garage onto Kalakaua Avenue, the main drag up and down Waikiki. To the west, the view was obscured by the hundreds of high-rise hotels and condominiums that extended to the office buildings of downtown Honolulu. In the other direction, Kalakaua stretched past the last hotel on Waikiki about a half mile away, where it passed the zoo and finally ran into Diamond Head, the massive extinct volcano that served as Honolulu's dominant landmark.

Teresa, followed by Mia and Lani, plunged into the throng of people crowding Kalakaua Avenue and crossed the road to Waikiki Beach. They passed a magnificent banyan tree and stepped onto the beach itself.

As Teresa searched for a spot big enough for the three of them, she heard people speaking Japanese, French, German, Spanish, and a few languages she couldn't place. Like all beaches in Hawaii, Waikiki was open to the public, so a mishmash of all walks of life mingled with the guests of the expensive resorts.

Two boys, both about sixteen, walked past. Tan and lean, they looked like younger versions of Brad. They gave the girls an appraising look and the taller of the boys spoke to them as they went by.

"The surf's a lot better by our condo." He pointed his thumb in the direction of Diamond Head.

The girls laughed, and the shorter boy yanked his friend and kept walking. Despite what Teresa had said earlier, the boys' attention to her daughter tickled her, but she hid her amusement.

They walked for a little while and stopped at an open patch near an impressive hotel called the Outrigger Waikiki. Teresa dropped her bag and started spreading out her towel. She had a clear view to the breakwaters on either side, and the waves coming in were good-sized, but still mild enough for safe boogie boarding.

"How's this?"

Mia made a show of propping up her boogie board in the sand. "Mom, Lani and I want to walk down the beach."

"We just got here. Don't you even want to get in the water? Look how blue it is. It's gorgeous."

"Yeah, it's great," Mia said, stripping down to her bikini. "But I saw some great T-shirts back there, and I want to get some souvenirs while we're here."

Lani piped in, now down to her bikini as well. "Yeah, and we want to get new dresses for the luau tonight."

Teresa wasn't very concerned about letting the girls go off on their own. Mia had been babysitting for a year now, so walking around the beach, especially with someone else, wasn't worrisome. Teresa looked at her watch. It was still a couple of hours until lunchtime.

"All right. But I don't want you to come back with a piercing."

Mia sighed. "I promise."

"How long do you think you'll be gone?"

The girls looked at each other and shrugged in unison.

"There's a lot to see," Mia said. "Maybe an hour or two."

"You have some money?"

Mia waved her wallet. The babysitting money she wasn't using to pay off her texting bill.

"Sunscreen?"

"We put it on at the house."

"Okay. But be back by eleven thirty. After a morning in the sun, I'm going to be starving."

"Thanks, Mom," Mia said as she and Lani turned toward Diamond Head and began walking. "You're the best."

"Bye, Aunt Teresa," said Lani.

Teresa gave them a wave. She was actually relieved to have a little uninterrupted time alone. After she liberally applied sunscreen, her plan was to immerse herself in a good mystery novel for a peaceful morning. As she spread out her towel, a beep caught her attention. She fished through her bag and saw that the display on her cell phone said, CHARGE PHONE. She powered it down and tossed it back in her bag.

CHAPTER 11

IT HAD BEEN HALF an hour since the tide gauge reading from Christmas Island was supposed to be transmitted, and Kai was growing more worried by the minute. Reggie's calls to Steve Bryant still went unanswered.

"What the hell is going on down there?" Reggie said to no one in particular.

The phone rang, and Kai swept the receiver up in the hope that it was the operator with good news.

"Dr. Tanaka, this is Shirley Nagle, the operator you spoke with earlier."

"You got through?" Kai asked hopefully.

"Well, no, I haven't," she said. Kai slumped in disappointment. "But I wanted to call you back, since you said it was so urgent. I asked another operator here, Chris, if he had any other ideas. He said that, in addition to the undersea cable, there's a backup satellite hookup on the island. But the funny thing is, I'm not getting through on that, either."

"Why is that funny?"

"Chris swears up and down that the satellite transmitter has a backup generator in case of power loss, so I should be getting a connection, even if the main island power is down. But I'm getting nothing. No signal whatsoever. It's like the island isn't there anymore."

"Jesus," Kai said, the implications too terrible to grasp. *It's like the island isn't there anymore.*

"Excuse me?" Shirley said.

"Nothing. Can you please keep trying to reach them?"

"Sure. We've already got a couple of other people on it. I'll let you know as soon as we get through."

Her voice sounded upbeat, but Kai didn't share her optimism. He had the terrible feeling that they'd never hear from anyone on the island again.

There were at least three thousand people on Christmas Island. Kai couldn't accept the possibility that it had been wiped out by a tsunami on his watch. He felt the beginnings of a headache and popped a couple of aspirins from a bottle in his desk.

Reggie saw the look on Kai's face. "What's the matter?" he asked.

Kai told him about the satellite transmitter.

"I think a tsunami hit Christmas Island," he said. "A big one."

"How is that possible?" Reggie said.

"I don't know. Could it have been a landslide? Maybe the seamount has been building for a while and now a major eruption triggered a landslide down the face of it."

"No way. There have been no major seismic disturbances in that region for the past ten years. I checked the database." Reggie was already working on his bid to get credit for his discovery. "The seamount couldn't be big enough to cause a major landslide at this point."

"And the quake magnitude? Have we gotten confirmation back from NEIC yet?"

"I just checked again," Reggie said. "NEIC estimates 6.9."

The Southeast Asian tsunami resulted from a quake

with a moment magnitude of 9.0, over one thousand times more powerful than this earthquake. An earthquake as small as 6.9 had never spawned an oceanwide tsunami. There just wasn't enough energy or motion of the seafloor to generate large waves that could travel great distances.

The conditions didn't add up. The earthquake shouldn't have spawned a tsunami, and yet they couldn't get any signal or communication from Christmas Island.

Kai picked up the sheet with the wave arrival times. Johnston Island would be next in about twenty minutes, then the Big Island twenty minutes after that, followed by Oahu an hour and twenty-five minutes from now. Johnston Island had a real-time tide gauge, so that would be their next chance to get data about a potential wave.

"When will we get the wave height data from the DART buoy?" Kai asked Reggie.

"The max wave height at the buoy will be about five minutes after it reaches Johnston. The captain on the *Miller Freeman* said they'll have the satellite uplink ready in ten minutes, which will be just enough time. So it looks like the tide gauge at Johnston is our first chance to see if it's really a tsunami."

Up to this point, Brad had quietly been watching events unfold, content merely to spectate, but now he couldn't resist interjecting.

"You mean, you're willing to wait more than twenty minutes until you know for sure?" he said.

"What do you want us to do?" Reggie responded. "Evacuate a million people because of a downed power line?"

"Do you want to take the chance that they could be killed because you thought it was just a downed power line?"

"I'm just saying that we need more evidence," Reggie said defensively. "I mean, sure, if we had a 9.0 earthquake on our hands, I'd issue the warning in a second. But to completely wipe out Christmas Island and our tide gauge, the tsunami would have to be huge—at least twenty feet high. There's no way a 6.9 quake causes a tsunami that big."

"Are you sure?"

"I've researched every major tsunami in the last sixty years," Reggie said. "There is absolutely no historic precedent for it. Besides, do you realize how much an evacuation costs? We'll be crucified if we're wrong, especially with this kind of flimsy data. I say we wait twenty minutes. If the tide gauge on Johnston craps out, too, then I'm all for a warning."

Twenty more minutes. For a massive evacuation, every minute would count. With less than an hour before a potential tsunami hit the southern tip of the Big Island, Kai had to make the call. In his mind he imagined the headlines vilifying him for a massive unnecessary evacuation. The internal NOAA investigations into why he ignored long-established procedures. The political reprisals condemning yet another federal employee who couldn't handle the position. As Kai thought about it, the retaliatory consequences became clear to him. His tenure would be cut short by what would be seen as a lack of judgment, that he didn't have the experience for the job.

On the other hand, something deep down was telling him that this wasn't just a power disruption. He couldn't pinpoint where the cognitive dissonance was coming from, the subtle clash of information that was telling his subconscious mind it didn't fit together. Logically, there was little reason to be worried about a major tsunami. But they couldn't rule it out, either, and that's what scared him the most.

In the end, Kai's choice simply came down to what was best for his family. His daughter was on the beach that morning. His wife was in a hotel no more than a hundred yards from the ocean. He could live with losing his job because he made a poor decision; he couldn't live with himself if his wife and daughter died because he made a poor decision.

"We've already waited thirty minutes," Kai said softly. "We can't wait any longer." His doubt made him sound unconvincing. When Kai realized Reggie and Brad were looking at him, hoping to see confidence, he cleared his throat and stood up straighter. "Reggie, send out the warning. I'll get on the phone and talk to the duty officer over at Hawaii State Civil Defense." Like the PTWC, HSCD would be minimally staffed on a holiday.

"Are you sure?" Reggie said. "We've got even less to go on than the one we issued last year."

A mixture of concern and support etched Brad's face. Even as a bystander, he knew this was a tough call.

But Kai's moment of hesitation was over. He couldn't let his misgivings influence others, diminishing the sense of urgency about the evacuation. If a real tsunami was coming, they needed to act quickly and decisively.

"I'm sure. Do it. Issue the warning."

"Okay," Reggie said. "I'm glad it's your call. I wouldn't want to be in your shoes."

Reggie went to the computer and started typing in the commands that would issue a tsunami warning to every government agency in the Pacific. Kai had just made a $50 million decision.

CHAPTER 12

KAI CALLED HAWAII STATE Civil Defense and the officer on duty, a junior staffer named Brian Renfro, answered the phone immediately.

"Brian, this is Kai Tanaka over at PTWC. I need to speak to Jim Dennis."

Dennis, the vice director of HSCD, was the person who normally made the big decisions there and coordinated all the efforts of the state's emergency services.

"Sorry, Kai, he took the weekend to visit some friends on Kauai. It's just me and a couple of others here today. What's wrong?"

On a normal working day, HSCD would have up to thirty people on staff. He knew Renfro from the first semiannual training scenario he had participated in. Renfro was a bright kid, but young, not much older than twenty-five. Kai could only hope that Renfro's thorough training at HSCD would prepare him for what was about to happen. He was about to get a big dose of responsibility.

At least Renfro was in a safer location than Kai. Rather than being built three hundred yards from the ocean like the PTWC was, HSCD was well ensconced in a bunker inside Diamond Head crater. Because Hawaii was exposed to so many different types of potential disasters—tsunamis, hurricanes, volcanoes, earthquakes—the state took civil defense very seriously. Situated inside an extinct volcano with sides over six hundred feet high, the bunker could withstand virtually any disaster nature could dish out.

"Brian," Kai said, "we've got a situation here. Did you see the bulletin we sent out earlier?"

"Sure did. What's the problem? Are you upgrading it?"

"Yes. We've lost contact with Christmas Island."

"You mean the tide gauge?"

"No, I mean the whole island, including the tide gauge."

"When?"

"The tide gauge was supposed to give us a reading over thirty minutes ago. Since then, we haven't been able to get in touch with anyone on the island." Kai took a deep breath. "We think it may have been wiped out by a tsunami."

There was a pause at the other end of the line.

"Okay," Renfro finally said. "Give me one minute. Then I'll call you back. I'm going to try to get in touch with the vice director."

Kai hung up the phone and told Brad and Reggie what Renfro said.

"What do we do now?" Brad said.

Reggie perked up as if he just remembered something. "My God!"

"What?" Kai said.

"There's a team of scientists on Johnston Island."

"But I thought it was abandoned," said Brad. "There was an article in the paper about the chemical weapons disposal facility being shut down in 2004. Now it's a nature sanctuary or something."

Johnston Island, a tiny coral atoll like Christmas Island, was only about twice the size of Central Park. Until 2001, it served as the United States' primary disposal facility for chemical weapons, but fortunately it had incinerated its last bomb. If this tsunami had happened before then, they might have faced the additional specter of having thousands of canisters of the deadliest chemicals known to man washed out to sea. That was one of the few things Kai felt relieved about at that moment.

The other good news was that, now that the facility was shut down, the thirteen hundred people who manned the station had packed up for good, with the last of them having left in 2004. Since then, it had been operated by the U.S. Fish and Wildlife Service as a wildlife preserve.

"How do you know someone's there?" Kai said, snatching the map of Johnston Island from its bin and unfurling it on a table.

"I wanted someone to check the tide gauge there because we've been having intermittent signal problems," Reggie said. "Alvin Peters over at U.S. Fish and Wildlife said a team was there for a month doing observational studies of turtle nesting on the island and that they could check on the equipment for me. Even gave me their sat phone number."

A quick scan of the map showed that the maximum elevation on the island was no more than forty-four feet, not high enough to ensure protection from a large tsunami. Kai didn't know the state of the buildings there or whether they would be able to stand up to the force of a tsunami. The only truly safe place was out at sea in deep water. Thank God the scientists on the island had a phone.

"They only have ten minutes," Kai said. "Call them right now. Let's hope they have a boat."

As Reggie ran to his cubicle to get the number and make the call, the office phone rang. It was Brian Renfro.

"I couldn't get in touch with the vice director," he said, "but I just got your tsunami warning, so I'm going to follow standard procedure. We're trying to contact the governor now. The sirens will go off in a minute, and then I'll start broadcasting our standard tsunami warning message on the EAS. Call me back if you get any new information. Especially if it's a false alarm." With that, he hung up.

"So HSCD is going to evacuate?" Brad said. "You know, your daughter—my niece—is at the beach today."

"I know. Along with a hundred thousand other people."

"So, shouldn't we call Rachel and Teresa and let them know?"

Kai was tempted to set aside the duties of the job and warn his own family. If everyone did that, though, the entire system—the government, fire department, police department, emergency services—would grind to a halt. He had to trust that the warning system in place would work. But that didn't mean that Brad couldn't call them.

"Try Teresa's cell. Her battery was dying, but she still might have it on. Then call Rachel and let her know what's happening. All the hotels are part of the warning system, but it can't hurt to call her anyway." Kai handed Brad his cell phone. "She's busy this morning, so she probably won't answer it unless she sees that it's my phone number. If she doesn't answer, choose the pager option when you get her greeting, then dial 999. That's our code for an emergency." Kai had instituted the code three years ago when Lani broke her leg playing soccer and he wasn't been able to get Rachel to answer her phone for two hours.

Brad took the phone and went into the conference room to make the call. Reggie almost knocked him over running into the ops center.

"I got 'em!" he said.

"The scientists? Thank God! How many are there?"

"Seven."

"Do they have a boat?"

"No, but they have a plane. The weekly supply flight from Hawaii didn't take the holiday off. But there's a problem."

Kai's stomach sank. "With the plane? It can't take off?"

"Oh, it can take off. In fact, they should be getting into the air in a few minutes. But it's just a small supply plane. It can only take five of the scientists. Two of them will have to stay behind."

At that exact moment, Kai heard the first wail of the tsunami siren.

Chapter 13

REALIZING SHE COULD DO nothing more for the Russian tour group until the interpreter arrived in about an hour, Rachel had turned her full attention to the most important event taking place at the hotel: the governor's veterans brunch.

The event had been under way for five minutes, right on time despite the ramp problem. Rachel stood at the back watching Governor Elizabeth Kalama give her speech, ready to make sure any potential issues were resolved quickly and quietly.

Because Rachel's job was all about communication, she carried a walkie-talkie and cell phone at all times. The walkie-talkie was for in-hotel communications with the staff, and the cell phone connected her with external vendors and clients. Either one could go off at any time. This time it was her cell phone. She had it set to vibrate mode so that it wouldn't interrupt the speech from the dais.

She pulled it from her belt and looked at the number. It was Kai's cell phone. She sighed and replaced it on her belt, letting it go to voice mail.

After another few seconds her cell phone's pager feature went off. She picked it up again and looked at the number typed in the display, expecting to see Kai's cell phone number again. Instead, she saw 999. Their emergency code.

She called him back immediately.

"Kai?" she whispered. "What's going on?"

"Rachel, it's Brad."

"Brad? Where's Kai?"

"He's busy. He wanted you to know that he just issued a tsunami warning."

"Oh, no! Right now?"

"Yeah, you should be getting the official warning in a few minutes."

"Oh my God! I'm at a brunch in our ballroom. The governor's here."

"Wait a sec." She heard Brad in the background say, "She's got the friggin' governor with her."

Kai's voice came on the line.

"It's me, hon."

"So, a tsunami is really coming?"

"We don't know for sure yet, but it looks like it."

"Jesus! When is it supposed to get here?"

"In a little more than an hour."

"An hour? You said that a tsunami from Alaska would take five hours to get here."

"It's not from Alaska."

"A local one? The Big Island?" Rachel knew that a tsunami caused by landslides or earthquakes in the Hawaiian Islands would take less than forty-five minutes to reach Oahu.

"No, somewhere in the Pacific. Listen, Rachel, I've got to go. I'll talk to you soon. Here's Brad again. Be safe."

A raspy sound came through as the phone got passed back.

"It's me."

"Hey, Brad," Rachel said, "I've got to get things in motion here."

"Wait, Rachel! Does Lani have a cell phone?"

Rachel just assumed Teresa had already been warned to take Lani and Mia to safety.

"Why?" she said. "What's wrong? Is she okay? Where is she?"

"Slow down. I don't know. I tried calling Teresa, but all I get is her voice mail. I was hoping Lani had a cell phone."

"No. She's going to get a new one for her birthday."

"Well, I'm sure they'll hear the sirens and get to high ground."

"Brad, make sure they're okay. Please? I won't have time. I've got to get the hotel ready."

"Don't worry. I got it covered."

Brad sounded confident, but then, he always sounded confident. She just had to trust him, so she hung up and turned her attention to her duties.

As the governor continued her speech, Rachel weaved her way through the tables of disabled vets. Because the Grand Hawaiian was a state-of-the-art Waikiki resort, it had a well-thought-out tsunami warning plan. The hotel ran drills every three months to familiarize the employees with the procedures in case of a tsunami. Rachel had been through two of them.

Procedure called for the first, second, and third floors to be evacuated and for all guests to be moved to a level higher than that. The ballroom was on the sixth floor, so she wouldn't have to evacuate anyone at the brunch.

She spotted the governor's assistant, William Kim, with whom she had coordinated the banquet. He had been an annoyance to her for a week now, changing every detail of the governor's appearance five times. Giving him this news wasn't going to be pretty.

"Mr. Kim," she said in a low whisper, "I need to talk to you. Right now."

She pulled him to the side of the room.

"What is it? I'm missing the governor's speech."

"A tsunami might be coming."

"Are you serious?"

"Yes. The tsunami warning should come out any minute. You have to tell the governor."

"In the middle of her speech?"

"Don't you think it might be something she'd like to know as soon as possible?"

"So the tsunami warning hasn't been issued?"

"It has. We just don't have the official announcement."

"Then how do you know—"

"My husband told me. He's the—"

"Your husband?" he said with a snotty tone. "Mrs. Tanaka, the governor is running for the U.S. Senate next year, and there are some very important donors in the room. If I interrupt her, and you're wrong—"

"Please, Mr. Kim, I'm not an idiot. As I was trying to say, my husband is the assistant director of Pacific Tsunami Warning Center."

"Fine. Come back when we get the actual tsunami warning. The governor can at least finish the speech."

"Look, I don't have time for this, and neither does the governor." With that, she strode onto the stage with Kim following her. He stopped short of holding her back, not wanting to make a scene.

As Rachel reached the podium, she thought she could

hear the faint peal of a siren through the ballroom's insulated walls. She put her hand lightly on the governor's shoulder. The governor stopped her speech to look at who was interrupting her and put her hand over the microphone.

"Yes?" she said. "Who are you?"

"Governor, I tried to stop her—" Kim began.

Rachel talked over him. "Governor, I'm Rachel Tanaka, the hotel manager. A tsunami warning has been issued for Hawaii."

"What?"

"Ma'am, my husband is Kai Tanaka, the—"

"Kai Tanaka? From the PTWC?"

"That's right, ma'am. You know him?"

"I met him four months ago during a tsunami drill."

"Governor, he told me that there's a good likelihood that a tsunami is heading this way and will be here in a little more than an hour."

"An hour?" Kim said, startled. Then he went on the defensive. "Governor, she didn't tell me that—"

"Be quiet, William," the governor said. The hush of the crowd was starting to give way to murmurs. "Mrs. Tanaka, you're sure about this?"

Kai might be new to the job, but he was one of the smartest people Rachel had ever met. He wouldn't have issued the warning if he didn't have a good reason.

"Ma'am, my husband knows tsunamis. If he says there might be one coming, then we need to get ready."

"I agree. William, get my car. I'll tell the audience what's happening and then turn it over to Mrs. Tanaka."

"Certainly, ma'am," Kim said, and hurried off the stage. If he'd had a tail, it would have been between his legs. Rachel stayed on the dais.

The governor turned back to the crowd with a somber face, and the audience fell silent immediately.

"I apologize for the interruption. I have just been informed that a tsunami warning has been issued for the Hawaiian Islands." A buzz ran through the crowd, and the governor raised her hands to quiet them. "Now, as you might have guessed, this will require me to cut the speech off here so that I may attend to the emergency—"

Rachel's walkie-talkie squawked to life, and she stepped off the dais to answer it. It was Max.

"Rachel, are you there?"

"Max, did we get a tsunami warning?"

"It just came in a few seconds ago. How did you know?"

"That's not important. Get the book out and start following the emergency procedures. Make sure you notify the staff first. They need to keep the guests from panicking. I've already informed the governor."

"Got it."

"Hopefully, it's just a false alarm, so let's make sure this goes as smoothly as possible. I'll be down when I can."

"But—" Max sputtered.

"The governor's wrapping up. I've got to go. Just keep calm." She replaced the walkie-talkie and stepped back onto the dais next to the governor.

". . . so I urge you to stay where you are, and Mrs. Tanaka, the hotel manager, will see to it that you are well taken care of. Let us all pray that this is a false alarm so that we can continue with our holiday remembrances at the Hawaii State Veterans Cemetery later this afternoon. I hope to see you there. God bless us and God bless the United States of America."

The crowd applauded as the governor left with her gaggle of assistants, and Rachel took the podium. Hundreds of concerned faces looked up at her. She paused to make sure she could keep her voice calm and professional.

"Ladies and gentlemen, my name is Rachel Tanaka, the hotel manager. This tsunami warning is an unfortunate development, but we'll try to do our best to make you comfortable until this is over. This hotel has been designed with the latest in tsunami safety design elements, and you are more than sixty feet above the ground here. Of course, you are free to leave if you desire, but we recommend that you stay where you are, enjoy our hospitality, and wait for the all-clear to sound. We will inform you about further developments as we get them. So sit back, relax, and I'm sure this will all be over quickly."

CHAPTER 14

TERESA HAD JUST DOZED off, soothed by the warm sand and light breeze from the ocean. When the warning siren went off, it startled her so much that the book resting on her hand went flying and landed next to an elderly couple sitting in beach chairs five feet away.

She sat up and looked around to see where the sound was coming from. After a few seconds she spotted a bright yellow siren atop a pole a few hundred feet along the beach. The wail rose and dropped in pitch, reminding her of the air raid sirens she had heard in movies.

The man in the chair rose and picked up the book. Although he wore a hat and had slathered his nose with zinc oxide, the poor guy was only another hour from a severe sunburn on the rest of his body. He handed the book to her.

"Here you go," he said with a thick southern drawl. "You look pretty surprised."

"I was taking a nap," she said. "What the hell is that?"

"Yeah, I wonder what the heck is going on. We getting bombed by the Japs again? And on Memorial Day too." He laughed at what he thought was a good joke.

Teresa didn't smile back. "Maybe it's some kind of drill."

"Oh, yeah, tsunami warning test. I read about that

on the plane over here from Mississippi. Hattiesburg is where we're from. Never been out to Hawaii before. Wanted to read all about it. Couldn't get Eunice here to read a bit of the book. Said she just wants to relax."

"Did they have to schedule it for the middle of the morning?"

"Don't know. Thought the book said it was sometime around the beginning of the month. Maybe I didn't read it right."

The siren continued to wail. Teresa thought it would go off after just a minute, but the minute passed. It didn't stop.

"Darryl," Eunice said, "what is that siren?" She picked up a radio that had been at her side and nervously twiddled with the knobs.

Darryl patted her reassuringly. "It's a tsunami warning. Don't worry about it, Eunice."

Teresa scanned the beach; few of the other beachgoers even seemed to notice the siren. Most of them went on with whatever they were doing: playing, sunbathing, swimming. The siren seemed to have no effect on them, except that she saw several small children with their hands over their ears.

"That's funny," said Eunice. "The radio just said there was a salami warning. I thought that meant there was something wrong with the lunch meat on the island."

"It's just a test. And it's tsunami, not salami. You know, a tidal wave."

"They didn't say it was a test. It just keeps repeating."

Teresa walked over to the radio to hear it for herself. An even, measured male voice issued from the ancient-looking device. She supposed the voice was intended to convey a sense of calm about the situation, to prevent panic, but she thought it seemed mechanical, too detached, as if he were describing the potential for afternoon showers.

". . . warning for the Hawaiian Islands. This is not a drill. The Pacific Tsunami Warning Center has advised that a destructive tsunami may be approaching the coastline of Hawaii. Evacuation procedures are under way. It is recommended that you move to high ground immediately. All Hawaii telephone books include maps that show evacuation routes and safe areas under the section called 'Disaster Preparedness Info.' The earliest arrival time for the tsunami is listed as follows: For the Big Island, the wave arrival time is approximately 10:44 a.m. For Maui, Lanai, and Molokai, the wave arrival time is approximately 11:14 a.m. For Oahu, the wave arrival time is approximately 11:22 a.m. . . ."

Teresa fumbled through her purse to get her watch. It was 10:08 a.m. Only an hour and fourteen minutes until the tsunami arrived.

". . . For Kauai, the wave arrival time is 11:35 a.m. Please follow all instructions given by your local authorities." A brief pause; then: "This is a tsunami warning for the Hawaiian Islands. This is not a . . ."

The message began to repeat.

Teresa felt her stomach go cold. "It's not a test," she said.

"Are you sure?" Darryl said.

She shook her head. "It wouldn't repeat. It would end with a message saying that it was only a test, and the siren would shut off."

"You mean there's a real tidal wave coming?" Eunice said, alarmed at the prospect. "What should we do?"

"Is your hotel nearby?"

"Yeah," Darryl said, "it's that big one over there. The Hilton." He pointed to a thirty-story building.

"What floor is your room on?"

"The twentieth."

"Good. Go back to your hotel room until they say it's over."

"You should come with us. Got plenty of room. Maybe even order up some room service."

"I can't. I have to find my daughter and her friend."

"Oh, my goodness, dear," Eunice said. "You don't know where they are?"

Teresa felt stung by the comment, even though she didn't think Eunice meant it as an criticism of her parenting skills.

"No. They went shopping."

"What store?" Darryl said.

Teresa shook her head. She pointed toward Diamond Head. "They went that way."

"How will you find them? They have a cell phone?"

Teresa was feeling worse as a mother by the minute. She had let her daughter go off to who-knew-where without any way of communicating with her. She didn't do anything differently from what a thousand other parents on this beach would have done. But the thought that she wasn't the only person who had lost track of her kids didn't make her feel any better.

Teresa put on her sarong and tank top. "No, they don't have a cell phone," she said, her voice cracking from worry. "And my cell phone battery is almost dead anyway."

Eunice put a hand on Teresa's shoulder. "I'm sure they'll come back, dear, now that they've heard the sirens. We still have over an hour."

Teresa nodded in agreement. The best thing for her to do was stay calm and stay where she was. If she left in search of them, she would surely miss them. And if they returned while she was gone, they might do something stupid, like go in search of her.

All she could do was pace back and forth along the sand, straining to see any sign of her daughter.

CHAPTER 15

LANI PADDLED HER KAYAK next to Mia and the two boys they had met only thirty minutes ago. By this time they had to be at least a half mile from shore. Lani was still bewildered at the sequence of events that had gotten her out there.

After they had left Teresa to read her book, she and Mia had wandered along the beach, looking at the vast horde of sunbathers, the families playing in the water, the surfers paddling out to take on their first attempts at waves, the college students playing Frisbee, the vendors of all sorts hawking snacks and kitschy souvenirs. Lani loved it. She didn't know anywhere else you could find such a cross section of humanity.

The day was glorious. The strong smell of suntan lotion complemented the salty breeze coming off the ocean. As they walked, Lani noticed how Mia kept eyeing the boys who passed them. A raucous crowd of boys played beach volleyball, and Mia waved at one of them. Lani pulled Mia's arm down and raced forward, giggling. But inside, Lani could only wish for that kind of confidence.

Of the two of them, Lani had always been the tomboy, excellent at athletics, ready to try every sport. She played soccer and volleyball, surfed, loved any kind of water sport. She had even been star shortstop on the otherwise all-boy Little League baseball team, where some of her teammates would barely talk to her because they resented her athletic skills. And because Lani was shy, making friends with girls was even harder.

Mia, on the other hand, was a girly girl. Other girls wanted to hang out with her because she was so cool and pretty and seemed to know the latest trends in fashion, even though her mom still didn't have much money to spend on clothes. She danced on the drill team, took ballet lessons, and had even been out on a date. Her mom had driven her to the mall movie theater and back, but Mia found a secluded moment and made out with the boy. Lani felt like she was falling behind Mia.

When she and Mia were about half a mile from Teresa, Mia pulled her to a stop.

"Look."

Mia pointed at the two boys who had passed them earlier when they were looking for a spot on the beach with Teresa. Now that she had a better look at them, Lani thought she recognized one of them. He was taller than the other boy and seemed more sure of himself. His mocha-colored hair tousled in a mop, he sported the deep brown skin of a native islander, while the other boy, blond and three inches shorter, still had the remnants of a farmer's tan. The boys were listening to iPods as they walked.

"What about them?"

"Let's go say hi," Mia said, pushing Lani forward. Lani dug her feet into the sand.

"No. I don't want to."

"Come on. It'll be fun."

"But I know one of them."

"Really? Which one?"

"The one on the left."

"The tall one? He's cute. But not as cute as the other one. Introduce me."

"How?" Lani was no good at that kind of thing.

"Say my name," Mia said.

"I don't know."

"Well, if you want, I'll do the talking. Come on."

Lani reluctantly went along. They cut in front of the boys, who took out their earbuds when Mia practically stopped them in their tracks.

"Hi!" the tall boy said in recognition. "Where are your boogie boards?"

"We're not boogie boarding right now," Mia said. "We're going shopping."

"Hey, don't I know you?" he said, looking at Lani.

"Me?" Lani said, gulping silently. He had actually noticed her!

"Yeah, you go to my school, right? IPA?"

The boy looked different out of his school uniform, but it was definitely him. He was a couple of grades ahead of her at Island Pacific Academy, so she never thought she'd actually meet him, that he'd never be more than a hallway crush.

"Yes. I'm a freshman."

"Her name is Lani. I'm Mia."

"Cool. My name's Tom. This is Jake. He's visiting from Michigan." Jake nodded at them. "Hey, we were thinking of heading out onto the water."

Lani felt herself uncharacteristically speaking up, perhaps in competition with Mia.

"Surfing?"

Jake jumped into the conversation. "We rented some sea kayaks for the week," he said. "Have you ever been on a kayak?"

"We both have," Lani said, bluffing with increasing boldness. Lani had paddled sea kayaks six or seven times since moving to Hawaii, but as far as she knew, Mia had never even seen one.

"Sweet," said Tom. "You want to come with us?"

Mia turned and shook her head at Lani. When Mia had suggested talking to the boys, Lani was sure that doing something athletic was the last thing on her mind. Lani beseeched her silently, and this time it was Mia who relented.

"Yeah," Mia said with little enthusiasm. "We'd love to."

"Awesome. The kayaks are just up the beach." He started walking, and the girls and Jake followed.

"You both from around here?" said Tom.

"Mia's just visiting from Seattle."

"Must be good to get out of the rain."

"Yeah," Mia said, "it's pretty cool here." And for the first time since she'd moved there, Lani felt like it *was* cool. "Are the kayaks big enough to fit two people?"

"They're single-seaters, but we have four of them," Tom said. "My parents are away for the day at some Memorial Day ceremony."

After a few minutes of walking, Tom stopped on the beach next to a large condominium.

"Okay," he said. "You wait here."

"I thought you said we were going to kayak," Mia said.

"The kayaks are back at our condo," Tom said. "We were going to go this afternoon when my parents got back."

"They're sit-on-tops," Jake said. "And we've got life jackets and paddles."

"We'll be back in a minute," Tom said.

While Tom and Jake sprinted across the street and disappeared into a parking garage, Lani gave Mia a crash course on the kayaks. Instead of enclosing the kayaker inside like a river kayak, the plastic shell of a sit-on-top kayak was molded so that the seat perched on top. Although sit-on-tops were better for warm weather because you didn't get as hot, they were also less stable. Mia wasn't happy to hear that, given her inexperience, but Lani tried to reassure her that paddling in them was easy.

Tom and Jake came trotting back carrying one kayak each over their heads. The kayaks didn't look that much different from the ones Lani had been on before: about eleven feet long and bright yellow, with black nylon around the seating area.

"Maybe when we're done kayaking," Tom said, "we could go get some lunch somewhere. My mom left her credit card for us."

"In that case, definitely!" Mia said.

The boys high-fived, then turned and ran back to get the other kayaks and gear.

"What about your mom?" Lani said, awed at Mia's brazen flirting.

"I'll think of something."

In another five minutes, all of them had their life vests on, and the kayaks were bobbing in the gentle surf. To the left were the enclosed waters of Kuhio Beach, protected by a breakwater. To the right, waves crashed into the beach, but the sea was mild where the kayaks floated.

"Shouldn't be too bad getting past the waves today," Jake said.

Lani saw that Mia was apprehensive. She lowered her voice to give Mia some tips.

"Just keep the kayak pointed straight out. There's an undertow at this point, so the waves will be small."

Mia waded up to her knees and sat on the side of the kayak to get in. She slipped off and sank to her shoulders. Jake laughed but rushed over to pick her up. She tentatively balanced herself on his arm as she climbed in. After two more false starts, she finally perched primly on the kayak.

"You sure you've done this before?" Jake said.

Mia nodded. "It's been a while since I did it the last time."

"We'll head out past the breakers," Tom said. "Then maybe we could turn and head up toward Diamond Head. I've heard there are some killer houses along the beach there, but they're hard to see except from the ocean."

They started paddling. When the first waves broke over the front of their kayaks, Mia let out a little scream. Lani laughed. She was finally in her element.

"Come on," Lani said. "It's not that bad."

"Remember to put the paddle sideways into the water, Mia!" Tom yelled. "Come on!"

The boys pulled forward easily, and they looked a little surprised to see Lani keep up with them. Mia fell behind immediately, her paddling technique abysmal. But with a few more minutes of practice, and with the others slowing down, she was able to keep up. The trip out took longer than expected as they fought the stiffened breeze coming off the ocean. After twenty minutes they were about a half mile out and turned east toward the towering walls of Diamond Head.

As they came around, Lani thought for a second that she heard a sound coming from the direction of the shore. But the wind picked up again, whistling as it whipped over the water, and she couldn't even hear the roar of the surf.

CHAPTER 16

REGGIE MADE CONTACT WITH Dr. Niles Aspen, the lead scientist on Johnston Island. After Reggie explained the situation over the satellite link, the scientists scrambled to get as many people into the supply plane as they could. But two would have to stay behind, including Aspen. Kai just had to hope the biologist could find a building sturdy enough to withstand a potential tsunami. Aspen would call back when he was at a safer location.

Brad had no more success getting in touch with Teresa and the kids, but the sirens would be impossible to ignore. Kai was confident that they'd follow the other tourists off the beach. Still, he'd feel better when he knew Lani was safe. He tried not to let his worries distract him from his work.

"Let's go over this again," Kai said, turning his attention back to the problem at hand. "We're still missing something."

Reggie leaned back in his chair and put his hands behind his head as he thought out loud.

"Okay, let's see. There is virtually no chance that an undersea earthquake that small could cause any kind of sizable tsunami, let alone one that could destroy Christmas Island."

"Why not?" asked Brad. Kai started to tell Brad to butt out from habit but changed his mind when he realized Brad's questions might help them look at the situation in a new light.

"No quake that small has ever generated an ocean-wide tsunami," Kai said, "unless the earthquake triggered a landslide."

"Okay. So what about a landslide?"

Reggie and Kai looked at each other and shook their heads.

"Maybe," Kai said.

"'Maybe'?" Brad said. "All you have is 'Maybe'?"

"Look, we just don't have any reason to suspect that that region of the Pacific would be prone to landslides. Underwater landslides usually occur near the edge of a continental shelf, but the region we're talking about is nowhere near a continental shelf."

Reggie threw up his hands. "So we have an earthquake that's too small to generate a tsunami, no known landslide risks, no sensor reading from Christmas Island, and no way to get in touch with anyone there."

"And," Kai said, "the earthquake was in a location where no quake has ever been recorded before."

"So you're saying the tsunami came out of nowhere?" Brad said.

At that moment, Kai happened to look up at one of the TVs. CNN was running the story of the missing TransPacific flight, the TransPac logo prominent in the corner. Then the image shifted to a graphic of the Pacific Ocean. A line stretched from Los Angeles and abruptly ended in the middle of the ocean due south of Hawaii.

"That's funny," Kai said. "It looks like the plane went down where the earthquake epicenter . . ."

And that's when it hit him. It was incredible, but it was the only explanation they hadn't considered.

"It can't be," he said.

"What?" Reggie said.

"We've completely ignored one possibility. It's crazy, but everything fits. I hope to God I'm wrong—knock on wood." Though not normally superstitious, Kai rapped the frame of the cork bulletin board on the wall. But it didn't matter: he knew he was right.

"What are you talking about?" Reggie said.

"Okay," Kai said, "here's the deal. Remember that discussion we had about Crawford and Mader?"

Reggie furrowed his brow for a second, then snapped his fingers and smiled. "Right! Yeah, I said their research was fun, but it was a waste of time. You said—"

Reggie abruptly stopped, his smile vanishing. He looked at Kai incredulously, and Kai could tell he'd struck a nerve. Kai nodded toward the TV, which still showed the map. For a moment Reggie looked at the television, baffled at the connection. Then his expression changed to horror.

In that instant, he knew too.

Reggie launched himself out of his chair. "You're not serious!"

"We have to consider it."

"No! No, no, no, no, no!" Reggie said with a look of stunned disbelief. "I just finished remodeling my house last month. Took me close to two years."

Brad, who had been watching this exchange in confused silence, couldn't take it any longer. "Not serious about what? Who are Crawford and Mader? What's going on?"

"You don't want to know," Reggie said.

"Yes I do! What the hell does this have to do with Reggie's house?"

"In about an hour," Kai said, "Reggie's house won't be there anymore."

Chapter 17

Since Renfro's call with Kai, the Hawaii State Civil Defense staffer and his two colleagues on the holiday skeleton crew, Michelle Rankin and Ronald Deakins, had been on the phone nonstop.

Renfro had the governor and the mayor of Honolulu on conference call. Both were on their way downtown to their offices.

"What's your ETA, Governor?" Renfro said.

"I'll be back at the Capitol in a few minutes. The holiday traffic was already bad, and more people are getting on the road every minute. My cabinet is spread out all over the city. We've been trying to get in touch with them since we left the hotel."

"And you, Mayor?"

The smooth, patrician voice of Mayor Carl Rutledge came over the line. "I was over at Pearl, so it's looking more like fifteen minutes if the traffic doesn't get worse, even with the police escort."

"Who's in charge there?" the governor asked.

"Well, I am, ma'am," said Renfro. "Vice Director Dennis is on Kauai, and there's no way he can get back in time."

"Renfro, what are we looking at here?" the mayor asked. "Is this going to be another false alarm?"

"Sir, you know I can't tell that for sure. What I do know is that we lost contact with Christmas Island, including the tide sensor, and the PTWC issued a tsunami warning."

"Better safe than sorry, Carl," Governor Kalama said.

"I suppose," the mayor said, "but dammit, we're already looking at a budget deficit. We can't have this happen every year."

"Sir, we should know more in a few minutes when the wave is supposed to reach Johnston Island."

On the other side of the room, Rankin was talking to Pearl Harbor's military liaison, an aide to the commander of U.S. Pacific Command. The leader of the USPACOM was responsible for all U.S. armed forces over half the world's surface.

"Lieutenant, we do have procedures for this—" Rankin began.

"But the last drill was for a three-hour window. Now you're telling me I have about an hour?"

"That's right."

"Ma'am, do you know what it takes for a Navy ship to set sail? It ain't like hopping in your Sea Ray and shooting out of the marina."

"How long would it take if you started right now?"

"Two hours, minimum. The engines aren't even hot."

"Look, I'm just telling you how much time you have. You can protest all you want: it's not going to change. Plus, you need to get all of the aircraft out of the coastal air bases. We're recommending moving them to Wheeler."

"Well, you see, that's another problem: most of our pilots are out on leave or at ceremonies away from the bases. We can try to get them back to base, but the way the traffic is moving, we'll be lucky to get a quarter of them up in the air."

Rankin scribbled a note about the military aircraft and handed it to Deakins, who had the responsibility for coordinating with the civilian airports and seaports. He was on the phone with the chief of operations at Honolulu International, which shared runways with Hickam Air Force Base.

"That's right, sir," Deakins said. "You've got about an hour before the wave arrives."

"And the all-clear? When will that be?"

"I can't say for sure."

"Well, I can't keep the planes circling forever."

"Believe me, sir, we will let you know as soon as the danger has passed."

"Flights are going to be backed up all day because of this, you know."

"I realize that, sir."

"Do we need to evacuate the terminals?"

"Not at this time. They're far enough from shore to be out of immediate danger. We're only concerned about the runways at this point. But we recommend that you take everyone off the planes just in case."

"What a headache. You better hope you're not making us do all this for nothing."

"And you, sir, better hope we are."

CHAPTER 18

TWO MINUTES BEFORE THE tsunami was expected to arrive at Johnston Island, Niles Aspen was on speaker phone in the ops center. He and Brent Featherstone, the other scientist staying behind, were both biologists from the University of London.

Kai had wanted them on the line to describe the tsunami in case they lost the feed from the tide gauge, which was in real time. But Aspen had a surprising source of information for them.

"Dr. Tanaka, to help educate our students, we have equipped ourselves with a video camera linked to the satellite network to broadcast photos at sixty-second intervals. But we could change that to a real-time video broadcast." He gave Reggie the web address of the video feed.

Reggie typed it in and they saw a jittery picture of the Johnston Island runway. The twin-engine supply plane carrying their five comrades was on its takeoff roll. In a few seconds it lifted into the air and circled the island to wait until it was clear to land again.

"Can we record what we're seeing?" asked Kai.

In a flurry of mouse clicks too fast for Kai to follow, Reggie started a recording application. "This will let us analyze the data later," he said.

Kai had already told Aspen about the loss of contact with Christmas Island. The British scientist seemed remarkably composed.

"Well," came Aspen's voice through the speaker, "we have Charlotte and the rest safely away. I have to say, Dr. Tanaka, this is all quite exciting for us. Just what we needed to liven up our normal routine." A muffled voice came through behind Aspen's. "And Brent reminds me that we even have a thermos of tea to help us weather the storm, as it were."

"Believe me, Dr. Aspen," Kai said, "I hope I'm wrong."

"I don't know what more we could do."

"You'll be our first confirmation as to whether we're dealing with a true tsunami or not. You're on a concrete structure, correct?"

"It couldn't be more solid. You Americans certainly don't mind wasting construction material. This is the safest place we can be within walking distance. It might be the strongest structure on the island, by the look of it. We didn't bring any vehicles, of course."

"How high are you?"

"I would say we're thirty feet above the ground."

The camera panned around to show a wide, flat roof, and then the jaunty figure of Aspen in a wide-brimmed hat, T-shirt, and shorts, holding a large phone to his ear as he waved to the camera. The voice came out slightly ahead of the image from the camera, so it looked like a badly dubbed foreign film.

"We are now moving the camera to the edge of the roof facing the ocean. As you mentioned, the tsunami should arrive from the southeast, so that is the direction that you will be looking."

After a few more seconds of nausea-inducing wobbles, the camera came to a stop atop a tripod, with Aspen now out of the picture. A narrow road led away from the building, passing several structures before it petered out at the beach. In the distance, breakers could be seen curling over the reef that encircled the island.

"To give you a sense of perspective," Aspen said, "the two buildings you see directly in front of us are single-story wooden structures roughly fifteen feet in height. I would estimate that the shoreline is about five hundred yards away. That is about as far as we could get from the ocean and still find a strong building. I'd be quite surprised if the water got even this far inland."

Another indistinct mumbling in the background.

"Brent thought he spotted a wave on the horizon, but it was just another big breaker on the reef."

"Dr. Aspen," Kai said, "it's likely that the first thing you'll see is the water receding from the shore."

"Right. We'll keep on the lookout . . . Wait a minute. I think I see what you're talking about."

A second later Kai could see the ocean noticeably receding from the beach, visible even with the poor video. He had seen similar video and pictures from other tsunamis, particularly the Asian tsunami, but seeing it in real time was literally breathtaking.

"It's a spectacular sight, really," Aspen said. "It's like no ebb tide I've ever seen."

Kai watched in wide-eyed wonder as the water went out. By the time it had withdrawn a couple hundred yards, he expected the tide to start reversing and come back. But to his astonishment it kept going out.

"Sweet Jesus," said Reggie. "It's happening."

Aspen continued to cheerfully report what he was observing.

"I'd guess the water has gone out one thousand yards by now. Is this the kind of phenomenon you were expecting, Dr. Tanaka?"

All Kai could say was, "No." This was beyond his wildest nightmares. Until that point, he thought Aspen's retreat to the rooftop would provide all the protection he needed. Now Kai clearly saw that the situation was dire, but he didn't know what to tell Aspen. There was nowhere else for the man to go.

"The water has stopped receding, I believe."

The video confirmed his words. The extreme ebb tide bubbled out past the reef. With better camera resolution, Kai would have expected to see thousands of fish flopping around on the newly exposed ocean bottom.

"My word, look at the birds."

That got Kai's attention. It seemed like an odd thing to say, considering everything else clamoring for attention. "Excuse me, Dr. Aspen?"

"I've never seen anything like it, really. All the birds on the island seemed to have taken flight simultaneously. I hope the pilot notices and steers clear of them."

A yell in the background.

"Brent just noticed that the water is starting to come back. At an alarming pace, too, I'm afraid."

In the distance, a frothy white line stretched across the horizon and out of the field of view of the camera. After a few seconds the white froth had risen visibly and seemed to be racing for the camera.

"Dr. Aspen," Kai said, "you need to find something to tie yourselves to. Anything permanently affixed to the structure."

"We have no rope."

"Use your belts, nylon from a backpack—anything."

"I'm afraid the best we can do is to wrap our arms around a metal ladder bolted into the side of the building. Excuse me while we do so." Kai marveled that the man continued to use common courtesies in such a dire situation.

The wave now approached the beach. The froth looked to be thirty feet high and still rising. A growing roar threatened to drown out Aspen's voice.

"As you can hear," he shouted, straining to make himself audible, "we are listening to what sounds like twenty approaching freight trains. How big is this tsunami going to get, Dr. Tanaka?"

He deserved the truth. "I don't know, Dr. Aspen. Maybe too big."

A pause. He knew what Kai meant.

"Well, Dr. Tanaka," Aspen yelled over the din, "it seems Brent and I may not get to enjoy that cup of tea after all."

As he said that, a wall of water smashed into the palm trees closest to the beach, completely engulfing them, and the wave finally showed signs of curling over. Kai could only watch in shock as the tsunami collapsed and drove itself into the first building it encountered, shattering the wooden structure.

Whole trees and the debris from the building were driven forward by a wave that had to be at least one hundred feet high. It engulfed everything in its path. No building was even half the height of the wave. It was as if the world's largest dam had burst.

The howl of crashing water coming from the phone now made it almost impossible to hear what Aspen was saying.

"My Lord! Hold on, Brent!" Then a scream from Brent

in the background, and that was all Kai could make out before the phone went dead.

At the same time, the tsunami commanded the entire area of the screen. It was like peering through the window of a washing machine, water boiling and churning, with indistinct bits of detritus writhing around within it.

The camera pitched backward, probably from the force of air pushed in front of it by the wave. For a fraction of a second, all Kai could see was blue sky. Then a shadow loomed over the lens, and the image was gone.

Kai, Brad, and Reggie all stood in stunned silence. Nobody could muster the words to comment on what they had just seen. But they knew the implications. In less than an hour, Hawaii was going to experience a catastrophe of epic proportions.

CHAPTER 19

THE HORROR OF WATCHING Dr. Aspen's and Brent Featherstone's deaths confirmed Kai's nightmare scenario.

"What the hell is going on?" Brad said. Then he pointed at Kai with an accusing finger. "How did you know the tsunami would be so big?"

"I didn't know, all right?" Kai yelled. He calmed himself, but his pulse was still racing. "It was just a guess based on Crawford and Mader's research. I saw on the news that a TransPac jet went down somewhere over the Pacific. They showed a graphic of the plane going down in the exact same location as the earthquake."

"So?"

"I don't think that it's a coincidence. Brad, since it's just me and Reggie here, I'm going to need your help. Call the FAA and find out exactly what the latitude and longitude was where they lost contact. And see if there were any other planes in the area. And don't take no for an answer."

"Why?"

"I'll explain when you're off the phone."

"But who do I call? It's a holiday."

"I don't know. There's got to be an emergency number. Here." Kai gave him the number for Hawaii State Civil

Defense. "Call Brian Renfro at HSCD. Get the number from him. Tell him you're my brother."

Brad looked dubious, but he saw that Kai was serious and went into the other room to make the call.

"Kai," Reggie said, "do you know what the chances are of this happening?"

"I don't know. A million to one? But, Reggie, what if it did happen? We've got no scenarios for dealing with it."

"If we're wrong about this and word gets out, we are going to be the laughingstock of the seismic community."

"I know, Reggie, but . . ." Kai tapped his watch. He didn't have to tell Reggie the clock was ticking. "I'm going to get on the phone with NASA and find out if they have any satellite data or photos from the site of our earthquake."

"And me?"

"Start doing a search of relevant papers in the *Science of Tsunami Hazards*. See if you can find that formula from Crawford and Mader."

"Gotcha."

Kai dialed HSCD. Although the PTWC notified many different organizations throughout the Pacific about tsunami hazards, NASA was not one of them. Kai had no emergency number for them.

Brian Renfro picked up the phone on the other end.

"Brian, it's Kai Tanaka."

"Kai, what is going on? Your brother just called me asking for the number for the FAA."

"You gave it to him, right?"

"Sure, but that's a little weird, don't you think?"

"It's going to get weirder. Who would we call to get emergency satellite imagery?"

"Satellite imagery. Why do you need that?"

"I think the situation may be worse than we first imagined."

"Worse than a tsunami? Is there a hurricane coming too?"

Brad came back in holding a slip of paper.

"Hold on, Brian," Kai said. To Brad: "That was fast."

"While I was on the phone, I looked at CNN's Web site. They already had the latitude and longitude reported in the story."

He gave Kai the slip of paper with the coordinates. Kai gave it to Reggie, who took a red dot from the container and stuck it on the map at the indicated coordinates. It overlapped with the dot of the earthquake.

"Jesus!" said Reggie. "You've got to be kidding me."

"What do you think?" Kai asked.

"I think I'm wrong about the seamount."

"Brian," Kai said, "it's worse than a hurricane." He told Renfro about the video of the disaster at Johnston Island.

"And Christmas Island?" Renfro said.

"It's probably completely wiped out. Brian, the reason I wanted Brad to call the FAA was because I wanted to confirm that the TransPac flight went down at the same location as the earthquake."

"Why do you want to know that?"

Kai took a deep breath. It was the first time he'd say it out loud. "Because I think that we've had a meteor impact in the middle of the Pacific."

Renfro laughed. "Yeah, right." When Kai didn't laugh with him, he became silent. "You're serious?"

"That's the only explanation I can think of."

"You think satellite imagery can confirm it?"

"Yes. Who is the best to call? NASA? They operate Landsat. How about NESDIS?" NOAA's National Environmental Satellite, Data, and Information Service operated the GOES weather satellites that were used for all of the nation's hurricane forecasting.

"They're a good place to start," Renfro said. "I'll patch you in when I get someone on the line."

With that, he hung up.

"Wait a minute!" Brad said. "What did you just say? A meteor?"

"Actually, if it hit the earth, it's a meteorite," Reggie said.

"What are you, the language police?" Brad said. "Who cares?" He turned to Kai. "Come on! If a meteor or meteorite or asteroid or whatever was heading toward us, it would have been big news all over the TV for months."

"Not if no one saw it coming," Kai said.

"Maybe it came out of the sun," Reggie said.

"You mean they might have missed an asteroid big enough to cause a tsunami? I'd like to know who's in charge of that screwup."

"That's not important now," Kai said. "We'll just have to assume it's an asteroid impact and work from there."

"Why does it even matter?" Brad said.

"Because if it *was* an impact, we don't know how big the resulting tsunami would be when it reaches Hawaii. Asteroid impacts move water in a way completely different from earthquakes. That's why we need to get some data. Reggie's looking to see if he can find Crawford and Mader's latest projections."

Brad looked confused. Kai explained further, as much to help himself wrap his head around the scenario as for Brad's benefit.

"Crawford and Mader are researchers at the Los Alamos laboratory in New Mexico. They wrote a series of papers about computer models they had developed predicting how big tsunamis from an asteroid impact would be. Of course, they had to make a lot of assumptions, like material density, velocity of the asteroid, and angle of impact. But part of their research estimated how big the tsunamis would be as a function of the distance from the impact point and the diameter of the asteroid."

"But if the asteroid wasn't detected before it hit, how can you know how big it is?" Brad was quick.

"Because we know how big the earthquake was and how deep the water is in that part of the ocean," Kai said. "They developed a formula that would approximate the magnitude of the resulting earthquake depending on the size of the asteroid. We'll solve the formula in reverse based on the size of the quake. From that, we can estimate how big the waves would be at various distances from the impact zone."

"Fine," Brad said. "But how do you know they're right?"

"We don't," said Reggie. "We've never gotten seismic readings from an asteroid impact. There have been a lot of different papers written about asteroid-generated tsunamis, and the estimates are all over the map. Even the Johnston Island images only give us a minimum size."

"The data from the DART buoy should give us an accurate reading," Kai said.

"So until then," Brad said, "you're guessing."

"Educated guessing. It's better than nothing."

"So, if it is an asteroid, what do we do?"

Kai honestly didn't know. The PTWC had been founded to warn against tsunamis generated by earthquakes, the most frequent cause of Pacific-wide tsunamis that were a threat to Hawaii. Most of the dangerous quakes were centered in Alaska, Japan, or Chile, but tsunamis could also be generated locally by volcanic quakes and landslides. Tsunamis originating from the Pacific Rim would take five hours or more to get to the islands, leaving plenty of time to evacuate the coastline, even if it was extremely costly and time-consuming. Locally-generated tsunamis could arrive in a matter of minutes and were therefore much more dangerous. In either case, evacuation routes and procedures had been carefully planned out, based on the size of tsunamis typical for those sources.

But there were no procedures for dealing with an asteroid-generated tsunami. It was just too unlikely to spend the PTWC's limited time and resources on.

"I've got the formula," said Reggie. He started tapping it into the computer. "So, let's see. We registered an earthquake of 6.9. What's the depth of the ocean at that location?"

Using a map of the Pacific Ocean floor, Kai sounded out each digit to make sure Reggie understood. "Four nine two five."

"Got it." Reggie continued typing. "And now I just type in how far we are from the epicenter, and that should give us a ballpark height of the biggest wave."

When he was finished, he leaned forward and looked confused. Then his eyes widened suddenly, and he pulled his hands back from the keyboard as if it were hot.

"What is it?" Brad said.

"Maybe I did the calculation wrong." Reggie started over and typed all of the numbers in again. When he saw the results, he leaned back and shook his head.

"Oh, man," Reggie said, "if this model is anywhere close to being accurate, we're in serious trouble."

"How big?" Kai asked, already knowing that it was beyond his worst fears.

Reggie let out a heavy sigh. "At least seventy when it gets here."

"Holy shit!" Brad said. "The Asian tsunami didn't get bigger than thirty feet high, did it?"

Reggie shook his head. "There are some estimates that it got at least twice that high in Banda Aceh."

Brad's eyes goggled at the awe-inspiring thought. "So seventy feet will be huge."

Kai put his hand on Brad's shoulder. He didn't get it.

"Brad, all of our figures are in metric units. Meters, not feet. Seventy meters. The wave is going to be over two hundred feet high."

CHAPTER 20

THE PROSPECT OF A two-hundred-foot-high wall of water hitting a populated coastline was unmatched in recorded civilization. The biggest tsunami to hit any kind of populated area was the monster wave that resulted from the explosion of Krakatoa in 1883. The hundred-foot-high wave wiped out entire villages in the Sunda Strait of Indonesia, killing thirty-six thousand people.

Now they were facing the possibility of a wave at least twice that big hitting one of the most densely populated coastlines in the world.

The phone rang, and Kai picked it up slowly, his mind reeling.

"Tanaka," he said.

"Dr. Tanaka, this is Jeanette Leslie from CNN. I have some questions about the tsunami warning that was issued a few minutes ago."

"I'm sorry, but I don't have time to answer questions right now."

"But, Dr. Tanaka, you—"

Before she could get any further, Kai hung up. Within moments, the phone rang again.

"It's started," Reggie said.

"The phone's going to be ringing off the hook." Without a receptionist to field the calls, just answering the phone would take up all of their time. Kai turned to Brad.

"I need your help again."

"Answer the phones?"

"Yes. Reggie and I have too much to do."

"But what do I say? I don't know anything."

"Actually, you know a lot. Maybe too much. I can't have you giving out quotes to the media. Just tell them we will issue an official statement in"—Kai glanced at his watch—"ten minutes. Until then, no comment."

Dealing with the media was a double-edged sword. Fielding their calls would take precious minutes away from calculating wave arrival times for the rest of the Pacific islands. On the other hand, giving the media statements could be a powerful tool for warning the public to get to high ground. But Kai couldn't blindside HSCD. He needed to confer with them first. And it would definitely help to have some confirmation from NASA.

"What about the meteor impact?" Brad said. "Do you think we should mention that?"

"Look, Kai," said Reggie, "I'm buying into your theory. We've got a big tsunami coming. But I think talking about a meteorite impact at this point is premature."

"Right," Brad said. "Why should we jump to conclusions? We have, oh, fifty-three minutes left. No reason to panic!"

"I didn't say we shouldn't issue another warning!"

"Calm down, you two," Kai said quietly. "Reggie, send out an update that we have lost contact with Johnston Island and Christmas Island, and we believe a large tsunami may hit the coastline of Hawaii. We recommend that people get as far inland as possible."

"Large tsunami?" Reggie said.

"Okay, massive tsunami."

"I guess vertical evacuation is out."

In most tsunamis, the downtown and Waikiki areas of Honolulu were so densely populated that evacuation by road, or "horizontal evacuation," would cause huge traffic jams, essentially stopping all motion on the roads and inhibiting the movement of emergency vehicles and buses. For those who couldn't evacuate away from the beach on foot or by vehicle, they normally recommended taking refuge above the third floor of a building at least six stories tall.

But in this case, the biggest wave was going to be at least the height of a twenty-story building. People following the standard instructions would be sentenced to death.

Kai nodded. "Recommend that people should get to high ground and that they may not be safe on high floors of buildings."

"What about calling it a mega-tsunami?"

Mega-tsunami, a term used by the popular press, had no scientific definition, but the generally accepted understanding was that it was a tsunami over one hundred feet in height. Using the term would be a huge step. Warning about a tsunami was one thing. Warning about a mega-tsunami was unprecedented. The media would latch on to it like lampreys.

"Not until we get confirmation from NASA or the DART buoy. Just say that it's a massive tsunami and that we're not ready to estimate the height."

"Gotcha. Helluva holiday, huh?"

Brad tapped him on the shoulder.

"Kai, I've got NESDIS on hold with Brian Renfro."

"Good. Maybe they have something."

"I also have Harry Dupree, George Huntley, and Mary Grayson holding. They called in as soon as they heard about the tsunami warning."

"Where are they?" Kai was hoping George and Mary might be close enough to come in. Having two more scientists at the PTWC would be a big help.

"Harry's in the Maui County Police Department. George and Mary are on the North Shore, at least an hour's drive from here."

"Okay," Kai said. "They're not going to do us any good here. Transfer the NASA call over here, and tell the others to wait."

A few seconds later the phone at the monitoring desk rang. As Kai picked up the phone, he motioned to Reggie.

"Reggie, once you've sent out the new warning, keep an eye on the DART data. Let me know the minute we start to get a reading."

Reggie nodded and started typing at the terminal.

"Hello," Kai said, getting back on the line. "Brian, you there?"

"I'm here, Kai. I've also got someone from NASA."

"Hello. My name is Kai Tanaka, assistant director of the Pacific Tsunami Warning Center. Who's this?"

A woman's chipper voice responded. "This is Gail Wentworth, the duty scientist at NOAA's Satellite Analysis Branch. Mr. Renfro said it was important. How can I help you?"

"It *is* important. The lives of almost every person in Hawaii may be at risk. I need to know if you have any photos or video taken over the central Pacific in the last hour. Specifically, at 1841 GMT."

"Let me see. GOES-10 takes images every thirty minutes. I've got an image from 1830 GMT. There's also the MTSAT from Japan."

"No. You don't understand. I need an image from 1841 GMT or *after*. We have reason to believe a meteorite struck that area this morning, and that a massive tsunami is headed toward Hawaii."

Wentworth paused to take that in, then slowly said, "Why do you think a meteorite impact is the cause of it?"

"Several reasons I don't have time to go into," Kai said. "Do you have any images from the area of the Pacific with these coordinates?" He read Wentworth the longitude and latitude of the earthquake epicenter.

"The next GOES image is from 1900 GMT," she said, "but even that may not help you. I don't know if the resolution is great enough to see an impact like that. Besides, there's a storm in that area of the Pacific. It may obscure an impact."

Wentworth's pace was agonizing for Kai.

"We have fifty-three minutes until the wave gets here," Kai said impatiently. "Less to the Big Island. Are there any other options? What about the space shuttle?"

"Discovery is the only one in orbit. It's docked with the space station. They're over Egypt right now. As you know, the region you're talking about is hundreds of miles from the nearest inhabited island. A higher-resolution polar-orbiting satellite may have been over that region this morning, but it'll take me a little while to check and get any images we have to you."

"Please let me know as soon as you have confirmation. Minutes count."

"I'll do my best."

Kai thanked Wentworth and gave her the e-mail address where she could send the images. When Kai hung up, Reggie waved him over to his terminal.

"I'm getting the DART buoy data now."

Kai bent over Reggie's terminal, explaining to Brad what they were looking at.

"This graph shows the displacement of the height of the sea level as a function of time. As the line of the graph goes up, the height of the sea level increases."

"How can the buoy detect a change in sea level with all the regular waves going by?"

"The buoy is just a transmitting device. The scientific instrumentation is actually on the ocean floor, measuring changes in pressure of the water above it. Then it sends those readings by an acoustic modem to the buoy, where it links with a communications satellite. The wind-driven waves aren't big enough to affect the pressure sensor on the seafloor, so it normally only fluctuates with the tidal pull of the moon."

Kai pointed to an historical graph that showed the sea level height going up and down on a daily basis. "But if a tsunami passes over it, the entire column of water from the surface all the way down to the bottom is affected by the wave."

"Will you look at that," Reggie said, his voice weighted with awe.

The line on the graph had already started to climb. Kai held his breath, hoping it would stay small, nothing more than a blip. But the line inexorably rose higher, propelled by the five-hundred-mile-an-hour wave. In two minutes, the line had topped out at 0.65 meters above sea level.

"I guess we're sure now," Reggie said.

"Zero point six five meters?" Brad said. "But that's

great! Less than three feet!" His enthusiasm waned when he saw Reggie's grim face.

Reggie shook his head. "That's in the open ocean. In a boat, you wouldn't even notice the change in sea level."

Kai leaned back, finally coming to grips with the reality of the situation. "In the deep ocean," he said, "the wave goes all the way to the seafloor. Once it reaches shallow water, it'll start to bunch up, slow down, and grow in height. How high it gets on land depends on the run-up factor at that part of the coast. Multiply the run-up factor by the wave height at sea, and you get how high the wave will be on land."

"The run-up factor for Honolulu is forty," said Reggie.

Brad did a quick mental calculation. "That's twenty-five meters. Seventy-five feet. At least it's smaller than two hundred feet."

Kai shook his head. "A seventy-five-foot wave is huge. Besides, that's just the first wave. There might be more—maybe two or three more."

"The computer models from the lab at Los Alamos expected the first wave from an asteroid impact to be the biggest one," Reggie said. "But this has never happened before, so who knows? We'll know if and when we get the next DART reading. In any case, we have confirmation now, even without the NASA photos."

Kai nodded. "Brad, call Brian Renfro back and conference him in with Harry, George, and Mary."

After a few seconds, they were all on the line, with one added person Kai hadn't been expecting.

"Kai," Brian said, "when you first told me your theory, I took the precaution of asking the governor to make her way to the HSCD bunker. She's still on her way, so I asked her to conference in from her car."

The governor didn't waste time with chitchat.

"Dr. Tanaka," the governor said, "is this a false alarm?"

"I'm sorry to say it isn't, Governor," Kai said. "We don't have much time. I got you all on the line so I would only have to say this once. We believe an asteroid struck the central Pacific about an hour ago, although we don't have confirmation from NASA just yet. What we do know is that a major tsunami is headed our way. And when I say *major,* I mean one that will make the Asian tsunami look like a kiddie pool. The first wave will be over twenty meters. If we get more waves, the max wave height could be over seventy meters, but we won't know for sure until we get the DART buoy readings for any follow-up waves."

"But you're sure about the first wave, Dr. Tanaka?" the governor said.

"Yes, ma'am. No doubt."

"Okay. Good work catching this in time. Brian tells me that was a gutsy call."

"Thank you, ma'am, but we've still got a lot of work to do."

"I know. I'm getting off the phone now so I can mobilize the National Guard. You guys keep doing what you need to do. And let me know if you need anything from me. I'll be at the HSCD in ten minutes." With a click, the governor was gone.

"Is everyone else still there?" Kai said.

"I am," Mary said, her voice quavering. "But George got off the phone to call his mother. She lives near the beach in Hilo."

Kai looked at Brad, who shook his head. No word from Teresa.

"You should all take a minute to call your families," Kai said. "Mary, you and George are too far away to do us any good right now, so I don't want you to try to get back here."

"Dammit!" Mary said. "Isn't there anything we can do?"

"Eventually, we'll have to leave the center and relocate somewhere up island. I'm thinking that Wheeler is the best option, so you can try heading in that direction. I don't know how long cell phones will work, but keep them handy. Harry, since you're already at the Maui Police Department, you can help coordinate there. All we can tell people is to get as far inland and as high up as possible."

"Our houses will be hit by the first wave," Harry said. Every person on the conference call would be homeless in a little less than an hour.

"I know. And we don't have any time to get your personal stuff out. I'm sorry." It was the same story for Kai. Fifteen years of his family's memories would soon be lost forever.

"What about you guys?" Harry said, the concern in his voice apparent. "Don't hang around there too long."

"I will evacuate us in time to get to safety. But until then we have a job to do and very little time to do it. We're going to have to throw our normal procedures out the window. At this point, all we can do is get as many people out of Honolulu as we can."

The clock on the wall said 10:32.

"Fifty minutes," Kai said. "That's how long we've got to evacuate over half a million people."

CHAPTER 21

KAI CALLED RACHEL HIMSELF this time. He needed her to know how dangerous the situation was, especially because what he was telling her sounded so improbable.

"It's good you didn't have Brad call me," Rachel said. "I'd think it was a joke."

"I know this sounds crazy, but it's what the data are telling us."

"An asteroid? I can't believe it."

"I know. But if I'm right, nobody is safe in that hotel."

"What about the Starlight restaurant on the twenty-eighth floor? We've got lots of room up there."

"Rachel, even if the wave doesn't reach that high, the building might collapse."

"But we have over a thousand guests staying in the hotel! Not to mention a ballroom full of disabled veterans."

"You've got to start evacuating them now. Do you have any buses for them?"

"I had some scheduled to pick them up and take them to the cemetery for the ceremony this afternoon, but they're not supposed to be here for another hour."

"Look, it's at least a fifteen-minute walk to a safe zone from there. That means you've only got about thirty minutes left to get everyone out."

"That's not enough time—"

"Rachel, the tsunami doesn't care if it's enough time. That's when it's going to get here, and anyone left in the hotel after that time won't make it."

Kai could hear a pause while she tried to accept what he was telling her.

"Okay," she finally said. "Where should they go?"

"They should use one of the west bridges off of Waikiki and then just head uphill until they can't go any farther. The best would be for them to try to get up to the Punchbowl or into one of the hillside neighborhoods. If they aren't safe there, I don't know where they'll be safe." The National Memorial Cemetery of the Pacific, known locally as the Punchbowl, was an extinct volcanic crater holding vast rows of veterans' graves. The sides of it were over four hundred feet high.

"What about Lani? What about Teresa and Mia?"

"I haven't heard from them. I'm sure they've heard the warnings and are heading to high ground as we speak."

"Then why haven't they called?"

"The phone lines are jammed. I'm lucky I got through to you. Plus, Teresa's phone battery is dead. She probably doesn't want to stop and call us from a landline until she's safe. Which is the right thing to do."

"Okay. But let me know the minute you hear anything. I better get going. I've got a lot of people to evacuate."

"Rachel, promise me you'll be walking in thirty minutes."

"I promise that as soon as I get everyone out, I'll get out too."

"If you don't get out before that, you'll be stuck in the hotel. There won't be time to get to safety between the waves. They're too big."

"I understand that, Kai, but I am responsible for these people. I have to do my job."

"I know. Go do it. And, honey, I love you."

"I love you too," Rachel said. "I'll see you when this is over."

She hung up. Kai stared at the phone, hoping to hell that she was right.

Rachel immediately got on her walkie-talkie.

"Max, come in."

"This is Max. Rachel, are you watching the TV?"

"No, I'm up in the ballroom."

"They just issued a new tsunami warning. But now they're saying—"

"They're saying it's going to be a lot bigger, and they're telling us to evacuate the hotel."

"So you are watching it."

"It doesn't matter. We've got to evacuate."

"I was having problems just getting people to go back to their rooms. We're swamped down here in the lobby."

"I know. You've been sending the guests with rooms on the first, second, and third floors to the Wailea Ballroom, right?"

"Yes, that's the procedure."

"Not anymore. Go up and tell them to leave the hotel. They should head up Kalakaua Avenue. Then have them go up Manoa Road to Woodlawn."

"Woodlawn? That's got to be at least three miles away."

"I know. That might be far enough inland."

"Are you kidding?"

How many people are going to ask me that today? Rachel thought.

"I'm not kidding," she said. "Just do it."

"Okay, but how do I convince the guests? Some of them have asked me where the best place to view the tsunami is." Max paused for a moment. "What if we set off the fire alarm?"

"I thought about that," Rachel said, "but it might make people more confused. They might think it's an alarm for the tsunami and stay where they are."

"Then what about the people already in their rooms?"

"First, spread the word to the staff that we're evacuating the hotel. Then, after you've informed the guests in the Wailea Ballroom of what's going on, take as many of the front desk staff as you can spare and go room to room to make sure people know to evacuate."

"What if they won't?"

"We can't force them to leave, but make sure they understand how dangerous the situation is. Remember, my husband works at the PTWC. If he says to get out, we're going to damn well do it."

"And what about you?"

"I've got five hundred guests in the Kamehameha Ballroom. I don't leave until they do."

CHAPTER 22

HONOLULU HAD FORTY-EIGHT MINUTES, but the Big Island had only eleven minutes. Renfro knew that many on Hawaii wouldn't be able to reach safety, especially if they hadn't already started to evacuate, but they had to try. And they had one advantage that Christmas Island and Johnston Island didn't have: the Hawaiian Islands were built by volcanoes, so they were very steep. If people walked quickly or ran, they might be able to get to a safe height.

Renfro realized that every second ticking away was precious. The governor was still on her way, but he couldn't wait even the last few minutes it would take for her to arrive. He would have to make the new announcement himself from the broadcast booth.

By this time, several others on staff had made it in to help him out. But there were still only six of them, so he gathered them around to give the most important briefing of their lives.

"Okay, here it is," he said, his voice shaking. "In eleven minutes, a massive tsunami will hit the south tip of the Big Island. In a little more than thirty minutes after that, Honolulu will be hit. I will be updating the warning immediately after I'm done here."

One of the new arrivals, Chet Herman, spoke up. "Shouldn't you wait for the governor—"

"No. She'll make another announcement later, but it'll be at least fifteen minutes before she gets here and has a script in hand. As it is, we basically have to write off the Big Island. Nobody in this room should spend any more time on it."

There was murmuring at that.

"I know it seems heartless, but I don't think we have enough time to coordinate anything from here. They'll have to take the warning and do their best. We'll concentrate on Oahu."

Some of them nodded. With this kind of crisis, the objective was to save as many as possible. Eighty percent of the state's population was concentrated here. There was still time to accomplish something on Oahu.

Renfro had no idea whether people would pay attention to the new warning. The previous plans that had been broadcast were now useless or, even worse, dangerous. If the populace didn't listen to his instructions, thousands would needlessly die.

Cathy Aiko raised her hand.

"What do you want me on?" she said.

"Cathy, you need to call all the hotels and get them to evacuate the tourists. Vertical evacuation is out of the question at this point."

The newest hotels and office buildings were constructed to withstand anything that was within the reasonable realm of possibility, including resisting 150-mile-per-hour hurricane winds with no more than a slight sway. The lower floors would allow the water from a storm surge or tsunami to pass through the building and blow out the back wall, so that the water pressure would not put undue structural stress on the load-bearing systems.

But no building was built to bear the impact of a twenty-story wall of water. For a wave that tall, the structure would have to survive fifty thousand tons of pressure, the weight of one hundred fully loaded 747s. Most buildings would simply collapse when the lower floors buckled, if they weren't completely torn apart. Fleeing to a higher floor would be no refuge.

The obstacles to getting the population to safety in such a short amount of time were too numerous for Renfro to address. After his announcement was made, many roads would become completely jammed with vehicles, despite their pleas to flee on foot. The traffic would make it that much more difficult for emergency vehicles and buses to evacuate those who couldn't walk.

Which led to the next problem: evacuating low-lying hospitals and nursing homes.

Renfro pointed at the last newcomer, Thomas Kamala. "Tom, you coordinate with The Queen's Medical Center. They need to get everyone out. They might have a little more time. They won't be hit until we get a third or fourth wave. Make sure Tripler is ready for them. You also need to alert all of the nursing homes."

With over five hundred beds, The Queen's Medical Center, located next to the Capitol building in downtown Honolulu, was the largest medical facility on the islands. Many ICU patients and premature babies would be on life support, not to mention the surgeries that were under way. They would all have to be moved to Tripler Army Medical Center, which thankfully sat on a small plateau northeast of Pearl Harbor. The patients who were not critical would have to be moved by bus, along with nursing home patients who were too feeble to move on their own. Others would have to be moved by helicopter.

The military presence on Oahu would be especially helpful in this crisis. The fleet of Army, Navy, and Air Force helicopters—as many as could get off the ground before the first wave arrived—and the numerous commercial helicopters on the islands would be pressed into service to evacuate the hospital patients and others who couldn't get to safety in time.

"Michelle, you're in charge of coordinating with the military. Get the bases around Pearl evacuated and get as many aircraft into the air as you can. We'll need the helicopters badly, I'm guessing. The other planes can go up to Wheeler." Wheeler Army Airfield was in mid-island Oahu. Not knowing exactly how big the waves would get, even Wheeler might not be safe, but it was the only option.

"Ronald, you're in charge of the airports, Honolulu International in particular. Even though the Kahului Airport is on the north side of Maui, it's also in danger because the wave will wrap around the island. You need to get everyone out of the airports. If there are planes all ready to go, get them in the air. But they don't have time to start boarding. We don't want to have them standing on the runway when the wave gets here."

"What about the planes coming in?" Deakins said.

"If they don't have the fuel to turn back to the mainland, they need to land at Wheeler. I don't want anything landing at the commercial airports after ten minutes from now."

Renfro got up, and except for Chet Herman the group dispersed.

"What about me?" Herman said.

Renfro paused. The equipment in the broadcast room was designed to be easy to use, but he still needed to have someone operate it while he was on air. The current warning was on a loop, and he would have to break in.

"I need you to help me with the broadcast," Renfro said.

Renfro seated himself in front of the camera and clenched his hands tightly on his knees. He nodded at Herman, who hit a few buttons and then pointed at Renfro. The red light on the camera came on, and Renfro began the announcement.

"Hello, I am Brian Renfro, duty officer at Hawaii State Civil Defense." He cleared his throat. "A tsunami warning has been issued for the entire Pacific, including the Hawaiian Islands. I am here to update that warning. The Pacific Tsunami Warning Center now has clear evidence from a deep-sea buoy that a massive tsunami is headed toward Hawaii. When it makes landfall, the tsunami is expected to be over eighty feet in height. We have lost contact with Christmas Island, and we know that a huge tsunami has hit Johnston Island. At 10:45 a.m. local time, the wave is expected to make landfall at the southern tip of the Big Island. It will hit Oahu and Honolulu at 11:22 this morning. The wave arrival times for the other islands will be scrolling across the bottom of the screen. If you are listening to this on the radio, the arrival times will be broadcast at the end of this announcement."

He took a deep breath to steel himself for what he would say next.

"Larger waves may follow. Again, there is a strong possibility of multiple waves, and the first wave may not be the largest wave. The biggest wave could reach over two hundred feet in height. Therefore, we are urging all residents of the Hawaiian Islands to immediately leave their present locations and evacuate as far inland as possible. If you are already in a seagoing vessel, do not return to shore. Get as far out in the ocean as you can."

At this point, he decided not to mention the asteroid. Without proof, he couldn't be sure that people would take the warning seriously if he told them that an asteroid strike had caused the tsunami.

"If you have evacuated to the upper floors of a building, you are *not* safe. Please leave the building immediately and walk to high ground. Only those who are incapable of walking should take vehicles.

"Please do not panic. If you begin to walk now, you will have time to get to high ground. When we have further information, we will broadcast a new warning. But do not stay by your television. Take a portable TV or radio with you as you evacuate. Authorities will be assisting the evacuation.

"Good luck. That is all."

CHAPTER 23

CAPTAIN MARTIN WAINWRIGHT PEERED through the cockpit window of his C-130E at the bright blue ocean below. The chatter coming over the radio was like nothing he had ever heard in his eight years of flying for the 314th Airlift Wing. Reports were being thrown around about an immense tsunami heading toward Hawaii, but from an altitude of thirty-one thousand feet, the sea looked as calm and flat as a pond in his native Tennessee.

The Air Force transport under his command had been flying for more than three hours on a mission from San Diego to Hickam Air Force Base carrying three brand-new Humvees for delivery to the naval base at Pearl Harbor. He was expecting the usual milk run for him and his four crewmates: land at Hickam, secure the aircraft, get off base for a few hours of sightseeing at Waikiki, hit the barracks for some sack time, then ferry a load of equipment back to the mainland the next day. Nothing that he hadn't done a dozen times before. But the order he was now being given by the Honolulu Air Traffic Control Center was extraordinary.

"This is Air Force 547," Wainwright said. He wasn't sure he'd heard correctly. "Say again, Honolulu control. You're closing Hickam?"

"Roger that, 547," the controller said, his voice clipped and strained. "You are instructed to turn back immediately to the mainland and make for the nearest possible landing site."

"That's a negative, Honolulu control. We're past the point of no return." The four-engine turboprop had already sucked up over half the fuel in its tanks. They wouldn't make it within three hundred miles of San Diego before they ran out of gas. Hawaii was one of the most remote archipelagos in the world, which meant that there weren't any other choices to land.

"Roger that, 547. You aren't the only one. Continue on your current heading. We'll try to make room at Wheeler for you."

"Affirmative, Honolulu control."

"And 547, be advised that we'll be evacuating Honolulu control in thirty minutes. We'll be turning control over to Wheeler Field at that time."

Wainwright glanced at his copilot in disbelief. To close down the airport was one thing, but shutting down the control center was unprecedented. The troubled look on his copilot's face reflected his own. Their routine run to the islands had just become a nail-biter.

Teresa had been waiting for thirty minutes, and there was still no sign of Mia and Lani. The sirens kept wailing at regular intervals, but without a radio, she didn't know what was going on. Even though it was critically low on battery power, she had turned her cell phone back on. She had to take the chance in case the girls called her.

The situation on the beach had changed dramatically in the last half hour. When the beachgoers finally realized that the warning siren was not a test, many of them had quickly gathered their belongings and started heading out. But many others, much to her surprise, kept on doing what they were doing. They seemed completely unconcerned about the fact that a monster wave could be headed their way.

Even when the police had started to arrive about ten minutes after the first siren had gone off and blared their loudspeakers at the beach, some people still did not heed the warning.

As he was making his way up the beach, one of the policemen had stopped when he reached Teresa.

"Ma'am, you need to leave the beach immediately. There is a tsunami coming."

"I can't. My daughter and her friend are somewhere on the beach, and they're probably going to be coming back at any minute. The radio said the tsunami would be here within the hour.. Is that right?"

"We're getting a lot of conflicting information. All I know is that we were told to get everyone off the beach as soon as possible. But I've done these kinds of evacuations before. We've got a few hours to go. You should be okay."

"Why isn't everybody leaving?"

"We always get the nuts who want to come down and see the tsunami. They figure that they'll head up to one of the hotels and have a party when the tsunami gets here."

"Even after the Asian tsunami?"

"Well, not as many nuts now, but a lot of kids think they're invincible. I see it every time. We can't force them to leave. It's still a free country. Even if that means they're free to die. I'm sorry, ma'am. Good luck."

He continued on at a deliberate pace. His comment about teens feeling invincible worried her.

Surely if Mia and Lani had heard the sirens, they would have had plenty of time to get back to her by now. She had been torn about whether to leave her location and chance missing the girls if they returned to find her. But by this time, the waiting had become agonizing. She just couldn't sit there and hope they came back. She had to do something

She rummaged through her bag until she found a Post-it pad and a pen. On the pad, she scribbled a note to the girls:

> *Mia and Lani, I have gone to find you. If you find this*
> *note, go to the Grand Hawaiian and find Rachel. I*
> *will meet you there. Teresa.*

The Grand Hawaiian seemed like the best place to meet if they were able to rendezvous. She certainly didn't want them waiting around on the beach until she came back.

Teresa took her keys and wallet out of her purse, placed the notepad at the top of the purse, and wrapped it in her towel. She could only hope that no one would steal the purse before the kids saw the note.

She then began jogging toward Diamond Head, the direction in which she saw the girls go, yelling their names as she went.

Within a minute, her phone rang. She looked at the number on the caller ID, hoping it was the girls. The number came up as unknown. They could have been calling from a pay phone.

When she answered, it was a familiar voice, but one that surprised her.

"Teresa, it's Brad. Thank God, I finally got through to you. The lines have been jammed. Did you get my text?"

"No. Have the girls called you?"

"What? Aren't they with you?"

"They went shopping about forty minutes before the siren went off, and they haven't come back. I'm looking for them now."

"Jesus! Teresa, you have to get as far away from the beach as you can. The tsunami is going to be huge."

"I can't leave them here! What if they can't hear the warning?"

"With all those sirens going off? I'm inside a concrete building three hundred yards from the beach, and I can hear them. Come on, they had to have heard it."

"Then why didn't they come back to me? Something's wrong! I'm not leaving until I find them!"

"Okay! Calm down. We'll figure out something. Where are you?"

"I'm on Waikiki. But my phone's battery is drained."

"I know. I got the message. If the kids call us, we'll tell them to meet you and Rachel at the Grand Hawaiian, but you've got to be there before—"

Teresa's cell phone beeped, and Brad's voice cut out. The display showed a blinking battery graphic and then went dead.

She closed the phone and began calling out Mia's and Lani's names again, angling up to Kalakaua Avenue so that she would have both the shops on the streets and the beach in view. She had only gotten a block when she saw a clothing store called Sweet that looked like it catered to teens. She entered the store and looked toward the back. She yelled the girls' names in a manner that would have raised eyebrows on any other occasion.

Televisions mounted along the walls normally showed music videos in a store as hip as this, but they were now all turned to various news stations. Most displayed the tsunami emergency broadcast warning. Others were tuned to national news networks that didn't carry the signal.

A young saleswoman who had been entranced by the broadcast whipped around when she heard Teresa call for the girls.

"Ma'am,' she said, smacking gum as she talked, "we're closing for the evacuation."

Teresa took a photo of Mia from her wallet. It was a year old, but it was good enough.

"Have you seen this girl?"

The saleswoman looked at it and shook her head.

"She probably took off. I'm leaving in a minute myself. Can you believe what they're saying?"

"I don't live here, so this all new for me." Teresa headed for the door to continue her search.

"Yeah, but two hundred feet high? It's scary."

That stopped Teresa in her tracks.

"Two hundred feet?" she said. "What are you talking about?"

"That's how big they're saying the tsunami is going to be. It's got to be some kind of hoax, right?"

Teresa thought about what Brad had said. "Oh my God! When he said it was going to be huge, I thought—"

"What's that?" The saleswoman pointed at one of the TVs.

On one of the national feeds, the view had changed to a camera in a helicopter. It focused on the rocky black coastline. Two people could be seen waving to the camera from a cliff top high above the waves breaking on the rocks below. A graphic at the bottom of the picture said KA LAE, HAWAII, SOUTHERNMOST POINT IN THE US, LIVE.

"Turn it up," Teresa said.

The woman aimed the remote at the TV, and they could hear the announcer's voice.

". . . should not attempt what you see these people doing. Again, we are looking at a helicopter camera shot of the southern tip of the Big Island of Hawaii, the first place where we are expecting the tsunami to make landfall. Our exclusive coverage comes courtesy of KHAI, whose helicopter was over the volcano at Kilauea for another story today. Apparently, two intrepid hikers have decided they wanted to be the first to see the tsunami and have chosen a cliff-side vantage point. They appear to be at least fifty feet above the water, so we'll have to hope they'll be okay. They have not responded to repeated requests to leave the area."

The camera panned away from the hikers and to the sea. Nothing unusual was visible, but the announcer's mood changed noticeably.

"What's that? I'm sorry, ladies and gentlemen, but we are having some technical difficulties getting audio from the helicopter. We do have reports coming in that several airliners over the Pacific have reported seeing waves moving across the water in the direction of Hawaii at an incredibly high rate of speed, but none of those reports have been confirmed at this point."

The camera panned back down to the cliff. The announcer continued his inane narration but didn't add anything beyond what they could see. The waterline had pulled back significantly from just a few seconds ago. The view shifted back out to the ocean again, and now they could see the first glimpse of white water far out to sea. It seemed to be moving slowly, but in just a few seconds it had moved much closer to shore. The camera continued to follow it, but Teresa couldn't get a good sense of the size of the wave because there was no frame of reference.

Finally, the camera had panned far enough as it followed the wave so that the shore was in view, but without houses or other buildings for comparison, it still looked unimpressive. The two people on the cliff's edge must have thought so, too, since they didn't move.

But when the wave broke against the rocks, Teresa realized that they weren't going to make it. She expected the wave to bounce against the rocks and reflect back into the ocean. Instead, it simply covered the rocks and continued to sweep up the cliff. Too late, the hikers realized the size of the wave and turned to run. Before they could get more than a few steps, the wave washed over them, and they disappeared as if they were ants being washed down a drain.

Teresa gasped, and the saleswoman started to cough uncontrollably.

"Are you all right?" Teresa asked.

"Swallowed   my . . . gum," the saleswoman said between coughs.

Teresa ran out of the store, leaving the saleswoman to fumble with her keys, intent on locking the door to a store that would soon no longer exist.

CHAPTER 24

THE ESTABLISHED PROCEDURE OF the tsunami warning system included notifying the Civil Air Patrol, an auxiliary of the U.S. Air Force that flew search-and-rescue missions and other operations that the military and government didn't have the resources to do on their own. In the event of a tsunami warning, their duty was simple.

Offshore and in remote locations, it was likely that surfers and boaters would not hear the sirens. Helicopters and planes that were equipped with loudspeakers would fly over the coastlines, broadcasting the warning. Each aircraft was responsible for a particular section of the coastline.

During past tsunami warnings, the CAP had met with moderate success. In many cases, the surfers would heed the warnings and paddle in to shore. But there were plenty of others who just waved at the aircraft, obviously enjoying the chance to say they had surfed a tsunami.

One of the CAP volunteers, an eager nineteen-year-old pilot named Matthew Perkins, flew a Cessna outfitted with a loudspeaker that he had installed himself. Although he had tested it extensively on the ground at Hickam, he hadn't had an opportunity to drill with it yet. The tsunami warning would be his first chance to try it in action.

He had made all the required preflight checks and then took off from the runway that Hickam Air Base shared with Honolulu International. It only took him a few minutes to get to his designated patrol area along Waikiki Beach.

Off the coast of Diamond Head, Lani and Mia continued paddling alongside their two new friends. The view from this far out was spectacular. Lani was having a great time, but Mia was struggling.

After having paddled all the way to Sans Souci Beach, Mia had gotten tired and asked the rest of them if they could turn back. Although Lani was getting sore, she could have gone on awhile longer and was disappointed Mia had given up so soon.

The breeze had picked up, and the previously calm water now rocked their kayaks on undulating waves. At the rate they were paddling, their tired arms would take another half hour at least to get them back to their starting point on Waikiki.

Lani was surprised to see all kinds of aircraft buzzing around. Tourist, news, and military helicopters were everywhere—way more than usual.

Then she heard a small plane approach. It was flying parallel to the beach, almost as if it were coming in for a landing, but the runway was miles away.

"What is that guy doing?" Tom said.

"I don't know," Jake said.

"Is he going to crash?" Mia asked.

"No, look," Lani said, "he's just flying straight and level."

"Then what's he doing?"

As it got closer, Lani could hear words cutting in and

out. She couldn't understand what was being said. In between the words, there was nothing but static.

"It's probably just some kind of advertisement," Tom said.

"Yeah," Jake said, "but the doofus's speaker is broken or something."

Lani heard a word more distinctly.

"Did he say *onami*?" she said.

"See," Tom said. "It's probably *Konami*. That's a video game company. It's an ad."

"Well, it's not working," Jake said.

The plane passed over them two more times, but they ignored the annoying whine of the engine and kept paddling lazily back to Waikiki.

CHAPTER 25

As Reggie analyzed the data from the DART buoy, Kai had been keeping an eye on the evacuation via one of the cable channels and was horrified by what he had seen. On most channels, the Emergency Alert System broadcast was being repeated over and over. In the last few minutes a new warning from the governor had been broadcast, perhaps to give the warning more weight, but the content wasn't significantly changed from the one Brian Renfro had so powerfully relayed.

There was still no mention of a meteor impact, and that may have been one reason that so many people were either ignoring the warning or were confused about what to do.

About ten minutes before, Kai had begun watching the TV more closely because he wanted to see how the evacuation was progressing. He tuned to the national MSNBC feed, which didn't broadcast the EAS warning because their main audience was the continental United States. The network relayed the feed from one of their affiliate's local Honolulu camera crews.

A reporter standing on Waikiki Beach motioned to the scene behind him. Some people ran in panic. Packed with cars, the road along the beach moved so slowly that the vehicles were almost idling. Many more cars could be seen trying to merge into the traffic from the garages of hotels lining the strip. Police attempted to direct the traffic at several of the intersections, but the sheer volume made it virtually impossible for the vehicles to make headway.

Still other people strolled along the beach completely unperturbed by the evacuation. The reporter, his close-cropped hair rigidly resisting the wind swaying the trees behind him, stopped an obese man in swim trunks and a towel slung over his shoulder.

"Sir," the reporter said, "you don't seem particularly concerned by the tsunami warning. Can I ask why?"

The man shook his head dismissively. "It seems like we get these warnings once a year. I just wait until about fifteen minutes before the wave is supposed to get here, and then I head back to my condo."

"Your condo?"

"Yeah, it's right over there," the obese man said, pointing at a white building behind him. "Eight stories up with a great view of the beach, so I just watch from there. Usually there isn't much to see, but hey, maybe today will be different."

"You sound like you consider it entertainment."

"Well, it'd be pretty amazing to see a real tsunami, don't you think? But I'm sure this is another false alarm."

"Are you aware that the warning now says the wave could be two hundred feet high?"

"That's just crazy. What are the chances of that?"

The man continued his walk, leaving the reporter to head over to a Lexus SUV, one of the cars making tortured progress along Kalakaua Avenue. In the background, along with a few individuals running in terror, crowds of people could be seen walking leisurely along the street, as if they were being herded in a particular direction by some unseen guide. Kai found the scene infuriating, but he knew it was typical behavior in an evacuation.

The Lexus owner, a deeply tanned man in a tank top and a hideous comb-over, had his window down. His eyes kept darting in the direction of the ocean as he talked. At first, Kai thought he was concerned that the tsunami might come in while he was still in his car.

"Sir," the reporter said, "do you think the traffic will let you get to a safe location in time?"

"Oh, I'll be safe," the driver said, his eyes continuing to flick away from the camera. "I'm heading down to the Ala Wai marina to get my sailboat. I don't want to see it get sunk because of some stupid tsunami."

"Are you planning to tow it back home?"

"No, I don't have a trailer. I'm going to take it out to sea. I gotta protect my property."

"What about your car?"

"My car?" It looked like the first time the guy had considered what would happen to his car.

"Yes, you'll have to leave it at the marina, right?"

"Dammit!" he yelled, pounding on the steering wheel. "I knew I should have brought my son with me."

The camera pulled back to the reporter, but Kai had seen enough. He turned to Reggie.

"These people aren't getting it. We need to do something."

"Like what? The inundation maps we have are worthless. Even if we could develop new ones in the next few minutes, we don't have enough time to distribute them. Besides, we don't even know for sure how large the biggest wave will be."

Kai sighed at the futility of the situation. The published inundation maps and evacuation signs were now woefully inadequate. They would lead the evacuees to supposedly safe locations that would be wiped out by the first seventy-five-foot tsunami. Kai didn't want to think about what would happen when those areas were hit by a two-hundred-foot monster.

And it looked as if some people weren't following even the established instructions, let alone the new warning telling them that the current inundation maps were useless. They didn't understand the severity of the situation, and unless Kai did something fast, many of those people would be killed.

Brad, who had been manning the phones, came back into the operations room. When he told Kai about his conversation with Teresa, Kai felt the blood drain from his face. His daughter was somewhere out there, and he had no idea whether she was safe or not. That was when the personal nature of the upcoming disaster fully hit him.

"Isn't there something we can do to help her?" Brad said. "Call the police to find her?"

"Are you kidding?" Reggie said. "Half the people on the island are probably calling the police right now."

"Well, we've got to do something! What about the governor? She said we should call if she could do anything for us."

"Oh, that'll look great," Reggie said, "using our connections for personal reasons while the rest of the people fend for themselves!"

Brad raced over to Reggie, who had a good four inches and a hundred pounds on Brad, and got within an inch of his face. "I don't give a shit how it looks! That's my niece!"

A snarl twisted Reggie's face, and Kai pushed himself between them before it got ugly.

"Hey! Hey!" he said, pulling Brad back. "Ease up! I know it's tense in here, but let's just bring it down."

Brad's idea was tempting, but even if Kai called the police or the governor, what could he tell them? That the girls were somewhere on Waikiki—maybe? Kai didn't even know that for sure.

"We're not calling them," he said. "The police are already doing what they should be doing. They have a duty, just like I do."

All Kai could do was hope that Teresa would find them in time or that they would call to tell him they were in a safe place, if they knew what that was.

Reggie went back to the computer. Kai escorted Brad to the other side of the room so he could cool off for a minute.

"Brad," he said, "I want to thank you for everything you're doing today."

"Lucky for you, I was free today. And I don't have to warn my employees. They have the day off."

Kai realized what he meant. Hopkins Realty had its corporate offices across from the Ala Moana shopping center, which was located only a few hundred feet from the beach in Waikiki. Outwardly, Brad might have seemed blasé about the business, but Kai knew it meant a lot to him to run the company his father had started.

"I'm sorry. I didn't think about Hopkins Realty until you said that."

Brad shrugged. "It's no big deal."

"But the office. The files . . ." Kai said.

Brad smiled. "Believe it or not, my insurance covers tsunamis."

Kai stared at Brad in disbelief. Most insurance policies didn't cover tsunamis unless you specifically purchased an expensive rider. They were more popular now, especially after the Asian tsunami, but still pretty uncommon.

"Hey," Brad said, "my big brother is the assistant director of the Pacific Tsunami Warning Center. I had to get it."

Kai smiled at that. At least there was one thing he could feel good about.

"The phones have been ringing nonstop," Brad said, looking at notes he had written. "We've gotten calls from everyone. *New York Times,* CNN, Fox, ABC, NBC. CBS even has a crew out by the front gate. I told them they couldn't come in—"

"You mean they're here?"

"They were filming some story over in Ewa and got over here as soon as the warning went out. They've been trying to get in to interview you. I told them you were too busy."

"All the data analysis in the world won't help if people don't understand what's going on. What do you think, Reggie?"

Reggie grudgingly nodded. "Why not? It might be better than a phone interview."

"We'll show them the video from Johnston Island. Maybe that will convince some people to move faster. Brad, open the gate and tell them that only the reporter and the cameraman can come into the building. Anyone else will have to wait outside. I don't want a mass of people in here."

In two minutes Brad ushered in a slender Asian woman in a blue blazer, followed by a bearded cameraman wearing jeans and a Detroit Tigers baseball cap.

"Dr. Tanaka, I'm Lara Pimalo," the reporter said, shaking Kai's hand firmly. She nodded toward the cameraman. "This is Roger Ames. Thank you for meeting with us. I know you must be extremely busy."

"We are," Kai said. He held up a finger. "My one condition on you being here: if I ask you to stop filming, you'll do so immediately. Okay?"

"Of course," she said.

"Good. The reason I'm letting you in here is because the evacuation is going poorly. We need to motivate more people to leave. Quickly. I believe I have something here that will help."

"What is it?"

"Can you show video of something on a computer screen?"

"Sure. It won't look great, but it should be recognizable. But, Doctor, graphs and such don't make for great—"

"It's not a graph. It's video from Johnston Island this morning. It shows a massive tsunami obliterating it. I want you to broadcast it."

She and Ames were stunned for a moment, but Pimalo couldn't hide her excitement about getting such a great scoop. She frantically gestured to Ames to start filming.

"Just tell us what monitor it will be on," he said, "and we'll set up for the shot."

As Ames got the camera ready, Pimalo said, "Why don't you just e-mail the video to someone at the studio? Not that I mind the exclusive."

"Can you make sure they broadcast this live?"

"Oh, we're planning to."

"With a live broadcast, I know the video will be seen.

If I e-mailed it, how do I know it wouldn't just sit there, waiting for someone to open it?"

"Good point. I'll let the station know to be ready for the broadcast."

In another minute the camera was in position and they were rolling. As the video from Johnston ran, Kai narrated what was happening on screen.

As the tsunami approached the camera, Pimalo spoke to the anchorman through the microphone, "Are you seeing this, Phil?" Kai couldn't hear the response, but her rapt attention told him it was getting through.

When the video went to black, Kai motioned for her to put the camera on him.

"Ms. Pimalo, I'd like to make another statement."

"Of course, Dr. Tanaka. Those were incredible pictures."

Kai thought to himself, *It's about to get a lot more incredible.* He couldn't believe he was about to say it on national television, with the possibility of making a fool of himself. After a moment of hesitation, he saw Brad and Reggie look at each other. They both nodded at Kai's unspoken question, and he felt some comfort knowing they were with him. He cleared his throat and began speaking.

"My name is Kai Tanaka, and I am the assistant director of the Pacific Tsunami Warning Center in Ewa Beach, Hawaii. About forty minutes ago, I issued a tsunami warning for the Hawaiian Islands. I cannot overemphasize how dangerous this situation is. To this point, we have not released the cause of this tsunami because we did not have the data to verify it. However, I am concerned that the evacuation is not moving fast enough because people don't understand how unusual this tsunami is. At 8:41 a.m. this morning Hawaii time, we suspect that a meteorite struck the central Pacific Ocean. If this turns out to be true, we can expect a disaster of unprecedented scale for the Hawaiian Islands because meteor strikes can generate gigantic waves, much larger than those from earthquakes. As we speak, the southern tip of the Big Island should be experiencing the brunt of the first wave. In a little more than fifteen minutes, it should reach Kona and then Hilo. Fifteen minutes after that, Honolulu will be hit."

One TV was set to a local station broadcasting the EAS and the other continued the feed from Waikiki. Neither of them showed video from the southern tip of Hawaii.

The phone rang yet again, and Brad picked it up.

"Excuse me, Dr. Tanaka," said Pimalo, "but these are incredible assertions. What evidence do you have that a meteorite struck the Pacific this morning?"

This was the touchiest part of the interview. Kai knew that if he went into a lot of detail, he might lose the viewer. But he also knew that the audience needed something if they were to believe this crazy notion.

"We have very little time left, so I don't want to go into all of the details. We don't have any direct evidence to support—"

"You do now," Brad broke in, putting his hand over the receiver. "Gail Wentworth from NOAA is on the line. You have eight images in your e-mail that they're about to release to the news agencies. It's a series of shots from Landsat-8 showing a massive explosion in the central Pacific. NASA is confirming that we were hit by an asteroid."

CHAPTER 26

IN THE COCKPIT OF his Cessna, Matthew Perkins frowned. Nobody seemed to be listening to his warning, even though he was flying low enough to be easily heard. On one of his passes, he told the kayakers below to wave with both hands if they could hear him. They simply looked up as he flew past.

Perkins opened the window of the plane, stuck the handset out of the window, and keyed it to on. The resulting feedback should have been loud enough to hear even over the roar of the engine. Nothing.

Damn! The loudspeaker wasn't working, he realized. The past twenty-five minutes of warning passes hadn't been heard by anyone. He radioed in to Civil Air Patrol headquarters to tell them about the problem and that no one off the Waikiki coast had yet been warned by the CAP.

As he set a course back to the airport to fix his loudspeaker, he was informed that another plane was on the way to Waikiki to take over.

"Wouldn't NASA see an asteroid headed toward earth?" Pimalo asked as Kai went to his computer. "We should have heard about this days ago, maybe even months ago."

Reggie scooped up one of the memos from his desk and pointed at the text.

"You see the period at the end of that sentence? Now imagine being two miles away from it. That's what it's like trying to find a five-hundred-meter-wide asteroid that's five million miles away."

"But as it gets closer to earth, wouldn't it get easier to see?"

"Asteroids move at twenty-five thousand miles per hour. It would get here in less than ten days. And there aren't nearly enough telescopes around the world to find every chunk of rock flying around out there. In 2002, an asteroid came within seventy-five thousand miles of earth, well within the orbit of the moon. The asteroid was one hundred meters in diameter, big enough to destroy a major city if it had collided with earth."

"But it missed," Pimalo said.

"Right. Barely. But the date of closest approach was June 14. The asteroid was detected on June 17. Three days *after* it had gone by. It's completely believable that the first we would know about an asteroid was after an impact. In fact, it's lucky it hasn't happened up until now."

Kai's e-mail pinged, and there was the message from Gail Wentworth. Eight JPEG images were attached to the e-mail. Pimalo's cameraman shot over Kai's shoulder as he opened the pictures.

He clicked through them in the sequence that Wentworth had labeled them. The first image showed a viewpoint looking straight down on a mass of clouds covering a wide swath of the Pacific. Two barely visible lines could be seen over the storm, as if someone had slashed a pen across the picture. At the bottom right, a time stamp showed GMT 18:40:00.

Kai pointed at the numbers and said, "Greenwich

Mean Time, which is ten hours ahead of Hawaii. That would make the time 8:40 a.m. in Honolulu."

In the photo stamped 18:40:30, the previous two lines were gone, but taking their place was a much brighter line, and Kai finally understood what he was seeing: the trails of asteroids burning up in the atmosphere.

"It wasn't just one meteor," he said. "It was a meteor shower."

Reggie pointed at the bright trail in the second picture. "That one must have caused our earthquake. If the first two were small enough, they would have exploded before they hit the water."

"They all must have been pieces of the same asteroid," Kai said.

"Just like Shoemaker-Levy," Reggie said. When he got puzzled looks from the others, he went on. "It was a comet that hit Jupiter in '94. It didn't hit all at once but in pieces. Looks like the same thing might have happened here, but the first two pieces were small. Relatively."

"Any of them could have destroyed the airliner," Kai said.

Reggie nodded. "Sure, but the third one—the one that caused the bright streak in that second photo—was big enough to make it intact all the way to the seafloor."

Kai could hardly imagine the amount of energy it would take to enable an asteroid to plunge more than three miles to the bottom of the ocean and cause a major earthquake. For a moment, his finger hovered above the mouse. He dreaded what he would see next, but he forced himself to continue through the photos.

In the third picture, the line was gone, replaced with a small bright dot at the center of the storm clouds.

As Kai opened each successive image, which the time stamp showed to be in thirty-second increments, the dot grew larger until, in the final image, the explosion was plainly visible for what it was: the asteroid strike ejecting billions of tons of superheated rock and steam into the atmosphere. On this last image, Wentworth had drawn a line parallel to the explosion and under it had written: *15 miles.*

"Good God!" Pimalo asked. "The explosion was fifteen miles across?"

"At least the mushroom cloud was," said Reggie.

Kai grimaced. He had hoped that the certainty that it was an asteroid would help him grasp the situation better, but if anything, he was in a daze. The abstract number crunching they had done when they were theorizing about the size of the asteroid was no longer abstract: it was real, and Kai sat for a moment processing it.

Reggie's voice snapped him out of his trance.

"We're getting another wave!" Reggie said, looking at the data coming in from the DART buoy. As before, the line rose inexorably, but this time it didn't stop until it had reached 1.3 meters.

Brad, now knowing the implications of the reading, said, "Jesus!"

"What!" said the reporter Pimalo. "What does that mean?"

"The second tsunami," Kai said, "is going to be over 150 feet high."

"The *second* one? What do you mean, Dr. Tanaka? How many are there going to be?"

"There's no way to know for sure. But we do know now that they are coming about twenty-five minutes apart."

"So now we know what we're dealing with," Reggie said. "It's not just a theory anymore."

"Maybe people will realize they have to leave the high-rises now and get to high ground," Kai said.

Lara Pimalo put a hand to her ear to listen to what the producer was saying to her. She waved to the cameraman to stop filming. After a second, she ran over to the TV and turned it to MSNBC. They were just rerunning the video of the wave hitting Ka Lae, the southern tip of the Big Island, with the two hikers consumed by the tsunami. Then the picture switched to the photos they had just seen from Landsat-8.

After the sequence of photos was shown, they kept repeating those shots in the upper right corner and switched back to video of Waikiki, where people were pouring out of buildings and running through the streets, some screaming, some lugging a ridiculous number of suitcases and electronics.

"I guess it worked," Reggie said. "People are definitely leaving."

"Not all of them," Brad said.

For Kai, it was amazing and sad to see how quickly circumstances like these brought out the worst in some people who saw the disaster as an opportunity to take advantage of the situation. Farther down the street, two youths smashed in a plate glass window and grabbed several unidentifiable objects from the storefront. A policeman who had been directing traffic ran after them around the corner and out of sight.

"That stuff is going to be gone in a half hour anyway," Brad said. "Might as well let them have it."

The main picture then switched to an overhead shot from a helicopter hovering over Waikiki. It zoomed in to show Ala Wai Boulevard, which ran parallel to the Ala Wai Canal on the north side of Waikiki. People could be seen streaming toward it and then turning to follow it westward.

"Tourists who don't know the city," said Reggie. "It seems like the most direct route from the beach, but they don't know there are no bridges over it. Locals would."

"The closest bridge is McCully Street," Kai said. "That could be a mile away if you're heading from the east end of the canal."

The view then changed to the camera in another helicopter, this one flying over the water off shore from Waikiki. The camera panned around and showed people still out in the water, some in boats, most on surfboards or small watercraft.

"What are they doing?" Kai said, turning up the volume. A woman's voice, distressed, described the scene.

". . . have apparently ignored warnings from the Civil Air Patrol to evacuate to land. I would like to repeat that this is an extremely dangerous situation, and you are recommended to stay as far away from the shore as possible."

"Don't those idiots hear the sirens?" Brad said.

"They might be too far from shore," Reggie said. "That's why the CAP does flyovers."

The camera zoomed in on a surfer kicking lazily back to shore. Then it moved across two more surfers and slid over until it focused on four kayakers. They were paddling slowly back in the direction of Waikiki, parallel to the beach. The camera zoomed in.

"Oh my God," Brad said.

On TV, the faces of the four were clearly visible now.

Kai didn't know the boys, but he instantly recognized the two girls with them. With little more than half an hour before the largest tsunami in recorded history would strike Honolulu, his own daughter looked directly at the camera and happily waved.

CHAPTER 27

IT TOOK KAI A minute to catch his breath after the shock of seeing Lani. The news report had gone on to another topic, but the video of her and Mia blithely kayaking, obviously unaware of the danger, still played in his mind's eye. Fear gripped him, but he controlled it. It simmered just below the surface, propelling his actions. He leapt to his feet, certain about what he had to do next.

"We're leaving!" Kai said, herding everyone toward the door. "Reggie, how long would it take to transfer what we need to a laptop?"

"I'm way ahead of you. I've already copied everything over the network."

"Good. You take it."

"Who's leaving?" said Lara Pimalo.

"You, me, everybody," Kai said.

"But you said we have thirty minutes left."

"We *only* have thirty minutes left," Kai said, "and we're on a flat section of land. You saw the traffic jams. It'll take a while to get to high ground. You should drive as far as you can. But when you reach a backup, get out and start walking."

"It sounds like we're not going together," said Reggie.

"We're not," Kai said, looking at Brad. "How fast could you get us to Waikiki on that thing?"

Brad raised an eyebrow, then nodded. Going after Lani was the only thing that would get Kai on that motorcycle; it was the only way to get through the traffic quickly. "You know how I drive. We'll get there in time."

Kai had made the decision to leave his post quickly, but that didn't mean it had been easy. It was his duty versus his daughter, and his daughter would win every time.

"You're going after Lani on that crotch rocket in this traffic?" Reggie said, sounding incredulous. "That's suicide!"

"Maybe." He just didn't see any other option.

"We could try calling someone—"

Kai cut him off quickly. "No. With the way the phone lines are tied up, it might take half the time just contacting someone, let alone convincing them to go find her. I'm not taking that chance."

"Then I can just go and you can stay with Reggie," Brad said.

"That won't work, and I don't have time to explain why. It has to be both of us."

Reggie nodded in agreement. "It's what I'd do. But what about the tsunami data? What about warning the other Pacific islands? We still don't know for sure if there are more waves coming."

"I'm leaving that in good hands. You're in charge now."

"Me?" Reggie shook his head, his eyes wide at the thought of the responsibility. His face was two shades paler than a moment before. "But I don't want—"

"Listen, I know I'm abandoning you at a critical time, and I'm sorry. But I need to do this."

"Maybe Harry should take over. I know he's on Maui, but—"

"Which is why you need to do it. Who knows what

the situation on Maui is like? They may not even have phone service after the first wave hits. Come on, Reggie. You know as much as I do—probably more. What's the problem?"

"I didn't make the right call on the tsunami warning."

"Neither did I, at first."

"But if you hadn't been here, we'd just be issuing the first warning now. What if I'm wrong again?"

"You did exactly what you were trained to do. It could have gone either way. Look, you'll do fine. I wouldn't leave if I didn't trust you to do the job." Kai honestly didn't know if that was true—he might have left in any case—but he did trust Reggie, so it didn't matter. "Use Wheeler Field as your base. You're still going to have to interpret the data coming in."

Reggie still looked like he had eaten a live roach, but reluctantly nodded. "I'll do my best."

"I'm going to be on my cell phone. You go with Ms. Pimalo. We were going to have to switch control over to Palmer at some point anyway. Might as well be now. You keep in contact with them and let me know when you get new readings. You've got my number."

The West Coast/Alaska Tsunami Warning Center in Palmer, Alaska, would continue to get all the same readings. They would be warning the west coast of the United States of the danger by now, even though the size of the waves would be diminished by a factor of ten once they went as far as California. At least they would have the hours of warning that Hawaii didn't get.

"Should we do the transition before we go?" Reggie asked.

"There's not enough time," Kai said. "I'll call Palmer

on the way and tell them you're the man now. Come on! Let's go!"

The five of them scrambled out of the PTWC. By now Bilbo was excited by all the commotion and barked as he followed them out. At the door, Kai stopped to take one last look at the ops room, knowing it would be the last time he saw it.

"At least we'll get the chance to build the next one in a better location," Reggie said.

Pimalo and her cameraman ran to their truck. Reggie said, "Don't leave yet," and sprinted to his house. Kai assumed he wanted to rescue a few mementos, and he didn't blame him. Kai sprinted to his house too. Bilbo came running after him.

As Kai reached the front door, he didn't know what he was doing. He wasn't thinking that clearly. He just knew he had to take something with him. He couldn't let everything in his family's life disappear.

Kai threw open the door, ran in, and stopped, considering all the things he could and couldn't take with him. Electronics, computers, jewelry, and other tangible objects of value didn't occur to him. Those weren't the things he wanted. In that moment, he knew he could only choose one, maybe two objects that he could take.

Of course, they had souvenirs from vacations they had taken. Valuable antiques that had been passed down through both Rachel and Kai's families, like his father's medals from the Vietnam War, a silver set Rachel's mother had given her, an Etruscan vase they had found at a garage sale that had turned out to be worth thousands of dollars, Kai's old baseball card collection. All of them were meaningful and valuable to him, but each of them was also too big and bulky to carry.

The only things that he considered truly irreplaceable were the photos from their life. The old photos of his parents when they were young and in love. Rachel's family photos from years ago. Their wedding. Lani's baby photos. The good times on holidays. That's when Kai understood what was really important to him. Of all the memories in the house, photos were the only things he wanted to keep.

Unfortunately, they had boxes and boxes of old photos. There was no way he could take them all. Kai hurried over and pulled out one of their family albums, the one they looked at the most. He gazed longingly at the rest and felt himself holding back tears because he wouldn't be able to take them.

Kai made his way back to the door and came to a halt when he saw the photos they had hung on the wall near the kitchen. One was an eight-by-ten wedding photo of him and Rachel. She looked beautiful in her beaded white dress, and both of them beamed with happiness. It always reminded him of their early days together: their introduction at the University of Washington Bookstore while they stood in line to sell their used textbooks; their first date at a comedy club; the awkward proposal on a Thanksgiving trip to see her parents when Kai popped the question on the plane because he couldn't wait for the candlelight dinner he had planned.

The other photo was a candid picture of the three of them on vacation at Disneyland. When Lani was born a little more than a year into their marriage, complications during the delivery made it impossible for Rachel to have more children. But the news didn't discourage them. In fact, it brought them even closer together. As soon as Rachel and Kai finished grad school and started making money, their major indulgence was to take yearly trips that they could share as a family.

Like many people, their favorite destination was Disneyland. The photo showed all three of them wearing Mickey Mouse ears and laughing, childlike in their disregard for the camera. They looked like one of those photos that you would see in a frame at the store. It wasn't staged. It just showed what a great time they had had.

Kai took both photos off the wall and smashed the glass against the counter. He wrenched the pictures out of their frames and inserted them in the album, tossing the frames onto the floor. The final thing he grabbed was Bilbo's leash.

"Come here, buddy." Bilbo wagged as he came and sat in front of Kai, who attached the leash and gave him a pat.

Kai took one last look around, and then he heard Brad call from outside.

"Kai, we have to go! Now!"

Kai sprinted with Bilbo back to the van and motorcycle, both now idling in front of the PTWC building. Reggie was just coming back at the same time. But what he was carrying caught Kai by surprise.

"You'll need this if you're riding with Brad," he said, handing Kai a motorcycle helmet. "I don't use it much anymore. I hope it's not too big on you."

"What about your stuff?" Kai said, picturing Reggie's remodeled house, soon to be wiped away. "Don't you have anything you want to take?"

"Nope. They're just things. I'll get more. Oh, and I got you a couple of other items."

He pressed some kind of tote bag and a small length of wire into Kai's hands. Kai was overwhelmed that all

Reggie could think of in this disaster was helping him. He'd never realized before how thoughtful Reggie was.

"That's my kayaking dry bag. It's the best thing for carrying your stuff. And that's an earpiece for your cell phone. It'll fit under the helmet so you can talk on the road."

"Thanks, Reggie," Kai said. "This means a lot to me."

"Hey, I'm just lending that stuff to you. I want it back."

"Can you do one more thing for me?" Kai said, holding out the leash. "Bilbo won't fit on the bike."

"No problem. If the news guys give me any trouble, I'll sic him on them." Bilbo licked Reggie's hand as if to show how dangerous he really was.

"You take care of yourself," Kai said, and then hugged him. Reggie seemed a little surprised at first, but returned the hug.

"You too. I'll see you in a couple of hours," Reggie said confidently, as if he didn't want to believe Kai might be in danger. Then he held his hand out to Brad. "No hard feelings, huh?"

Brad took Reggie's meaty paw without hesitation. "I want you to know I don't pick fights with three-hundred-pound football players often."

"I understand. Just go get her." Reggie climbed into the news van with Bilbo, and they pulled away, headed for the front gate.

Kai put the photo album in the dry bag and slung it over his shoulder. He plugged the headset into his phone and placed the helmet on his head. It was about three sizes too big, but Kai snugged the strap down until it didn't float around too much.

Brad leapt onto the bike and revved the engine. Kai

tentatively threw his leg over the tiny pad of leather that qualified as the backseat.

"Where do I put my feet?" Kai said.

"Man, you really have never ridden one of these before."

"I wouldn't be now if it weren't an emergency."

"Just put your feet on the dead pedals back there and put your arms around my waist."

"Just tell me if you can't breathe."

"I'll be fine, but I'm going to have to do some tricky driving if we're going to get there in time. By the way, where are we going? We need a boat if we're going out into the bay, and mine's in my driveway."

"I have an idea. Go to the Grand Hawaiian. I'll explain on the way."

"With the wind noise, we won't be able to talk much. Explain when we get there. Hang on tight. If you fall off, I'll stop and get you."

Kai didn't appreciate Brad's sense of humor. Kai had never ridden a motorcycle and didn't want to. But his determination to find his daughter was stronger than his terror of riding 140 horsepower of exposed metal when, in an impact with even a Mini, the Harley would lose.

As Brad gunned the engine and roared off, Kai gripped him like a vine wrapped around an oak, the cell phone clenched in one hand. The g-forces were incredible, but surprisingly, Kai didn't feel in danger of falling off the bike. He did feel like throwing up, but at least that was something he had control over.

Kai reluctantly loosened his right hand and felt for the keypad on the phone as they whipped through the gate and turned onto Fort Weaver Road, the main drag leading to the H1. Cars packed the road, but the traffic moved steadily, albeit slowly. In a few seconds they caught up with the news van and passed it like it was standing still.

Kai punched in the speed dial number for the West Coast/Alaska Tsunami Warning Center. All he got was an out-of-range beep. As he expected, the cell phone lines were stretched to the limit with people calling loved ones about the oncoming tsunami.

The road turned north and they ran into more traffic, moving at no more than ten miles per hour. Brad swung the motorcycle onto the shoulder and rocketed forward at an insane speed only inches from the cars on their left. Occasionally they would hit a patch of sand or a bump, and Kai would feel the bike skid a little. He glanced over Brad's shoulder. The speedometer hovered around sixty.

Kai hit redial on the cell phone again and again. After at least seven tries, he finally heard the call go through. The director, Frank Manetti, answered. He must have had caller ID, because Kai didn't have to say anything before Manetti spoke.

"Kai, is that you?"

Even with the helmet, the wind noise buffeted Kai's ears, but he could still hear Manetti's voice easily over the headset. He silently thanked Reggie.

"Yes, it's me," Kai said.

"What's that noise? I can barely hear you."

"It's the wind. Did you get the latest readings from the DART buoy?"

"What?"

"The DART buoy!" Kai shouted.

"We sure as hell did. That's a monster of a wave headed your way."

Kai had to let Manetti know that he had left the

PTWC and that Manetti was now in charge of the only operating warning center. Not only that, but HSCD wouldn't get any new warnings until Palmer took over. Kai hadn't taken the time to call Renfro before they left to let him know that they were going off-line.

"Listen, Frank, you need to take over now."

"Say that again, Kai? I didn't get that."

Kai raised his voice as loud as he could. "I said you're going to have to—"

Brad turned his head left to look for cross traffic at an intersection. He didn't see the Volkswagen Beetle with the enormous surfboard tied to the roof turn in front of them.

Kai reached up with both hands and pushed Brad's head down just as they passed under the surfboard, which barely missed decapitating both of them. The board grazed his hand, knocking the cell phone into the air. It clattered as it bounced once and then smashed into the curb, shattering into pieces.

"Dammit!" Kai yelled as he flexed his stinging hand.

"That was close!" Brad shouted over his shoulder. "Are you okay?"

"I'm fine. I dropped my phone!"

"I've got one. Do you want me to stop so you can use it?" He started to slow down.

Brad's telephone was virtually useless to Kai, because he didn't know anyone's number from memory—not the warning center in Palmer, not Hawaii State Civil Defense, not even Reggie's. It was all in his cell phone address book, which was now destroyed.

The only alternative was to turn back and find the TV van again to tell Reggie that he hadn't been able to complete the transition. It might be an hour before Reggie was able to get to Wheeler and establish contact with everyone—critical time when additional information from the DART buoy would not be getting to HSCD or other Pacific island nations.

But if they turned around now, it would add at least ten minutes to their ride to Waikiki. They'd never get there in time.

Kai felt Brad downshift, and the bike slowed.

"No!" Kai yelled. "We don't have time! Keep going!"

Brad revved the engine, and soon they were up to seventy.

In another minute they had reached the entrance ramp for the H1. It was clogged with cars and buses. But there was enough room for a motorcycle to get through on the shoulder, and in no time they were cruising along at eighty.

CHAPTER 28

AS THEY ROUNDED DIAMOND Head, Lani's attention was drawn to a big commotion along Kalakaua Avenue, which was even more jammed than usual. From their position a mile out in Waikiki Bay near Kuhio Beach, she could see people running in both directions. Few were left on the beach.

"Mia," she said, pointing, "what's going on over there?"

The two boys also followed her finger.

"I don't know," Mia said tersely. Her face had turned ashen.

"Are you okay?"

Mia nodded, but Lani recognized seasickness when she saw it.

"Is there a parade today?" Jake asked.

"Not that I know of."

Tom shook his head in puzzlement as well.

"Well, something's going on."

Across Waikiki Bay at the Ala Wai marina, a huge number of boats streamed from the harbor at a pace that seemed frantic. In fact, it looked as if two of the boats had collided, although they were so far away, it was hard to tell for sure.

Then there was the large number of aircraft. First,

the low-flying plane that had passed over them. Then a news helicopter that seemed to be training its camera on them. That one Lani had waved to. Now it seemed like another small plane was headed in their direction. Within another few seconds she thought she heard a voice coming from the plane. It turned and began to circle them, and the voice became clearer. There was one word that was unmistakable:

". . . *a tsunami warning has been issued for Hawaii. You must head for shore immediately and get to high ground. I repeat, a tsunami warning has been issued for Hawaii. This is not a drill. You must get to land immediately. The wave will reach Honolulu in twenty-three minutes. If you understand this warning, raise both your arms and wave.*"

All four of them looked at each other and then started waving their arms frantically while still holding their paddles. The plane waggled its wings and banked toward a group of surfers about five hundred yards away.

"Why didn't we hear the sirens?" Jake said.

"We're too far from the beach," Lani said. "The wind is blowing in that direction."

"It doesn't matter why!" Mia screamed. "Let's just go!"

"Come on!" yelled Tom. "This way!"

Lani and the boys quickly turned their kayaks to the closest beach and began paddling furiously. Mia, who was not as skilled with the kayaks, took longer to turn.

Mia was barely paddling at half the speed of the rest of them. At that rate, they would be in danger of not making it.

"Faster!" said Jake. "We don't have much time!"

"My arms are too tired!" Mia yelled, distraught. "I can't go faster!"

Tom pointed at Jake. "Kayak back as fast as you can and find somebody to get a boat or something out here."

"Like who?" Jake said. "Your parents are gone for the day."

"My mom," Lani said. "She works at the Grand Hawaiian. It's that hotel right there." She pointed at the distinctive double towers with the walkway between. They looked tantalizingly close until she saw the cars parked at their base, no bigger than toys.

"You go as fast as you can," Tom said. "We'll follow you."

Jake began to paddle furiously in the direction of the beach.

Within three minutes, Jake was already a few hundred yards ahead of them. By this time, the stress, inexperience, and rocking of the kayak was too much for Mia. She leaned to her left and threw up over the side of the kayak. Mia drastically changed the center of gravity while she vomited, and before she finished heaving, the kayak tipped over, tumbling her into the water.

"Mia!" Lani yelled.

Mia bobbed in the water, buoyed by her life vest. She coughed out some salt water and retched again.

"I fell out!" she screamed. "I fell out!"

Tom paddled over to her and stabilized the kayak.

"We've got to get you back in the kayak," he said. He turned around and shouted, "Jake! Jake!"

Jake, already far ahead, continued paddling, oblivious to Tom's yells in the constantly changing breeze.

"Don't call him back!" Lani said. "He's got to keep

going. If he hears you and turns back, he won't be able to get help for us."

Lani could see Tom measuring the distance with his eyes. "You're right," he said reluctantly. He let Jake keep going.

Mia, who wasn't a strong swimmer, dog-paddled over to her drifting kayak. When she got to it, she pulled on one of the nylon cords, but her strength was so sapped that she couldn't lift herself more than a foot out of the water. She slumped back into the ocean, choking on more salt water in the process.

"I'll never get back in," she sobbed. "I'm not strong enough."

"Yes, you are," Lani said, seeing that she was going to lose Mia if she didn't calm her down. "They make them so you can get back in. Right, Tom?"

Tom eyed Lani and shrugged dubiously. Then he said, "We can try."

Tom and Lani paddled over to Mia and twice tried to lift her onto her kayak, but their awkward position made it difficult. Both times Mia fell back into the water before she was halfway on.

"This isn't going to work," Tom said.

"What am I going to do?" Mia cried.

"What about putting her on *your* kayak?" Lani said.

"This kayak's pretty small. I'm afraid she'll tip both of us over."

"Please don't leave me!" Mia cried.

"We're not leaving you," Lani said. "Tom is going to tow you."

"Tow me?"

"Yes. He's stronger than me."

Tom nodded. "Good idea. Mia, hang on to this strap."

He loosened one of the seat straps and threw it to Mia. "Tie it to your life vest. I'll pull you." He turned to Lani. "Are you okay? Can you paddle?"

Lani nodded. "I'll keep up. Let's go."

They started paddling. Jake was far ahead. Lani looked at her watch. Only nineteen minutes left. She paddled harder.

CHAPTER 29

AFTER LEAVING THE CLOTHING store where she had watched the first tsunami wave engulf the hikers on the Big Island, Teresa had returned to the beach to check the note in her bag. To her dismay, the bag was still there, with no sign from the girls.

Her first thought had been to find another phone so that she could call someone for help. But without the phone book in her dead cell phone, she didn't know any numbers to call. When she finally convinced an obliging tourist to let her use his cell phone, her calls to information went unanswered, as had her calls to the Grand Hawaiian. There was no way for her to contact anyone she knew.

By this time, the evacuation had reached its peak. People walked and ran in all directions, some calm, others crying or screaming. Many of them were families, the children struggling to keep up with their parents. Teresa hadn't taken the time to get an update on the tsunami, but whatever people were seeing on TV was spurring them to get out fast. When she tried to stop passersby to show Mia's photo, most people brushed her aside, immersed in their own problems. Of the ones who did take the time to look at the picture carefully, none recognized Mia.

Numerous possibilities for where Mia and Lani had gone fluttered through Teresa's mind. The most likely explanation was that they were in one of the hotels or condos lining the beach, either oblivious to the mass panic below or dismissive of the danger. Or they could have gotten a ride in someone's car. Teresa didn't think Mia would do something like that, but given her own state of dread, she wasn't ruling out anything.

If the girls were in a vehicle or a hotel room, she'd never find them in time. Her only hope was that the girls would become aware of what was going on and come back to find her.

Teresa's search led her back to the east end of Waikiki Beach, where she came to a stop at the corner of Ohua and Kalakaua. While the midday sun blazed unimpeded by clouds, the ocean breeze kept the temperature to a comfortable eighty degrees. Nevertheless, sweat glistened on Teresa's arms and brow, more a result of her anxiety than the climate.

She scanned the two blocks between her and the end of the developed part of Waikiki where the Kapiʻolani Park began.

"Mia!" she yelled. "Lani!"

A few heads turned, but none of them belonged to her daughter. She was about to turn and head back in the other direction when a muffled sob caught her attention.

Tucked in an alcove was a little boy no older than six. He was hunkered down against the wall, tears streaming down his pale face, the wind tousling his ash-blond hair. The people hurrying by were so engrossed in the evacuation that he had escaped attention. If Teresa hadn't stopped there, she most likely wouldn't have seen him either.

She knelt down in front of the boy, forgetting about her own lost child for a moment.

"Hey there, kiddo. Are you lost?"

He nodded glumly between sobs.

"What's your name?"

"David."

"Hi, David, I'm Teresa."

He looked at her dubiously, as if he had already told her too much.

"My mom said I shouldn't talk to strangers."

"That's usually a good idea, David. Where is your mom?"

He paused. Teresa could see that he was unsure whether to trust her.

"David, I'm a doctor, and doctors help people, right? And all I want to do is help you find your mom."

"You don't look like a doctor."

"What do doctors look like?"

"Like my doctor, Dr. Rayburn. He's old, and he has a funny nose."

Teresa smiled at that.

"I swear I'm a doctor. Here, let me show you." She plucked her medical ID from her wallet. It showed her in her white lab coat. Apparently, that was enough for David, and the information poured out.

"We're from California and we heard about the tsunami, so we were running out of our hotel with some other people and I let go of my mom's hand by accident and I couldn't see her or my dad, so I followed the other people. But she wasn't there, so I turned around to try and get back, but I got lost and now I don't know where she is."

The last statement set off another round of tears, and Teresa gave him a hug.

"We'll find her, David. Do you know the name of your hotel?"

"Hana."

"The Hana Hotel?"

"It's pink."

"Your hotel is pink?"

He nodded.

This being Teresa's first trip to Honolulu, she had no idea where the Hana Hotel was. She looked each way along Kalakaua Avenue but couldn't see any pink buildings lining the beachfront road.

"Is your hotel right on the beach?" she asked, wanting to make sure she hadn't missed it.

David shook his head. "We had to walk down a street to get to the beach."

Since she was at Ohua Avenue, Teresa thought that was as good a street as any to try. She led David by the hand and hurried along the sidewalk away from the beach, joining the other evacuees.

"Tell me if you see your hotel," she said to David.

The boy trotted at Teresa's side, occasionally tucking behind her to get out of the way of another fleeing tourist. She asked a few people if they knew where the Hana Hotel was, but none of them did. She spotted a phone booth across the street and angled toward it.

"I don't see the hotel yet," David said.

"I know. We're going to try to get the address."

Teresa tried not to think about what would happen if she couldn't find David's parents. She certainly couldn't abandon the little boy, but his plight was derailing her search for Mia.

A yellow pages hung from the bottom of the phone booth, and she flipped it open to the hotel section. She scanned the *H*s until she came to the place where Hana should have been listed. It wasn't there.

"David," she said, "are you sure it's called the Hana Hotel?"

The boy screwed up his face in concentration.

"I'm pretty sure."

The hotel section of the yellow pages was huge, but she didn't think David would have invented that name on his own. She quickly scanned down the list until she got to the *W*s. There it was. The Waikiki Hana on Koa Avenue.

The front of the phone book had a map of the Waikiki area. Koa Avenue didn't intersect with Ohua, so she would have missed it heading in this direction. She took David back down to Kalakaua and jogged the two blocks to a road that would intersect with Koa. In another minute she spotted the pink façade of the Waikiki Hana.

Stragglers still emerged from the hotel. She went into the hotel lobby, and even before she could ask David what his mother's name was, a woman screamed "David!" and swept the boy up in her arms, weeping with joy at holding her lost son. She turned to Teresa and clasped her shoulder.

"Thank you for finding him," the woman said. "I don't know what happened. One second he was there, and the next he was gone."

"You're welcome. Now you need to get out of here."

"But my husband—he went out to find David! I don't know where he is!"

"I'm sorry. But—"

"How will I find him?"

Teresa saw the woman's desperation and realized that her own search for her daughter was futile. There was no way she would find Mia or Lani running around on the streets. She needed to go where they might go.

"How will I find my husband?" the anguished woman repeated.

"I'm sorry," Teresa said. "I don't know."

She took one last look at the little boy and mother she had reunited. Then she sprinted out the front of the lobby and ran toward the Grand Hawaiian.

Chapter 30

THE LOBBY OF THE Grand Hawaiian seethed with scared and confused tourists. One couple from New York argued with a staff member about retrieving their luggage from their room. When they were told that no bellman would have time to get it for them, they became irate, demanding that they get, in writing, the promise of a full refund for their stay. Rachel told them personally that they could get their own damn luggage or leave and that they were not to talk to any of her staff again.

Most of Rachel's employees were busy running from room to room, knocking on doors to make sure that no one was left behind. They were almost done. Only the top two floors were left, but Rachel knew time was running out. Luckily, those were the floors with suites, so there weren't many doors to knock on.

The interpreter for the Russian tour group had never shown up. Rachel tried to explain to the group that they had to leave, but when she shooed them out of the front of the hotel, they stoically came to a stop, as if they were waiting for further instructions.

The Russians watched as Rachel helped some of the disabled vets into one of the buses she had hastily arranged to pick them up. Only about half the buses she needed had shown up. When she realized the deficiency, she tried to triage so that the most disabled would go first. Many of the vets could walk well enough that she sent them with the crowds now making their way up Kalakaua Avenue. That left her with about seventy-five vets and their wives who would need to be evacuated somehow. Bob Lateen, the chairman of the conference, was one of them.

"Mrs. Tanaka," he said, "when is the next bus coming?"

"We're working on that right now, Mr. Lateen."

"But they said we only have fifteen minutes left to evacuate. You've got a lot of scared people here."

Rachel used her most reassuring voice, but she couldn't help letting some testiness through. "I'm aware of that, Mr. Lateen. We're doing the best we can."

She saw Max, whose tailored gray suit and slick black hair looked as perfect as ever, despite the chaos. He hadn't even deigned to loosen his tie. Rachel's suit, on the other hand, was already rumpled, and small sweat stains peeked out from under the arms of her jacket.

"Excuse me," Rachel said to Lateen. "I'll be right back." Despite Lateen's protests, she left him and pulled Max into a quiet niche.

"What about the hotel airport shuttle?" she said.

"Just checked. It's still over at Honolulu International. It got caught there when the initial warning went out."

"Maybe we could take them in our own cars."

"We don't have enough drivers left. Besides, we wouldn't make it far in this traffic."

"Well, do you have any suggestions?"

"Yes," Max said. "I suggest we get ourselves the hell out of here."

"You're not serious."

"Rachel, what else can we do?"

They had already seen many cars abandoned by their drivers, leaving the road a mess, littered with unattended vehicles. That was one of the reasons that the last bus had come and gone more than twenty minutes ago. The rest simply couldn't get to the hotel. In fact, one bus that had already left reported back that it had resorted to pushing abandoned cars aside just to get through.

Guests continued to stream out of the hotel, but anyone moving at less than a jog was not going to make it to high ground in time, since the first wave might well reach more than a mile inland in some places.

"You have to help me get these guests up to a higher floor."

Max's jaw fell open.

"What? But you said the building wasn't safe! It might collapse."

"Keep your voice down!" Rachel said. "Look at these people." Many of the vets left in the lobby were on walkers or in wheelchairs. Some had their wives with them because the women wouldn't leave their husbands. "They wouldn't make it to the Ala Wai Canal before the wave hit, let alone to a safe distance."

"But there are more waves coming. The TV said they're twenty-five minutes apart. That's not enough time to get to safety before the next wave comes in, is it?"

"I don't know," Rachel said. "But we have less than fifteen minutes left now. Unless we do something, they're going to be sitting in the lobby when the wave comes in."

A few moments later, the elevator opened and Adrian Micton, one of the front desk clerks she had conscripted to warn the guests still in their rooms, stepped out. Rachel expected to see five staffers, but only Melissa Clark was with him.

"Where are the others?" she said.

Adrian hesitated, then said, "They . . . left. Out the back. I guess they didn't want to run into you."

Rachel couldn't blame them. They were hotel workers, not firefighters. Risking their lives wasn't in the job description. A part of her wanted to join them.

"Did you finish the sweep of the hotel?" she said.

"Yes. Every room's been notified."

"Are all the guests leaving?"

"No. There are twelve rooms where the guests said they wanted to stay here."

"Dammit! You couldn't get them to leave?"

"For whatever reason, they thought they were safer staying in their rooms. You want me to try again?"

"No, we can't make them go. You've done enough. I want you to get everyone down here and leave the hotel immediately. And I mean run. You don't have much time left."

"What about you?" Adrian said.

"We've got a bunch of people down here who can't leave. We're going to take them upstairs."

"I'll help."

"Thanks, but we need you to lead everyone who can get out to safety. They may get lost."

"I'm staying," Adrian said. "Melissa can take the others out."

Rachel smiled. "Okay, you and Max start taking the vets up to Starlight." Starlight was the restaurant on top of the Moana tower.

"All of them?" Max said. "That'll take longer with just the express elevator. What about the Akamai tower?"

"No, we should stick together. Divide them up between you and use the service elevators. They're bigger and faster. Shouldn't take you more than five minutes to get them all up there."

"Then what? What happens when the next wave comes?"

"I don't know, all right?" Rachel said, exasperated at his bickering. "We'll deal with that when the time comes. All I know is that they are not going to make it if they try to walk."

"But how do you know? How can you be sure?"

"Because if my husband says that the wave is going to be eighty feet high, I believe him. And if it's that high, they won't make it to safety in time. Now, just do it, okay?"

Max reluctantly started gathering up the guests.

Rachel looked outside and saw the Russians still milling around. Melissa was futilely trying to answer questions from a couple of the disabled vets' wives.

"Melissa," she said to the tall cashier, "come with me. I need you to help me."

One of the Russian men, probably the leader, immediately started barking in Russian at Rachel and gesticulating wildly. She put up her hands to quiet them down. Speaking to them would be useless. She tried the one word she thought they might understand.

"Tsunami. Tsunami?"

They stared at her with blank expressions. She curled one arm over the other in a motion that she hoped would convey a wave crashing while saying "Booooosh!" Then a small woman in the back with an equally small voice said, "Tsunami."

Rachel seized on that and repeated the word. The petite Russian woman spoke rapidly to the others, with the word "tsunami" sprinkled through it.

After a moment, the entire tour group realized that they were in danger and surrounded Rachel, screeching at her in panic. Rachel motioned them toward Melissa, who waved for them to come with her. Thankfully, that calmed them, and they followed her.

"Good luck," Rachel said. "And, Melissa?"

Melissa turned back to see the deadly serious look on Rachel's face.

"Run."

Lani took a second from paddling to look up and saw Jake reach shore far ahead of her. He curled out of the kayak and splashed up to the beach. He fell to the sand for a moment, and Lani was afraid he would be too exhausted to go on. But he quickly clambered to his feet and jogged off in the direction of the Grand Hawaiian as his kayak floated along the shore.

"Hold on, Mia. Jake's reached the shore. He's running to the hotel for help."

Mia could only sputter in response. The wake from Tom's paddling continually got her in the face, and she heaved up salt water periodically. However, with the strap firmly tied to her life vest, she wasn't in danger of being left behind.

"How did Jake get so far ahead?" Tom said, huffing and puffing, Mia's drag requiring him to more than double his effort.

"What?" Lani said. "Towing Mia is slowing you down a lot."

"No, that doesn't explain it all. Sure, he should be ahead of us, but not that far. It seems like we're standing still."

Lani looked to where Jake had made landfall. To this point, it had looked like he was directly in front of them. But now she realized that he was at an angle to them, and she knew what was wrong.

"We're in a riptide. That's why we're not making any headway."

"A riptide? Here?"

"It may not be strong, but it might be enough to keep us from getting farther."

"How do you know?"

"I've been boogie boarding a lot and got caught in a rip one time. We need to go parallel to the beach to get out of it."

They began paddling westward, and in a minute Lani could feel a shift in the current.

"I think we're out of it."

"Thank God," Tom said. "We've got a little more than ten minutes left."

Lani willed her tired arms to pull as hard as they could. She didn't want to say anything to discourage them, but judging from how far they were from the shore, ten minutes didn't seem like nearly enough time to get there.

CHAPTER 31

WHEN BRAD AND KAI reached the exit for Waikiki, the roads were packed, with all lanes going in the direction of the mountains. Even using the shoulder, they got bogged down by the traffic as they neared downtown Honolulu; but thanks to Brad's breakneck driving, they'd been able to make the trip in a record twenty minutes.

Kai noted with surprise that they didn't seem to be the only ones headed down to Waikiki. Some were misguided tourists intent on saving luggage or money that had been left behind on their day out, and others were locals heading to workplaces to save materials that they thought were vital. Like the man in the Lexus on TV, still others were trying to make it to the marina to get to boats they didn't want destroyed by the wave.

The thought of all those people blatantly disregarding his warnings appalled Kai. The vast majority of them would not live to see the end of the day.

The traffic coming from the shore was at a standstill. Hundreds of abandoned cars lined the side of the road, but Kai saw plenty of other vehicles filled with people desperately trying to make headway through the gridlock: a family of four in an SUV crammed with suitcases and other bric-a-brac; a lone woman in a small Toyota, her two border collies jumping back and forth between the windows; a wizened hippie in a scuba shop van; the driver of a Coca-Cola truck shouting into his radio handset. Kai wished he could stop and tell each of them to get out of their vehicles, but he knew it wouldn't do any good even if he had the time.

Throngs of people were on foot, and Brad had to slow to avoid hitting them. Most walked calmly but briskly on the sidewalk or the side of the road, but some in the horde were screaming or running or otherwise panicking. There didn't seem to be any pattern to it. Many called out names of those they'd been separated from. The scene reminded Kai of old photos showing refugees fleeing bomb-ravaged cities during World War II.

As they approached the hotel, Kai was relieved to see that the crowds thinned until there were just stragglers and the police who were trying to gather them up. One of the policemen tried to flag them down, but Brad simply passed him.

He screeched to a stop in front of the Grand Hawaiian lobby. Brad leapt off the bike and tossed his helmet onto the ground. Kai dropped his as well and ran with Brad to the front door.

Before Kai could go into the hotel, a clap of thunder ripped the air, visibly shaking the glass in the hotel's window. It was so loud that the few people still around halted where they were, searching the clear blue sky for the source of the din. Brad stopped as well, and Kai looked toward the ocean with dread. The sound continued to peal like a battleship's cannonade for more than ten seconds before it finally faded.

"What the hell was that?" Brad asked.

Kai had read stories about how islanders thousands of

miles from Krakatoa had heard the blast of the eruption, so he knew what it was instantly.

"The asteroid impact. That's the shock wave."

"Jesus!"

Traveling twelve hundred miles, it had taken more than two hours for the sound of the explosion to reach them. But what really scared Kai was that in open ocean, tsunamis traveled only slightly slower than the speed of sound. The wave wouldn't be far behind the sonic boom.

"Come on," he said. "We don't have much time."

They sprinted into the hotel. Kai yelled Rachel's name as they entered the lobby. It was deserted, with the few TVs in the lobby showing either the EAS broadcast or video from the other islands, including Johnston Island. Then another picture came on the TV with the word LIVE in the upper right corner and LAHAINA, MAUI at the bottom. Kai recognized the waterfront from several visits there. As he watched, every building—none bigger than five stories tall—was washed away by a gigantic tsunami. He sucked in his breath as he saw one of his favorite places destroyed. Their time was running out.

On the far end of the lobby, twenty people, some of them in wheelchairs, were making their way toward a bank of elevators. Kai recognized Rachel's red hair cascasing down the back of her business suit. He called her name again, and she turned. When she saw that it was Kai, her eyes went wide with surprise, and she ran to him.

"Kai!"

She threw her arms around his neck and buried her face in his shoulder. Then she pulled away. The people in the group she had been leading stopped, appraising them from across the lobby.

"What are you two doing here?" Her voice rose an octave when she realized they wouldn't have come without good reason. "What's wrong? Oh my God! Lani! Where is she?"

"Have you seen Teresa?" Kai asked. "Brad told her to come here."

"No. Where are they? Didn't they get away?"

"We saw Lani and Mia. They're in the ocean, kayaking off Waikiki somewhere."

"What! How do you know that?"

"There's no time to explain. We need to get to them before the tsunami arrives. We've got about ten minutes—"

As Kai spoke, Teresa blew into the hotel lobby. She had been running and was obviously frantic. The girls weren't with her.

"Thank God you're here!" Teresa said. "Have you seen Mia or Lani? I can't find them anywhere."

"They're on kayaks somewhere in the bay."

"What? Did they call you?"

"Where in the bay?" Rachel said.

"I don't know," Kai said. "The recreational equipment—is it still out?"

Rachel immediately understood what he meant. "Yes, down by the beach—"

A boy who was about fifteen years old ran into the lobby. Kai had never seen him before, but he looked exhausted.

"Lani's mom!" the boy yelled. "Lani's mom!"

For a moment they all stood stock-still, their mouths agape. Brad was the first to go over to him.

"You're the kid from the video," he said. "On the kayaks."

In his shock at seeing Lani and Mia on TV, Kai had barely registered the boys with them, but Brad had always been more observant than he was.

Teresa, Rachel, and Kai rushed over and began to pepper him with questions.

"Where are they?"

"Aren't they with you?"

"Can you show us where they are?"

The boy looked befuddled. He was tired and his chest was heaving.

"They're still out there," he gasped. He could barely get the words out between breaths. "In the bay. Mia was paddling too slow, so I went ahead. When I got to shore, I could only see two of them. I don't know what happened."

Kai grabbed his arm. "You're going to show us where they are."

"What?" Rachel said. "This kid can barely walk."

"Rachel," Kai said, "without him, we may not find Lani in time."

"I'm fine," the boy said. "How are we going to get them? Do you have a boat?"

"The hotel rents Jet Skis down at the beach. Let's hope they're still there."

"Then what?" Rachel said. "The wave—"

"I've got a plan." Kai nodded at Rachel and Teresa. "But you two need to leave now. Rachel, take the hotel's rental bikes—"

"I'm going with you," said Teresa.

"I don't have time to argue—"

"Then don't. That's my daughter out there. You can't stop me. I'm going."

Kai didn't waste time on it. She was coming.

"And I've got to stay with my guests," Rachel said.

Kai pulled Rachel aside.

"You can't stay here," he said. "The biggest wave might be over two hundred feet high. This hotel is right on the beach. I don't know if it can stand up to a tsunami that big."

"I've got to help these people. I'm responsible for them. I'll get them out. Somehow."

Kai felt his heart skip a beat, and his eyes welled with tears. He couldn't bear the thought of never seeing her again. He didn't know what was going to happen, but he was never more proud of her. In those few seconds, Kai could see the same thing flashing through her mind.

Rachel slipped her walkie-talkie off her belt and tucked it into Kai's dry bag.

"I'll use Max's. I may not be able to get through to you on the cell phone. I want to know that you're all right."

"Thanks."

They shared a tender, warm kiss, the one they had missed earlier in the morning. Kai wanted to hold her longer, but neither of them could linger another moment.

"I love you."

"I love you too."

He looked at her one last time and then sprinted for the door, following Brad, Teresa, and the boy.

Rachel yelled after Kai, "Call me when you're safe!"

On hearing that, Kai's mind flashed back to Lani eagerly waving to the camera on the news chopper, and it became clear to him how Rachel should get her guests out of the hotel. Just before he dashed out into the sunlight, Kai stopped and shouted one word to her:

"Helicopter!"

CHAPTER 32

BRAD, TERESA, THE BOY, and Kai tore down to the beach as fast as they could. The sun neared its apex, and the bright blue sky and perfect temperature posed an odd juxtaposition to the panic Kai felt. The path was littered with objects people had tossed aside as they made their mad dash to escape. Beach towels, various types of clothing, sunglasses, a volleyball, pool chairs—the kinds of items that would normally signal a fine day of vacation were now useless, even a hindrance.

"What's your name?" Kai asked the boy between breaths.

"Jake."

"Thanks, Jake. Thanks for coming."

"No problem."

"I'm Kai, Lani's dad."

They huffed to a stop in front of four Jet Skis that rested on the beach undisturbed. Because all the beaches in Hawaii were public, the Grand Hawaiian couldn't build an outbuilding or pier on its property, so they rolled the Jet Skis down to the beach every morning on trailers and left them there all day to be used by the guests. The Jet Skis would typically be watched over by someone from the hotel, but now the beach was nearly deserted.

Three of the four in front of Kai were the smaller, two-person variety, the other a larger, three-person craft. The staff had left in such a hurry that they hadn't bothered to get the trailers to move all of them back to the hotel—just as Kai had hoped.

"Where are the girls?" he said to Jake.

Jake pointed toward Diamond Head. "That way. I came ashore near the Marriott."

"Can you see them?" Kai said.

"I think so," said Brad, his hand shielding his eyes from the sun.

"Do you know how to ride one of these?" Kai said to Teresa. He didn't have to ask Brad, who Kai knew had one of his own sitting in his garage.

"No," she said. "I've never ridden one before."

"I do," said Jake. "I know how to ride one."

When Kai had said that he wanted Jake to show them where the girls were, he only intended for Jake to point them out. Then Kai was going to send the boy back to the relative safety of the hotel.

"No," Kai said. "I don't want you out there. It's too dangerous."

"Kai, we need him," Brad said. "We don't have time to teach Teresa how to drive one of these things. And if she comes with you or me, we won't have room for everyone."

"And I *am* coming," Teresa said, her eyes fierce with determination.

Kai wanted to argue, but they had no time.

"You sure?" Kai said to Jake.

"Yeah. My dad takes us on them every summer."

"Okay, you take that one," Kai said, pointing to one of the small ones. He jumped on the three-person Jet

Ski, and Teresa got on the back with him. Brad pushed a third out into the water.

When they got them afloat, Brad was the first to notice a potentially fatal problem.

"Holy crap, Kai!" he said. "None of these Jet Skis have keys!"

In their haste, they had forgotten to check whether the keys were still in the ignition. Normally, the keys would stay with the Jet Skis all day because they were always attended by the hotel staff. But some enterprising employee had decided to take the keys in case someone tried to go joyriding during the evacuation.

"Dammit!" Kai said. "Stay here. I'll get them."

He jumped off and splashed up to the beach in a mad scramble to find the recreational shack where the keys would be kept. But as he raced from the water, Kai heard a yell from the direction of the hotel.

"Kai! I've got them!"

Rachel ran toward him, waving a handful of keys.

"I remembered that I told Craig to take the keys when he said he didn't have time to get the Jet Skis back to storage. I brought them all." She thrust one into Kai's hand and threw two more to Brad and Jake. The key was labeled with the number on the Jet Ski.

"You're amazing," Kai said.

"Just get our daughter." She put a hand on his cheek, and then sprinted back to the hotel.

They fired up the Jet Skis and roared off at top speed.

The few people remaining on the beach ran in different directions, but the masses had by this time left. Some small groups and individuals stood on the shore, looking out to sea. Many others had gathered on balconies to watch the wave come in. Kai noted with distress that most of them were no higher than the fourth floor.

"Idiots!" he said under his breath. There was nothing he could do for them now.

They soon reached the group that Kai thought Brad had been pointing to. It turned out to be four surfers paddling idly, chatting among themselves. Kai slowed, and Brad and Jake followed suit.

"You guys need to get to shore right now!" Kai shouted at the surfers. "There's a tsunami coming."

"We know," one of the surfers shot back. "Just like last year!"

The other surfers laughed at that. Kai looked at his watch, then at Brad, and shook his head.

"Let's go," he said.

Leaving them went against Kai's urge to save everyone he could, but there simply wasn't time. His first responsibility was to save his family.

As they throttled back up to full speed, Brad called out, "You morons are going to die!" The surfers just laughed again.

A minute later they passed another small group of surfers, and this time Kai didn't even slow down. He didn't have time to convince people who didn't want to be convinced.

Before they had gone another two hundred yards, Jake shouted, "There's Tom!"

Up ahead, Kai could make out two bright yellow kayaks. They were still three hundred yards from shore.

The kayakers heard the noise from the Jet Skis and turned. Kai and the others all started waving at them. At first they didn't recognize Kai, but as they got closer, Kai heard Lani shout:

"Daddy!"

With that one word, Kai knew how desperate Lani felt. She never called him Daddy anymore.

They slowed so that their wakes wouldn't swamp the kayaks. By this time they could see Mia's head bobbing above an orange life vest behind the boy's kayak.

"Oh my God!" Teresa said. "Get Mia!"

Kai pulled his Jet Ski up to the stern of Tom's kayak.

"Brad, get Lani," he said. He untied Mia from the nylon rope, and Teresa grabbed one arm while Kai pulled on the other. They lifted her onto the Jet Ski and placed her between them. Teresa hugged her tightly.

"I'm so glad I found you. Are you okay?"

In response, Mia threw up over the side of the Jet Ski, but all that came up was salt water. Apart from her pallor and exhaustion, she seemed all right. She wiped her mouth and swiveled in the seat to hug her mother.

"Mom!" she said, weeping uncontrollably. "You're here."

"You're safe now, honey. I won't let anything happen to you." Kai knew that Teresa's response was reflexive, but her promise was empty. They were all in grave danger.

Brad pulled Lani onto his Jet Ski, and Tom climbed on with Jake. Brad circled around to them, and Kai held out his hand to Lani, who grabbed it and held it like a vise.

"Are you all right?" he said.

Lani sobbed with relief and nodded.

Kai checked his watch; they had less than three minutes left.

"Let's go!" Kai yelled to everyone. "Hold on, guys!"

He goosed the throttle, and Brad and Jake did the same.

"Where are we going?" Brad asked over the roar of the Jet Skis.

Kai pointed at a new twenty-story hotel next to Kapiʻolani Park. It was only a block from the beach, right behind a condo building half its height. As long as it didn't collapse, the shorter building might provide a buffer against the tsunami.

"But the third wave . . . !" Brad yelled.

"I know!" Kai yelled back.

They had no confirmation a third wave was coming, but their calculations made one likely. If the first wave was really eighty feet high, they would be able to survive as long as the building remained standing. It wouldn't hold up against a two-hundred-foot wave, but Kai was worried that they weren't going to make it to the hotel as it was, and he didn't want to take the chance that they would be caught on the ground when the wave came in. At ground level, even a twenty-foot wave would be deadly.

They were making good progress, coming in just south of the Kuhio Beach breakwater, when Kai's Jet Ski inexplicably started to slow down. He already had the throttle pushed to the limit, but they were still losing speed. He thought he had a mechanical failure, but the other Jet Skis seemed to be slowing as well.

"Something's wrong with my ride!" said Jake.

"Mine too," said Brad.

Kai looked at Waikiki and realized that they weren't slowing down. Their speed in relation to the beach was indeed slowing, but it wasn't because their Jet Skis were decelerating. It was because the water was receding, and they were struggling to maintain forward motion. The tide was ebbing, the classic trough preceding the wave.

The tsunami had arrived.

CHAPTER 33

THE EXPRESS ELEVATOR TO the penthouse restaurant in the Grand Hawaiian opened to dispense the last of the guests from the lobby, Rachel among them. According to the list in front of her, seven rooms below the tenth floor still had guests in them, but it was too late to do anything about that now. They were on their own.

The Starlight restaurant had a panoramic view of Honolulu, with glass in every direction except toward the north. To the west was the other Grand Hawaiian building—the Akamai tower—and downtown Honolulu. To the east was Diamond Head. And to the south, a magnificent view of the Pacific Ocean out to the horizon. The stunning vistas, not to mention the world-class cuisine, made the Starlight one of the most sought-after reservations in Honolulu. Celebrities visiting Oahu would often stop there to nosh on crab Rangoon or shallot-infused mahi mahi and take in the spectacular scenery.

Rachel paid no attention to the view. She walked around the restaurant, trying to calm the guests and answering questions.

"When can we leave?"

"Is someone coming for us?"

"Are we safe up here?"

Rachel tried to be as positive as she could without promising anything.

"Please calm down, everyone," she said. "We're perfectly safe up here for now."

A few of the women cried, but most of the guests took the situation well. The battle-hardened veterans in particular seemed to be taking it in stride.

A woman at the window screamed, and a man on crutches next to her pointed outside. All heads turned in the direction of the beach.

Max, who was also standing at the window, waved her over.

"Rachel, come here quick!"

She ran over and gasped when she saw what they were looking at. The water had receded from the beach, exposing a great swath of sand for miles up and down the coast. The yachts that remained in the Ala Wai marina rested on the bare seafloor, most of them leaning over on their sides. The Ala Wai Canal, which extended from the marina under three bridges and angled behind Waikiki, had been completely drained, revealing its silty brown bed. A few of the sightseers that were left leaned over the bridges' railings to watch the fish flopping around in the empty canal. Some of the bystanders finally understood that the coming tsunami was real and ran across the bridges, seeking refuge they could no longer reach.

Several boats that had left the marina late were now stranded on ocean floor that hadn't been exposed to the air since before the first Polynesians had settled in Hawaii. In all, five sailboats, seven motorboats, a 150-foot white luxury yacht, and a massive dredging barge were left high and dry. Some of the passengers stood dumbfounded on the decks of the boats, while others jumped overboard in an attempt to get to high ground.

To the east, only a scattered few stayed on the beach, either not realizing the danger or ignoring it. As she surveyed the scene, she spotted three minuscule objects racing for the shore.

"Kai!" she cried out.

"What?" said Max.

"My husband and daughter. That's them right there."

"You're kidding!"

The Jet Skis were just about to reach the waterline. But that would leave them still a hundred yards from the nearest building.

"Oh my God!" said Max. "They're not going to make it. Look!"

"Don't say that!" Rachel said, clasping his arm. "They *will* make it!"

With the water still flowing out, an even more ominous sign approached. The sun reflected off a line of water stretching from horizon to horizon. The line seemed to be coming toward them at an impossible speed, but just as it began to slow, it started to grow in height.

Rachel put her other hand on the window and leaned her head against it.

"Come on, Kai!" she said, pleading, her eyes wide with terror. "You can do it!"

She clutched Max's arm and could do nothing more than watch as the tsunami loomed in the distance, no more than a minute from engulfing the tiny specks below.

"Hold on!" Kai yelled.

The Jet Ski hit the exposed beach more gently than

he thought it would, sliding along the wet sand easily for at least fifteen feet. By the time they had all jumped off, the water was already another forty feet behind them, as if a giant vacuum were sucking the ocean away.

Kai grabbed Lani's hand and, with the dry bag flapping uncomfortably against his back, sprinted for the hotel in front of them. The distance seemed vaster than the Sahara Desert, but he knew they could cross that span in less than a minute. It was all they had.

Brad held Mia's hand and pulled her along, followed by Teresa, Tom, and Jake. The going was slower than Kai wanted, because the sand was wet and their feet sank into it all too easily. To make matters worse, the shore inclined significantly, so they felt as if they were practically climbing it.

Twice, Lani slipped and fell. Kai looked down and saw the reason: she and Mia were wearing flip-flops, while the rest of them wore sneakers except for Brad, who had on boots.

"Kick those flip-flops off!" Kai said.

The girls did as they were told without hesitation.

In a few more seconds they reached what was normally the surfline. To Kai's astonishment, a massive Hawaiian woman dressed in a flowing muumuu walked slowly out toward the ocean, her arms outstretched.

He stopped, mesmerized by the sight.

"Hey!" he yelled. "Ma'am! A tsunami is coming!"

She turned to him. She was in her fifties, her skin wrinkled from exposure to the sun, a beatific smile revealing stunning white teeth.

"This is God's will," she calmly said, and then continued her march to the sea and certain death.

"Come on!" Brad screamed. "Forget her!"

Before Kai turned to run, he stole a look at the sea and with his own eyes saw the phenomenon he had studied for years in cramped offices with abstract mathematical formulas.

A frothy white mass churned toward them in horrifying splendor, building and collapsing as it reached the shallows surrounding the island. At first the sound was very much like the crashing of waves on the shore, but the difference was that the roar never abated: it just kept growing, continually topping itself, reminding Kai of a jet engine throttling up for takeoff.

He might have stayed there, transfixed, until the tsunami took him if Brad hadn't grabbed his shoulder.

"Come on!" he repeated.

The others were already ahead of Kai, but Lani lagged behind. He grabbed her hand as he ran by.

The girls were exhausted from their ordeal in the kayaks, and they slowed the group down. Mia sobbed from the fatigue, but she didn't complain, and neither did Lani.

"You're doing great!" Kai yelled in encouragement.

They reached Kalakaua Avenue, the sound of the tsunami behind them so loud that it was hard to hear each other. Tom and Jake started sprinting for the building directly in front of them, and Teresa followed with Mia. They were headed for the wrong building. The twenty-story hotel Kai had intended to go to was a hundred yards farther up the street. The condo in front of them was only ten stories high.

"No!" he yelled. "That one!" He pointed at the taller hotel.

The boys either didn't hear or ignored him.

He followed to try to keep them from going into the

smaller building. Although it looked strong, with a solid concrete base, it was too short to be a refuge from more than the first wave. The wave now towered high above Waikiki Bay, casting a shadow even though it was mid-day. To the southeast, the point of Diamond Head was struck by the tsunami. Geysers of water plumed into the air as it plunged against the steep sides of the extinct volcano, where million-dollar homes were now being pummeled into splinters by one of the most powerful forces in nature.

The boys had too much of a head start, and Kai didn't get to them until he reached the front of the building. Brad grabbed them before they ran in.

"This is the wrong building!" he yelled.

Brad started to run with the boys away from the condo and toward the hotel, but Kai shouted for them to stop. They had run out of time. If they ran for the hotel, they weren't going to make it. The boys got to the corner of the condo building before they turned and headed back toward Kai, who was now at the condo entrance.

He threw open the doors etched with the name "The Seaside" and frantically searched for the stairs. The unfashionable decor and peeling paint revealed the Seaside's age, but the building also looked sturdy, and that's all Kai cared about at the moment.

Teresa shouted, "There!" and wrenched Lani toward a staircase on the east side of the building. Kai followed, with Mia in tow.

The emergency stairwell was obviously built before new building codes required stairs to be protected within the interior of the building. These stairs were airy and bright and actually more attractive than the lobby because they were completely encased in glass.

To his right, Kai could see the tsunami crash with a mammoth splash onto Waikiki Beach. The wave reached the shore to the southeast first, smashing everything in its path. Instead of a vertical wall of water, the ocean rose like the world's fastest-rising tide. At first the palm trees resisted, but the water was too powerful and bent them over like toothpicks. A five-story hotel farther down the beach was hit and the wave poured through it. Ranch-style homes near it were covered within seconds. Closer to Kai, surfboards bounced above the churning foam, their owners nowhere to be seen. The Jet Skis flipped over and disappeared. Then the woman in the muumuu was engulfed by the wave.

The sight made Kai gasp in terror. He raced up the stairs as fast as he could.

Before he reached the second floor, Kai could tell that Mia was completely spent. He grabbed her and held her in his arms like a toddler, sprinting up the stairs two at a time, the adrenaline kicking his energy to a level he had never before experienced. In any other circumstance, carrying an extra ninety pounds would have slowed him to a crawl, but with the wave about to crash down on them, Mia seemed to weigh no more than a sack of groceries.

Kai kept Teresa and Lani in front of him, willing them to go faster. The door on the first floor banged open. He knew it had to be Brad and the boys, but he didn't take even a second to glance down at them. They had to get much higher.

He was on the eighth-floor landing when Kai heard a chilling sound. Over the roar of the water, the noise of glass shattering on the first floor signaled that their time was up. In quick succession, the wave blew out the windows on one floor after another, like a sharpshooter at a rifle range systematically shooting bottles on a fence.

The building lurched, throwing Kai off balance as he stepped onto the ninth-floor landing, and he slammed against the railing, almost dumping Mia over the side. He regained his footing and made it up the last flight of stairs to the top floor. He set Mia on her feet and looked down.

Brad pushed Jake and Tom in front of him at the sixth floor, the churning mass of water now only two floors below him and rising fast.

They all yelled at Brad from their perch. "Hurry! Come on!"

Kai held the railing in a death grip, hoping that their luck wouldn't give out now. All he could do was watch as the tsunami stalked his brother from below.

Chapter 34

Rachel had watched in horror as Kai and Lani fled the wave and lost sight of them when they got to Kalakaua Avenue, the buildings obstructing her view. She immediately tried to call Kai's cell phone to see if they were all right, but all she got was a fast busy signal, indicating all lines were jammed. She tried Max's walkie-talkie with no success.

When she couldn't see them anymore, she turned her attention back to the tsunami coming in. From her vantage point on the twenty-eighth floor, she was far above the maximum height of this tsunami, but as the wave grew, it looked like it would never stop.

"Will you look at the size of that thing?" said Max.

The boats that had been left stranded were picked up by the wave. The smaller boats capsized immediately or were borne by the wave as it rammed into the shoreline and buildings, smashing them into unrecognizable pieces. The people who had been running from the water were simply swallowed up.

The tsunami crashed into the white luxury yacht's bow, driving it backward, but most of the wave's force went around the yacht, and it floated on top of the water only a short distance from where it had been resting, its propellers churning at full speed to keep it from coming ashore.

The dredging barge that had been attempting to leave the inlet to the Ala Wai Canal was not so fortunate.

The barge was part of a project to dredge the accumulated sludge at the entrance of the canal. The captain had tried to get the barge and its equipment out to sea before the tsunami hit. However, the barge lacked quick maneuverability, and in the chaos during its escape, it had drifted too close to shore. The receding water left it stranded broadside to the wave, helpless. When the tsunami reached it, the wave picked up the three-hundred-foot-long vessel like a toy and threw it back toward the hotels lining the beach, on a direct collision course with the Grand Hawaiian.

"It's coming right at us!" Rachel said. "Hold on, everyone!"

Many of the guests had crowded up to the window to see the wave come in, but most of them ran to the back of the room when they realized what was happening. Screams and yells filled the restaurant. Max and Rachel stayed at the window, transfixed by the ease with which the tsunami tossed the massive barge.

As the water rumbled toward them, the building shook as if a minor earthquake had jolted it. The glass vibrated in sympathy with the motion.

When the wave reached the original shoreline, the barge rotated so that its bow pointed straight inland. As the wave was about to smash into the Grand Hawaiian, the barge rotated just enough so that it cleared the building they were standing in, but now it headed for the second of the Grand Hawaiian's twin towers.

The barge's bow plunged into the Akamai tower with immense force. The sound of pulverized steel, glass, and concrete was audible twenty-eight stories up in the

Moana tower. The top of the barge crashed through the sixth-floor balcony and came to a stop after fifty feet of the ship had disappeared into the interior. The tsunami kept up the pressure as it climbed higher and inundated the barge, sweeping the jumble of dredging equipment on its deck into the building. The stern half of the barge, buoyed by the water, rose up and snapped off, leaving the bow firmly wedged in the building. Detached from the rest of the barge, the stern glanced off the building and floated around the Akamai tower and out of view.

Vast amounts of debris choked the water. Cars, boats, pieces of buildings, trees, all combined into a morass of detritus flowing inland. Rachel knew that bodies must be mixed in with the wreckage, but thankfully she was too far up to make out those details clearly. For as far as she could see on either side of the hotel, water seven stories high filled the streets of Honolulu. Anyone caught in that would have needed a miracle to survive.

Rachel mentally reviewed her options. Evacuating the guests by going back downstairs would be futile. Even assuming the wave would retreat enough to let them out onto the streets, there wouldn't be enough time before the next wave for them to reach safety. Their only hope was to be saved by air.

She gestured toward the helicopters, both military and civilian, buzzing around the city. Her best hope was to follow Kai's suggestion.

"We have to try to get one of them," she said to Max.

As she opened her cell phone to dial 911, the only way she could think of to get help, she happened to glance across at the Akamai tower. With a gasp, she pointed to a window about three floors below them where a man with a goatee leaned against it, a cell phone in his hand, peering down at the barge sticking out of the lower stories. The sun reflected off his bald spot, and his flowered shirt rippled in the breeze. Even from this distance, the desperation on his face was apparent.

"He's trapped," Rachel said, "and he knows it."

The dredging barge had been driven into the middle of the tower like an enormous spike, most likely crushing the stairwell and any escape in that direction. The distinctive spire roof of the Akumai tower, in contrast to the flat roof of the Moana tower, provided no place for a helicopter to land.

"My God!" Max said. "He's not going to jump, is he?"

"I don't know," Rachel said, waving her arms and banging on the window, trying to get the man's attention.

A woman, as dark as the man was fair, ran to the man and hugged him, followed by three children. The man didn't seem to hear Rachel, but the biggest of the children, a boy, caught sight of her in the restaurant and pointed. The man returned Rachel's wave and motioned with his hands, asking what they should do.

"What now?" Max said.

"I don't know. But if we don't get a helicopter, none of us is getting out of here alive."

She had just started dialing again when shouts of alarm coursed through the room. Every light in the restaurant went dark, and the air handling system fell silent. The power was out.

From the Hawaiian State Civil Defense's bunker, Renfro had been monitoring Oahu's major power stations with growing apprehension. All three of them sat on the coast, the biggest in Nanakuli, the others at Barbers Point and Honolulu. Of course, HSCD disaster planners had considered their proximity to the coast, but the most urgent concern was hurricanes, which battered the Hawaiian Islands periodically. In those cases, the tidal surge was never higher than fifteen feet. Tsunamis rarely reached more than thirty feet in height, and the power plants were above that level.

A mega-tsunami was unprecedented, so large that HSCD had not considered it a realistic possibility. The chances of it happening were so remote that planning for it was not deemed economically prudent.

And so, when the eighty-foot-high tsunami struck the coast of Oahu, the wave submerged all three power plants to a depth of thirty feet, shutting all of them down. The higher waves to come would destroy them completely.

Renfro shook his head as the reports came in. Not only were the power plants smashed, but the wave had washed away most of the power lines and their towers. Where lines remained intact, the water caused short circuits in the system. The power substations that weren't submerged couldn't handle the massive overloads, and the surviving circuit breakers were tripped.

The island of Oahu was in a blackout.

A few locations, however, still had power. Backup generators and batteries continued to power HSCD, hospitals, and the air traffic control tower at Wheeler Army Airfield.

Renfro knew only one other major system continued to function: small backup generators or batteries were included in the design of every cell phone tower.

On the tenth floor of the Seaside, next to the stairwell, a second set of stairs led up to the roof. Brad, Jake, and

Tom had reached the top of the stairs without getting injured by the flying shards of glass. With the rushing water just below them, Kai ushered everyone up the last flight of stairs and onto the roof.

The flat expanse of faded and peeling white paint was broken up by a few large air-conditioning units and not much else. Kai ran to the edge of the building and looked down. At that height, he would normally see multitudes of beachgoers thronging the promenade far below. Instead, breathtakingly, the water was now only fifteen feet beneath them, the top floor dry by a few inches. Water surged like a river around the corner of the building, taking all kinds of debris with it.

Kai was relieved that the building hadn't collapsed with the first wave. But he had no idea if it would stand up to the next one. Not that it would matter: the next wave was going to be another five stories high, completely covering this building.

He knelt by Lani.

"Are you all right, honey?" Kai said.

She nodded and gave him a tight hug. "I can't believe you came to get us. How did you know where we were?"

"You were on TV. Then Jake led us to you when we got to the Grand Hawaiian. Was it your idea to send him there?"

She nodded again. She was a smart kid.

"Is Mom okay?"

"She was at the hotel. I'm sure she's fine." Although Kai tried to project a confident calm, he was in fact sick with worry about Rachel. He knew this thing was far from over, and he didn't think she'd be safe for long where she was. Neither would they.

Kai took out the walkie-talkie and tried it first. After a few attempts he got through to his wife and breathed a sigh of relief.

"Rachel, are you all right?"

"Kai! Thank God! Please tell me you got Lani."

"I have her right here. She has an exciting story to tell you."

Kai passed the walkie-talkie to Lani and walked over to Brad. He was taking pictures of the flooding with his cell phone, which had been in the dry bag.

"What do we do now?" Brad said, snapping a photo of a boat floating past the eighth story of the building behind them, the twenty-story building they would have been in if only they'd had another minute to run over to it. Kai took Brad aside so that the kids wouldn't hear them. Teresa joined them.

"We wait," Kai said. "The water will recede. When it does, we need to make a run for higher ground. In the meantime, maybe we can wave one of those helicopters down."

"We're not the only ones," Teresa said. "Look."

She gestured to the other buildings around Waikiki and Honolulu. As far as the eye could see, buildings were topped with people leaning over the sides or waving to the skies. There had to be hundreds of them, if not thousands. Seeing that, it struck Kai as strange that they were the only ones on the top of this building. He had the awful thought that perhaps The Seaside held other people who hadn't tried to evacuate their condos until the water was upon them.

To Kai's surprise, Teresa grabbed both him and Brad in an embrace.

"I can't ever thank you enough for saving Mia," she

sobbed. "I don't know what I would have done if you hadn't come along."

"Hey, it finally got Lame-o here on a motorcycle," Brad joked. "Of course, my Harley is now rusting away under about eighty feet of Pacific seawater. But it was a helluva last ride."

Kai wanted to say it was going to be okay, that they were all safe now, but it couldn't have been further from the truth. They couldn't stay, but at the moment they couldn't go, either.

Kai borrowed Brad's cell phone and dialed 911. The line was jammed and all he got was a busy signal. He tried again, with the same result.

He was about to call Reggie when Kai realized that it wasn't his own phone. His was in pieces on the side of Fort Stewart Road, washed away by now. Reggie's cell number, of course, wasn't in Brad's cell phone list, and Kai had become so reliant on that feature that he had no idea what Reggie's number was.

He resorted to calling his own number, knowing he would be routed to voice mail, since his phone wouldn't answer. It rang through, and Kai punched in the remote access code while his greeting played. He had one message. It had been received less than five minutes ago.

"Kai, this is Reggie." Kai heard Reggie wheezing. "I sure as hell hope you get this, because that means you survived. We're running up Fort Stewart Road right now. It is a madhouse. People everywhere. I haven't been able to get in touch with Alaska. I assume you got through to them or I would have heard from you, but I'll keep trying. Once I get to Wheeler, we should have some dedicated phone lines."

Kai berated himself for leaving without making the

transfer. He could only hope that HSCD was in contact with the warning center in Palmer. For all he knew, they and the rest of the Pacific island nations were now ignorant of any new information because he had abandoned his post without even making sure someone else would pick up his responsibilities. His stomach twisted with guilt.

"I'll keep my phone on," Reggie continued. "The service has been spotty. I'm lucky I got through to your voice mail. If you're out there, give me a call and let me know you're okay. I hope I hear from you, Kai."

The message ended. Kai memorized the number rattled off by the voice mail's caller ID and saved it in Brad's phone's list before dialing it.

"Who are you calling?" Brad asked.

"Reggie," Kai said. "Maybe he can send us a chopper."

The call immediately went to voice mail.

"Quick," Kai said to Brad, "what are the cross streets of this building?"

"It's hard to tell with all the streets gone. I know we're on Kalakaua." He pointed in the direction of the mountains behind them. "Lemon is that way. I think this might be Laka'laina running perpendicular."

Great, Kai thought. *The only real estate developer in Honolulu who doesn't know the streets.*

Lani came over, holding the walkie-talkie in front of her.

"Mom wants to talk to you."

Kai motioned for Brad to take it. "Tell her what we're doing and that we're all right." He didn't have to add "For now."

Reggie's voice came on and Kai left the message.

"Reggie, this is Kai. If you get this in the next ten minutes, we are on top of a white ten-story condo building called The Seaside on the east end of Waikiki. We think the cross streets are Kalakaua and Laka'laina. If you get this, send a helicopter to come get us. And call me. I lost my cell phone, so I'm on Brad's." Kai gave him the number and hung up.

"Do you think he'll be able to send one?" Teresa said.

"I don't know. But if he doesn't, we're going to have to try running for it."

"'Running for it'?"

Kai forgot that Teresa didn't know anything about tsunamis.

"This wave will recede as the next trough in the series of tsunamis reaches us."

"Series! You mean there are going to be more?"

Kai didn't have time to cushion the news.

"We cannot stay on this building. We've got about twenty minutes before the next wave comes in and covers this condo."

"How many more are there?"

"I don't know." If Kai had made sure Reggie was in touch with Palmer, maybe he would have known. "At least two. Maybe more. We've got to leave one way or another."

"How?"

"If a helicopter flies near us, we need to try to wave it down. If not, we'll go down the stairwell as the water ebbs. Once we reach the ground floor, we'll have ten minutes before the next wave comes in."

"How far can we get in ten minutes?"

Under the best of conditions, they could run maybe a mile in ten minutes. But given their exhaustion and the debris that would be littering the way, that estimate was way too optimistic. And with waves this size, the water would surely reach more than a mile inland.

Kai studied the buildings around him. About five blocks away from the beach was another apartment building that was about twice the height of The Seaside.

"That building is twenty stories tall. If we make it up that one, it's a little farther inland. We can sort of leapfrog our way up to the Punchbowl as the next wave recedes. That's the closest point that's safe."

It wasn't a great plan, but it was all he had.

The smell of seawater was strong—much stronger than it should have been this high up. It reminded Kai that they were still in mortal danger.

He looked to the sky, trying to will one of those distant helicopters to come their way. He wanted to do something but couldn't. Only twenty minutes until the next wave, and he was completely helpless.

CHAPTER 35

AFTER BRAD FINISHED FILLING Rachel in on their situation, she had a last word with Kai and then signed off to deal with her latest problem.

There was no way a helicopter could land on the pointed top of the Akamai tower to rescue the family across from Rachel and Max. The only way for the family to escape was to go down. But with the dredging barge embedded in the building, probably blocking the stairwell in the center of the structure, they might not be able to make it all the way to the ground.

"Do you think they can get out?" Max said.

"There's no way to know from here," Rachel replied. "They'll just have to try it."

"Even if they get all the way down, can they get to safety? You said there's another wave coming, and it's even bigger than the last one."

"There's one other possibility," she said. "They might be able to go across the skybridge."

They searched for signs of the sixth-floor skybridge, but the water level was still well above it. The skybridge, designed like a suspension bridge, hung from cables that extended up to the eighth floor. Sixteen cables, eight anchored to each side of the bridge's floor, held it in place, half the cables attached to the Moana tower and the other half attached to the Akamai tower. The cables were still intact, but it was impossible to tell whether they were still connected to anything substantial enough to walk across.

"The skybridge?" Max said. "Do you think it's still there? That would be convenient."

"Convenient? You think anything about this morning is convenient?"

Max dropped his head in embarrassment. "I just meant that it would be lucky for them," he said sheepishly.

Rachel sighed. "I know, Max. I'm sorry. I shouldn't take it out on you. Look, we won't know about the skybridge until the water recedes, but if it is still there, they might be able to get to it and get across. It'll take them a few minutes to get down twenty stories."

The family didn't budge. They just looked at Rachel and waved frantically, not knowing what to do. They were in a panic.

"We have to tell them to move now."

"But how?" Max said. "With the power out, we can't use the hotel phones."

"We'll write it on something." Rachel looked around, then realized what they needed was right in front of them. She ran over to the maître d's desk and grabbed the grease pencil he used to mark the seating plan. She took it to one of the dining tables, threw the glasses and utensils on the floor, and began scrawling on the white tablecloth in huge letters.

In a minute she completed the crude message.

"Help me," she said to Max, and whipped the tablecloth off. They carried it over to the window. It said: GO TO SKYBRIDGE 6TH FLOOR.

"Wait a minute," Rachel said, keeping the tablecloth out of view of the window.

"What?" Max said.

"We need to make sure the skybridge is actually there."

The water had begun to flow back toward the ocean, carrying anything that floated. In another minute, the level was down to the sixth floor. They held their breath to see whether the skybridge was still intact.

As the water dropped farther, the debris started to get caught on something. When it began to pile up in a line between the buildings, Rachel knew the skybridge had survived.

"Okay, let's put the sign up," Rachel said. "And let's hope they speak English."

They held the tablecloth against the window so that the family could read it. After seeing it, both the man and woman nodded furiously and gave a thumbs-up. In a second, the whole family was gone.

"Looks like they got the message. Max, you need to get everyone here up to the roof. It won't be easy because of the stairs. You'll have to leave the wheelchairs behind. Keep calling for a helicopter. And take some of the tablecloths to wave as a signal."

"You're not going down there, are you?"

"They may need help getting across. Besides, once they get over to our building, they may try to go down instead of up. That would be a bad decision. Max, do whatever you have to do to get that helicopter."

He nodded. "Be careful."

"You too. I'll see you in twenty minutes. If I'm not back by then, that means . . ." She trailed off, not wanting to actually say the words.

"You better be," Max said.

With that, Rachel ran to the door marked by the emergency exit sign and started down the stairs.

Over the skies of Honolulu, Kai saw more helicopters than he even knew existed. Army Black Hawks and huge Navy HH-53s were the biggest, but there were news choppers, scenic tour helicopters with their logos emblazoned on their sides, and everything in between. At one point he counted over a dozen helicopters buzzing around the city in all directions. All seven of Kai's group waved their arms wildly, but even with that many helicopters in the air, not one of them came in their direction. There were just too many other people clamoring for their attention.

The only other option was to go down. The water swirling below made that an unpleasant prospect. Along with the inorganic wreckage, Kai now saw bodies being drawn back to the ocean. Most of them were facedown, so he was spared looking at their last expressions, but he could see the tsunami had been indiscriminate.

In the short time that the water had begun to withdraw, Kai saw at least thirty bodies of men and women, some still in flowered shirts or bathing suits, others stripped completely naked. But the most horrible sight was the children. The first one was a girl about Lani's age, her long blond hair floating around her. Kai felt the urge to jump in and pull her out, but he restrained himself, knowing it would be a pointless gesture that would not only get him killed but would also mean he'd no longer be there for Lani. Each time he saw a child float by, Kai looked for signs of life in the hope that he might save him or her, but each body remained still. He told Lani not to look, but he knew he couldn't protect her for long. Eventually, they would have to go out in that.

Almost as horrible was seeing the pets that had been taken by the wave. Dogs and cats were mixed in with the people. Some of the dogs still had their leashes on. It made Kai wonder for the first time how Bilbo was, but he realized with relief that if Reggie was okay, his dog was too.

Then they saw another carcass, one so out of place amid all of the other carnage that Kai blinked several times before realizing what it was.

"Is that what I think it is?" said Brad.

Below them, swirling next to a Volkswagen Beetle, was an enormous orange and white giraffe, floating on its side.

"What on earth . . . ?" Teresa said.

"The zoo is right over there in the park," Kai said, pointing in the direction of Diamond Head. "It must have gotten swept away by the wave and pulled over here."

"Poor thing," she said. "They must not have had time to get the animals evacuated." Kai shook his head. Every animal in the zoo must be dead.

On the building behind them, the water level was now half a floor below the high-water mark. It was definitely receding.

"Come on, everyone," Kai said quietly. "We need to make our move now."

He led them down to the main stairwell, where he peered over the side to inspect the damage. The surface of the ninth-floor landing dripped with water and silt, but the steps looked otherwise intact. Pieces of trash were caught in the railings and wrapped around the pillars that held up the outer part of the stairwell.

A pungent smell surrounded them. The bodies hadn't begun to decay yet, but the tsunami had mixed sewage, gasoline, garbage, and assorted chemicals into an odor that Kai had never before experienced. He coughed at the stench.

The water drained surprisingly quickly off the eighth-floor platform. The flow past the building must have been greater than ten knots, much faster than a person could swim—even faster than the currents of many rivers. Occasionally a large object would bang off a pillar, startling them.

Instead of following the receding water down the steps, Kai opened the door leading to the tenth-story condos, the only dry floor left.

"What are you doing?" Brad said.

"With all that debris outside, Mia and Lani are going to need shoes."

"You mean, we get to bust down some doors?" he said, a little too delighted at the prospect of Kai's proposed thievery.

"This building won't be here in an hour, so we might as well help ourselves. Teresa, you stay here with Tom and Jake. Lani, you and Mia come with us."

"I want Mia to stay with me," Teresa said with a hint of fear.

"She needs to try on the shoes," Kai said calmly, trying to ease her mind. "And I need Brad to help me break down the doors. If Reggie gets my message and sends a helicopter, someone will need to run up to the roof as fast as possible to flag it down. It's okay. We'll be right back."

The hall was dark from the lack of power, so Teresa held the fire door open while Tom and Jake went to the mid-story landing to get a better view outside. Kai walked down the hall to the first condo door on the left, 1001, facing the ocean to the south. He lashed out with a kick, but the solid door just rang from the impact.

"Let me try," Brad said.

Brad threw his weight into a kick, and the door frame cracked. Two more kicks, and the door swung open with a crash. Kai shot him a curious look.

Brad shrugged. "Karate classes," he said.

They passed a kitchen in which the sink was piled high with dishes and entered a living room that held little more than a massive leather couch, a coffee table littered with issues of *Maxim* magazine and Xbox controllers, and a big-screen television. Kai immediately thought, *Bachelor pad,* but they headed straight to the bedrooms and looked in the closets anyway. Just as he thought: all the shoes were men's size twelve.

Frustrated in their search, Kai and the others emerged into the hall for another try.

"Any luck?" Teresa said.

"Dude's apartment," Brad said.

"The water's down to the sixth floor now!" Jake yelled from the stairwell. He and Tom followed the water farther down.

"This is taking too long," Kai said. "We need to be ready to run once the water reaches the bottom. Let's try two apartments at a time."

Brad nodded, and this time they both kicked open the door of condo 1002, directly opposite 1001. It opened right away. Brad proceeded to the next condo with Mia while Lani followed Kai into 1002, the expression on her face betraying her tension.

"Remember," Kai said, trying to lighten the mood, "we're not looking for cute strappy heels. Just sneakers."

She gave him a look that said his attempt at humor was not well received.

The patio door to the balcony was wide open, as was the custom in Hawaii, to let the breeze ventilate the condo. Kai heard Brad yell from the adjoining condo's patio door.

"Looks like a family lives here! We might get lucky."

"Mine too!" Kai yelled back.

Lani had already made her way into the bedroom and was rooting through the closet.

"Find anything?" Kai asked from the doorway.

She held up a pair of white sneakers. The rest of the shoes were either high heels or sandals.

"Are they your size?"

"Close enough," she said.

"Okay, put them on."

Kai went back to the living room to let Brad know they'd found some. When he got there, he heard a strange hissing sound coming from the direction of the balcony. The high-pitched whine of escaping gas was unmistakable and was soon supplemented by the roar of fire. Kai dashed out onto the balcony to find out where it was coming from. He skidded to a halt at the railing when he saw what was causing the noise.

Directly in front of him, the twenty-story high-rise to the north obstructed The Seaside's view of the mountains. On the ninth floor of the structure, a giant propane tank jutted out of a window. The tank had apparently plunged through one side of the glass building and then got stuck in the side closest to The Seaside. A jet of gas six inches across shot out of a hole at one end, where it instantly transformed into a blazing torch.

"Brad, get out of there!" Kai yelled.

"What happened?" Brad said, racing out to the balcony to see what he was talking about. "Oh my God!"

The propane tank had probably been ripped from its spot at a gas station and pierced the high-rise while being swept along by the water. Then any spark could have set it off. The receding water had left it hanging high and dry in a corner of the window, with no chance that it would be doused before the next wave came in. It could blow up any second.

"It's going to explode!" Kai shouted out the door of the apartment. "Run!"

"Mia!" Teresa said from the stairwell.

Without answering, Kai ran back to the bedroom and grabbed Lani's hand, yanking her to her feet without letting her finish tying the other shoe.

As they ran out, Teresa flashed past the front door of the condo, headed for Brad and Mia.

"Teresa! Come back!"

She ignored Kai and flew through the door of the next condo down to find Mia. Lani and Kai ran across the hall to condo 1001, and Kai slammed the door behind them. He pushed Lani over the couch and dove after her. As they hit the floor with a thud, the tank blew up.

Despite the several walls separating them from the tank, the noise from the blast assaulted Kai's ears. The building shook from the impact. The door to the condo was ripped from its hinges, flying over them and out the window. Kai instinctively covered Lani with his body. Pieces of debris and shrapnel from the tank peppered the wall. A tremendous heat wave singed the hairs on Kai's arms. He felt a sizzling burn crease his thigh, and he screamed in pain. A chunk of white-hot metal ricocheted off the wall.

"Are you okay?" he said to Lani as the noise subsided.

"Oh my God, Daddy!" Lani said, pointing at his leg. "You're bleeding."

Kai looked at his pants. A five-inch gash ran laterally across his thigh. Blood dripped from the wound, but it wasn't deep. The shrapnel had just grazed the skin. A few inches to the left, and it would have gone right through his leg, tearing through the femoral artery.

"I'm fine. It's nothing to worry about." Once the adrenaline was gone, Kai knew the pain would come, but it didn't look like he'd bleed to death, so he ignored it. "Are you okay?" he repeated.

"Yes," Lani said. "But where are the others?"

"I think they were in the other apartment."

They ran back into the hall, and the sight that greeted them was appalling. Part of the hallway wall on the north side had disintegrated, spilling bits of plaster and drywall all over the floor. Through the doorway of the facing condo, they could see that the entire northern exterior wall had been shattered. Visible out of that gaping hole, the remains of the high-rise burned, covered with what was left of the liquefied propane. One half of the high-rise simply wasn't there anymore. A jagged wound was carved out of the other half, but it wouldn't last long. As Lani and Kai watched, the remaining steel and concrete buckled in what seemed like slow motion, and in a hail of dust and a low rumble, the building collapsed into the water below.

It was like seeing their fate played out in front of them. The building they were standing in was stronger than the one that had collapsed, but Kai was worried now that it also had sustained significant structural damage.

He and Lani began yelling for the others.

"Brad! Teresa! Mia! Jake! Tom!"

Kai heard coughing from the stairwell and ran over to it. The fire door was off its hinges, but the building had shielded the main stairwell from significant damage. The stairs to the roof were a mangled mess of twisted railings and pulverized concrete.

He looked down to see Tom peering from the doorway on the eighth floor. Tom's face was contorted in a rictus of confusion and agony. With his right hand he held his left arm, which hung at a grotesque angle at his side. His complexion was ashen.

"Tom!" Kai said. "Where's Jake?"

Tom nodded toward the hallway. "In there. I think he's dead!"

Kai wanted to comfort him, but they didn't have time. There were only fifteen minutes left before the next tsunami.

"Are you sure?" Kai said.

Tom shook his head. "No, but he's not moving."

A yell came from the other end of the hallway.

"Kai! Help!"

It was Teresa.

"Teresa! We're out here."

Teresa poked her head out of the condo Brad had been in. The look of alarm on her face was enough to tell Kai something terrible had happened.

"Are you okay?" he said.

"It's Brad and Mia. The wall fell down. They're trapped."

CHAPTER 36

11:34 A.M.
13 MINUTES TO SECOND WAVE

THE STAIRS LEADING TO the roof of the flat-topped Moana tower in the Grand Hawaiian were steep but wide. Normally, the access was strictly limited to hotel employees who needed to maintain the rooftop air-conditioning units, but Max was forced to herd the guests up the steps. The only good news was that they had just one floor to climb.

Max conferred with Bob Lateen before deciding that, one at a time, Max and Adrian would carry each of the eight disabled veterans remaining in the restaurant. Some of the wives—none of them under seventy— volunteered to help, but Max was afraid one of them would fall, and he didn't need any more problems than he had already.

In the meantime, Max asked all of those with cell phones to try calling the police, fire department, or any-one else who could send a helicopter to rescue them. Of course, he could go up to the roof and try to flag one down, but that would delay the movement of the disabled guests. He asked three of the ladies to leave their husbands to signal for help by waving a tablecloth.

It took two minutes to get the first wheelchair-bound guest up and situated comfortably on the roof—much more time than Max had expected. At that rate, it would take over fifteen minutes to get them all up, so he decided to send the elderly who could walk up the stairs first.

While Adrian finished helping those guests up the stairs, Max went to the window to look at the devastation below.

The streets were unrecognizable. A steady stream of water flowed back toward the ocean, dragging all kinds of flotsam with it. It would be only a matter of minutes before the land was completely drained.

He could clearly see the skybridge now. A huge gash in the roof exposed part of the walkway to the bright sunlight. Max couldn't see the piece of debris responsible, but it must have been something big. Anything large enough to leave that mark could have easily torn the skybridge from its moorings. As it was, the bridge appeared to be hanging by the thinnest of threads. *Anyone willing to cross that would have to be pretty desperate,* he thought as he made his way back to the stairwell.

Rachel reached the sixth-floor conference center. The skybridge in front of her looked like it had been blasted by a truck bomb. Every shard of glass had been torn out of the windows, exposing the walkway to the ocean breeze from floor to ceiling. The skybridge itself was tilted at an extreme angle, with the beach side higher, as if the wave had pushed up one edge but couldn't wrest it from its steel cables.

The midday sun poured through the hole in the skybridge roof, illuminating the sorry state of the floor itself. Like every other surface the tsunami had touched, a fine layer of soupy silt coated the decking. In many places, holes had been punched through the floor as well as the ceiling. Fifty feet below, the outflow of water was now only ten feet deep. They were lucky the skybridge was still there at all. It certainly wouldn't stand up to another onslaught of water.

As Rachel approached the bridge, the family appeared on the other end of the sixty-foot walkway. They heaved visibly from the exertion of racing down twenty flights of stairs. The father carried a small girl, while an eleven-year-old boy and another girl several years younger than the boy leaned on their mother. All three kids had their mother's black hair and lean figure, but their light-mocha skin was obviously a combination of their parents' complexions. The man, slightly jowly, towered over them. His shirt draped over a beer gut past its infancy.

The family hadn't started across the skybridge yet; they were terrified by the creaking structure. The railing along the beach side of the slanted walkway had been ripped off and rested atop the railing on the other side.

Rachel yelled down the hall, "I'm the hotel manager! My name is Rachel Tanaka! Are you all right?"

"Yes," the father said.

"What are your names?" In her line of work, Rachel found that it always made things go more smoothly if she knew the names of the people she was dealing with.

"I'm Bill Rogers," the father of the three children said. "My wife is Paige, and my kids are Wyatt, Hannah, and the little one is Ashley."

"Is it safe to cross?" Paige asked.

"I don't know," Rachel said. "The incline is going to make it difficult to get across. Bill, can you get down the stairs in your tower?"

"No," Bill said. "I checked. It's totally blocked by that barge."

"Then you don't have a choice. You'll have to come over here."

"Maybe we should just stay here. That bridge looks rickety."

"We're trying to get a helicopter to come to our roof-top—"

"Then we can do the same thing in this tower."

"That won't work," Rachel said. "There's nowhere for a helicopter to land on your roof."

"Yeah, Dad," Wyatt said. "Remember that big spike on the top of the building?"

"Then we'll just go back up to the top floor and wait until this is over."

"Look," Rachel said, "I don't want to frighten you more than you already are, but there are more waves coming, and they're going to be much bigger than the last one. Maybe even taller than this building. We need to get out of here."

They still hesitated.

"Come on! We don't have much time left!"

"But how do we get the kids across?" Paige said with a slight accent suggesting a Caribbean Island origin. "I'm not letting any of them cross on their own."

"And it's too shaky for you to all come at once," Rachel said.

"I'll come back and get them," Bill said.

"That will take too long. You see that water going out? That means another wave is coming soon. We have ten minutes at most."

"We don't even know if the bridge is strong enough," Paige said.

Rachel looked at the slick floor of the skybridge and realized she'd have to go out there if she was going to save those children. Her maternal instinct overrode the fear she felt.

"How about if I come and meet Wyatt halfway and bring him back with me?"

Without waiting for an answer, she kicked off her shoes and stepped onto the bridge. Her arm span was wide enough that she could keep hold of one pillar while she inched along to grab the next one. She made her way carefully, keeping her toes along the edge for more grip.

"See," she said. "It's still sturdy enough. Come on, Wyatt. Come to me."

Bill and Paige exchanged looks and nodded.

Paige held Wyatt's shoulders. "Can you do this, Wyatt?"

Wyatt looked scared, but he nodded.

Paige hugged him. "Okay, but if it's too hard, you come right back."

Wyatt grabbed one of the floor-to-ceiling pillars and pulled himself toward Rachel.

"Come on, honey," Rachel said as she continued edging across. "You can do it."

Wyatt gingerly pulled himself along. When he was almost to Rachel, the skybridge creaked ominously. He stopped, and they all held their breath. The creaking subsided, and Wyatt continued to make his way until Rachel took his hand.

"Great job, Wyatt," she said. "Now hold on to me."

Wyatt nodded again. Rachel had Wyatt hold on to one pillar, and when she had safely grabbed the next, she pulled him with her. They paused when they heard another shriek of grinding metal. Paige covered her mouth in terror, but there was nothing she could do to help them without endangering them further.

The grinding stopped, but it was another reminder of how precarious the walkway was.

As they proceeded across, Rachel and Wyatt got into a steady rhythm. They had reached the last pillar when Wyatt suddenly slipped on the muck as he was moving from one pillar to another. Both his feet flew out from under him and he went down, pulling Rachel down as well.

Shouts of *"No!"* came from the other end of the walkway.

With one hand, Rachel clung to the bottom of the pillar with a fierce grip. If she let go, nothing would keep them from sliding to the opposite side of the skybridge. Only the pillars on the other side would stand between them and a six-story fall to the water below.

CHAPTER 37

THE CONDITIONS AT WHEELER Army Airfield were spartan, but Reggie Pona had power for his laptop and an Internet connection, thanks to the Air Force's backup electrical system. As soon as power had been lost from the island's main plants, the base's own generators had taken over.

Reggie had been able to outrun the first wave and had finally gotten in contact with Renfro at Hawaii State Civil Defense, which sent one of the trucks evacuating from Pearl to Wheeler to pick him up. In the chaos, HSCD had gone thirty minutes before realizing that they weren't getting updates from the PTWC anymore. When they finally called the Alaska warning center, Palmer immediately took over updating the Pacific nations about further tsunami readings, including the *Miller Freeman*'s DART buoy. While Reggie was en route, the DART buoy had registered a third wave at the height that they had projected an hour before. It would be two hundred feet high when it hit Honolulu.

Wheeler sprawled across the midsection of Oahu, at least five miles from the nearest shoreline. Already, the air base's taxiways were jammed with Boeings and Airbuses from seventeen different airlines.

Reggie shared space with countless other displaced

government agencies, including other NOAA officials, the National Weather Service, FEMA, even the FBI, all of whose offices were located in the heart of downtown Honolulu. Most of those buildings had already been inundated, and the rest would be underwater in the next hour.

The only working landline telephones were reserved for the U.S. military, and they were in short supply. The cell phone tower that Reggie's service linked to was still operating, and his cell phone had provided his best news of the day so far.

Reggie had listened to the message from Kai three times to make sure he had the correct information. He tried calling Brad's cell phone back repeatedly, with no success. He had no way of knowing if the subsequent messages he left had been received, but it didn't matter: unless he could get a helicopter to them, all the messages in the world wouldn't save them.

The number of helicopters available was not what it could have been. The sightseeing helicopters were ready to fly because they had been fully booked for the holiday, but many of the armed forces' helicopters were overseas, lacked pilots, or had been destroyed by the first wave.

The choppers that were left zipped over all the Islands, not just Oahu. With thousands of square miles of shoreline and ocean to cover, even the combined forces of the Army, Navy, Air Force, Coast Guard, civilian, and tourist helicopters were stretched thin.

The evacuation had happened so quickly that coordination was nonexistent at the outset. Only now was there some effort to deploy the available aircraft with some sort of organization. Even so, many pilots simply flew around, looking for survivors who were still in the path of the tsunamis.

While he had been trying to find a helicopter for Kai, Reggie had also been hard at work in the midst of all this chaos. Not only did he have to keep the Hawaiian authorities informed of new tsunami activity, but he had to keep the rest of the Pacific apprised of the danger. During the emergency, confusion had reigned. Some agencies hadn't gotten the updates from the West Coast/ Alaska Tsunami Warning Center, so Reggie had been serving as the local contact in Hawaii.

The PTWC was responsible for warning nations on half the earth's surface about the coming waves. It still wasn't over for Hawaii, but it was just starting for twenty other countries and the mainland United States. Reggie assisted Palmer in communicating with every major branch of the government, preparing them for what was about to happen. And the person from the government who offered the best possibility for a helicopter was standing right in front of him.

"What about islands like Wake?" asked Stuart Johnson, an Air National Guard colonel who was acting as the military liaison to all of the American territories in the Pacific for the duration of the disaster. "We've got two hundred contractor personnel stationed there."

"Look," Reggie said, "Wake is way too flat for people to find any ground high enough to survive. The only thing they can do is get on a plane or a ship and get off the island." He hoped that building whatever rapport he could with Colonel Johnson would help pave the way for his request.

"We're already doing that."

"They'd better be fast. The first wave will get there in about forty minutes."

"What about Guam?"

"They've got a few hours left. If it has land that's over two hundred feet above sea level, they'll probably be okay."

"Probably?"

"Colonel, we're talking about a Pacific-wide mega-tsunami. It's unprecedented in human history. This isn't an exact science. We're taking our best guesses with the data we have. But we estimate that the wave will substantially decrease in size as it gets farther from the impact zone."

"Why? I thought waves could cross the entire ocean without losing much of their energy. You said that on an old file tape they showed on CNN twenty minutes ago."

"Oh, man. If *you're* confused, I can imagine what's happening on the mainland right now. That's for an earthquake-generated tsunami." Reggie drew a crude representation of a fault on his notepad, showing waves issuing from it. "It only goes in one direction, in a line. It's very focused. The waves from the meteor impact are in concentric circles, so the energy is spread out over the entire circumference of that circle. As the circle gets bigger, the same energy is spread out over a larger area, and the wave gets smaller."

"So it'll be a lot smaller when it reaches the naval base at San Diego?"

"I wouldn't call a thirty-foot tsunami small. That's still huge, but it's nowhere near what we're seeing on TV now. With the amount of time they have to evacuate, everyone should be able to get to safety before it hits."

"Dammit! What a mess." The colonel shot Reggie a nasty look, as if this were all his fault. "I guess I have a lot of work to do." He turned on his heel to leave, but before he got two steps toward the door, Reggie shoved his huge bulk in front of him.

"Colonel," Reggie said, "I need a favor."

"I don't have time right now."

"You'll make time. My friend is stuck on a building in Waikiki. I need a helicopter."

"Everybody needs a helicopter."

"This isn't just anybody! He's the assistant director of the PTWC!"

"I've got orders from General Lambert at CINCPAC that says our highest priorities are the major population centers. Besides that, I've got to warn every single base in the Pacific to evacuate."

"But Waikiki *is* the biggest population center!"

"Then the helicopters will get to them eventually."

"Eventually?"

"Look, Mr. Pona, I'm sorry about your friend, but I've got my orders and so do my helicopter pilots. Excuse me." He went around Reggie and into the next room, where he started talking with another officer.

Fuming about being brushed off, Reggie made another phone call, this one to the HSCD. After less than a minute of discussion, he walked into the room with Colonel Johnson, interrupting his conversation.

"Pardon me, Colonel, but luckily I had another person who owed me a favor."

"Look," the colonel said, exasperated at Reggie's persistence, "I already told you I can't help you."

"I really think you'd better take this phone call." Reggie thrust the cell phone toward the officer. Colonel Johnson eyed it suspiciously.

"Why? Who is it?"

"It's the governor. She wants you to give me a helicopter."

* * *

Teresa practically dragged Kai to where Mia was trapped. Instead of finding refuge in one of the ocean-side rooms, Brad, Mia, and Teresa had hunkered down in the kitchen of condo 1004, on the north side of the building facing the explosion.

Kai was stunned by the sight of the ravaged condo. The entire exterior wall was in tatters, and bits of furniture and metal had been propelled into every surface. Even though the kitchen had been shielded from the worst of the blast, it hadn't come through unscathed.

As Kai had covered Lani during the explosion, Brad had done the same for Mia. When the blast caused a piece of the ceiling to cave in, a steel girder slashed into the wall on one side and smashed the counter on the other, pinning Mia and Brad at their midsections. Although Teresa had been only five feet away, the falling girder had missed her.

"Are you okay?" Kai said to Brad.

"Except for the fact that I can't move, I'm fine. I think Mia might have a broken leg."

"Let's try pulling you." Kai gripped Brad by both hands and pulled until his full weight was into it.

"Stop!" Brad cried. "It's not working. You're going to pull my arms off."

Teresa bent over and caressed Mia's hair.

"You're going to be all right, honey."

Kai quickly inspected the foot-wide girder. The situation looked grim. The wall between the kitchen and the condo hallway had kept it from hitting the floor and crushing them, but that was about the only good news. Moving it was going to be a big job, and they only had a few minutes.

"This thing must weigh a thousand pounds," Brad said.

"And," Kai said, "it looks like the girder is wedged into that wall pretty solidly." To Mia he said, "You can't move at all, sweetie?"

Mia shook her head. "My leg hurts. Please don't leave us here."

"No one's going to leave you," Kai said. "We're going to get you out."

He led Teresa back to the hallway.

"I'll be right back, Mia," she said as they left.

"I need you to go down and check out Jake. Let us know what you find."

"What about Mia?" Kai could see the desperation in her face.

"I'll stay and try to figure out something."

"How long do we have?"

"Not long. No more than ten minutes to the next wave. But that means we need to be out of here in five minutes so that we can get down and find another building to climb." Kai pulled the fire ax off the wall. It had survived the explosion, although the protective glass was gone.

"What are you going to do with that?" Teresa said.

"I don't know."

Teresa whispered to Kai. "You're not thinking of amputation, are you?"

"That's not an option."

"Good."

"But we've got to figure out a way to get that girder off of them."

"I didn't come all this way to lose her now, Kai."

Kai held her head in his hands. As gently as possible, he said, "I know. You are not going to lose her. But we need you to keep it together, okay?"

She nodded. "You figure something out."

"I will." He hugged her, and she hurried down the stairs. Kai headed back to Brad and Mia, ax in hand.

Teresa met Tom on the eighth-floor landing and quickly assessed his awkwardly dangling arm.

"Jake was already into the hallway when I slipped on the stairs and fell," he said. "Is it broken?"

"No, it's dislocated. Where's Jake?"

With his other arm, Tom pointed down the hall. It looked like a bomb had hit it, which was essentially what had happened.

Other than the dislocation, Tom seemed uninjured, but Jake had not been so lucky.

A jagged piece of metal about two feet in length had sliced through the wall like it was tissue. Jake sat against the opposite wall, the metal protruding from his chest, his hair filthy from rubbing against the muck coating everything. Blood covered the wall behind him and oozed from the wound. Teresa bent down to examine Jake. His breath was shallow, but it was there.

"Can you help him?" Tom asked plaintively. "Is he dead?"

Teresa was devastated at the sight of the injured boy. She had to make a decision, and her options were not good. It was a no-win situation. If she did nothing, he would die in minutes. If she moved him, the shock might kill him. He'd already lost a lot of blood, and any movement might cause further disruption of the wound. Ideally, paramedics would be brought in to stabilize him before he was taken away in an ambulance. But the likelihood of getting any kind of professional medics here in the next ten minutes was nil.

That left her no choice. She had to try to get him out. But before she did that, she had to take care of Tom.

"Tom, I'm going to have to put that arm back in place because I need your help."

"Will it hurt?"

"Yes."

"Okay. But do it quick."

"Lie down."

Tom lay down on the floor on his back. Teresa positioned herself behind him. She put her left hand on his shoulder and her right hand on his elbow.

"I'll count to three, and then I'm going to push your arm back into the socket. Okay?"

"Yeah."

"One . . . two . . . three." With a fast rotation, she snapped the arm back into place. Tom screamed and then relaxed, the pain greatly reduced now that the arm was in its socket.

Teresa heard Kai yell from upstairs. "Are you all right?"

"Don't worry about us!" she shouted, then turned her attention back to Tom. "Better?"

He nodded in relief.

"You did well, Tom."

"What about Jake? Should we take that thing out?"

Teresa knelt down, shaking her head at the hopelessness of the situation. "If we do, he'll bleed to death."

As she said that, Jake's eyes fluttered open. A hoarse whisper came out of his mouth.

"Where am I?" He was in shock. He felt no pain, probably wasn't even aware that he had been through an explosion.

"You're injured, Jake. We're going to get you out of here."

"I'm so tired."

"I know, sweetie. But you need to stay awake."

"So tired . . ."

Jake closed his eyes, leaned his head back, and slipped into unconsciousness.

"Jake!" Tom yelled. "Jake!" He grabbed Teresa's shoulders. "Do something!"

She wanted to, but she could see that Jake was too far gone. She put her ear quickly to each side of his chest and heard shallow gasps on only one side. The metal shard had collapsed his lung and nicked a major artery. Resuscitation wouldn't work. If she had the proper instruments and a hospital staff, they might be able to remove the metal, control the bleeding, and re-expand the lung so that he could be revived. Without them, any attempt at saving him was futile.

Jake let out a gurgling wheeze, and a trickle of blood ran from the corner of his mouth. His body shuddered for a moment and then was still. Teresa checked for a pulse, but found none.

"There's nothing I can do, Tom. He's gone."

"No! You can do CPR or something."

"Tom, I'm a doctor—"

"Then help him!"

"I can't. The injury was too severe. I'm sorry."

As a teenage boy, Tom was probably unaccustomed to crying, but he sobbed uncontrollably at the sight of his dead friend. All Teresa could do was comfort him.

"I know, honey," she said, hugging Tom, who buried his head in her shoulder.

"It's my fault," Tom said between sobs. "I convinced my mom and dad to let Jake visit us. He moved away two years ago . . ." He broke down again.

"It's not your fault. And I'm sure your mom and dad will be proud of what you did today. You saved the lives of my daughter and Lani. And so did Jake. You're heroes. I owe you everything for that."

"Do you think my mom and dad are okay?"

Teresa didn't want to make any promises she couldn't keep, but he needed some reassurance. Besides, his parents would have evacuated at the first sirens. She thought back to her own search for Mia and hoped they hadn't tried to get to Waikiki to find him.

"I'm sure they're all right and worrying about you," she said. "Now I need you to focus on seeing your parents again. Can you do that?"

"I'll try. What about Jake? Are we just going to leave him there?"

"We have to," Teresa said. There was no way that they could carry Jake's body with them. She thought about covering him, but even that minor attempt at decency would be rendered moot when the next tsunami came through, washing him to a watery grave.

Kai was in the hallway looking for something, anything, to help him pry Brad and Mia loose when Teresa and Tom emerged from the stairwell.

Tom's face was flushed and tear-stained. He winced as he leaned against her, but his arm no longer dangled awkwardly.

Kai saw the bleak look on Teresa's face.

"Jake?" he said, knowing the awful answer.

She simply shook her head.

With that small movement, the reality of the situation solidified. Somebody Kai knew had died. A kid no more than fifteen years old. It hadn't been Jake's fault.

In fact, if he hadn't done so much to help them, Jake could have gotten to high ground and saved himself. Kai felt the blood drain from his face as guilt for his role in the boy's death overtook him, but he fought to stifle the feeling. If he didn't send it to the back of his mind, he wouldn't be able to think of anything else. He needed to concentrate on the next task, which was saving his brother and Mia.

"How is she?" Teresa asked.

"She's holding up like a trouper, but she's in pain. I managed to clear off the lighter pieces of rubble, but I couldn't budge the girder. The ax didn't serve as much of a lever."

"Maybe the four of us can lift it."

Kai was dubious about that prospect. "It's wedged in pretty good."

"We won't know if we don't try."

Kai nodded. "You're right. Let's give it a go."

"Me too," Tom said. He didn't look like he was in any condition to contribute much strength, but anything would help.

They lined themselves up along the more exposed part of the beam: Teresa and Lani on one side, Tom and Kai on the other.

"On three," Kai said.

On cue, they heaved with all their strength, which had by now been sapped by the rowing, running, and general stress of the situation. The girder didn't move. They tried again, but the effort was pointless. They weren't going to get Brad and Mia out this way.

"It's no use," Kai said.

"We need something stronger to jack it up," Teresa said.

When she mentioned the word "jack," Kai and Teresa looked at each other and realized what the answer was.

"Car jack!" they said simultaneously.

They were going to have to make it quick. By this time the streets were empty of water. The large number of cars strewn everywhere outside meant that there would be plenty of places to look for a jack, but the search might be hampered by the debris. And they wouldn't be able to get at a jack if a car was overturned, as many of them would be.

Kai glanced at his watch. Only seven minutes left. He did a quick calculation in his head. Assume one minute to get down to the street. Say three minutes to find a jack if they were lucky. Another two minutes to get back up. That only left one minute to jack up the girder, get down the building, run to another building, and run up the stairs. When Kai finished the mental arithmetic, he was stunned. They simply couldn't do it in time. Brad and Mia were going to die. And unless they left and didn't come back, the rest of them would too.

"There isn't enough time," Kai said.

"I'm not leaving without Mia," Teresa said. "We are going to try, damn you!"

Kai looked at Teresa, Lani, and Tom. All of them looked ready to risk their lives to save Brad and Mia.

"All right. We can do this," he said, trying to sound more positive than he felt. "But I need all of you. The search for the jack will go faster."

Kai couldn't help feeling that their efforts would be futile. But when they got to the open air of the stairwell, the glass windows long gone, he happened to glance past the now-destroyed building behind them and felt a surge of hope recharge him.

Along the base of another building still standing a hundred yards away, Kai saw a partially obliterated sign, some of the letters washed away.

The sign said, "Re f K ngs." A red rectangle with a white diagonal line through it flapped to the side. He had seen the same thing on a truck as they were entering Waikiki.

The symbol was easily recognizable to divers. The store was a scuba shop.

CHAPTER 38

MAX HAD TO TAKE a few seconds' rest after the first two trips carrying the disabled veterans up the stairs to the roof. Adrian looked just as tired as Max, who had finally taken off his jacket and tie. Three of the vets were grossly overweight, tipping the scales at three hundred pounds, and the exertion required was overwhelming. If they didn't take a break, they might drop some of the people they were carrying.

Only ten people were left downstairs: the veterans who couldn't walk up on their own, plus the spouses or loved ones who wouldn't come up without them. Those with cell phones had continued to try to call out, but without success.

While Adrian rested, Max went over to the edge of the roof and looked at the skybridge twenty stories below. Rachel was taking far too long. Through the gash in the roof of the walkway, he couldn't see any movement. Maybe that meant she was on her way up. She had taken his walkie-talkie, so he didn't have any way to contact her.

The noise of helicopters had been a constant but distant companion when they were on the roof. The sight of so many helicopters landing on crowded rooftops reminded him of photos he'd seen of the evacuation of

Saigon just before it fell after the Vietnam War. This evacuation was no less haphazard, but with an even harsher deadline.

The sound of beating rotor blades seemed to be getting louder. Max looked up, shielding his eyes from the noon sun. The buildings and surrounding mountains could make the direction and distance of sound deceiving. He searched the sky and then saw some of the guests pointing in the direction of downtown Honolulu.

A small sightseeing helicopter with no more than six seats was headed in their direction. Along with the other guests, he waved his arms like a madman and yelled loudly, even though it would have been impossible for anyone in the helicopter to hear them.

When the chopper got within one hundred yards, Max could see the pilot's face. He could also see that the helicopter was already carrying several passengers, although he couldn't tell how many.

The pilot brought the helicopter lower until it hovered about thirty feet above the roof, where it held steady. He waved with his hands to back off. Max understood, but many of the hotel guests had thronged to where the pilot was trying to land. Everybody wanted to be the first on the helicopter.

"Adrian!" Max said. "Help me get these people back!"

They pushed the guests back toward the roof edge, despite some protests. When they were safely away from the landing zone, the pilot eased the helicopter down.

"Stay here!" Max yelled above the din of the rotors.

He ran over to the helicopter, and the pilot popped his door open.

"Are we glad to see *you*!"

"How many you got?" the no-nonsense pilot said.

"Maybe sixty, sixty-five. I haven't counted."

"Jesus. All right. I'll see if I can get some more choppers headed this way. A lot of the Marine helicopters got caught on the ground by the first wave. The radio waves are jammed. It may take a few minutes."

Max looked around the cabin. Three passengers sat in the back. It looked like two seats were still available.

"Do you have room for more?"

"Yeah. Give me two, but no more; I don't want to be mobbed. I've already seen that happen to one helicopter. Crashed when it tried to take off. It won't be the last one, either, and I don't want it to happen to me. If I see more than two people run over here, I'm taking off before they get here."

"Gotcha."

Max went back over to the guests.

"Okay. This helicopter can only take two people," he announced. Groans and curse words erupted from the crowd. Max put up his hands to calm them.

"More helicopters are on the way. But we don't have time for a lottery, so I'm just going to choose two people at random." He pointed at a septuagenarian couple standing right in front of him. They were obviously husband and wife, the man on crutches because he was missing his right leg.

"Come on, you two."

He expected a revolt from the others who weren't selected, but perhaps because they were veterans, they knew how to take orders. Although there was a lot of grousing, no one tried to make a break for the helicopter.

Instead, the man who had been selected protested.

"I'm not going when there are still women here. What kind of a man do you think I am?"

"Sir, this isn't the *Titanic*, and we don't have time to argue—"

"I don't care. I'm not going until all these women are gone."

"Mr. Lateen, can you help me here?"

Bob Lateen, who sat to the side, his wheelchair now a floor below him, quickly glanced around the crowd and shook his head.

"I think I can speak for every one of us when I say that not one man is getting on a helicopter until all the women are gone. You're just wasting your time if you think something else will happen. And I'm going last."

Max started to protest again, but he could see that Lateen was not going to budge. The other battle-hardened veterans seemed equally stubborn. Max knew he had no time to argue, so he pointed at a woman standing on the other side of the man.

"Fine. You, then. Let's go."

Each of the women hugged her husband good-bye. Max escorted them over to the helicopter, instinctively ducking his head under the blades. The women climbed aboard and tearfully waved to their husbands after they strapped in.

"Come back quick," Max said.

The pilot nodded.

"We're dropping people off at Tripler Medical Center, or Wheeler Field if Tripler is too busy. I'll be back as soon as I can."

Max backed off as the helicopter's blades spun up. It lifted off gracefully, made a neat turn, and headed northwest.

The crowd behind him let out an unexpected cheer at the first good sign they'd seen since the end of the brunch.

Max got Adrian and went back to bring the rest of the guests up, hoping what he'd told the guests was true: that more helicopters really were on the way.

Rachel dangled from the pillar with one hand and held Wyatt with the other. When she saw Bill start to come over, she yelled, "Wait! The bridge might collapse if you get on too!"

Bill saw that she was right and stayed on his side, wringing his hands in frustration.

Wyatt was too heavy for Rachel to pull him back up.

"Wyatt," she said. "Grab my legs and climb up my back."

"Okay," he said.

Rachel felt him let go of her hand and grab her legs. She gripped the pillar with her free hand, securing herself. Wyatt clambered up her back until he could pull himself to a standing position. When he was out of the way, Rachel swung her leg up until she had some purchase. Carefully, she inched up the pillar until she was on her feet. Together they completed the last few steps of the journey and collapsed onto the floor of the lobby, stunned from the ordeal.

Wyatt's family cheered from the other end of the skybridge. Rachel looked up to see that neither of the parents had made a move to come across.

"Maybe we should just stay over here until this is over," Bill said.

"No, Dad!" Wyatt begged, terrified by his near fall. "Don't leave me here!"

Rachel tried to comfort the boy. He lunged as if to go back on to the bridge, but she restrained him.

"Stay there, Wyatt!" Bill yelled. "It's not safe."

Wyatt dissolved into tears and sagged to the floor. Paige cried at the sight of her distraught son but didn't move.

"I'm telling you," Rachel said, "my husband works at the Pacific Tsunami Warning Center. He says that more waves are coming, and they're going to be massive."

"Maybe he's wrong—"

"He's not wrong. Just look below you if you don't believe me. There's nowhere for a helicopter to land on your roof, so you have to decide right now. And this is your last chance. The skybridge won't last through the next tsunami."

Bill and Paige conferred.

"Are they coming?" Wyatt asked Rachel.

"I hope so, honey."

"Okay," Bill said. "Paige's coming first with Hannah. Then I'll carry Ashley." He took the five-year-old from Paige's arms so that Paige could grab Hannah.

"Good. Hurry up. We don't have much time left."

Using the method Rachel had used with Wyatt, Paige cautiously began the trip across the skybridge, holding the hand of her eight-year-old daughter. Not wanting to frighten Paige into making a mistake, Rachel suppressed the urge to shout for her to move faster. Because they were being so careful, the crossing took much longer than it should have. Finally, Paige and Hannah made it to the Moana tower without incident.

Bill put Ashley down and squatted so she could put her arms around his neck from behind. Then he stood, holding her piggyback style, and started to cross.

"Paige," Rachel said, "the kids should start climbing up the stairs. The next wave is supposed to be a hundred and fifty feet high. We need to get at least to the fifteenth floor to be safe."

Paige was obviously torn. Keeping the children with her meant a slower climb up those ten stories once Bill and Ashley were across. But she didn't want to leave her husband and other child, either. And sending the children up alone wasn't an option. They were already scared, and having them by themselves was a recipe for confusion or worse.

In the end, the idea of having two of her children safe was more important than having them with her.

"Will you take them for me?" Paige said. "I can't leave Ashley and Bill here. What if something happens?"

"I understand," Rachel said. "I have a daughter myself. I'd do the same."

Paige hugged her two kids.

"Remember," Rachel said, "you've only got a few minutes left. Besides, you'll know when it's time to head up. We'll wait for you on the sixteenth floor."

"If you don't see me in ten minutes . . ." Paige's voice trailed off.

"I'll take care of them."

"Thank you."

Rachel led Wyatt and Hannah to the stairwell.

"Where are we going?" said Hannah.

Rachel forced a smile. "We're going up the stairs so we can ride in a helicopter. Won't that be fun?"

She opened the door to the stairwell and the children hesitated at the gloom, with little more than a faint glow filtering down from above. Thankfully, the emergency lights in the stairwell above the eighth floor were still on, powered by the batteries in each unit as soon as the hotel power was lost. Below that level, all of the lights had been short-circuited by the water.

"It's spooky," Wyatt said.

"That's just the emergency lights."

"Aren't Mommy and Daddy coming?" Hannah said.

I don't know, Rachel thought as she looked back at Bill tentatively stepping onto the skybridge with Ashley riding piggyback. *I hope. I pray. But I don't know.*

"Yes, sweetie," Rachel said confidently and started up the stairs holding both children's hands. "Your parents will be with us again soon."

CHAPTER 39

GIVEN ALL OF THE obstacles they had encountered up to this point, Kai had no reason to expect that their luck would improve. Even if they simply found a jack and managed to pry Brad and Mia out from under the steel beam, there wouldn't be time to escape to a taller building. They would all be caught in the ten-story condominium when the next tsunami hit.

But on seeing the scuba shop, he felt a rush of optimism. If he could find what he needed in the ruined shop, they might be able to buy themselves more time.

That depended, of course, on the condo building withstanding another tsunami impact. Kai had no illusions about their chances, but the only other option was to leave Brad and Mia to their fates, and he wouldn't even contemplate that.

Lani, Teresa, and Tom went with Kai to search. He had considered sending Lani and Tom toward high ground on their own, but at this point the thought of Lani fending for herself was frightening. Kai wanted her with him where he could keep an eye on her. And sending Tom off by himself, injured, seemed like a poor idea. Besides, Kai needed their help to gather supplies. They would have to survive with whatever they could carry in one trip; they wouldn't have time for a second.

When they got outside, Kai divided up the group, dispatching Teresa on a search for as many car jacks as she could find. At least two, maybe three, if she could carry them. Tom and Lani would accompany Kai to the scuba shop.

The street by the condo looked like Sarajevo during the worst years of the Balkan war. Pieces of wood, metal, concrete, vegetation, and, worst of all, human bodies littered the pavement and sidewalks. Cars and other vehicles had been thrown into every conceivable orientation, many of them smashed beyond recognition. One car, a Mini, defied gravity, hovering twenty feet above the ground, skewered like a kebob by a steel pole jutting out of the second story of a building.

Most surprisingly, several people wandered the streets unscathed. Kai supposed he shouldn't have been amazed—if he had survived, others would have as well—but the utter devastation made it difficult to believe anyone else had lived through it.

An Asian woman babbling in a language Kai didn't recognize led a boy of about ten toward a hotel and disappeared through the front door. Several teenagers emerged from another hotel and began running wildly in the direction of the mountains. Two people on a tenth-floor balcony about two hundred yards away waved to them.

A man, sopping wet and completely naked except for a pair of running shoes, darted up to them and said, "Where's Emily?"

"Who?" Kai said, dumbfounded.

The naked man grabbed Kai's shirt and yanked Kai toward him. "Emily. Have you seen her?"

Kai looked at the others, who were as shocked as he

was. He shook his head, and without another word the man released him and kept going down the street, peering into every open doorway and window. Kai could only guess that he had been caught by the tsunami with his girlfriend or wife or daughter. The scope of the tragedy continued to grow in Kai's mind.

"Don't stop to talk to anyone else," he said, and the rest of them understood what he meant.

They just didn't have time to help others. It was now the law of the jungle: every man for himself. The thought that civilized behavior could degenerate so rapidly was sobering to Kai, but reasoning with panicked people or guiding them to safety would keep them from saving the people they loved. None of them was going to let that happen. No more needed to be said.

Leaving Teresa to rummage through the cars, Kai and the others sprinted to where he had seen the scuba shop. As they got closer, Kai could see more clearly the extensive damage to the building that housed the store. He wasn't encouraged by its condition.

He ran through the door to find the interior completely gutted. None of the store's original complement of supplies remained. Instead, it had been replaced by junk swept inside by the wave: chairs, garbage cans, and minor bits of scrap littered the floor. The only recognizable bit from the shop was a Professional Association of Diving Instructors plaque that had been nailed to the wall.

"No!" Kai cried in frustration. "There's got to be something!"

He began to toss the refuse around, looking under it for the scuba tanks and other equipment that he had imagined would be their lifesavers. But with each piece he threw aside, his hope ebbed further.

Then Lani pointed at something Kai hadn't noticed in his frenzied search.

"Dad. There's another door."

Along the back wall of the store, a large plywood sheet had been slammed against the wall, covering the door. Only a sliver of the door and the doorknob showed. Kai pulled the plywood, which had dug into the Sheetrock, and it clattered to the floor, revealing an undamaged handle. He pushed the door open, and his effort was rewarded.

The plywood had kept the back room of the shop from getting washed away. At the opposite end of the room stood a metal emergency door that was still intact. It opened outward, so the receding water hadn't been able to push it open.

Nevertheless, the room was still wet from floor to ceiling, which explained why it had come through the tsunami relatively unscathed. If the room had been watertight, the pressure from the water outside would have been far greater than the air in the room, and the water would have blasted the doors inward, sweeping everything away. But something had equalized the pressure, and Kai saw the source: a rivulet of water drained through a three-foot wide hole near the floor where the pole propping up the Mini had initially penetrated the building.

Kai had hit the jackpot he desperately wanted to find. The room was a tangled mess of air tanks, hoses, buoyancy compensators, weight belts, and everything else needed for diving. Kai stole a look at his watch. Five minutes.

"Okay. We're going to be out of here in ninety seconds. We need three air tanks, three octopus air hoses, and some nylon rope. Make sure the hoses have two regulators on them. There are six of us."

"You mean we're going to scuba dive?" Lani said.

"Get to work," Kai said, picking up the closest air tank and screwing a loose air hose onto it. "It's Brad and Mia's only chance. We can't get them out and up to a safe height in another building in time. We're going to have to ride out the next wave. That's why we need the rope."

Kai saw Tom following his lead, screwing a hose onto another tank.

"You've done this before?" Kai said.

"I'm certified. Logged twenty hours."

"Good. Make sure it's pressurized. We can't come back if we find out the tank is empty."

Lani returned with a yellow nylon rope. Given the number of loops, Kai guessed it was about a hundred feet of line.

"This is the only one I could find."

It would take too long to tie one long piece of rope.

"See if you can find a dive knife and masks. And a flashlight or two would come in handy."

While Lani searched, Kai took a third tank and attached the last hose, activating the pressure gauge. Empty. Damn!

He tossed it aside. Tom carried over another tank.

"It's the last one," he said. "The valves on all the others are snapped or bent."

Kai screwed the hose on quickly, praying that the gauge wouldn't be in the red.

The gauge read two thousand pounds per square inch. Full. Thank God.

"I got a knife!" Lani said with joy.

"What about masks?"

"They're all smashed, but I did find a flashlight. It works."

"Good. We've got what we came for. Let's go."

Kai picked up two of the tanks and staggered under the sixty-five-pound load, while Tom carried the third with his good arm.

As Kai ushered Lani and Tom out, he spotted something else: a yellow package about the size of a large watermelon. It had a red handle on it and the words PULL HERE TO INFLATE. It was an old life raft.

Despite the raft's apparent age, the CO_2 cartridge seemed to be new. If they couldn't get a helicopter, maybe they could float out on one of the waves. It wasn't a great idea, more of a last resort, but it was better than swimming. Kai pointed at it.

"Lani, can you carry that too?"

"I think so," she said. She hoisted the raft into her arms, and they scrambled out of the store.

Teresa tried for a car jack in the first car she saw. The door was smashed in, so she reached into the open window and pulled on the trunk release.

Nothing happened. She tried again, with the same result. She ran around to the back and kicked at the trunk a couple of times, but it wouldn't budge.

She didn't have time to keep trying on one car, so she ran to the next one, an overturned Chevy with a crushed roof. This one looked even less encouraging. She skipped it.

Finally, she found a car that seemed promising. A minivan lay on its side, the rear window gone. She wriggled through it and examined the floor that was now on its side. The third row of seating was still in place, so she had to get that out of the way. She found the release handle, and the bench seat dropped away, almost falling on her. She pushed it against the second row of seats, leaving enough room to get at the floor covering.

Teresa pried the soaked covering off and saw what she was looking for. A gleaming copper-colored car jack was screwed into the floor pan next to the skinny spare tire.

The jack was held in place by a wing nut that was normally easy to twist off. But while it was being tossed around, the minivan's frame had bent, tightening the nut. Teresa tried with all her strength to turn it, but it wouldn't move. She needed some leverage.

She snaked back out of the van and looked around for anything that could be used as a lever. Ideally she would miraculously find a pair of pliers on the ground, but that was wishful thinking. Instead, she would have to make do with what she could scrounge from the area immediately around her. That happened to be a metal chair leg. The smooth round caster still dangled from one end of it. She twisted the caster until it popped out of the leg. She also picked up a heavy piece of broken concrete to hammer the chair leg with.

When Teresa got back in the minivan, she carefully placed the chair leg on one side of the wing nut and braced herself against the vehicle. She made sure it was not on the bolt itself. One wrong hit, and it would bend hopelessly askew.

Teresa reared back with the concrete block and whacked it against the end of the chair leg. She felt the nut give way. In two more taps, the nut was loose enough to unscrew by hand. When it finally came off, she fumbled the jack, and it fell to the ground.

As she bent to pick it up, she heard movement outside the car. She assumed Kai had returned from the scuba shop.

Teresa emerged from the minivan triumphantly holding the jack and jack handle above her head.

"I got one!"

But instead of Kai, she found a scruffy man with a patchy beard. The smell of alcohol wafted through teeth yellowed from years of smoking. His soiled T-shirt couldn't hide the enormous gut protruding over his low-hanging shorts.

"Damn looter!" he said, slurring his words. "I knew I'd find some out here."

Teresa lowered her hands to show she wasn't dangerous. She had dealt with patients like him many times at the hospital.

"I'm not a looter."

"You look like a looter to me. Tearing through someone's car. Stealing their stuff."

"I need a car jack to help—"

"Don't give me that crap! I seen it on TV. I know what to do with people like you."

She hadn't noticed what he was carrying in his right hand. He raised an automatic pistol and pointed it at her.

"Sir," she said, "listen to me—"

"You come with me and we'll find the police. They'll sort you out."

"A tsunami is coming!"

"Yeah, I bet you're glad it came. That way, you can take whatever you want."

"Sir—"

"Police!" the man began to yell. "Police! Looter! Police!"

"Do you see any police around? There is another tsunami coming."

"Do you think I'm stupid? Police!"

As he continued to yell for the police, Teresa saw Kai,

Tom, and Lani coming toward her from the scuba shop.

"Kai! Get back!"

The man spun around to see who she was yelling at. He raised the gun even higher as if to threaten this new group with it. Kai and the others were nonplussed at what was going on. All they saw was a grubby-looking man holding a gun in his hand. They stopped abruptly.

The man, possibly unbalanced by his quick movement, possibly on purpose, pulled the trigger. A crack ripped the air, and the bullet whizzed by Kai's head, pinging off a piece of metal behind him. The three of them hit the ground.

This man was obviously unhinged. Trying to reason with him would just make things worse, and any further discussion would eat into the precious time Teresa had to somehow pry Mia free. The man was a danger not just to her but to her daughter. She didn't hesitate; with the man facing away from her, Teresa swung the heavy metal car jack with both hands and bashed him in the back of the head.

The effect was instant. The man dropped the gun and fell to his knees, where he swayed groggily. Teresa picked up the pistol, ejected the magazine onto the pavement, and threw the gun into a pile of debris. The man pitched forward and lay on the ground, still conscious but moaning.

"Bitch," he slurred in a low rumble. "You hit me."

Teresa waved to Kai.

"Come on! I got a jack. Let's go."

"What happened?" Kai said, rushing up to her. "What the hell is going on? Who is that guy?"

Teresa, shaking from the rush of adrenaline, stared at the prone man.

"I'll tell you later," she said. "Let's go get Mia and Brad."

CHAPTER 40

ON THE SKYBRIDGE BETWEEN the Grand Hawaiian buildings, Ashley clung to Bill's shoulders as they crossed from the Akamai tower to the Moana tower. They had been making good progress, suffering only one or two minor slips. However, the creaking of the walkway became more frequent, in part due to Bill's two-hundred-fifty-pound frame.

"You're doing great, Ashley," Paige said, trying to keep her daughter's spirits up. She had to dig her fingernails into her palms to keep herself together. She could do nothing to help them other than provide encouragement. "Just keep holding tight."

The decision to send her two children off with a stranger had been agonizing for her, but she couldn't bear the thought of leaving Ashley and her husband behind. The image of Wyatt nearly falling off the skybridge was burned into her memory. If anything like that happened to Ashley, she'd rather depend on herself to save her child.

As Bill was ready to take his final steps toward the safety of the building, Paige heard a commotion on the other side of the bridge.

Five college-aged men stumbled to a stop at the end of the bridge. Each of them talked in a sloppy midwestern twang fueled by at least a twelve-pack of beer apiece.

"Hey, look," one of the guys said. "See, I told you I could see people crossing from our room."

"Come on," said another one. "Let's get the hell out of here."

Before Paige and Bill could shout more than "No!" all five of the drunken frat boys stepped onto the bridge. They hadn't gotten more than a few feet before one fell, dragging two of the others down with him. The impact resonated on the already fragile skybridge. It started to bounce, snapping cables, swaying sickeningly over the courtyard below, now drained of water.

"Bill!" Paige shouted. "Jump!"

But Bill wasn't going to be able to get to the Moana tower without falling, possibly losing Ashley, so he grabbed the child's arm and pulled her off his back. He swung her around and hurled the small girl toward the waiting arms of Paige six feet away.

At that moment the center of the skybridge snapped from the added load. The two halves, still attached at the ends, swung toward their respective towers. All five of the drunken men slid off the deck and screamed until dull thuds marked their passing. Paige turned Ashley's head away so that she didn't see the resulting impacts. The opposite end of the walkway crashed against the building and then sheared off, collapsing into a pile of bent metal far below, burying the bodies.

Bill had wrapped both arms around the pillar he was holding. When his end of the bridge slammed into the tower, the floor of the walkway detached from the roof at its base, smashing into the courtyard below. But the roof, along with the vertical pillars, remained attached to the Moana tower, suspended by only two surviving steel rods.

Paige peered cautiously over the edge, fearing what she would see below. To her relief, she saw Bill still clinging to the pillar, but it was only a matter of minutes before he either lost his grip or was engulfed by the next massive wave.

Rachel, exhausted from running up and down the stairs and the ordeal at the skybridge, rested her head against the metal fire door of the sixteenth-floor stairwell. She had been trying to raise Kai on the walkie talkie and was terrified because he wouldn't answer.

"Kai, are you there? Kai, come in, please."

"Who's Kai?" Wyatt asked.

"He's my husband. He's with my daughter, Lani."

"What happened to them?" Hannah asked.

"I don't . . ." Rachel started to answer but a sob caught in her throat, and before she could stop herself, she began to cry.

She buried her face in her hands as it all came rushing out. The stress. The responsibility for all the hotel guests. Not knowing whether her family was safe or She didn't want to think about the possibility of the worst case, but it came anyway. And now she was responsible for someone else's children.

Hannah hugged her. "It'll be okay, Rachel. Lani and Kai will be okay."

Rachel sobbed again and held the little girl to her tightly. *How can a child keep it together while I'm such a mess,* she thought. Teresa was right. There was nothing glamorous about saving lives, but the outcome was worth the toll.

After another moment Rachel caught her breath and calmed down.

"Thank you, Hannah," she said, stroking Hannah's hair. "I'm sure they'll be okay too."

Wyatt, who was standing behind Hannah, looked embarrassed by the emotional display.

"Can I try the walkie-talkie?" he said. "I have one like it at home. Maybe I can get him."

Rachel smiled and wiped her face on her sleeve. "Sure, Wyatt." She handed the walkie-talkie to him. "Just press the red button and talk."

"Kai, are you there?" he said. He waited for a response. None came.

"Try again, and make sure . . ." Rachel stopped in midsentence and cocked her head.

"And make sure what?" Wyatt said.

Rachel raised her hands.

"Shhh!"

"What?" Hannah said.

"Be quiet for a second. I think I hear something."

Rachel turned her head so that her ear pressed against the door. Wyatt and Hannah followed suit.

After a moment of silence, a thudding sound was distinctly audible. Normally the whirring of fans and the rush of air movement throughout the hotel's ductwork masked low-level sounds. But with the power off, the hotel was bathed in an eerie stillness.

The noise repeated at regular intervals. One, two, three, four. Silence for four counts. Then again: one, two, three, four. The faint pounding reverberated through the metal door. The sound was definitely manmade.

"What is that?" Hannah asked.

"I don't know," said Rachel, "but it sounds like it's coming from the hallway."

She sprang to her feet and opened the door. The sound was louder now and more distinct. It seemed to be emanating from somewhere in the deserted corridor.

"You guys wait here," Rachel said.

"Where are you going?" Hannah said.

"I need to find out what that sound is. I'll be right back. Don't go anywhere unless your parents come back. And keep the door open."

Rachel walked down the hall, stopping every few seconds to get her bearings on the noise. As she went farther into the building, the pounding got louder, until she was able to zero in on it without stopping. About halfway down the corridor, she rounded the corner to the elevator lobby. It was now obvious where the sound was coming from.

The sound of a voice accompanied the pounding.

"Help! Is anyone out there?"

Someone was trapped in the elevator.

Carrying all of the equipment slowed them down more than Kai thought it would. Time was short as they hurried out of The Seaside's tenth-floor stairwell and into the condo.

"We were beginning to think you forgot about us," Brad said. His voice had a façade of cheer, but Kai could sense the despair just underneath the surface. He was trying to keep up Mia's spirits.

"Not a chance, haole," Kai said. "We're going to get you out of there."

Teresa showed him the jack.

"That's a beautiful sight," Brad said.

"Let's try it," she said.

"Wait," Kai said. "We don't have time for that yet."

"What are those for?" Brad said, noticing the scuba tanks.

"For us. All of us."

"Why don't you get us out first?"

"We have two minutes at most," Kai said as he cut the rope into ten-foot segments with the dive knife. "We need to get ourselves tied down first."

"Kai, you're kidding, right?"

"No." Kai didn't have time to cushion the news. His mind flashed back to Brad trapped in that shipwreck and the panicked rapping at the door before Kai had been able to free him. Brad hadn't dived since, his fear of the depths approaching phobia.

"I'm not staying here," Brad said.

"Unfortunately, Brad, you're going to have to."

"Kai, get us out of here!" Brad began to struggle against the girder. "I can't stay here."

"Stop it!" Kai said, trying to calm Brad. He gave the ropes to Teresa. "Start tying yourselves to the girder. Tightly! It's the strongest thing here. Don't forget Brad and Mia."

"Why didn't you tell me?" Brad yelled.

Kai leaned closer to speak softly into his ear. "Because I knew this is how you would react, and you're scaring Mia."

"But the water . . . !"

"Yes, we're going to be under at least fifty feet of water. I know it's not what you want, but it's going to happen."

"I can't!"

"You can and you will, because there's no other choice. Now, are you going to be quiet, or do I have to stick the regulator in your mouth right now?"

Brad's weak nod did nothing to hide his terror.

"What's his problem?" said Tom.

"He had a bad experience scuba diving one time."

"What happened?"

"He got stuck in a shipwreck and almost drowned."

Kai took some of the rope and lashed the tanks to the girder. Only now did it occur to him that they should have also brought buoyancy compensators—the vests that support scuba tanks during a dive—to strap the tanks to. He hadn't thought about it while they were in the dive shop, even though he remembered seeing some. The nylon rope was certainly strong, but his technique for tying them down was lacking. He had never been in the Boy Scouts, so he was just winging it on the knots. He didn't really care if they would be easy to untie. They could always use the knife to cut themselves free.

Kai was more concerned about the building's structural integrity, but there was nothing he could do about that. Either it would withstand the wave or it wouldn't. All he could do was make sure that if it did stay put, they would too.

"I've got Tom and Lani secured," Teresa said.

Kai quickly inspected her work.

"Nice job," he said. "Those should hold. Let's get Mia and Brad tied up too."

"Why? They're already stuck there."

"You don't understand the power of water. The pressure alone might drag one of them out. If that happens, they'd be swept away."

They rapidly tied the ropes around Brad and Mia together.

"Now it's your turn," Kai said.

He threw the rope around the girder and encircled her midsection with it.

"What about you?" she said.

"I'll do my own. I want to be next to Lani."

Tom had already screwed the regulator hoses onto each tank. Each unit had an octopus hose with a second breathing regulator attached to it. In scuba diving, you always had one regulator for yourself and a spare one that dragged along behind you to be used by your buddy if his air ran out.

In this case, that meant they only needed three tanks for the six of them: one for Brad and Mia, one for Teresa and Tom, and one for Kai and Lani.

"Test them out," Kai said to all of them. "Make sure they work."

If they didn't, the only thing they could do was share a regulator, but buddy-breathing with the water pulling at them would be difficult, if not impossible. Fortunately, all of the regulators were delivering air.

Kai secured the dive light to his wrist and snaked the last of the rope around the girder and the life raft. Since they hadn't had time to get Mia and Brad free, they wouldn't have a chance to use the raft with the coming wave. He snapped the nylon strap from Reggie's dry bag—which still held Brad's cell phone, the walkie-talkie, and the photo album—around one of the ropes.

As they finished tying themselves down, Kai heard a sound that was both uplifting and heartbreaking.

"Just in time," Brad said.

Through the open windows came the sound of beating helicopter rotors hovering directly above them: the chopper Kai had requested from Reggie. He had come through for them, but the timing couldn't have been worse.

Kai wouldn't have left Brad or Mia anyway, even if the

helicopter had come earlier, but he briefly considered sending Tom and Lani up. With all of them tied up, it would take them minutes to get untangled and attempt to climb the blast-shattered stairs to the roof. He dismissed the idea, no matter how tempting the helicopter sounded. They'd certainly be caught by the wave before they got to the roof.

After a few seconds the helicopter crew must have decided that no one was there to be rescued and went on to another building.

"They were so close," Lani said.

As depressing as the situation was, there was no reason to dwell on it. They had more pressing issues.

"Okay, everyone," Kai said. "The current is going to be stronger than anything you've ever felt. The important thing is to keep your regulator in your mouth. Keep it clenched tightly between your teeth, and use your hands to hold it on. We don't have masks, so keep your eyes closed. There's going to be a lot of debris flowing past us, so try to protect your head as much as you can. This is going to be tough, but it's not impossible. We can do it."

"And we'll jack them out when the water recedes?" Teresa said.

"Absolutely." Kai patted the jack, which he had lashed against the girder, just next to his tank.

Everyone grew silent as they sensed something change in the air. In the distance, Kai could make out the first inklings of the now-familiar roar they had heard only twenty minutes before.

He strained against his ropes and could barely see through the blown-out door of the condo on the other side of the hallway. The window frame twenty-five feet away perfectly framed the blue sky to the south. Normally, this far from the ocean-side window ledge, he'd be able to see the water only at the distant horizon. But even from his awkward vantage point, Kai could see that the crest of the second tsunami, rushing across Waikiki Bay at forty miles per hour, was already higher than they were. Although seeing a tsunami firsthand was no longer novel to him, it was breathtaking nonetheless.

Kai gripped Lani's hand tightly.

"Here it comes!" he yelled. "Everybody brace yourselves!"

Then Kai clenched the regulator in his mouth and steeled himself for the impact of a billion gallons of water.

CHAPTER 41

THE REMNANTS OF THE skybridge swayed in the breeze, screeching where the metal rubbed against the side of the Moana tower of the Grand Hawaiian. Bill Rogers had been able to hold on, but he struggled to pull himself up onto the pillar that he was dangling from. Paige looked down helplessly from the safety of the building not more than ten feet away.

"Mommy, help Daddy!"

Paige's daughter Ashley had wandered away and was now standing at the edge of the broken skybridge. Paige yelped and snatched the girl back from the six-story precipice.

"Honey, wait over by that door." Paige pointed at the stairwell exit sign.

"But Daddy—"

"You have to do what I tell you so that I can get Daddy, okay?"

Ashley grudgingly nodded and retreated to the door.

Paige returned to see Bill clinging to the tenuously attached remnants of metal. The pillar was bending from his 250-pound weight now that it was not firmly anchored at both ends. It was all he could do to keep from falling. There was no way he'd be able to climb up on his own.

"Bill, I'm going to find something to lower down to you."

"Is Ashley okay?" Bill yelled.

"She's fine."

"Good. Hurry. I can't hold on much longer."

Paige went to find the only thing she could think of that would be both strong enough and likely to be found somewhere nearby. A fire hose.

"Stay there!" she told Ashley.

She ran toward the ocean side of the building, hoping to find a hose still in its hallway glass storage case. Given the extent of damage from the previous wave, it could be in any state.

That's when she heard the tsunami. Paige saw the foamy white line building and cascading across the bay and realized that she had no more time to find something to lower to Bill. She would have to do it herself.

Paige ran back to the skybridge. From his vantage point, Bill had already seen the tsunami.

"Did you find anything?" he said.

"I didn't have time. I'm going to climb down onto that pillar above you and grab your hand." She began to lower herself over the edge.

"No!" screamed Bill. "The skybridge can't take your weight too. We'll both go down."

"Then what should I do?"

As the freight-train roar of the wave got louder, Bill gave Paige a look that was both sad and loving.

"Go."

"No!" Paige sobbed when she understood what her husband meant. "I'm not doing it!"

"Paige, you have to get Ashley to safety. You have to be their mom."

"No! No! You're coming with me!"

"Paige, I won't let you die trying to save me. Go!"

"You don't have a choice. I'm not leaving you!"

The wave was no more than five hundred yards away.

"I'm not leaving you!" she repeated.

"I understand. It's not your fault. I love you!"

And with that, he let go.

"Bill!"

The six-story plunge was mercifully short. His broken body lay motionless on the debris below. Paige stepped back, wailing in anger and grief. She leaned against the wall, rooted to the spot as she sobbed.

The riotous sound of the wave shook her loose. The water was almost upon them. She had to make sure that her daughter was safe, that her husband hadn't sacrificed himself in vain.

Still crying uncontrollably, Paige swept Ashley up in her arms and dashed into the stairwell.

The view from Wheeler Army Airfield was far removed from the action, but Reggie had a front-row seat, courtesy of a TV hastily set up at the front of the crowded office. He was talking with Frank Manetti, his contact at the West Coast/Alaska Tsunami Warning Center, on his cell phone.

"You seeing this?" Reggie said, absently patting Bilbo, who panted beside him. When Reggie had snagged his ride during the evacuation, his only condition had been that Bilbo would be allowed to come with him. Lying obediently at Reggie's feet, the dog never took his eager brown eyes off the commotion around him.

The TV showed a helicopter view of the second tsunami coming in. The TV stations, which weren't going to let a little thing like complete destruction of their facilities get in the way of covering one of the biggest disasters in history, had quickly moved their satellite uplink vans to high ground. Any cameras still operating in the islands were now broadcasting via those vans.

When Manetti didn't respond, Reggie said, "Frank, you still there?"

"Yes. I just can't believe what I'm seeing."

"Believe it. Kai's still somewhere out in that." *I hope,* Reggie thought. The news from the Black Hawk that Colonel Johnson had sent wasn't encouraging.

"You found him?" Manetti said.

"Not yet. I haven't heard from him since his last message. The helicopter didn't find anyone on the rooftop. The building next to it was blown to hell. Maybe they got out in time and made a run for it."

"If they did, they've got a bigger problem headed their way."

"I know," Reggie said. "The third tsunami."

"That's not what I mean."

"What could be a bigger problem than a two-hundred-foot tsunami?"

"There's a fourth wave."

"A fourth wave!" Reggie blurted out. "Are you sure?"

"We just got the reading from the DART buoy a minute ago. But the really bad news is its size. The wave is going to be over three hundred feet high."

"Dear God!"

As Reggie said that, the second wave slammed into the buildings lining Waikiki.

Kai closed his eyes as the seawater bashed in the front windows and engulfed the condo. The noise bombarded his eardrums, and it got even worse as the water found them. It crashed into the hallway from multiple directions, converging on their position, where it smacked into them with tremendous force.

Anyone who has ever ridden one of those water slides that plunges hundreds of feet in seconds has experienced the discomfort and indignity of having their bathing suit ride up during the deceleration from sixty miles per hour to zero at the end of the ride. Although tsunamis only travel at forty miles per hour on land, the effect from the current is similar. The shoes of people caught in tsunamis are the article of clothing most easily ripped from their bodies, but they are lucky if they aren't stripped completely naked by the water, as the man Kai had seen earlier had been.

Because they were inside the building, the current did not flow steadily past them. Instead, it was a turbulent mess that would rush in one direction one second, then reverse itself. The effect whipped them around like they were in a washing machine.

Pieces of debris pummeled Kai. Most were small, but a sharp piece of glass stung his cheek as it tore by. He heard a bang as something large hurtled past over his head and struck a hard surface. Somehow it had missed him. Many deaths in a tsunami are not the result of drowning but from being crushed by large objects. The respirators that Kai and the others were relying on wouldn't protect them from that.

Kai braced his feet against the girder in the hope that he could keep his shoes on. He would definitely need them to clamber over the debris in their escape from the building, if they made it that far.

His ears popped several times as the water above them got higher and higher. Every thirty-three feet under the water equaled one atmosphere of pressure, and they had been submerged to twice that depth in a matter of seconds. Kai just hoped none of them suffered punctured eardrums. They didn't need to add to their problems.

Kai opened his eyes and shut them again immediately, the filthy water stinging them. After what seemed like forever, the worst of the current eased, although it continued in the general direction away from the ocean. To Kai's relief, the building had been able to sustain the initial impact, but that didn't mean much. It could still collapse at any moment, undermined by the ebb and flow of the wave.

He tried opening his eyes again, and although the water was still foul, it didn't scratch his eyes as much as before. According to the dim glow of his dive watch, little more than thirty seconds had passed. As the water continued to rise above them, the light from the sun became more and more indistinct until the gloom was virtually complete.

Kai felt for the dive light that he had lashed to his wrist. It was still there. He turned it on.

The murk of the silt did not obstruct as much of the view as he had expected, but the visibility was still minimal. The fuzzy outline of the light played over a scene that seemed unfamiliar to him, even though he had seen it in broad daylight not a minute before.

He searched for Lani. Kai's chest tightened for a moment when he didn't see her face where he had been expecting it. He rotated the light over a larger area until he saw her floating above him. Her eyes were screwed shut, but Kai could see that her mouth was still tightly clamped around the regulator. Then a string of bubbles emerged from the mouthpiece, and he knew she had made it through the worst of it.

Kai gripped her arm to let her know that he was still

there. Her eyes fluttered open for a second, and Kai gave her the okay sign, which she returned.

On the other side, Brad and Mia seemed to be all right, although Brad still had a look of terror on his face. Teresa and Tom were discernible at the edges of the dive light, but Kai couldn't make out their condition.

He focused the light on the air tank he and Lani shared to make sure it was still intact. It was in one piece, but Kai found the source of the impact sound that he had heard.

Just to the right of the air tank, the car jack that he had strapped to the girder dangled from its rope. Some unseen object had crushed it. The jack was now completely useless.

They had no way to free Mia and Brad.

"Hello!" Rachel yelled through the closed elevator door. "Are you all right?"

"Thank God!" A man's voice replied. "Yes. I'm fine. I'm on top of the elevator cab roof."

The building shuddered from the tsunami impact.

"Oh my God!" the man said, his voice rising an octave. "What was that?"

"It's another tsunami. Are there others with you?"

"My sister and my mother are still in the elevator. I climbed out through the hatch to see if I could reach the outer door, but I can't get it open. The elevator shaft is pitch-black. I can't see a thing."

"Hold on. I'll get something to pry the door open."

A fire ax hung just around the corner from the elevator. Rachel broke the glass and wrenched it out.

She put the ax head into the space between the doors and used the leverage to separate them. When they were six feet apart, she wedged the ax under one door to hold them open.

About three feet below her stood a bald man of about forty-five. He was gangly and holding a metal cane. The man squinted and blinked at the first light he'd seen in twenty minutes.

"Thank God you came. I couldn't get the doors open from here. Without any light, I couldn't tell what to do."

Voices below him shouted. "Help us! Jerry! Get us out of here!"

"Jerry, you all need to climb up and get out right now. Look!" Rachel pointed at the water shooting up the elevator shaft next to him from below.

"Oh, crap!" He began to babble. "They can't. It was hard enough for me to get out with their help. My sister isn't exactly thin, and this is my mom's cane. She's seventy-eight."

"Listen to me," Rachel said as the water continued to rise at an astonishing speed. "You're in an express elevator. It only serves the sixteenth to twenty-eighth floors. There are no doors for that elevator between here and the lobby. This is the only way out."

"Maybe we should wait for the fire department."

"Nobody else is coming. You're lucky I heard you."

The water rose inexorably.

"I already tried lifting them," the man said. "I can't do it myself. Please!"

Rachel ran around the corner and shouted to the kids at the end of the hall.

"Wyatt and Hannah, stay there. There are some people stuck here. I'll be back in a minute. If the water keeps coming up, go up the stairs."

Rachel came back around and dropped down onto the

elevator roof. She peered through the emergency hatch. A plump woman in her forties and a frail elderly lady looked up at her.

"Who are you?" the elderly woman asked.

"I'm Rachel Tanaka, the hotel manager. The power is out in the hotel. We have to get you out of there immediately."

"How? We don't exactly have a ladder in here.."

"The water is almost here," Jerry said.

Rachel looked over the edge of the elevator. The water no longer shot up, but it was still rising. It looked to be to the thirteenth floor, only twenty feet below the bottom of the elevator.

"Can you both swim?"

"Are you kidding?" the younger woman said.

"No," Rachel said.

"There's water coming up, Sheila," Jerry said. "She's right. You may not have a choice."

"Can you swim?" Rachel repeated.

"Just because I have a cane doesn't mean I'm a cripple," the older woman said. "Of course I can swim. If you kids had let us leave when I wanted to, we wouldn't be in this mess."

"This is Jerry's fault!" Sheila said. "He's the idiot who wanted us to stay."

"If we had taken the stairs like I wanted to," Jerry said, "you wouldn't be stuck down there!"

"Shut up!" Rachel said. The last thing she needed was a bickering family. "What we'll do is wait to see how high the water gets. If it comes into the elevator cab, you'll float up and we can pull you out. If it starts to go down before then, we'll have to figure out something else."

The water reached the bottom of the cab.

"It's coming in!" Sheila said.

But the water didn't stop rising. The level crept up the side of the cab.

"How high is this going to get?" Jerry said.

"I don't know," Rachel replied.

"What if it comes over the top?

"I don't know," she repeated. "Do you have a better suggestion?"

He shook his head meekly.

The water level had risen three-quarters of the way up the exterior of the elevator cab, but the water inside was still only two feet high, trickling in slowly through the doors.

Paige appeared at the doorway of the elevator with Wyatt, Hannah, and Ashley.

"Paige! Thank God you made it! Where's Bill?"

Paige said nothing, but the stream of tears running down her face said it all.

"I'm sorry, Paige. I'm really sorry, but we need your help down here."

But Paige could only stand there, crying. The children started crying too.

"Okay," Rachel said. "You stay up there. There are three people down here. You can help pull them up."

The water kept rising. When it reached the top of the elevator, the water inside was only three feet high, still too shallow to float in. The seawater poured over the edge of the cab's roof and across the flat surface, where it lapped at Rachel's feet, drained through the emergency trapdoor, and filled the elevator at three times the previous rate. The rush of falling water was not loud enough to mask the screams of the two women trapped inside.

CHAPTER 42

WHEN THE SECOND WAVE hit the Moana tower of the Grand Hawaiian, the swaying of the building had caused panic among the people still on top. The evacuation had been going smoothly, with a helicopter arriving every five minutes to pick up new passengers. At one point, an Army Black Hawk helicopter was able to pick up fifteen of them, including the men who were the most disabled. Now just a handful were left.

Max leaned over the edge and saw the surface of the water flowing past the fifteenth floor. Rachel had not come back, and they had heard the collapse of the sky-bridge.

Another tourist helicopter landed. It had enough room for the rest of them, including Bob Lateen, who had insisted on remaining until everyone else was gone.

"Adrian," Max said as they hauled Lateen into the chopper, "tell them to wait for a minute." He hopped out onto the roof.

"Where are you going?" Adrian asked.

"Rachel should have been back by now. I'm going to check the stairs."

Max flung the door open and looked down the stairwell. He couldn't make out any movement between him and the water a hundred feet below. He yelled down.

"Hello! Rachel! Are you there?"

No response. But the sound from the helicopter could have masked an answer. He closed the door, ran down two floors, and tried again.

"Rachel! Are you there? Anyone?"

Still nothing. Surely, if Rachel had made it, she would be climbing the stairs right now.

Adrian opened the rooftop door.

"Max, the pilot says they've got lots of other people still to rescue. He needs to go now."

With a heavy sigh, Max went back out onto the roof and got in the helicopter with Adrian.

"What happened to Rachel?" Adrian asked.

"I don't know. She must have gotten caught in it. I shouldn't have let her go. Okay, pilot. Let's go. There's no one left here."

They took off, leaving the empty roof behind them.

When Kai saw the ruined car jack, he was crushed. It meant another trip down to find a jack in another car. Of course there was no guarantee they would find one, and they would have the same time crunch getting it back here and getting Brad and Mia out before the building either collapsed or a third wave came in.

By this time the water had reached its peak height. Kai could feel the water stop flowing away from the ocean and begin its inevitable slide back where it came from. Flooding Honolulu to a depth of 150 feet had taken less than three minutes.

Kai felt something pulling on him. It was Lani. She grabbed his hand and pointed it and the dive light in the direction of the jack. He turned the light on his own face and nodded that he understood the situation. But then she did something completely unexpected: she patted the life raft and then pointed at Kai.

He shook his head, thinking that she wanted to use the raft to float up to the surface. She focused the light on herself and made a wide gesture with her hands, mimicking the inflation of the raft. She then pointed at the girder and pretended to push it up.

Of course! Leave it to a kid to think outside the box. She wasn't saying that they should use the raft as a boat. She was suggesting using the raft as a jack.

That's my girl, Kai thought. He raised his hand and nodded. He needed a minute to think.

The raft was attached to a CO_2 cartridge, so it would inflate itself in seconds. Kai focused the light on the side of the raft. It was rated to hold eight people. That meant at least 1,600 pounds of displacement on the surface. Underwater, it was at least twice that. If it was placed in the right location, it might be enough to lift the girder.

But there were also great risks with that plan. First, they'd only get one chance. If it wasn't placed properly, the raft would inflate, pop out of position, and float right out of the building. Second, there was no guarantee that it wouldn't burst if it was pinned in one spot by the girder. To make matters worse, the inflation would not be controlled. Once Kai pulled the trigger, the raft would inflate completely. If the girder fell off or the raft exploded, the beam might fall on any one of them, including Brad and Mia. They would be pushing their luck.

Kai felt himself being pulled toward the ocean. They didn't have much time before the water finished flowing back into the bay, leaving them high and dry. Once the water was gone, the raft would be ineffective. If he was going to try it, it would have to be now.

The building groaned under the changing motion of the water, indicating that it only had a few minutes of life left. It wasn't going to stand up to a third wave. The raft was their only option. Kai had to take the chance.

Kai pulled out the dive knife and sawed carefully at the rope tied around the life raft, making sure not to nick the raft's fabric. It took him about a minute to cut through. By that time the pull of the water had strengthened, and Kai wasn't expecting the raft to come loose so easily. It dropped from his hands and threatened to float away.

Lani had been watching him, and her hands shot out to catch the raft. Kai stuffed the knife back in its sheath and took the raft from her.

The girder was horizontal, with each end embedded in the drywall on either side. It looked like the explosion had ripped both ends of the girder from its welds, but the end Kai was closest to—the end extending toward the demolished building outside—left no space between the wall and Brad. Inflating the raft there would risk crushing him. That meant Kai would have to place the raft under the girder on the south wall.

But that side of the girder was out of reach.

Kai thought he could explain what he was planning well enough with hand gestures so that everyone would be ready, but he didn't trust his signing ability enough to tell someone else where to place the raft. He would have to get free of the rope and place it himself.

Kai tapped Brad on the shoulder and showed him the life raft. Kai motioned that he should be ready to get himself and Mia out when the girder lifted up. Brad gave a thumbs-up. Kai took it to mean that Brad wanted to get the damn thing off of him.

Since Teresa and Tom were the closest to where Kai would need to be to place the raft, he motioned to them to grab his feet. The flow of the water started to pick up, and he was afraid he'd be taken by the ebb if he wasn't secured. Kai didn't want to take the extra time to tie himself up again when he was in place.

Kai cut himself free, and as he was about to push off, he realized that the regulator hose wouldn't reach as far as he needed to go. Even if he were cut loose, he would have to go without air. Then he saw that Teresa could just barely reach his hose. Kai proposed trading regulators, and she nodded. They each took a deep breath and passed their regulators to each other.

With his ankles now held by Teresa and Tom, Kai paddled over to the other end of the girder, careful not to let go of the raft. The flow continued to accelerate, and the water tugged harder at his clothes. He'd have to make this quick.

The regulator attached to the tied-down air tank abruptly snapped his head back, still two feet short of the corner where he thought the raft should be placed. He had to hold it in position as it inflated, or it would pop out. There was no other way of keeping it there, no way to do this without leaving his air behind.

Kai took a last puff of air and dropped the regulator. He pulled himself even with the wall, shoved the raft into position, and ripped the inflation cord.

The sound from the rushing gas filled their chamber. The raft inflated asymmetrically, pushing one end out toward Kai while the other end was still flat. He had to push it farther in, or all this would be for nothing.

He braced his shoulder against the wall and pushed with his right hand until the raft was directly under the girder. With the dive light strapped to his wrist, Kai could see that the raft was beginning to compress as it reached the heavy steel above it.

At first nothing moved. If Kai wasn't already holding his breath, he would have done it then.

Then the miracle happened. The girder groaned and began to move ever so slightly. Kai had no idea how far it had to come up to let Brad and Mia get out, so he just kept his eye on the raft to make sure it didn't shift. Not that there was much he could do if it really wanted to squirt out.

As the raft continued to inflate, the girder moved up and up, guided by the slash in the wall that it had made. When it had risen a foot, Kai heard a grunt from Brad's direction. He was struggling to get free.

Kai was almost out of breath, but his work was complete. The pull of the retreating water was now as strong as the incoming tsunami had been. He struggled back to Tom and motioned for the regulator. Kai felt around for the tank and then followed the hose up to the mouthpiece. He stuck it in his mouth, and just before he couldn't hold his breath any longer, he pushed the button to clear the regulator. Clean, dry air filled his starved lungs.

Kai took several deep breaths, holding on to the tank with one hand. Tom clenched his arm with his good hand. But before Kai could grab on to Tom's rope with his other hand to steady himself, a huge piece of debris struck him on its way out of the building. Kai couldn't tell what it was—maybe something freed when the girder had been lifted up. But it hit him in the back, and the impact was enough to jar him loose from Tom's grip.

Kai's body swung around, and the regulator was

ripped from his mouth. He was about to be swept out to sea.

With the waterfall coursing through the elevator's escape hatch, the cavity filled quickly. Just as Rachel and Jerry could finally reach the outstretched arms of Jerry's mother, Doris, the water level began to drop. With the two of them pulling, they were able to carefully drag the drenched woman up onto the roof.

"Are you all right?" Rachel said.

"I'm fine," Doris said, panting. "Just let me catch my breath for a second." Her feet still dangled over the edge of the hatch, blocking access to Sheila, who splashed in the dark elevator below.

"Get me out of here!"

"Mama, move your feet," Jerry said.

"Okay! I am seventy-eight, you know."

"I know. You won't let us forget it."

Doris finally swung her feet out of the way, and Rachel and Jerry leaned down through the hole. The swirling water had taken Sheila to the side of the cab.

"Swim over here," Rachel said. "We can't reach you."

Sheila awkwardly swam over to their waiting arms. Her right hand grasped Rachel's, but she couldn't find purchase with Jerry.

The water level in the elevator shaft began to fall rapidly, but the water inside the cab could only escape through the narrow slit between the elevator doors. The cab lurched from the weight of the excess water.

Rachel, her hands slick from the water and sweat, almost dropped Sheila, whose thrashing made holding on even more difficult. Sheila finally found Jerry's hand, but with the water supporting less of her considerable heft, her weight threatened to pull both Rachel and Jerry down into the cab with her.

"Paige!" Rachel grunted. "Come down here quick! We need your help."

"No! My kids!"

"Please!" Doris said. "She's my child!"

"Paige! I'm losing hold of her!"

"All right!" Paige lowered herself from the sixteenth floor and lay down on the cab's roof. She grabbed Sheila's arm, and together she and Rachel pulled. Sheila must have weighed close to 200 pounds, so even with the three of them pulling, they were close to dropping her.

They hoisted Sheila high enough that her hand was even with the rim of the hatch.

"Grab on!" Rachel said.

"I'm trying!" Sheila said, coughing and sputtering salt water.

She steadied herself with both hands, allowing the three of them to adjust their grips. As they pulled her up like fishermen landing a prize bass, Sheila retched and vomited onto the roof.

She caught her breath, and the others heaved sighs of relief as they sat up and rested. Although the elevator shaft was three cabs wide, neither of the other cabs was visible in the darkness. The water outside the elevator was down to the fifteenth floor and falling quickly, but the elevator cab itself was still half-filled. Another screech of metal came from the elevator rails, and the cab shuddered. Rachel saw the mass of water still in the elevator and realized they needed to get off the cab's roof.

Because she had been involved in all hotel inspections, Rachel knew the elevators in the Grand Hawaiian were rated to carry 2,400 pounds. With half of the elevator full of water, it must have added thousands of pounds to the weight of the five people on the roof of the cab. Instead of the twelve passengers it was designed to hold, the elevator now supported the equivalent of eighty people, more than six times the weight limit.

Rachel stood, prodding Jerry up as well, and pointed at the opening to the lobby.

"Climb out that door now!" she yelled, but all she got was a confused look from the others before the bolt holding the elevator cable snapped.

The safety brakes on the elevator's guide rails automatically engaged, but not before the elevator dropped five feet, the bottom slamming into the surface of the water below.

The jolt threw Sheila and Doris flat. Paige was tossed toward the escape hatch, but she grabbed the rim before she fell in.

Rachel and Jerry, who had been standing closest to the edge, fell backward over the side of the elevator and splashed into the shaft's draining eddy of black water.

CHAPTER 43

THE FAST-FLOWING WATER DRAGGED Kai toward the doorway of the condo. He flailed his arms, hoping to find something solid to grasp. The wildly roving spot from the dive light tied to his arm illuminated the entry rushing by. As he tumbled through the hallway, his hand brushed against the doorway of the south-side condo unit. He whipped his body around and slapped his fingers onto the jamb's edge.

His progress stopped, but Kai was still without an air supply. He had less than ninety seconds before he inhaled water.

He thought about trying to swim back toward the air tanks, but the current had to be over twenty knots. It was all he could do just to hold on. Pieces of debris pelted his head, but he concentrated only on the weakening grip he had on the doorjamb.

Kai had two very simple choices, neither of which was appealing: he could either hold on until his breath ran out in the hope that the water flowing out would recede to his level, or he could let go and try to swim for the surface, getting towed out to sea in the process. He knew that very few people who were carried away by a tsunami lived to tell the tale. In fact, most of them were never even found.

On the other hand, if he did hold on and ran out of air, he would drown and be dragged out to sea anyway. Kai decided to take his chances at a few more minutes of life, so he prepared to let go and swim for it.

Just before he released his grip, he noticed that he could make out vague forms where the dive light wasn't pointing. The murky water was getting brighter; Kai had to be nearer to the surface than he thought. Sunlight streamed from the direction of the condo windows, meaning fresh air couldn't be more than ten or twenty feet above him. With that realization, he decided to stick it out for another minute or until he panicked, whichever came first.

The room got brighter and brighter until he could actually see some of the shapes around him without the light: the edge of the door, the pattern of the wood parquet on the floor, the pieces of flowered wallpaper that hadn't been ripped away. Just a few more seconds. His lungs were on fire, but he willed himself to make it.

Kai took a chance and inched himself up the edge of the door, hoping that he would be exposed to the air that much quicker. In short order, he reached the ceiling just as a new sound filled his ears: the unmistakable roar of water falling. At the same time a blessed air pocket opened above his head. Kai thrust his face upward, careful to maintain his grip, and gulped in a huge breath.

The water level dropped faster than an unplugged bathtub as it shot past him into Waikiki Bay. Kai maneuvered back down the doorjamb, and as the waterline reached about four feet above the floor, the flow abruptly shifted.

The walls on the south side of the condo were still intact, so when the water level reached the bottom of the windows, it had no way to continue draining on that side. But the wall on the north side of the building had been obliterated by the explosion, making an easy escape route for the remaining water.

The water stopped for just a few moments, and Kai knelt, his head just above the surface. Then the current changed direction to the north and charged back through the doorway. Because he wasn't expecting the change, Kai wasn't prepared. Although the rushing water was only a yard high, the force was enough to knock him down. It wrenched him off his knees, again sending him flailing. Kai was now in danger of being washed out the north side of the building like a log going down a flume.

Kai slammed into the north-side condo doorway, swung around, and saw the others in his group for a split second. Teresa tried to reach him, but she wasn't quick enough. His head went under again, and he thought for sure he was going right through the kitchen, after which there was nothing solid to grab on to. But then a hand latched onto his arm and stopped him with a jolt.

Kai put his foot against the kitchen wall to brace himself and splashed up to get another breath. When he did, he saw Brad's face, weary and terrified, but determined.

"You're not going anywhere," Brad rasped through clenched teeth.

In another few seconds the water drained enough so that Kai wasn't in danger of going with it. The air was rank with the smell of dirty seawater, but it couldn't have felt more refreshing. Kai stood to check whether he was in one piece. He had cuts and bruises all over, but all of the important parts worked.

"Thanks, Brad. For once I'm glad you spend all that time at the gym."

Brad looked like he was still in shock. Being pinned down and dependent on the scuba gear must have rattled him.

"You okay?" Kai said.

Brad just nodded and started untying himself. Mia was still on the floor beside him. She was also now free of the girder. The improvised plan had worked. The raft bulged out at the other end of the girder, no longer able to hold the weight. The girder had settled back down into its original position.

"Good idea with the raft," Tom said.

"It wasn't my idea," Kai said. "Lani deserves the credit."

Lani lay on the floor, and only now did he realize she hadn't moved since the water had gone.

"Lani, honey? Are you okay?"

He bent down and turned her over. The regulator was no longer in her mouth, and he saw why. The hose had been neatly severed by some floating object.

The suddenness of the cut gave Lani no warning that she would be inhaling water. In her struggle for air, she must have spit out the regulator. Her face was blue, and she wasn't breathing. Kai's daughter, his only child, was about to die.

CHAPTER 44

THE WATER ROILED AND churned as it was sucked down the Grand Hawaiian elevator shaft. After a moment of confusion and paralysis, Rachel found her bearings and swam for the surface, crying out as she broke into the air. She looked up to see Paige and Sheila peering over the side of the elevator roof. They were already twenty feet above her and receding away from her at an alarming rate. As she got farther removed from the light coming in through the open door on the fifteenth floor, the gloom got heavier.

"Rachel! Are you all right?" Paige yelled down.

"I'm okay," Rachel replied. "Where's Jerry? Jerry!" She spun around but couldn't find him.

"We can only see you. Maybe he's under us."

"I can't see him!"

Rachel paddled around the shaft, feeling for him under the water. Her leg brushed something in the middle of the shaft, and then it was gone.

"I think I touched him!" Rachel shouted.

More voices joined Paige's above, all of them calling, "Jerry! Jerry!"

Rachel dove under the water, but the light was non-existent. She felt around in the darkness, and her hand snagged on a piece of cloth. It was Jerry. Rachel kicked and pulled him to the surface.

Jerry was groggy, but conscious. He moaned and floundered, but he was able to keep his head above water.

"I found him!" Rachel yelled.

"Thank God!" someone cried back in relief.

"It's hard to see, but I think he's got a gash on his head. He must have hit it on something when he went over." She shook him. "Jerry! Can you hear me?"

His eyes rolled back, like he was about to lose it. Rachel slapped him.

"Jerry! Stay with me!"

That got his attention, but he couldn't manage more than a halfhearted dog paddle. They were still in the middle of the shaft, at least ten feet from any side.

"Where's that light coming from?" yelled Paige, who was now more than thirty feet above Rachel.

Rachel looked down to see what Paige was talking about. A ghostly light began to filter up from beneath them. It seemed to be concentrated on one side of the shaft. Then Rachel realized with a start what it was.

"Oh my God! One of the elevator doors must have come open. Come on, Jerry! We need to grab on to something or we'll be sucked right out of the hotel."

Even though the elevator Jerry had been in was an express, the two next to it were not, so that part of the shaft had doors at every floor below.

Rachel pulled Jerry's shirt. He gracelessly thrashed after her. The tug toward the open door strengthened. Their only chance was to get to the shaft's emergency ladder before they were whipped through the door and out the lobby window. Rachel had picked up enough knowledge from being married to a tsunami scientist to know that being caught in open water during a tsunami was deadly.

If she let go of Jerry, she could make it to the ladder easily. But she wouldn't release her grip. There was no way he could make it on his own.

The light wasn't bright, but it was enough to see that there were only a few feet separating them from the open elevator door. Rachel reached for the ladder with one hand and grasped it. Jerry's shirt became taut with the strain, but he made one last kick as well and grabbed on to a rung just as the water surface broke through the elevator door.

They steadied themselves on the ladder as the water rushed out with the sound of Niagara Falls.

"Are you okay?" Sheila yelled.

"We're alive!" That was as good as it could get at that point.

After another few seconds the water reached an equilibrium with the open door, and the extra water on that floor rushed back through. Rachel could now read the floor number on the outside of the door.

"We're at the eleventh floor."

"Can you climb back up?"

"Jerry's going to be lucky to be able to climb out right here. You'll have to come down and help me. Hold on, Jerry."

Jerry nodded hazily. He was in no condition to do much more than wait there.

It took a few minutes for the others to climb off the cab at the sixteenth floor and make it down to them by the stairs.

Guided by Rachel, Jerry stumbled down the ladder toward the eleventh floor. Hands snaked from just outside the door to grab on to him and pull him inside, where he collapsed on the floor of the elevator lobby.

Rachel crawled out, exhausted, and sat on the floor to catch her breath.

She looked at Paige, who was comforting her children.

"Paige," Rachel said between gasps, "I'm so sorry about Bill."

"You should be."

"What?"

"It's your fault!" Paige said, spitting her words at Rachel. "If it wasn't for you, I never would have let us try to cross that rickety bridge. If we had stayed on the other side, he'd be alive right now."

"Paige, I—"

A massive cracking sound came from the direction of the floor-to-ceiling elevator lobby window that faced the Akamai tower. It started as a few sporadic snaps and pops, but quickly merged into a grinding cacophony of agitated metal and concrete that overwhelmed the sound of the rushing water.

Except for Jerry, they all raced to the window to see what was happening. Dust began to puff out all over the building, as if its seams were popping. The scene was instantly recognizable to anyone who had seen the events of 9/11 unfold on TV.

Rachel turned to the others and yelled, "Get back!"

They dragged Jerry to the end of the lobby as the Akamai tower, weakened by the impact of the barge that had struck it, collapsed into a pile of rubble. They watched in horror as a building that just an hour before had seemed so solid—virtually indestructible, built to withstand hurricane-force winds, a state-of-the-art twenty-first-century exemplar of modern engineering—crumble in front of their eyes. And the worst part was that the Moana tower was identical.

CHAPTER 45

KAI DROPPED TO HIS knees and cradled Lani's head in his hands, his terror rising when he saw water spill from her mouth. Panic seized him.

"Teresa, what do I do?" he cried out, the desperation in his voice verging on hysteria.

Without thinking, Kai repositioned Lani's top, which had fallen embarrassingly low. That meager gesture to protect her dignity only magnified his helplessness. Despite his scientific training and his extensive education, he had never bothered to learn CPR.

"Cut me loose!" Teresa yelled, struggling to untie the rope that encumbered her.

Kai sliced through the main rope linking her to the girder, not bothering with the loops still dangling around her midsection.

Teresa bent over Lani, feeling for a pulse.

"How long has she been out?"

"I don't know. She was fine before I went over to inflate the raft. Two, maybe three minutes. Maybe less."

"I knew something like this would happen!" Brad said, his voice cracking under the strain.

"Will you shut up!" Kai barked at him. He pointed the knife at Brad. Kai didn't have time for Brad's panic as well as his own. "Do something useful."

Brad took the knife and began to cut himself and the others loose.

"She's got a pulse," Teresa said, "but it's almost gone."

Without another word, Teresa tilted Lani's head back and cleared her tongue, making sure nothing was obstructing her throat, then turned her head to the side to drain any water left in her mouth. Once the last of the water gurgled out, Teresa leaned over and began to force air into Lani's lungs using mouth-to-mouth.

After two deep breaths, she pulled back and turned Lani's head again. She pushed on Lani's chest, forcing more water to gush out.

"She took in a lot of water. We've got to clear it."

Kai was a wreck. There wasn't anything he could do. He never felt more useless. He simply held his daughter's hand and called her name.

"Lani! Come on! Lani! Can you hear me? Wake up!"

Suddenly, Teresa drew back. "We lost her pulse!"

Instead of slamming her fist onto Lani's chest as Kai had seen done on TV, Teresa carefully placed the heel of her hand on Lani's sternum and rhythmically pressed firmly but gently. After thirty beats, she breathed twice into Lani's mouth.

"Come on, Lani!" Teresa huffed as she continued the compressions. "We've come this far."

Kai felt the tears streaming from his eyes and mingling with the salt water still dripping from his hair.

"Please, Lani," Kai said. "Don't do this to me. Don't leave me."

As if answering him, Lani emitted a slight wheeze. Her eyes fluttered open. Then a small cough escaped her, and the cough became a fit. She turned over, gasping for breath. But Kai couldn't have been happier to see her wracked with coughs. All that mattered was that she was alive.

Lani vomited about a quart of water amid the coughs. After the fit was over, Kai sat her up and gripped her shoulders.

"Feel better?" he said.

She nodded. "What happened?" Her voice was still a hoarse croak and talking started another round of coughs. Kai wiped her mouth on his shirttail.

"Your hose was cut. You inhaled some seawater."

"Did the raft work?" she said.

"Just like you thought it would. I'm so proud of you." Kai took her in his arms, relishing the warmth that was missing from her skin just a few moments ago.

"She'll be okay," Teresa said. "We'll just have to make sure she doesn't get pneumonia from all the seawater in her lungs."

She turned her attention to her own daughter. Mia cradled her right leg but otherwise seemed intact.

"Thank God we got you out," she said, holding Mia. "How's your leg?"

"It hurts. Is it broken?"

"Let me look." Teresa touched her leg tenderly. "I don't see any broken bones. Can you wiggle your toes?"

Mia tried it and nodded. She repeated the same for her ankle. When she got to the knee, she winced and cried out.

"Looks like you might have a torn ligament in your knee. In any case, you're going to need help moving."

"Look, I don't want to be a jerk," said Brad, focusing the point on Kai, "but we're currently sitting in the world's largest game of Jenga. Can we go now?"

He was right. The condo building was precarious at best. It could collapse at any time.

"You," Kai said, pointing at Brad, "are going to carry Mia." He cut the dry bag loose and slung it over his shoulder. "Lani, can you walk?"

"I can make it."

Kai applauded her guts, but he didn't think she would get far without help. Her lungs would be raw from the near drowning, and the debris outside would make the walk anything but easy.

"All right, let's move."

They made it out to the hallway when Kai heard a squeal behind him. The life raft that had been pinned under the girder had been slowly sliding out, lubricated by the water. It finally shot out like a balloon from the pressure, bouncing around the room before going through the open wall and over the side of the balcony.

They all chuckled at the silly spectacle and then stopped when they heard a more ominous noise coming from all around them.

"Down! Down!" Kai yelled.

Leading Lani by the hand, he tore down the stairs, constantly sliding on the muck left behind by the water. Several times he slipped and caught himself with what was left of the railing.

When Kai got to the third-story landing, he heard Tom crash to the floor. Kai turned and yanked him up.

"No time for that."

As they ran, the groaning of the building grew, and Kai knew they didn't have more than a few seconds left. When they got to the first floor, Kai and Lani jumped through the open space where the windows used to be and ran in the direction that was most clear of debris: toward the beach.

Kai looked over his shoulder to make sure everyone

was behind him; he wasn't going to let anyone fall back. Brad carried Mia piggyback, with Tom in front of him and Teresa close on his heels. Out of the corner of Kai's eye, he saw the condo building tilt at a strange angle. Lani ran too slowly, so he gathered her up like a baby and pumped his legs as fast as they would carry him across Kalakaua Avenue.

An immense bang of snapping steel erupted behind him, and Kai felt a whoosh of air pound his back. He dove into the sand of Waikiki, now covered with a slimy ooze, and shielded Lani with his body. Pulverized pieces of the disintegrating building pummeled his back, but nothing bigger than a small pebble landed on him.

When the sound died, Kai pushed himself up. His back and head were coated in fine powder that clung to his wet skin. Instead of seeing the building they were just in, all he could make out was a fog of dust and a pile of debris. The entire ten-story Seaside condominium tower was now a pancake of rubble twenty feet high.

Kai sat on the sand, surveying the now-unfamiliar surroundings. The landscape of Waikiki had been utterly changed in the thirty minutes since they had entered The Seaside. Shattered structures littered the streets like crumpled beer cans. Other buildings were nothing more than skeletons stripped bare of their innards. Massive piles of junk had been caught against the various mountains of wreckage that used to be hotels and condominiums.

But even without the landmarks, the outline of the mountains behind was familiar. Kai recognized the pattern where they had come ashore with the Jet Skis. Of course, the watercraft were nowhere to be seen.

"Nice job, Kai," Brad said, squeezing the water from his filthy T-shirt. "We're back where we started."

Chapter 46

Jerry had fallen unconscious, his head wound more severe than Rachel had first thought. After spending a few minutes trying to wake him, they decided to carry him up the stairs. Even though he was skinny, it took all three of them—Rachel, Paige, and Sheila—to pull him down the hall and up the stairs. At each landing, they stopped for thirty seconds to catch their breath. They had only made it up one flight to the twelfth floor.

As they carried him, Doris kept the children occupied and told them about herself and her kids. Their last name was Wendel, and Doris had been widowed two years earlier when her husband, Herbert, had been stricken with cancer. Neither of her children, Sheila and Jerry, were married, so they had all come out to Hawaii for a family vacation. When the tsunami warning was issued, they had returned to their room as they were initially instructed. When the warning changed, Jerry had thought it was best to stay put.

After the first tsunami, they realized that staying was a bad idea, so they got in the elevator to get up to the roof. That's when the power went out, and they'd been left stranded. As Rachel listened to the story, it dawned on her that she was risking her life for people who had blatantly disregarded her warnings to leave. She wanted to shake these people and say, *Why didn't you listen?* But dwelling on their ignorance wasn't going to help.

Their progress climbing the stairs was slow; at the rate they were going, they wouldn't be on the roof until the next tsunami hit. They needed help carrying Jerry.

As they took another breather, Rachel heard voices coming from the stairway above them. The voices were getting louder: people headed down toward them.

"Hello!" Rachel called out.

The movement above froze. She saw two faces peer over the railing about sixty feet above her at the twentieth floor. One of the strangers waved. Then they began coming down the steps even quicker than before.

In less than a minute they had covered the distance. A thirty-something couple, obviously happy at finding other survivors, smiled at Rachel, their bright red faces burned from exposure to sun they weren't accustomed to.

"Are you coming from the roof?" Rachel said.

The couple looked at each other and shrugged. The man in the couple then started speaking rapid-fire in a language that sounded Slavic.

"Oh, no," Rachel said. "Are you with the Russian group? Russki?"

The man repeated the word "Russki" and pointed at him and the woman. He then started speaking in Russian again.

"Do you speak English?"

"Nyet." He shook his head. "No English." Rachel guessed that it was the only English phrase he knew.

They were two more of the hotel guests who had failed to leave their rooms when the evacuation was taking place. Either that, or they had gotten separated from their group when they had been shuffled around the lobby. In any case, they were going the wrong way.

Rachel pointed down and said, *"Nyet."*

At this, the smiles disappeared. The man's voice became angry, even indignant. Perhaps he didn't like being told what to do by a woman. Whatever the reason, he gesticulated and nodded vigorously as he pointed down.

Rachel motioned to her badge, which was still attached to her soggy suit. It said: *Rachel Tanaka, Hotel Manager.* Under those words was an image of the Grand Hawaiian logo. She hoped that would lend her an air of authority.

She pointed at Jerry's inert form and tried to indicate that they needed help carrying him. The man, who was fairly burly, nodded and grabbed his arms.

"Good. He understands." She turned to the Russian man. "Thank you. *Spasibo."*

Rachel grabbed one leg, and Sheila got the other. But instead of continuing up, the man rotated Jerry around and made as if to carry him down the stairs. Rachel immediately put his leg down and grabbed the man's arm. She shook her head.

"Nyet!"

The Russian became furious and practically dropped Jerry onto the cement. He made a rude gesture and took his girlfriend, who had been watching all of this silently, by the shoulder. They continued down the stairs, the man muttering to himself.

"Where are they going?" Sheila said.

"They're going to die," Rachel said, the weariness evident in her voice. She was too tired to sugarcoat anything. "They don't know another tsunami is coming, and that it's going to be bigger than the last one."

"Shouldn't we try to stop them?" Doris said.

"How? That guy is bigger than any of us. And you heard all the Russian I know. If you can make them understand, be my guest. Our bigger problem is that this is taking too long." She waved her hand at Jerry. "It would go a lot faster if we got some help."

"From that guy? You just said—"

"No. From Max."

"Who's Max?"

"He's my assistant manager. He's up on the roof with the other guests."

"But if one of us goes," Paige said, "there's no way two of us can carry him."

"No, but we can still make progress if Wyatt goes. He can run up those stairs in just a few minutes."

"Sure I can!" Wyatt said.

"What if something happens to him?" Paige said. "What if he gets lost?"

"There aren't many choices. They're either still in the restaurant or they're on the roof. He just needs to tell Max to come down and help us."

Paige pulled Wyatt close to her, sheltering him from some unseen enemy. She buried her face in his hair and then faced Rachel, her eyebrows arched in despair.

"I'm sorry about what I said earlier. About you being responsible for Bill."

"Don't be."

"When that building fell down, all I could think . . ." Paige broke down without finishing.

"It's okay," Rachel said, placing her hand gently on Paige's shoulder.

"You saved our lives," Paige said. Then she squared her shoulders in renewed determination and knelt beside Wyatt.

"This is very important, honey. Do you understand what we want you to do?"

"Go and get Max."

"Or any other adult up there. But you come right back down as soon as you find him, you understand?"

He nodded.

She hugged him. "I'm so proud of you. I'll see you in a few minutes."

Wyatt padded up the stairs. The rest of the group picked up Jerry again and renewed the slog upward.

"How are you doing?" Kai asked Lani. Her breathing was a ragged rasp.

"Hurts a little."

"I'll give you a lift in a minute." Even though they were jogging, Kai needed at least a little bit of a break. He ached all over from being twisted and turned by the water. He had strained his shoulder when he was holding on to the doorway, trying to keep from going out to sea. Not to mention cuts and bruises too numerous to count. Still, it could have been much worse.

Teresa put her hand on his shoulder and squeezed. Kai winced but didn't pull away.

"Thanks, Kai. For Mia. If you hadn't gotten her free . . ." Her voice trailed off, the implications too much for her to bear.

Kai put his arm around her and returned the hug. "I know. Same for Lani."

"Where are we going?" Brad said. "Isn't that building closer?" He pointed at the building directly in front of them, about three hundred yards away.

"It's closer, but it's only twenty stories tall. I'm not sure that's high enough. Besides, it's going to get the brunt force of the next wave. I'd rather be in one that has a little protection and doesn't get a direct blast. Remember, the next wave is going to be the biggest yet."

"I wish you'd stop saying that," Brad said. "So which one are we going to?"

"To that one," Kai said, nodding.

"Which one?"

"The one with the boat sticking out of it."

On the ocean side of a thirty-story apartment building, the aft end of a sixty-foot charter fishing boat was suspended ten stories above the street. Its twin propellers were easily visible from their current position about a quarter mile away.

"Man!" Tom said.

"If that doesn't show the power of a tsunami," Kai said, "I don't know what does."

"Yeah," said Brad, "we sure haven't seen enough examples of that yet." He jumped in front of Kai and led the way, Mia still clinging to his back.

Lani began coughing again from the exertion.

"That's enough jogging for you," Kai said. "Hop on." She jumped on his back, and he continued to trot, albeit a bit more slowly. The debris was getting treacherous. The terrain was literally postapocalyptic. They continually detoured around large heaps of splintered wood, twisted metal, and dislodged concrete that impeded their progress.

They were still two blocks from their designated refuge when they found an intersection piled three deep with cars, buses, and trucks that had gotten wedged against the bottom of a cement foundation. Brad skirted it and stopped when he rounded the corner of the pile.

"You've got to be kidding," Brad said.

"What?" Kai said, coming to a stop beside him.

"There's a couple of people up ahead. They're heading this way."

Sure enough, two young men were making their way through the debris toward them. Kai couldn't tell if they were high school or college students, but they couldn't have been older than twenty. They looked like they were in good shape, and both had their shirts off and sticking out of the back of their shorts, as if they were on an afternoon stroll. One of them held a video camera.

"Hey!" Brad yelled. "You're going the wrong way."

The men looked in their direction, appraising the motley crew.

"No we're not, man," the one with the camera said.

"You are if you don't want to die."

"Look, we're not stupid, you know. We're heading to that building on the beach."

"You *are* stupid," Kai said. "There's another tsunami coming." He kept going, and the others followed. He wasn't stopping to chat with these bozos.

"Why do you think we're taking this with us?" the one without the camera said. "We're gonna sell the video. We've already got some good stuff of that building coming down over there." He pointed at the remains of The Seaside.

"You idiots," Brad said. "We were in that building."

"Cool," the cameraman said, and turned his camera on them.

Their comment got Kai to stop. He turned and stared at them, unable to comprehend how crass and greedy some people were.

"You two little shits look at all this destruction and death," Kai said, "and all you can see is some money for yourselves?"

"Hey, the TV networks are making money off this. Why shouldn't we?"

"You're not going to make any money because you are going to die. That building is not going to stand against a wave two hundred feet in height."

The two men laughed at that.

"You think this is funny?"

"Man, this is going to be great footage."

"Turn that camera off, you asshole!" Brad yelled. He moved as if he were going to try to take it away from them, but Kai stopped him.

"Forget it, Brad. No one's ever going to see that footage anyway. If they're too dumb to take good advice, they're on their own. We don't have time for it. Let's go."

The two men stumbled off in the direction of the beach, talking in low voices and laughing.

Kai was angry at them, not just because they were cold opportunists, but because they made him see how futile his job could be in some cases. Kai's job was to warn people of danger. The people could do with that warning what they wished. He couldn't force them to get to safety. He couldn't save them if they didn't want to be saved. Now he was seeing that reality up close. And what made Kai feel even worse was that he didn't want to save them. They deserved whatever happened to them.

As Kai's group got close to the "boat building," as he had come to think of it, Lani tapped him on the back.

"Daddy, I hear something."

"What?"

"A voice, I think. It's coming from your bag."

My bag? Then Kai realized how stupid he had been. In all the rush, he hadn't remembered to check the phone or the walkie-talkie. Someone was trying to reach them.

CHAPTER 47

JERRY MADE IT TO the twenty-first floor before the women carrying him were too fatigued to continue. Even for three of them, Jerry's deadweight was too much. They were spent.

"What are we going to do now?" Jerry's sister, Sheila, said, her voice strained from fatigue and worry. "We can't just leave him."

"He's too heavy. We need some help. We'll have to wait for Wyatt to get back."

"What's taking him so long?" Paige said. "He should have been back by now. I shouldn't have let him go. I should have trusted my instincts. I'm going to look for him."

Despite her exhaustion, Paige forced herself up the stairs, but before she could get to the next landing, a door slammed and the sound of light feet drifted toward them. She stopped.

"Wyatt?"

"Yeah?" Wyatt replied. They could hear him crying as he came down.

"Are you all right?"

"No!"

Paige quickened her pace upward, and Rachel followed. They met him on the twenty-third-floor landing. His eyes were red, his cheeks stained with tears.

"What's the matter, honey?" Paige ran her hands over him, looking for injuries. "Are you hurt?"

Wyatt shook his head.

"Then what's wrong?"

"I couldn't find anyone," Wyatt said between sobs.

"No one anywhere?" Rachel said.

"I swear, I looked all over. They're all gone."

He took out the walkie-talkie that Rachel had given him before the incident at the elevator.

"I even tried this. I couldn't find anyone. I'm sorry!" He wailed, the experience too much for him. "I'm sorry! I tried!"

Paige held him to her. "It's okay, sweetie. You did great."

"They must have found a helicopter," Rachel said.

"Why didn't they wait for us?" Paige said, her voice pleading.

"I don't know. Maybe they thought we didn't make it."

"So now we're stranded?"

Paige was on the brink of hysterics. Rachel tried to soothe her.

"If they found one, we can too. We just have to let them know we're here. Who knows? Maybe they're planning on coming back."

"So what do we do? We can't carry Jerry."

"We'll have to go up there and try to flag down a helicopter. There's nothing else we can do."

A faint voice called from the walkie-talkie still in Wyatt's hand.

"Rachel! Rachel! It's Kai, are you there?"

Kai had stopped at the lobby of the boat building so that he could get at the dry pack. He lowered Lani and let her walk on her own. While Kai climbed the stairs of the apartment complex, he opened the bag to retrieve the walkie-talkie.

When he got it out, the walkie-talkie felt moist to the touch. He inspected the bag and found a tiny tear in the seam. It must have happened when he was battered by the wave. The bag wasn't soaked inside, but it was damp. He didn't bother looking at the photo album, the only thing he'd saved from his house. It was either intact or it wasn't, and now wasn't the time to see. The most important thing was the electronics. Kai opened the cell phone. The LCD display was cracked, another victim of debris impact. He tried calling 911, but there was no sound. It was useless.

Kai keyed the Talk button on the walkie-talkie.

"Rachel! Come in!"

He didn't know if he was getting through because he couldn't hear more than a crackling hiss. The voice that they had heard before sounded like a kid, so Kai wasn't even sure whether they were getting the signal from Rachel or from someone else.

"Rachel! Rachel! It's Kai, are you there?"

He listened carefully, trying to hold his breath as he climbed. The volume was turned up all the way. Then, loud and clear, Kai heard her voice.

"Kai, it's me. Are you all right? How's Lani?"

"We had a close shave, but she's fine. Teresa, Mia, and Brad are okay too. But Jake, the boy you saw at the Grand Hawaiian? He didn't make it."

"Oh my God!"

"How are you?" he asked.

"I'm better now that I hear you," she said, the relief in her voice palpable. "It's been a little rough. I'm just glad you two are all right. When the other tower collapsed, I couldn't—"

"What? The tower collapsed? You're still at the hotel? I thought you would have caught a helicopter by now."

"There were some people in trouble. It's been crazy. We're heading to the roof now. Where are you? Did you get out of Waikiki?"

"No," Kai said. "It's been crazy for us too. We're about a mile from you. Of course, the tsunami has obliterated all the street signs, so I don't know exactly where we are, but it's a white thirty-story apartment complex. There's a big boat sticking out of it, if that helps."

"Okay. We're on the roof now. I'm not sure if I see your building. I don't see a boat sticking out."

"You may not be able to from your angle. When we get to the top, I'll see if we can wave to you."

"Everyone else is gone on this building. They must have found a helicopter."

"Can you see one to flag down?"

"I see a few," Rachel said, "but they're not close enough to see us."

"We're going to have the same problem. Listen, is anyone with you?"

"Yes, there are eight of us in all, including three children."

"Eight? Jesus. Does anyone with you have a cell phone? I lost mine and Brad's got smashed."

A pause, and then: "Yes, Paige has a cell phone. We've tried 911 and can't get anything."

"Reggie left me a message earlier. You can try him."

"What's his number?"

It was in Brad's now-smashed cell phone. Kai had a pretty good memory for numbers, but he couldn't quite nail down the sequence Reggie had left in his message. He gave Rachel three variations he thought were close.

"Try all of those. It's got to be one of them. See if he can find a free chopper."

"Okay. I'll call Reggie."

"And, Rachel, the next one may be at least two hundred feet tall. Stay on the roof. Get a helicopter as soon as you can. If one tower has already fallen—"

"I know," she said. "We all watched it collapse. None of us wants to stay here longer than we have to."

"I'm so glad to hear your voice, honey."

"Me too. I'll radio back after I get Reggie."

Kai had fallen behind the others as he talked to Rachel, so he sped up until he caught up to them on the twentieth floor. He filled them in as they continued trudging up the stairs.

When Kai opened the door to the roof, he expected to see another empty expanse of concrete, devoid of people. Instead, a couple stood at the edge of the roof, looking up at the sky. When the door banged into the wall, they turned. The woman, dressed in a stylish gray jogging suit, looked like someone in her forties who hoped that cosmetic surgery would keep her in her thirties. Her oversized breasts strained against her top, and her forehead showed the unmistakable rigidity of frequent Botox injections.

The man with her wore a shiny silk shirt and Italian slacks, more expensive than tasteful. His curly hair was too jet-black for his age, and he had the wiry build of a fitness buff. He strode over to Kai, pulling a rolling carry-on suitcase behind him.

Kai smiled and said, "We're glad to see that we're not the only ones—"

The man interrupted him. "We were here first."

Kai's smile faltered. "What?"

"Are you deaf? I said, we were here first."

Brad stopped next to Kai. "What's that supposed to mean?" Brad said.

"It means that any helicopter that lands here is ours. You can ride along if there's room."

"Are you serious?" Teresa said. "Don't even think about getting on a helicopter before these girls do."

"They have kids, for God's sake," the woman said. "Be human for once."

The man looked at Mia and Lani and then grudgingly said, "The girls can go first. Then us."

Brad jabbed his thumb at the man. "Who *is* this guy?" he said to Kai.

"Chuck is my soon-to-be ex-husband," the woman said with venom. "We were out shopping when we heard about the tsunami warning. Genius here thought we had all the time in the world to come back to the apartment and get into his safe—"

"Denise," Chuck said with a warning tone.

"—a safe I didn't even know we had—"

"Don't tell them about that."

Brad pointed at the suitcase. "So, Chuck, what's with the luggage?"

Chuck paused and narrowed his eyes at Denise. "It's important papers," he said through clenched teeth.

"I'll tell you what's in it," Denise said, happy to sell Chuck out. "His collection of signed baseballs is in there. Babe Ruth, Mickey Mantle. Must be dozens of them. But that's not all he had in that safe. When he was getting the baseballs out, he dropped some photos. Photos of him and his girlfriend."

"I wish I was stuck here with her instead of you," Chuck spat at Denise. He pointed at Kai. "And remember, we were here first."

Kai had heard enough. He showed the walkie-talkie to Chuck.

"Guess what, Chuck," he said. "I have a radio. If *we* get a helicopter, *you* are welcome to come along with us if there is room. Now excuse me while I try to get our butts rescued."

Kai nodded to the others to follow him and walked to the edge of the roof to get as far from Chuck as he could. He pressed the walkie-talkie's Talk button.

"To anyone who can hear this, we are trapped on the roof of a building in Waikiki . . ."

Reggie Pona had already tried calling Brad's cell phone nine times, with no success. He left several messages to call, but he didn't really think that they were still alive to get them. The helicopter—the same one he had sent for Kai the first time—had done a fly-by thirty minutes later and reported that the building had completely collapsed. There was no chance that anyone inside had survived.

The devastation across the Hawaiian Islands so far had been unbelievable, even to those like Reggie who had seen the effects of the Asian tsunami firsthand. He had taken a trip to Thailand and Indonesia two weeks after the tsunami to help document the destruction, so that the PTWC would know what to expect if it ever happened in Hawaii.

The construction in South Asia was not up to the standards in the United States. Banda Aceh, on the northern tip of Sumatra, had been wiped off the map, and the majority of the deaths occurred in that area. The only building still standing after the tsunami was a sturdy white stone mosque. Previously it had stood among hundreds of shops, businesses, and homes; after the tsunami, it rose alone from a plain of mud and fractured wood.

In Hawaii, buildings near the ocean were primarily hotels and other structures made of concrete and steel. Many of them withstood the first and second tsunamis, a testament to the solidity of their designs. But a great number had already been swept away or fallen when their foundations were undermined by the water, and any buildings made of flimsier materials no longer existed. Pictures and video from Hawaii, Maui, Oahu, and Kauai now unspooling on the major networks showed miles and miles of shoreline blasted free of the monuments of man, as if God's own eraser had rubbed them out.

Hilo, on the Big Island, had endured two tsunamis in the twentieth century, events that sparked the creation of the Pacific Tsunami Warning Center. The awful pictures from those earlier disasters looked quaint compared to what Reggie saw now. Little was left of that small city, despite being located on the east side of the island, out of the direct path of the tsunami. The wave had wrapped around Hawaii, capturing the island in a deadly embrace.

Lahaina was the Maui beach town best known as the place to see the humpback whales that came to breed each year. The pictures from a helicopter were labeled LAHAINA, but Reggie couldn't make out anything familiar, and he had been there at least seven times on vacation. The only things left to signify that there might have actually been a town were the outlines of concrete foundations poking out of the scoured sand.

And then there was Oahu, home to 80 percent of the state's population. The current CBS feed from a helicopter hovering near Waikiki showed the devastation in stark clarity. Reggie could barely recognize some parts of the city. Honolulu was the most crowded part of the island; combining residents and tourists, some areas of Waikiki had a population density rivaling that of Hong Kong and Manhattan. Over the years, the suburbs had stretched around the shoreline in both directions, so that there was virtually no uninhabited land along the southern coast.

Hundreds of thousands had heeded the warnings and evacuated to high land all along the coast. Frightened masses hunkered on the sides of Diamond Head and inside the protected crater itself. The mountains were lined with people. So many had retreated to the confines of the Punchbowl National Cemetery that no room was left for helicopters to unload the people they rescued from skyscrapers, remote beaches, and overturned sea vessels.

Tripler Army Medical Center was filled to the brim with evacuees from other hospitals on lower ground. It received one helicopter after another dropping off the injured, a makeshift triage station set up on the grass next to the parking lot.

With little safe flat ground left, most of those rescued by helicopter were taken to Wheeler Field, a ten-minute round trip from Waikiki, not including the time it took to get people loaded and unloaded. It was possible Kai and the others had been picked up by another chopper and been deposited there. Possible, Reggie knew, but not likely. He had practically given up when he heard about the collapsed building.

Reggie's cell phone rang. He forced his eyes away from the TV and looked at the caller ID. He didn't recognize the number; it had a California area code. He flipped the phone open.

"Hello?"

He was shocked to hear the voice on the line.

"Reggie, it's Rachel."

"Rachel!" he shouted. When he saw others in the office staring, he brought his voice back to normal. "Thank God you're all right. Kai was . . ." Reggie hesitated, not knowing how to tell her. "I'm not sure, but—"

"Kai's fine."

"He is? I mean, that's fantastic—"

"We're all in trouble. We're still in Waikiki."

"You're together? Where?"

"No. I'm on the roof of the Grand Hawaiian. He's on the roof of a white building about a mile northeast of me. I can reach him by walkie-talkie. We need a helicopter. We don't have time to run away on foot, and both buildings are shaky. I don't know if they'll stand up to the next tsunami."

"Don't worry. I'll get something to you. What's the name of the building Kai's in?"

"He doesn't know what the cross streets are or what the building is called, but he said there's a boat sticking out of the tenth floor."

"God, I saw that on some news footage a few minutes ago. I'll find out where it is."

"Please hurry. We've only got a few minutes until the last tsunami, right?"

"I'll hurry. But Rachel, the next tsunami isn't the last one."

"What?"

"I got word from Alaska about twenty minutes ago. Tell Kai the last tsunami will arrive at 12:37, and it's going to be three hundred feet high."

There was silence on the other end of the line.

"Rachel? Are you there?"

"Just get someone here now, Reggie."

She hung up.

Reggie left the office to find Colonel Johnson. He was on his cell phone in the next room. He snapped it shut as Reggie approached.

"Colonel, I need your helicopter again."

"Mr. Pona," Johnson said, coming around his desk and putting on his jacket as if he were getting ready to leave. "I'm sorry about your friend, but the building is gone. There are other people to evacuate—"

"He's alive. I just got word."

Johnson stopped. "What? Where?"

"Waikiki."

He shook his head. "Mr. Pona, I can't—"

"Look, if it weren't for him, none of us would be standing here right now. You, me, your family, for God's sake. We'd all be dead."

"It's not that. That chopper is on the other side of Oahu. It'll take at least fifteen minutes to get back to Wheeler and unload."

"Damn!"

"Do you have that kind of time?"

"No. Don't you have anything else?"

"Look, I'll send out an alert, but I can't promise anything. It's absolute chaos out there. Most of the choppers are running low on gas, and Wheeler is overloaded trying to refuel them all." When he saw the pleading look on Reggie's face, Johnson said, "I'll see what I can do. But you might want to find another option."

"Thanks," Reggie said, looking around for ideas. He wasn't going to give up now that he actually had a chance to save them. Who besides the military would have access to a helicopter? Then he glanced through the office window and saw his solution. He ran outside.

Lara Pimalo, the CBS reporter who had broadcast from the PTWC, was just outside the building where Reggie had his temporary office. As thanks for evacuating him, Reggie had let Pimalo and her cameraman ride in the Humvee to Wheeler after they had abandoned the station's truck.

She looked like she had just wrapped up a report and was holding her microphone lazily at her side, but when she saw Reggie she gestured to the cameraman to start rolling. Reggie put up his hands to stop her.

"I'm not here to be interviewed," he said. "I need something."

"You need something from *me*?"

"You have a CBS helicopter over Waikiki."

"Well, we rented it from a sightseeing company. Cost a mint too."

"Kai Tanaka is stranded on top of a building in Waikiki. Do you know the reporter in that helicopter?"

"There's no reporter in it, just a camerawoman."

"Kai found his wife and daughter." Reggie had told her about Lani and Rachel on their ride to Wheeler.

"They're all alive? That's incredible."

"But now they're stranded, and the military won't give me another helicopter."

"I don't know if I have that much pull."

"He gave your station something no one else had. And now he has one of the best stories to tell the world about this disaster."

Pimalo exchanged glances with her cameraman. Reggie saw the hesitation, but he knew the phrase that would push her buttons.

"Ms. Pimalo," Reggie said, "how would your network like another exclusive?"

CHAPTER 48

A FEW MINUTES AFTER Rachel hung up with Reggie, a helicopter that had been flying along the coast angled over.

"Your friend is fast," Paige said to Rachel. Rachel was surprised and impressed at Reggie's feat.

The sightseeing chopper, one of the AStars popular with the tourists in her hotel, had *Wailea Tours* painted on the tail. It set down on the Grand Hawaiian roof, and Paige and Rachel ran over. Next to the pilot sat a fit woman who aimed a professional video camera at them. Rachel knew she looked bedraggled after her swim in the elevator shaft, but she didn't care what the camerawoman shot as long as the helicopter took them off the building.

"Are we glad to see you!" Rachel said. "Reggie must have gotten through to you."

"They did say something about a Reggie," the pilot said. "The station that hired me called to tell me to pick you up. You're lucky. I was about to head over to Portlock when we got the call about you. Hop in."

"Wait. There's more of us."

"How many more?"

"Five, including three kids." Rachel looked at the helicopter's cramped interior. "One of the adults is pretty heavy."

"That would make ten altogether."

"Can you get us all in?"

"This is only a seven-person chopper, including me. I might be able to squeeze more than that in, but one or two of you will have to stay behind."

Rachel didn't like the sound of that, but she guessed that he was being conservative. They'd deal with that when they were all on the roof.

"Fine," she said.

The pilot looked around the empty rooftop. "Where are they?"

"We need you to come with us."

"What? Where?"

"A man is injured. We can't carry him up on our own."

"Are you kidding?"

"What do you think?" Rachel said, wringing out the tail of her coat for effect.

"I can't leave the helicopter here."

"What about you?" Rachel said, pointing at the sinewy camerawoman. "He's too heavy for three of us to lift. He's unconscious. With four of us, it'll only take a few minutes."

Up to this point, the camerawoman had been silent.

"Hey, I'm not a medic," she said. "I'm supposed to be filming."

"We just need help carrying him."

The camerawoman turned to the pilot. "Nobody said anything about leaving the chopper when we got the call."

"Please," Rachel said. "He'll die."

"Do you know how many people have died already today?"

"Do you want there to be one more?" Rachel pointed

at the ocean, already receding from shore. "We don't have much time."

The camerawoman paused, and then sighed and put the camera down on the seat.

"I better get some good shots out of this. Where is he?"

"Thank you. He's this way."

Rachel led her down the stairs.

As they walked, she called Kai back to tell him what Reggie had said about the three-hundred-foot wave that was heading their way and that he had sent a helicopter for them.

"Are you boarding the chopper?" Kai said.

"No, we've got an injured man here. I asked someone to help us get him to the roof."

"Who are you talking to?" the camerawoman asked.

"My husband. He's on top of another building."

"We don't have room to take all of you, let alone another group."

"I know. Are there more choppers coming?"

The camerawoman shook her head. "We're it. Can you dial up other frequencies with that thing?" She nodded at the walkie-talkie.

"I don't know. They preprogram it for me." She keyed the button. "Hold on, Kai." She handed it to the camerawoman, who examined it for a moment and then returned it.

"Looks like you can. Just twist that knob on the side. You should be able to get the frequency the pilot's using. You might be able to reach someone who can get them."

"Kai," Rachel said, "there's not enough room on this helicopter for you guys, so you'll have to call another one." She relayed the frequency to him.

They arrived at the twenty-first floor, where Jerry still lay unconscious.

"Kai, we've got to start carrying Jerry now. I'll call you back on the new frequency."

"Okay. Rachel?" Kai said.

"What?"

"I see it. The tsunami. Get out of there as fast as you can."

"I will. And you get Lani out of there." She replaced the walkie-talkie on her belt.

The camerawoman took one of Jerry's arms, Rachel the other, and Paige and Sheila each took a leg. The climb was still awkward but proceeded much more rapidly.

When they reached the twenty-fourth floor, the tower shuddered as if it had been hit with a giant sledgehammer. For a moment they all staggered, thrown off balance.

"Jesus!" yelled the camerawoman. "Was that what I think it was?"

Rachel nodded grimly, now familiar with the sensation.

"Hurry," she said. "We don't have much time."

For the third time that day, Kai watched a giant tsunami tear into Honolulu. Only this time, he had a spectacular 360-degree view from their perch three hundred feet above the ground.

The wave's size was something only a handful of people in recorded history had ever seen. In 1958, a landslide at Lituya Bay, Alaska, unleashed a wall of water that climbed a quarter mile up the side of a cliff directly opposite of it. A smaller but still huge wave charged down the length of the bay. A father and son, fishing in their boat only a mile from the landslide that day, were borne by the wave over the tops of trees more than two hundred feet high and settled back in the bay upon the receding water. Two other people fishing the bay were not so lucky. Their bodies were never found.

Up to that point, it had been the only mega-tsunami that witnesses had lived to tell about. Now Kai was watching an even bigger one wipe out his home state.

The third wave swept in like a giant fist. The force of water topped ten tons per square foot. Many buildings, already weakened, didn't stand a chance. At 184 feet, the Aloha Tower had been for many years the tallest structure on the islands. The landmark had miraculously withstood the first and second waves, and Kai could just make out the top of it between other buildings. When the third wave hit, though, it folded like a straw. The Hyatt, the Waikiki Beachside, and the Hilton all collapsed into rubble.

"Darryl and Eunice," Teresa murmured. She and Brad propped Mia up, and Kai stood with his arm around Lani. Tom had joined them at the rooftop edge, but Denise and Chuck kept their distance on the other end.

"Who?" Kai said.

"A couple I met on the beach. They were staying at the Hilton. I hope they got out."

Kai waiting in agony to see what would happen when the wave struck the Grand Hawaiian. Just before the impact, Lani buried her head in Kai's chest.

The tsunami, its crest even with the fifteenth floor, exploded against the side of the hotel's remaining tower, the water spraying hundreds of feet in the air. For a moment it seemed like the top of the building tilted backward, and Kai held his breath, expecting it to topple.

But it didn't. The wave wrapped around it and continued on. Other buildings remained standing under the onslaught as well, including many of the behemoths downtown. Most of those buildings had been shielded by others that took the brunt of the wave.

Then the water reached the boat building, and Kai hoped it would hold up to the impact. Even three hundred feet up, the sound was like a dozen approaching tornados.

Two buildings stood directly in the path between the boat building and the full force of the wave. The first, the Moana Surfrider, was blasted by the wave and instantly collapsed. But it had done its part to mitigate the blow. The second building met the slowed wave and the debris from the first building. It was shorter than their building, but it was a stout apartment complex of gleaming steel. The glass that hadn't shattered during the previous impacts didn't stand a chance.

The water shot all the way through the building and rocketed out the back windows. It joined the water sweeping around the side and hit Kai's building.

The impact was not as intense as it had been with the other buildings, but it was still strong. Kai swayed sickeningly on his feet as the water sought to undermine the foundation of the structure. But the foundation held, unlike that of the apartment complex in front of them. When the surge reached the twentieth floor, just below the rooftop, the whole structure disappeared into the sea.

As the water continued to rush past, every few seconds another building would fall, its death signaled by a time-delayed roar, like thunder cracking after the flash of distant lightning.

Kai knew it was simply a matter of time before his building joined them.

CHAPTER 49

THE MOOD ON THE ROOF of the Grand Hawaiian while they boarded the chopper didn't register as panic, but Rachel could sense the fear.

To balance the load, the smallest people had to sit in the front, so Paige, Hannah, and Wyatt clambered in there with Ashley on Paige's lap. Stan, the pilot, helped Rachel, Sheila, and Paige load Jerry's frame into the backseat. The camerawoman, Deena, snatched up her video camera again as soon as Stan took Jerry's arm and began filming the process. They propped Jerry upright next to Doris, who sat in the rightmost seat.

Sheila climbed in next. Deena waited for Rachel, but Rachel shooed her in. As Deena climbed in, Stan said, "Lose the camera!"

"What?" Deena said. "Do you know how much this costs?"

"I don't care. It weighs too much, and we're overloaded. We need all the lift we can get."

Deena grudgingly dropped the camera from her shoulder and removed the tape. She handed the camera to Rachel, who was standing outside. Rachel set it gently on the roof.

"Get in!" Stan yelled to Rachel.

"I thought the weight was too much."

"It'll be close, but the kids are light, so we're going to try for it. This building isn't going to be here much longer."

"But it's jammed. Where should I sit?"

Stan pointed at Deena. "Get on her lap."

Rachel scrambled on top of Deena awkwardly. Her hand slipped and dug into Deena's leg. Deena flinched.

"Sorry." There was no way for Rachel to fasten a seat belt around herself, so she grabbed the seat in front of her as tightly as she could.

Stan secured himself in the pilot's seat on the right, with Paige and the kids squeezed next to him. He brought the engine up to speed.

"Okay," Stan said. "We're going to do this slowly."

With the engine at full speed, he pulled back on the stick. For a second, nothing happened. They simply sat there, the helicopter blades throbbing over their heads.

Stan pushed the throttle until the engine passed the redline. The helicopter jumped a yard into the air. Stan struggled with the collective, trying to keep the chopper level. But before he could get any more height, the aircraft skidded to the right, dangerously close to the huge rooftop air-conditioning unit. The helicopter rotated awkwardly, and for a moment the sound of grinding metal buzzed behind them, sending a cascade of sparks flying past them. Piercing screams filled the cabin.

Stan rotated the helicopter back around and dropped the stick. The helicopter thudded onto the roof, the main rotor blades sweeping past the machinery with only a foot to spare.

"I'm sorry, guys," he said. "This isn't going to work. Someone's going to have to get out."

"Only one of us?" Rachel said. "Will that make a difference?"

"I hope so. That sound you heard was our tail rotor brushing the air-conditioning unit. It seems okay, but I can't take any more chances of bumping it. Nine passengers is just too many. I'll be lucky to take off with only eight of you."

There was an uneasy silence for a second.

"If I drop these people at Tripler," Stan said, "I can be back in five minutes. I'd volunteer to stay behind, but unless one of you can fly a helicopter—"

"I'm staying," Rachel said with a resigned tone.

"Maybe you should draw straws," said Stan.

"No, this is my hotel. I'm responsible. I'm the one who should stay."

Everyone else remained quiet. Even if they had argued, Rachel wouldn't have let one of them stay behind while she was whisked to safety.

Before Rachel could climb out, Paige grabbed her arm and hugged her fiercely.

"Thank you for giving my family a chance."

"Thanks for helping me. Take care of those kids."

Rachel backed away to give the helicopter room to maneuver.

Stan brought the helicopter up to speed again. Without Rachel's added 120 pounds, the blades were able to claw more lift from the air. The chopper slowly rose and angled away from the air-conditioning machinery.

After it was clear of the hotel, it circled once thirty feet above Rachel. They waved, and Rachel gave them a thumbs-up.

Then the helicopter swung away and headed in the direction of downtown Honolulu, leaving Rachel on the roof of the Grand Hawaiian, alone.

CHAPTER 50

WHEN KAI AND THE others saw the helicopter take off from the Grand Hawaiian, they let out a weary but jubilant cheer. It was quickly cut short by a rumble from far below them. The building continued to resist the force of the water, but it protested mightily. The noise made Kai step up the broadcasting of his Mayday. It would be extremely risky to wait for Rachel's helicopter to get back.

"My name is Kai Tanaka, and we are standing on a white building approximately six blocks from the beach and eight blocks west of the Honolulu Zoo. To anyone who can hear us . . ."

The power of the walkie-talkie limited the radius to just a few miles, so he was hoping something would fly within range long enough to hear the message. After a couple of broadcasts on the new frequency Rachel had given him, he got an answer.

"Mr. Tanaka, this is CWO Henry Mitchell on Army flight one niner three. I see your party. What is your situation?"

Teresa hugged Mia, and Tom yelled, "All right!"

"You see us?" Kai said to the pilot.

"We're just passing over Diamond Head." Kai turned and looked to the east, where he saw a Black Hawk helicopter speeding toward them.

"Thank God! We've got eight people here." A huge antenna sprang from the center of the building's roof, a feature Kai hadn't noticed from the ground. Three microwave transmitters were perched on the antenna. Kai didn't see markings on it, but it couldn't be anything other than a cell phone tower. It would get in the way of any helicopter trying to land. "You'll have to hover next to the building to pick us up."

Chuck and Denise, the other couple on the roof with them, saw the commotion and edged closer.

"What's happening?" Chuck asked. "Did you get someone?"

"A helicopter," Brad said.

"Which one?" Chuck pointed at the Black Hawk. "That one? Why isn't it coming down?"

Kai expected the helicopter to start dipping down toward the building, but Chuck was right. It was maintaining its altitude. It would pass over them in a few seconds.

"I'm sorry, Mr. Tanaka," the pilot said, "but I don't have any room."

"Even for a few people?" Kai pleaded. "We have children here."

"I'm packed to the gills with injured from Maui. I'm heading over to Wheeler to drop them off. I'll be back for you as soon as I can."

"How long will that be?"

"I'm running low on fuel, so we need to gas up. That could take thirty minutes."

"Thirty minutes!"

"Maybe longer. Wheeler's jammed, and it's the only place that still has refueling equipment for choppers."

The Black Hawk roared overhead, tantalizingly close.

Chuck, who had been listening to the conversation, pushed next to Kai and snatched the walkie-talkie from Kai's hand. Kai stood in shock as Chuck keyed the Talk button.

"Pilot, this is Chuck Bender, and I have ten thousand dollars in cash here for you if you—"

Brad grabbed Chuck's wrist, pressing his fingers into Chuck's carpal tendon. Chuck screamed in pain and dropped the walkie-talkie into Brad's other hand.

"That's not yours," Brad said, and handed the walkie-talkie back to Kai. Chuck glared at Brad but thought better about taking it further.

"Did I hear that right?" Mitchell said. "Do you think I do this for money? Who was that?"

"I'm sorry, Chief Mitchell," Kai said. "That was another party here. He does not speak for me. We'd appreciate any help you can give us, but thirty minutes will be too long. There is another wave coming. And I'm not sure the building will even survive that long. We're hearing a lot of rumbling coming from it. It might go at any time."

"I'm sorry," Mitchell said. "I'll see if there are any other helicopters available. In the meantime, I suggest you keep sending out the SOS. Good luck."

The sound of the Black Hawk grew fainter, along with Kai's hopes.

The walkie-talkie squawked again, and Kai thought he'd given up too quickly.

"Kai," Rachel said, "I couldn't hear everything that pilot said. Did you get a ride?"

"Rachel?" Kai hadn't expected to hear her. He assumed she was on her way to being dropped off in the other helicopter, which would be out of range by now. "Where are you?"

"The helicopter was too full, and I drew the short straw."

"You mean you're still on top of the hotel?"

He looked at the roof of the Grand Hawaiian and could just make out her tiny figure waving at them. Kai nearly fainted. After all that, she still wasn't safe.

"Not the best place to be, I agree," she said, trying to sound brave in her plight. "Do you mind picking me up after the chopper arrives?"

"Honey, we can't. They don't have room on the Army helicopter. It won't be back for a while."

The pause at the other end was heartbreaking.

"That's okay," she finally said. "The pilot that was here said he'd come back for me." She paused again, then her voice came back more weakly. "But just in case, you better keep calling for help."

"I will," Kai said. "Trust me, Rachel. We're going to make it."

"I know," she said, but Kai could tell that she didn't really believe it.

Stan circled the helicopter over Tripler Army Medical Center looking for a flat space that hadn't been overrun by evacuees. Every inch of the massive hospital's grounds was occupied by people, thousands of them. Then he spotted a Navy Sea Stallion take off from a parking lot that had been cleared as a landing zone, and he zipped in to take its place before another helicopter could get it.

The hospital was just six miles northwest of Waikiki, so the trip had only taken a few minutes. Not only did Stan want to get his passengers to safety, he was starting to worry that the damage to his tail rotor was more serious than he initially thought. A high-pitched whine was coming from the tail, a faint sound that someone unfamiliar with the chopper wouldn't have noticed over the helicopter's turbine roar. But Stan, who had been flying for over ten years, knew every normal sound his craft made. He had never heard this one before.

After Stan dropped these people off, his plan was to head directly to Wheeler to get it checked out. If it was still okay, he'd refuel and head back.

He maneuvered the AStar until it hovered just above the lot's asphalt, and then the skids came to a rest on the surface. Two members of the hospital staff, burly men dressed in scrubs, ran over and began helping the passengers out of the helicopter.

Stan pointed at Jerry's slumped figure behind him and said, "That one first. He's injured." After retrieving a stretcher, the men pulled Jerry down and placed him gently on it. Sheila and Doris, who didn't even turn to thank Stan for his efforts, began to babble about Jerry's condition as the men wheeled him toward the hospital.

Paige, with the help of Deena, guided her kids down, and they ran straight in front of Stan, away from the tail rotor, as he had instructed.

Deena climbed back into the helicopter and was about to belt herself in, but Stan put out his hand.

"You need to stay here!" he yelled over the throb of the rotors.

Deena was stunned. "What?" she said. "I'm going back to the hotel with you. I'm getting my camera back." By this time Paige had returned to the helicopter. Her kids stood at the edge of the parking lot, watching them.

"I'm not going back," Stan said. "I'm afraid the chopper might be damaged."

"You're not going back?" Paige said. "You have to!"

"The tail rotor rubbed against something. It might go at any time."

"You can't just leave her there!" Paige screamed. "She's the reason my kids are alive!"

Stan was about to tell her that he was sorry, that he couldn't risk it, but he stopped when he saw tears streaming down Paige's face. He remembered the way that Rachel had so readily given up her seat to give the others a chance to get to safety, and he felt a moment of shame for considering not taking the same kind of risk for her.

He slowly nodded and said, "I'll get her."

Paige mouthed "Thank you," and backed away from the helicopter.

Shutting down the engine to do a visual inspection of the tail rotor would take too long. He'd just ignore the sound coming from it. Besides, he wasn't a pilot because it was the safest thing he could do for a living. His bird was tough; she'd make it.

He glanced at Deena.

"You still can't come. If I do go down, I'm not taking you with me."

Deena didn't glare at him or protest, like Stan expected. She didn't even mention her camera. She simply gave him a look of understanding. Without a word, she climbed out of the helicopter and walked away.

Stan increased power and lifted off. He waved to Paige and the kids, but they didn't wave back until he made his turn and headed back in the direction of the Grand Hawaiian.

CHAPTER 51

As THE WATER STARTED to flow back to the ocean, the creaking and rumbling from the apartment building increased. After every broadcast for help, Kai would release the Talk button. He heard lots of other voice traffic on the frequency, most of it garbled and unintelligible, but his calls continued to go unanswered. Everyone on the rooftop, including Chuck and Denise, crowded around him, hoping to hear a response.

He was about to try again when a choppy message mentioned the name Rachel. Several of the others started talking, but Kai shushed them. At first the communication faded in and out, then it became clearer, as if the transmission was getting closer.

"I repeat, Rachel at the . . . Hawaiian . . . returning from Trip . . . you up. Are you . . . there?"

Then Rachel's voice came through clearly. "You are breaking up. This is Rachel Tanaka on the Grand Hawaiian. Repeat your message."

Now the voice came through with no interruptions. "Rachel, this is Stan Milne from Wailea Tours. I am returning from Tripler to pick you up. Be prepared to jump aboard."

"Stan, listen to me," Rachel said. "You have to get my husband and daughter first."

"You have someone else with you?"

"No," she said, "they are on a white apartment building about a mile northeast of me." From the walkie-talkie, overpowering Rachel's voice for a moment, Kai could hear rumbling that was even louder than it was on his building. It was worse than he feared. The Grand Hawaiian was about to collapse. Suddenly, all he could think about was that his wife was in danger, and he couldn't help her.

"So I should go there first?" the pilot said.

"No, pilot!" Kai shouted. "Stan! Pick Rachel up first—"

Chuck grabbed Kai's wrist and yanked his thumb off the Talk button.

"Are you crazy?" Chuck said, a wild look on his face. "We need to get off this pile before it falls down."

Brad pushed Chuck away with a flick of his arm, but his face registered as much panic as Chuck's.

"Kai, unfortunately, I agree with the bozo here. We should be first."

Rachel's voice cried out through the tinny walkie-talkie speaker. "Kai, no! Get Lani out of there first. Pilot, if you can hear me, get my husband and daughter first."

To Brad, Kai said, "The Grand Hawaiian took the full force of the tsunami. We're lucky it's still standing as it is."

"We're lucky this building is too," Brad said. "And I'm not going back in the water."

"Stop thinking about yourself, you bastard. That's my wife over there."

"Kai, think straight. Your daughter is over here, along with seven other people."

"I agree with Brad, Kai," Teresa said. "We have to get the girls out of here."

"I may be a bastard," Brad said, "but you know I'm right. Rachel would never forgive you."

So that was the choice. Kai's wife or his daughter. There was no right answer, just a terrible decision. He looked at the haggard faces around him.

They were right, of course. Kai wasn't thinking straight. Lani was what mattered above all else. Kai keyed the walkie-talkie. His voice strained to keep from breaking.

"Okay, Stan. Come get us first. Are there any other helicopters in the area?"

"I haven't been able to get one."

"Then we'll get her ourselves."

"How many of you are there?"

"Eight."

There was a pause. Then Stan said, "I've burned up some fuel since the last trip. We'll give it a shot."

If someone had to stay behind on the Grand Hawaiian, Kai would gladly let Rachel take his spot when they got there.

"You should be able to see my AStar by now, northwest of your position."

Kai took a quick look and saw the helicopter speeding toward them. It was small. Kai could see why their numbers gave the pilot pause.

"Did you hear that, honey?" he said. "We'll be there in just a few minutes."

"Kai, let me speak to Lani."

He held the walkie-talkie up to his daughter.

"Hi, Mom."

"Hi, honey. Lani, I want you to know how much I love you."

"I love you, too, Mom," Lani sobbed.

"You are such a joy in my life. I couldn't be prouder to be your mother."

Lani was crying so hard, she couldn't answer.

"No matter what happens today," Rachel said, "you be strong. You're a smart, caring, beautiful girl, and I know you'll grow up to be a wonderful woman."

"Mom, we're coming to get you!"

"I know, Lani. Be good. I can't wait to give you a hug."

"Me too."

In the background behind her voice, Kai could hear loud crunching, as if the Grand Hawaiian were being eaten by an enormous monster.

"Rachel, what's that?" But he knew what it was, because the building they were standing on was making the same noise. Both buildings were in their death throes. "Are you okay?"

"Just hurry, Kai!"

The chopper hovered over them but didn't land. The pilot pointed at the antenna in the middle of the roof. The rotor blades would strike it if the helicopter tried to land. The railing all around the roof rose four feet above the deck. The best the pilot could do was lower the left side of the helicopter so that its skid was resting on the railing. With the pilot sitting on the right, both the front and rear doors were accessible. The sound of the rotors was deafening, and the downdraft from the blades buffeted the group mercilessly.

The building shuddered again. The structure was on the verge of collapse.

Before Kai could establish an order for getting in the helicopter, Chuck pushed past everyone and jumped into the backseat, pulling his small suitcase behind him. Denise stood next to Kai, as flabbergasted as he was.

"Hey!" Brad yelled and scrambled in after him. He wrestled with Chuck, trying to pull him out of the chopper. "You bastard! Children first!"

"Stop it!" Kai shouted. "Forget it! There's room for all of us. There's no time."

Brad stopped fighting, but before he moved back to the opposite side, he tore the bag away from Chuck.

"That's mine!" Chuck screamed.

"Not anymore!" Brad yelled back and threw it out the door. The rotor wash blew it sideways, where it smashed into the outer wall of the building, popping open. Just as Denise had said, baseballs, dozens of them, dropped to the water below.

Chuck threw a murderous glare at Brad.

"Don't even think about it, Chuckles," Brad said. "Or you'll follow them." Chuck buckled himself in, and Brad turned his attention back to the others trying to board.

Brad hoisted Tom by his good arm while Kai boosted him up from below and guided him into the seat next to the pilot. The breeze from the ocean challenged the pilot to keep a steady position. Despite Stan's efforts, the AStar kept moving back and forth in response, making it difficult to get a grip. Kai climbed up on the six-inch-wide railing of the building and held on to the helicopter as he gingerly pulled Mia up. Teresa and Lani supported her and tried not to hit her bad leg.

"Don't look down," Kai yelled over the sound of the rotors. He didn't follow his own advice and peered through the space between the helicopter and the skid. The water had reached its acme, but it was still a hundred feet below them. Kai looked away quickly before vertigo could claim him.

Once Mia was safely inside next to Tom, Kai grabbed Lani's hand and yanked. When she got onto the railing, she teetered for a second, and Kai thought for sure that she was going to fall. She screamed, and Brad grabbed her other hand, swinging her into the backseat.

Denise crammed herself into the front seat with Tom and Mia, leaving enough room in the backseat for the rest of them.

That left Teresa. As Kai pulled her up, a gust of wind blew the helicopter farther along the railing, which threw both of them off balance. She stumbled sideways, wobbling precariously on the railing, and Kai fell against the side of the chopper.

Mia yelled "No!" as Brad threw himself onto the floor of the helicopter and grabbed both of Kai's arms to keep him upright.

"Teresa!" Kai shouted. "Come on!"

She careened back toward him and latched onto his legs to keep herself upright. Suddenly her full weight pulled on him. The wind had changed direction and pushed the helicopter away from the building. They were suspended high above the water.

"Don't let go!" Kai screamed to Teresa, as if that would help.

Seeing that Teresa might be crushed against the building if the pilot tried to get even with it again, Brad yelled, "Up! Up! Up!"

The weight pulling Kai down seemed to double when the pilot maneuvered up. Kai felt Teresa slip down his legs and heard her scream.

"Hold on!" he yelled stupidly. The door banged against him as it fluttered back and forth in the rotor wash.

Teresa came to a stop, her arms wrapped around Kai's ankles.

"Pull me up!"

"I can't!" Brad said, straining from the weight.

Kai saw a belt dangling from the backseat. He gripped it with one hand and pulled himself up until his upper body was on the backseat of the AStar. Lani tried to pull him in, but with her strength sapped, she wasn't much help. Chuck sat there motionless, his eyes wide with terror.

Kai's legs hung over the side, still tightly held by Teresa.

"You can let go!" Kai yelled to Brad. "Get Teresa!"

Brad released him, and now Kai's grip was the only thing keeping him and Teresa from falling from the helicopter. Brad leaned out and strained to grab Teresa.

"I can't reach you!" Brad said. "Give me your hand!"

Kai felt Teresa release his left leg. Then he heard her shriek and let go of his right leg.

"No!" he yelled.

He pulled himself up, turned around, and saw that Brad was still draped over the side. With trepidation, he looked over the edge.

Teresa dangled by only one hand from Brad's hold. She had inadvertently let go when grabbing for Brad. Kai flattened himself onto the seat.

"Grab my hand," he said.

Teresa flailed until her palm reached his. He clenched it fiercely.

"Pull!"

With the two of them pulling, Teresa's light frame practically rocketed into the helicopter onto the seat next to Kai. He slammed the door behind her.

Brad continued to lay on the cramped floor, the only place there was room for him. Their feet rested on top of him. Teresa threw herself at Kai and wept with relief. He held her tightly, thankful that they hadn't lost anyone else.

"Are you okay?"

She nodded, panting from the exertion. "I think I've used up a lifetime's supply of adrenaline."

"Me too."

Teresa fished around for the seat belt. Kai did the same.

"Rachel," she said.

"Stan," Kai said as loud as he could.

The pilot pointed at a headset hanging from the ceiling. Kai put the earpieces on and depressed the cord's switch as he spoke into the attached microphone.

"Mr. Tanaka, I presume," Stan said through the onboard comm system. "We're headed to the Grand Hawaiian right now." The helicopter made a steep turn in the direction of Rachel's hotel. "I've got your wife on the radio."

"Kai?" Rachel said, the fear in her voice clear from that single word. "There's a lot of creaking and movement going on. It's like standing on the world's largest piece of Jell-O." He admired her for trying to make a joke even in this situation.

"We're on our way, Rachel. We'll be there in less than a minute."

"I don't think you'll make it." Even over the noise of the helicopter, Kai could hear the screech of distressed metal. He leaned into the cockpit and saw the Grand Hawaiian dead ahead less than a mile away. They would be there in seconds. But she was right: they were too late. Puffs of dust were erupting from all over the building, the telltale signs of imminent collapse he'd seen in the other buildings that had already gone down. Nevertheless, Kai clung to any shred of hope that they'd make it.

"Don't say that, sweetheart."

"Tell Teresa that I understand her job now."

"You can tell her yourself. I can see you."

"I know. Kai, I love you. I'll miss you."

"Rachel, no. We're coming."

"Take good care of Lani for me. I wish I could have seen her grow up. I'll miss her so much." He could hear the ache in her voice.

"Rachel."

"Honey. My honey."

Tears streamed down Kai's cheeks, but he kept his eyes riveted on the Grand Hawaiian.

"Oh, Rachel, I love you. Don't leave us."

"I don't want to. I love you, I love you. I—"

Her voice was abruptly cut off. It was followed by a colossal rumble.

"Rachel!" Kai screamed. "Rachel!" But there was no answer.

The Grand Hawaiian tower finally succumbed to the power of the water pounding at its frame. The south side buckled, sending the top pitching over toward the beach. Windows blew apart. Pieces of the hotel flew out in every direction. The pilot swung the helicopter around to avoid getting struck with debris.

With all of the dust billowing up, Kai lost sight of Rachel. But she didn't have a chance. The bulk of the structure splashed into the water with an enormous roar. For a moment it surged to a stop, halted by the impact with the water. And then, surrounded by white foam, it sank. The entire hotel slid below the surface. It was gone.

All Kai could do was slump in his seat and moan, only vaguely aware of Lani's screams. In shock, he sat there, mute, looking out the front of the cockpit as the chopper raced back in the direction they had come.

And that's when he saw the boat building, the tower they had been rescued from, tumble into the sea.

CHAPTER 52

*M*Y WIFE IS DEAD, *and it's all my fault.* That's all Kai's mind could comprehend at the moment. Not gone, not passed away, not any of the other euphemisms that people use to try to protect themselves from reality. She was dead. His job was to protect her and everyone else who had died in the last two hours. He had failed not only professionally but personally.

He had been her husband. His was the shoulder she had cried on after a tough day at work. He was the one she had snuggled up to for comfort. It had been his responsibility to keep her safe. And he knew she had felt equally protective of him.

Kai had never felt more miserable than at that moment, and he never cried harder. He howled from the pain in his chest, from the unfairness of it all. They had been so close to saving her. So close. Kai didn't know how he could endure the heartache.

But then he felt Lani burrow into the crook of his shoulder, still wailing. He tugged her close to him and along with the despair, felt a glimmer of pride. Rachel must have had a good reason for giving up her spot when the helicopter left the Grand Hawaiian. She would only have done it for someone else's family.

As for her own family, Rachel had know the risk she

was taking sending the AStar to them first. And, deep down, Kai understood her need to make that sacrifice. If the situation had been reversed, he would have done the same without hesitation.

Kai was holding the living, breathing embodiment of everything Rachel wanted in life. There was nothing more important to either of them. Lani's fragile little body shuddering against his arm reminded Kai that there was still good in the world and that he still had responsibilities. He had to get Lani to safety. With a fourth wave set to hit Honolulu in the next fifteen minutes, they were still in danger.

But he couldn't give up on Rachel yet, no matter how impossible the odds of her survival were. Once the danger of airborne projectiles had passed, Kai convinced Stan to fly back to where the Grand Hawaiian had been just a minute before and circle. The water was awash with debris and bodies, and Kai simultaneously hoped and feared he'd see Rachel's. He wanted to find her no matter what, but the idea of seeing her limp, lifeless form was too much to bear. He looked for any unusual movement at all, anything to indicate someone was alive in that brew.

They found no sign of her.

"I'm sorry, Kai," Brad said from his prone position. "She's gone."

"I know," Kai said, wiping his eyes. "I was just hoping—"

"Mr. Tanaka?" Stan interrupted. "We should get back. I just let your friend Reggie know that you were safe."

"Reggie sent you?"

"Yes, sir. He was the one who told us about your wi— about the Grand Hawaiian. We'll be back at Wheeler in seven minutes."

As they passed the downtown area and flew over Sand Island, Kai couldn't help but stare at the water as it receded into the ocean that was now his wife's graveyard. His mind replayed the last few minutes over and over, like a sick videotape that he couldn't turn off. He tried to distract himself by looking out the window, but it was almost worse seeing the terrible vista below.

In the distance, Pearl Harbor, the Navy base already synonymous with disaster, was once again dotted with smoke trails, this time from explosions kicked off by oil and other chemicals dispersed by the tsunami. The vast flat expanse of Honolulu International and Hickam Air Force Base was only recognizable because of the control tower jutting out of the water and the battered hulks of airliners crushed against the remains of the terminal.

They were crossing one of the airport's seaplane channels when a high-pitched whine spooled up from behind Kai's head. As it grew louder, the helicopter wobbled back and forth as if balancing on a slowly spinning top that was about to fall over.

"Dammit!" Stan shouted. "Not yet!"

"What's happening?" Kai said. The helicopter was quickly losing altitude.

Stan's finger's stabbed at a few switches on the control panel. The cyclic stick wagged to and fro as if trying to wrest itself from Stan's grip.

"The tail rotor's giving out!" Stan said, barely able to grunt the words. "If I don't get us down in the next thirty seconds, we're going to crash!"

CHAPTER 53

THE WATER HADN'T COMPLETELY receded yet, so the Honolulu International Airport runways were still awash. Several structures jutted above the surface, their frames intact. Airliners were scattered around the airport, most of them ripped to pieces, their aluminum frames no match for the power of a tsunami. The closest was a Hawaiian Airlines 767 that lay on the tarmac a hundred yards away, its landing gear and one wing ripped off, all the windows blown out.

If the helicopter landed in the water, they'd drown. Kai had no doubt about that. The only chance was to land on one of the buildings. Stan apparently had the same idea.

"I'm going for the terminal," Stan said.

The enormous main terminal stood about a mile to the north. Its gigantic roof would give them plenty of room to land. But then what? It was only three or four stories high. The next tsunami would completely engulf it, and it was much too far to run to high ground.

The airport control tower loomed in front of them, and Kai noticed that the roof of the tower's companion building was just peeking above the water's surface. Half of it was in tatters, ripped apart by the waves, but the other half seemed to have survived. The tower had to be at least 250 feet high. If they climbed to the top of it, they might have a chance.

"Stan!" Kai said into his microphone, "the building next to the tower. Land on it and we can use the stairs to get to the top."

Stan nodded and aimed the helicopter for the white roof of the tower's office building. The cabin shook like a paint mixer as they descended. The roof rose to meet them at a terrifying rate.

"Hold on!" Stan yelled.

The skids smacked into the roof, and Kai was afraid they'd go right through. Instead, they bounced off and careened toward the edge. They weren't going to get another shot at landing, so Stan forced the stick down, and the skids made contact again. Mia and Lani screamed as they slid along the roof, the skids scraping the poured concrete surface.

The chopper quickly scrubbed speed because of the friction, but they continued to approach the edge. Kai pulled Lani toward him and braced himself, ready for the plunge over the side, but the helicopter came to a halt two feet from the precipice.

Stan turned the engine off, and the turbine began to wind down. Kai removed his headset.

"Is everyone all right?" he said.

A few mumbles and nods were the only responses. Nobody seemed to be injured.

Kai unbuckled his belt and lifted his feet so Brad could pull himself up.

As they crawled out of the ruined helicopter, Chuck walked in circles. "What kind of rescue was that?" he said in a high-pitched keen.

"Will you shut up, you dimwit," Brad said in a weary voice. "You're fine."

"Fine? Fine?" Chuck said. "We almost get killed and you say we're fine!"

"We're alive, aren't we, Chuck?"

"No thanks to you."

"If you weren't in such a hurry to get on the helicopter, maybe we would have left your ass behind."

"If you hadn't overloaded the helicopter with all these people, we might have made it." Chuck strode over to the pilot, who was still sucking wind from the adrenaline rush of the emergency. "Thanks for picking us up in a faulty helicopter!" Stan looked at him as if he were crazy, which Kai thought he might be.

"Are you done?" Kai said.

"I'll tell you what I think—"

"We don't care what you think," Teresa said.

"And if you say one word about those stupid baseballs," Brad said, "I'm going to punch you in the face." When Chuck saw Brad's clenched fist, he quieted.

"What's the plan, Kai?" Brad said.

"Let's find a way off the roof," Kai said. "Then we'll climb the stairs to the top of the tower."

Brad looked up at the cooling tower. He turned back to Kai with a dubious expression. He didn't want to go into another building.

"What if it's not tall enough?" he asked.

"That's why Stan is going to stay here and use his radio to try to find another helicopter."

Stan nodded and got back into the chopper, where he started to transmit a Mayday.

"Everyone else, stay here," Kai said. "Brad and I will find a way down."

"Don't leave us!" Lani cried, and then broke into sobs. She ran to Kai and threw her arms around him.

"I'll be right back, honey." Kai wanted to comfort her—wanted *her* to comfort *him*—but there just wasn't time. He glanced at Teresa.

"I'll take care of Lani," she said. "Just hurry."

Kai broke away from Lani and jogged across the expansive roof in the direction of the tower with Brad next to him.

"I'm sorry, Kai," Brad said. "About Rachel."

Kai didn't say anything, not because he didn't appreciate Brad's sentiment, but because he couldn't afford to break down. He put his hand on Brad's shoulder for a moment and left it at that.

The roof of the office complex was multileveled, and they had landed on the lowest level. Kai could see where ladders to the higher levels had been ripped from their mountings.

After a minute they reached the edge of the roof nearest the tower. They hadn't been able to spot any stairs leading from the roof. Kai peered over the side.

The water had completely drained, leaving behind the ubiquitous ooze glistening on the few chunks of grass that were left. Next to the control tower, a pile of debris that looked like remnants of an airplane rested against the side of the building. It had been deposited in such a way that they might be able to climb down it.

"Come on," Kai said.

One at a time they picked their way down. The junk was sturdy, settling only a couple of times as they descended.

The outside of the tower was blocked by the debris. The only way in was through the office building. Kai couldn't see any doors, but all of the windows had been blown out, so he heaved himself over one of the sills and Brad followed.

The room was a standard office that had been swept clean by the water. They emerged into a hallway leading in the direction of the tower. Rounding the corner, they found that the door to the control tower stairwell had been ripped from its hinges.

Now Kai saw that the pile of debris didn't end outside. It was resting against the tower because it was part of a larger piece of the airplane that had broken through the tower's outer wall. On the piece of aluminum skin facing them, Kai could just make out a blue and white logo and the letters *Tra*. It was the remains of a TransPacific airliner.

A portion of a wing surface blocked the stairs for two stories. Kai couldn't see any way around it. There was no way to get to their refuge.

CHAPTER 54

KAI LEANED AGAINST THE wall and slowly shook his head. "It was my idea to land here," he said.

"Don't beat yourself up about it," Brad said. "It was a good idea."

"What was I thinking, Brad?"

"What do you mean?"

"I can't even save my own family. What made me think I could save everyone else?"

Brad started to speak, then stopped. His face had a puzzled look. "Did you really think you could save everyone? That that was your job?"

"Of course that was my job!"

"No. It wasn't. Your job was to give everyone else a chance. To warn them. You did that. I saw you do it. You can't save everyone. People have to save themselves. You gave them a chance to do that. After that, it's up to the Big Man upstairs."

Kai stared at Brad, truly surprised. He had never heard Brad mention any religious beliefs before. It just wasn't something they talked about.

Brad saw the stunned look and said, "Hey, how do you think I got through that scuba diving bit? Now, enough with the pep talk. Let's go figure out another way out of this mess."

With that, Kai pulled himself together. If they were going to get out of this, gnawing self-doubt would not help them.

They climbed the debris back onto the roof and ran to the now-silent helicopter.

"So can we get up there?" Teresa asked. The others looked at Kai expectantly.

He shook his head. "It's completely blocked. It'll take too much time to try moving it."

"Oh, this is just perfect!" Chuck exclaimed before Brad shot him a look and shut him up. Denise ignored him, as if she wanted nothing more to do with him.

Stan seemed to be having a conversation on his headset.

"Stan," Kai said, "please tell us you found a helicopter."

Stan wrapped up his discussion and removed the headset. He climbed out of the helicopter and looked up.

"No," Stan said, "I still can't find any. None will respond to my hails."

"Then who were you talking to?"

"I have another pilot who says he might be able to get us."

"You just said there weren't any other helicopters," Chuck said.

"There aren't." Stan pointed straight up. "Look there."

At first, Kai didn't see what Stan was talking about, mostly because he expected a helicopter. Then a glint of metal directly overhead flashed in the sun.

"That's a plane," Chuck said, master of the obvious.

"An Air Force C-130," Stan said. "He's got an alternative solution."

Kai spun around. The runway next to the office building was pitted with holes where the concrete was torn up. The sections that were still intact were strewn with garbage and airplane parts.

"He'll never be able to land here," Kai said.

"He says that he can spot a section of the reef runway that is clear—at least, clear enough for him. Those babies can land on anything as long as it's flat."

The control tower and its office building stood in the center of the airport. The reef runway was reclaimed land built on a coral outcropping at the airport's southernmost point.

"That's got to be a mile away," Kai said.

"Given where he said he'd have to land," Stan said, "I'd say more like a mile and a half."

Kai looked at his watch, which continued to tick despite all it had been through. Seven minutes left.

"We'll never make it, even if we all run."

"We're not going to run," Stan said. "We're going to drive."

CHAPTER 55

AS PROMISED, THE C-130 swooped down and, from Kai's vantage point, looked like it was landing on the water itself. It came to a stop, still far in the distance, and its rear cargo door lowered.

The transport had just entered Hawaiian airspace and was headed to Wheeler when the pilot, a Captain Martin Wainwright, heard Stan's plea over the radio. Wainwright had gotten a bright idea and volunteered to help.

It was the cargo that was particularly relevant: three Humvees headed for Pearl Harbor. The cargo door lowered to disgorge one of them.

"Come on," Kai said. "Let's cut the distance that guy has to come get us."

Brad spotted a section of the partially collapsed roof that they could easily slide down to get to ground level. When all of them were safely down, they started jogging in the direction of the reef runway. Brad carried Mia on his back, and Kai carried Lani. Teresa, Stan, and Tom jogged behind them. Chuck and Denise were in fairly good shape, so they could keep up—not that any of them could go fast anyway. The muck was slippery, and there was standing water everywhere.

Just a few seconds into their trot, Stan ran through what, on the surface, looked like just a shallow puddle.

But when he stepped into it, his leg sank up to his knee, and he fell facefirst into a pool of water two feet deep.

"Dammit!" he yelled, sputtering the filthy water from his mouth.

"You okay?" Kai said, helping him out.

"I'm fine. The water's so dirty, I couldn't see the hole."

"Well, let's try to steer around water where we can't see the bottom."

"You think?" said Chuck. "You're a genius." He kept running.

Brad made a move toward him, but Kai put his hand on Brad's shoulder and shook his head. They didn't need the distraction. After Stan's plunge, they had to constantly make detours around obvious holes, standing water, and wreckage. Their progress slowed considerably.

"This is a dumb idea," said Chuck. "I bet that pilot could have found a helicopter if he'd tried harder."

"Why don't you shut up?" said Brad. "I'm sick of your bitching. If you had been smart enough not to go back to your apartment, you wouldn't be out here with us."

"I don't have to shut up. I can say anything I want."

"Well, why don't you say thanks to me for not tossing you out of that helicopter?"

After inching down the cargo ramp for what seemed like an eternity, the Humvee roared off in their direction. With all the debris on the ground, it would still take a few minutes for the Humvee to get to them. They would be cutting it close.

The cargo ramp lifted, and the plane pivoted so that it would be ready for takeoff.

While Brad and Chuck verbally duked it out, Denise came closer to Kai.

"I'm sorry about my husband," Denise said. "He's a jerk."

"I noticed," Kai replied.

"I can't believe I've stayed with him so long. Listen, thanks for saving us. If it wasn't for you, we'd still be on that building."

"You're welcome."

"You know, you look really familiar," Denise said. "Have I seen you somewhere?"

"Maybe. My name's Kai. Kai Tanaka. I work at the Pacific Tsunami Warning Center. Or worked, I should say."

"Right!" she said. "I saw you on TV this morning."

"Wait a minute!" said Chuck, overhearing their conversation. "I saw you too. Whatever they were paying you, it was too much."

Brad grabbed Chuck from behind and wrenched him to a stop.

"If it wasn't for him," Brad said, "nobody would have had any time to evacuate."

"Get out of my face," Chuck said. "He screwed up, and now we're running for our lives because of it."

"He lost more than you'll ever know today."

"Well, he deserves it."

Anger flared across Brad's face, and without another word, he belted Chuck in the jaw. Chuck went down hard on his back. He lay there stunned for a moment and then picked himself up. None of the others moved a muscle to help him.

When Chuck was fully standing, he continued looking at the ground. Apparently he was a big mouth with nothing to back it up. Kai understood that the guy was scared, but that didn't mean he had to like him.

With Mia still clinging to his back, Brad walked to

within three inches of Chuck's face and loomed over him. Brad had a good four inches and thirty pounds on him.

"Now, you're going to keep your mouth shut, or we're going to leave your sorry butt out here. Got it?"

Chuck didn't look at him, but he didn't say anything, either. He got it.

"Come on," Kai said. "The farther we run, the sooner we'll be on that Humvee."

In a minute, the Humvee was less than a half mile from them. It closed in on them at a high speed that bordered on reckless. The mud was no match for its huge tires and ground clearance, so the driver took as straight a line toward them as the debris on the airfield would allow, instead of following what was left of the airstrip concrete. Splashes of water periodically shot into the air as it pounded through large pools.

"I know we're in a hurry," Teresa said, "but that guy better watch out—"

Before she could finish her sentence, the Humvee nose-dived into another pool. This time a massive plume sprayed twenty feet high in front of the vehicle and it came to a dead stop, its front submerged in a rut three feet deep. The engine sputtered and quit.

They all skidded to a halt, their mouths agape at seeing their only way to safety literally dead in the water.

CHAPTER 56

Kai sprinted to the Humvee. It was one of the models that look like an enormous pickup truck, with the back of the Humvee open to the air. The driver's door swung open. An airman in a green uniform stumbled out and fell into the pool. He was the only one in the vehicle. He clambered out of the hole, his hand over his forehead.

Brad and Kai got there first and let Mia lean on Lani.

"Are you all right?" Kai said.

"Yes, sir. Hit my head on the steering wheel. Guess I should have worn the seat belt. No air bag."

He lifted his hand, and Kai could see a nasty gash above his right eyebrow. The blood flowed down into his eye.

"That'll make a great scar," Brad said.

Chuck and Stan came to stop behind them, followed by Tom, Denise, and Teresa.

"Let me look at that," Teresa said, and put pressure on the wound.

"Are you the pilot?" Chuck asked. Why he thought the man would be the pilot, Kai had no idea.

"Loadmaster," the crewman replied. "Airman Darrin Peabody. Sorry about crashing the truck."

"How old are you?" Chuck asked. "Thirteen?"

"I'm twenty, sir."

"Great! They sent a teenager to save us."

"I said shut your mouth," Brad said, and Chuck did. "It's all right, Airman. Stan over there took a header a few minutes ago."

"I'd love to introduce you to everyone," Kai said, climbing into the Humvee's driver's seat, "but we need to get out of here right now." Peabody was in no condition to drive.

"Oh, no!" Brad said. "Move over. You drive like an old lady."

"What's the best way to get this thing unstuck?" Kai asked Peabody.

"Jeez, I don't know. I've only driven these things a couple of times, and that was just to get it on the plane. My job is to make sure it's loaded right."

"Never mind," Brad said, putting it into gear and starting it up. "It's like any other truck, just a lot bigger."

The engine wasn't entirely submerged, or they might really have been out of luck. The front of the Humvee rested against the edge of the hole, which looked like a less solid part of a taxiway that had been stripped away from the concrete where it met the runway. The back wheels were up on the remaining concrete, so the truck sat at a steep angle.

Everyone stepped back, and Brad threw it in reverse. The four-wheel drive bit at the pavement under the back wheels and the mud below the front. Water and mud sprayed high into the air in front of the vehicle. He put it in first, with the same sprinkler effect in the other direction. The Humvee rolled slightly back and forth but didn't make any progress.

The radio in the Humvee crackled.

"Dare! Are you all right? Dare, what happened?"

"That's our pilot, Captain Wainwright," Peabody said.

"Dare! Airman Peabody! Come in!"

Brad grabbed the mouthpiece.

"Captain, Dare's got a bump on his noggin, but he'll be okay."

"Who is this?"

"This is Brad. I'll get back to you in a minute. We're trying to get this SUV out of a hole."

"What do you mean? What's going on?" Captain Wainwright continued to call, but Brad was right. They didn't have time to waste explaining the situation.

"This isn't working," Kai said to Brad. "Try turning the wheel to the left. The hole doesn't look as steep on that side. If you can get the whole Humvee down in there, you might be able to climb out."

"Are you crazy?" said Chuck. "He'll stall out if he gets the whole thing down there."

"Shut up!" Kai said. "Brad, what do you think?"

"It's worth a try. My way still might work, but not in time."

Brad cranked the wheel to the left and floored the gas. The Humvee rotated a little to the left and then stopped.

"It's stuck on something. Everybody push on the back left of the truck. Even you, Chuckles. If I spin the wheels, the traction should be low enough on this mud to push it."

"This is a waste of time," Chuck said, although he lined up on the left rear fender with the rest of them except for Lani and Mia. "This thing must weigh a couple of tons."

"Ready?" Brad said.

"Yes!" they all yelled, their feet planted as firmly as possible.

"Start pushing as soon as I gun it."

Brad revved the engine and then dropped the clutch. The water didn't spray right at them because he had the front wheels turned, but they were getting soaked anyway from the backsplash on the undercarriage. The back wheels started spinning, and that was their cue to push.

"Go!" Kai yelled. He pushed, using up whatever adrenaline he had left. This was their one chance out of there, and he wasn't leaving anything in reserve.

At first, nothing seemed to happen. Kai was about to let up when he heard Brad yell.

"It's working!"

That gave Kai an extra burst of energy, and finally he felt the back end give. The rotation of the Humvee accelerated, and the right rear wheel slipped off the concrete.

"Come on, baby!" Brad yelled.

Then the left rear reached the edge of the hole. They gave one last heave, and with a big splash the back end of the Humvee dropped into the hole.

Brad didn't let up on the gas, and after an agonizing moment when it seemed like the Humvee would bog down, it sprang forward and launched itself out of the muck.

Everyone whooped with joy, and Brad leaned out of the window.

"Anyone want a ride?"

Kai put Mia in the backseat and jumped in the front passenger seat next to Brad. The rest of them climbed into the rear.

When they were all aboard, Brad jammed the pedal to the floor, and they hurtled forward.

"Why don't you let the captain know we're on our way? I'd better keep my eyes on the road."

Kai picked up the transmitter.

"Captain, this is Kai Tanaka, one of the people you so kindly agreed to pick up. We're out of the mud and on our way."

"Good. What's your ETA?"

"I think it took Peabody about two minutes to get here, so I'm guessing the same for the trip back. Captain, can you see if the water is receding?"

"What?"

"If you can see the shoreline moving seaward, that means the tsunami is almost here."

There was silence on the other end for a second, as if they were discussing something. Then he came back on.

"Uh, Mr. Tanaka," Wainwright said. "The shoreline is so far out, I can hardly see it. Make it quick. I mean *real* quick."

"You better believe it," Brad said.

Brad followed the tracks that Peabody had made getting to them as closely as he could, knowing that the path was safe. It was the bumpiest ride Kai had ever experienced, and the people in the back were thrown around viciously.

After another minute they were back on smooth concrete, and it was a straight shot to the plane directly in front of them.

"Look at that," said Peabody. The sight was familiar to everyone else, but he was in awe at seeing it for the first time. In the distance, the ocean rose precipitously. Kai had lost track of time, and now they were out of it. The massive tsunami kept climbing into the air as it rushed toward the runway. It looked to be about a half mile from the end of the runway where the C-130 sat.

Captain Wainwright came back on.

"Do you see that, Mr. Tanaka?"

"We see it. How long will it take you to lift off the runway from a dead stop?"

"It'll take a little longer because of the state of the runway. Maybe thirty seconds."

Kai did the mental calculation. Without time to analyze the data, he couldn't be sure of anything. But he couldn't take the chance, and so he made the call.

"Start your takeoff roll now," Kai said.

"What? But you're less than three hundred yards away! We're not leaving without you."

"Believe me, I don't plan on you leaving us."

"Then we'll wait."

"Captain, you don't understand. Waiting will kill us all. If you don't start your takeoff roll right now, that plane will never get off the ground."

CHAPTER 57

THE C-130'S PROPELLERS SPUN up to full speed in preparation for takeoff.

"Are you insane?" Chuck screamed. "You just told him to take off without us!"

Kai ignored him.

"Listen to me, Captain," he said, not only for Wainwright's benefit, but for everyone in the Humvee. "We're going to come up behind you and jump onto the cargo door, so keep it lowered." They couldn't drive onto the plane because, although the door was lowered, it couldn't contact the runway during takeoff. "That way, you can take off as soon as we're all on board."

"I get it. A running start. I'll keep the speed down as long as I can, but I've only got about six thousand feet of clear runway, and there's a big-ass hole at the end. We're on our way."

The plane lurched forward and started moving down the runway. The Humvee was now only two hundred yards behind and closing quickly.

"Let's change places," Kai said to Brad.

"No way! You know I'm the better driver."

"I don't care. Move!"

"It's too dangerous. And you're crazy if you think I'm stopping."

Kai lowered his voice.

"Brad, someone's got to be at the wheel to hold it steady while the rest of us get on. And I don't see a cruise control."

Brad let it hang there for a second without answering. "I'll figure something out," he finally said.

"What?"

"I've got an idea."

"What?"

"Dammit, Kai! I don't have time to explain. Let me concentrate."

The huge tail of the C-130 loomed in front of them. An Air Force crewman stood at the back of the plane, hanging on to a strap and beckoning them to get closer.

To their left, the tsunami grew to gigantic proportions, heading at them on an angle. It wouldn't swamp the runway all at once, but would hit the part in back of them first. Because of the angle, the wave would be chasing them down the runway at an effective speed of about 150 miles an hour, far above the Humvee's top speed of seventy.

Their closing speed with the aircraft slowed, but Brad had the accelerator floored. Kai could see the airman in the plane talking into a headset, and the plane decelerated a little, allowing them to catch up.

When the Humvee was within five feet of the plane, Chuck jumped up from the rear truck bed. He scrambled over the cab and onto the hood directly in front of Brad.

"You idiot!" Brad yelled. "I can't see!"

"Wait until he's closer!" Kai yelled to Chuck.

But Chuck didn't listen. In his impatience to get on the plane, he couldn't wait until they got closer than three feet. He ran forward, and just as he was about to jump, the Humvee hit a piece of debris on the runway.

The jolt sent Chuck reeling sideways, and before the airman in the plane could grab him, he fell off the side of the Humvee and tumbled onto the runway.

Denise screamed as she watched Chuck's cartwheeling body. Kai didn't say what he was thinking, which was that even if Chuck survived the fall, there was no time to turn around and get him.

The Humvee rammed against the back of the C-130.

"Now!" Kai said as he crawled into the backseat. "Hurry!"

Denise, Peabody, Tom, and Stan, who were in the back of the Humvee, climbed onto the roof. Kai followed Teresa and Lani out the open back window, then pulled Mia through.

Tom and then Denise quickly crossed to the plane without incident. Peabody was next. With his blurred vision, he misjudged the step onto the cargo door. He lost his footing on the front of the hood and dropped onto his back, his butt suspended in a space that had opened up between the C-130 and the Humvee.

There was no way Peabody could pull himself up. The airman inside the plane let go of his strap, but he couldn't reach Peabody's hand. Stan pulled Peabody up by his shoulders. Together they stood, and with Peabody's arm around his shoulder, Stan ran and jumped onto the deck of the C-130. They both went down spread-eagled, and the airman pulled them out of the way.

Teresa grabbed Kai, who now had Mia on his back.

"Be careful," she said.

"Don't worry. I've got her."

"Okay. I'll take Lani with me."

Kai looked at his daughter. He saw no fear, only determination. "I can do it, Dad," she said.

Kai's thoughts flashed through everything she'd accomplished today—towing Mia to safety, coming up with the idea for how to use the raft, showing such stamina after nearly drowning—and realized she was right.

"I know you can," he said. "Now, go!"

Using the wide rooftop rack as a brace, Teresa and Lani pulled themselves over the Humvee's roof.

Kai stole a quick look behind him. Chuck, who was futilely chasing the plane, slipped in the muck and fell. As he pushed himself up on his knees, he turned to see a wall of water three hundred feet high tower over him, blocking the midday sun. Chuck raised his arms as if he were Moses trying to part the Red Sea, and then he was absorbed by the wall as it surged onto the runway. He was gone.

Kai, numbed by the day's experiences, couldn't bring himself to feel sorry for Chuck.

Once Teresa and Lani were on the hood, Kai clambered over the Humvee's roof, pulling Mia sloppily with him. Holding Teresa's hand, Lani jumped onto the plane's cargo door, where she grabbed the airman's outstretched arm. She tottered for a second and then collapsed with Teresa to the deck, out of harm's way. Kai breathed a sigh of relief.

The airman frantically waved to Kai, so he knew there was little time left before the C-130 would have to take off. He stood and hoisted Mia onto his back. Even with the plane blocking the wind, the current of air was strong enough to push him to the side, and he misplaced his foot on an edge of the hood. He heard Teresa's scream faintly over the rush of air and the airplane's engines.

Mia tilted her body to the side, helping Kai right himself before he fell. With a last burst of adrenaline, he leaned toward the airplane and made a dash across the hood. He leapt onto the cargo floor, and the airman caught him.

Kai retained his footing and passed Mia to Teresa. He grabbed a strap that the airman handed to him and spun around to see what Brad had planned.

The tsunami was so close to their flank now that, with the tail of the aircraft blocking Kai's view, he couldn't see the top of it unless he looked straight back. The solid mass of water dwarfed the Humvee.

Brad was talking into the radio transmitter. He had a big smile on his face, but it belied the sadness in his eyes. The plane pulled away from the Humvee. That was his plan all along. Kai locked eyes with Brad and shook his head.

"Don't do this," he mouthed, knowing that Brad would never be able to hear him.

Brad pointed at Kai and gave him a thumbs-up. As Kai continued to stare at him, the plane lifted into the air. He could see Brad's smile grow even bigger when he saw the plane take flight. That was Kai's last image of Brad— smiling, his eyes shining with tears—as the tsunami overtook him and swallowed the Humvee.

They had barely gained the required three hundred feet before the tsunami passed underneath them by only a few yards, the turbulent air causing the plane to buck. The wave was so close that Kai tasted the salty spray.

"Are you Kai?" the airman on the plane asked.

Kai nodded dumbly, completely drained.

The airman handed Kai the headset.

"The captain wants to talk to you."

Kai put the headset on.

"Yes?"

"Kai? This is Captain Wainwright. Your brother told me that it was more important for you to get on the plane than him. I talked to him right before the end. He had a message for you. He said, quote, 'Kai, don't worry about me. I'm not afraid of the water anymore. Take care of my niece for me. I love you, brother.' End quote."

Captain Wainwright paused, but Kai didn't have anything to say.

"I'm very sorry for your loss," he said.

"Me too," Kai said, and tore the headset off.

He sagged to the deck of the aircraft, and for the last time that day, he cried.

Chapter 58

WHEN THE C-130 LANDED at Wheeler, Denise and Stan went their own ways, leaving Kai and Teresa to find treatment for the injuries that Tom, Lani, and Mia had sustained. They were in the same circumstance as thousands of others who crowded around the edges of the runway tarmac.

Wheeler had its own small oil power plant, so it was self-sufficient in case of island power outages. With all of the coastal power plants wiped out, it was one of the few places on Oahu that still had electricity.

Displaced residents and tourists from all over Oahu had converged on the air base as a safe haven. Thirty-five jets had been forced to land because they didn't have enough fuel to return to the mainland. They packed every bit of spare concrete at the air field, including a long-abandoned runway. Since the base didn't normally accommodate airliners, there were no motorized stairs or walkways for the planes to unload. Most sat there still full of passengers, while others had disgorged using their emergency slides.

Tripler Army Medical Center had rapidly filled to capacity with patients requiring use of its trauma center, so all other injuries and illnesses were routed to a temporary triage center set up in a hangar at Wheeler. That's where Kai took his daughter for treatment.

Kai stopped, speechless, as he took in the enormity of what had happened. Before him was an image he had seen previously only on TV. Row upon row of people were being tended to by dozens of men and women, some in uniform, some in scrubs, some in civilian clothing. Because the disaster had happened so fast, only a limited supply of cots was available. Most patients lay on blankets or stretchers on the hangar floor. Many of the victims moaned or wailed, some from injuries, others from the mental anguish of their loss.

An Army lieutenant directed them to a second hangar, where they saw a similar scene of woe. A nurse found an empty space for the children to lie down and gave them some blankets. When she found out that Teresa was a doctor, she took her aside, out of earshot of the kids, who dropped to the floor, exhausted from the ordeal.

After a minute, Teresa returned. "They're short of doctors," she said.

"I'm not surprised," Kai said. Hundreds of people lined the floor in this hangar alone. He could only guess how many more there were.

"I need to go. Lani will be okay. I don't think there's any permanent damage. Tom's shoulder will need to be checked out by an orthopedist. And Mia needs an MRI, but that won't happen until we can get back to the mainland. The nurse said nobody has any spare clothes yet, so we'll just have to dry out until we can get some."

Tom massaged his shoulder, but he seemed more intent on looking around the hangar.

"When you find someone in authority," Kai said, "let them know that Tom is looking for his parents." Then he realized that even after all he had gone through with the boy, Kai still didn't know one important detail about him.

"Tom," Kai said. "What's your last name?"

"Medlock," Tom replied, understanding why he was being asked. "My parents are Joseph and Belinda Medlock."

"I've got it," Teresa said. "We'll find them, Tom." More quietly, she said to Kai, "Listen, I'm just . . . Oh, God . . . I mean, Rachel . . ." Before she could finish, she burst into tears and grasped Kai in a hug. After a few moments she pulled away. "I'll be back as soon as I can."

Teresa took a breath to compose herself, then made her way toward the front of the hangar. Kai turned his attention back to Lani and Mia.

Neither of them spoke. Mia stared off into the distance, and Lani slowly flipped through the photo album Kai had saved. It was hard to believe these were the same girls who had been so chatty this morning.

Kai knelt down and smiled at Lani.

"How are you feeling?" he said.

"I'm just coughing a little."

"You're going to be fine," Kai said. "You're going to be fine."

"Why, Daddy?" Lani cried. "I want Mommy! I want Uncle Brad!"

Lani put her face in her hands and bawled loudly. Kai comforted her the best that he could, taking his own comfort in her vitality.

"I know, sweetie," Kai said. "I want them too."

Eventually, her sobs lessened until she just moaned into his shoulder.

A warm puff of air tickled Kai's ear. He turned just in time for Bilbo to lick his face energetically.

"Bilbo!" Lani said, and the dog sprang to her. Lani lavished him with coos and pats.

Kai looked up to see a massive brown hand held out to him.

"Glad you made it," Reggie Pona said, pulling Kai to his feet, then throwing his arms around him. "I thought we'd lost you a few times."

"If you hadn't sent help for us, you would have."

"I saw Teresa back there," Reggie said, pointing to the hangar entrance. "She seems okay. Are you girls all right?"

Lani and Mia nodded, focusing most of their interest on Bilbo. Kai knew Reggie wanted to hear about what happened. The dog was just what the girls needed to comfort them after the ordeal.

"Let's take a walk, Reggie. Lani, take care of Bilbo. I'll be back in a little bit." Kai saw her start to protest, so he held up his hand to stop her. "I swear that I will not drive or fly anywhere without you. We'll just be outside."

As they stepped out of the hangar, two trucks screeched to a halt and began unloading passengers and supplies.

"Let's get some privacy," Reggie said, leading the way down the tarmac. "I saw a good place on my way here. You don't know how glad I was to hear you landed."

Kai didn't answer. After a few moments of silence, he said, "Is it over?"

"The DART buoy says we're in the clear. That last monster was absolutely unbelievable. Three hundred feet! I mean, everything's gone for three miles inland in some places."

"I know. I saw it when we were in the air."

"Oh. Right."

Another silence.

"Teresa told me about Rachel and Brad," Reggie said. "I don't know what to say. I'm really sorry."

Reggie was tactfully leaving it open for him to say more, but Kai wasn't in the mood to discuss the details.

"Who's handling the warning duties now?" he said, knowing Reggie wouldn't have left his post without making sure it was covered.

"George and Mary finally showed up. They're on the phone with Alaska. I left them in charge so I could take a break and come find you. The first wave won't reach California for another two hours. The West Coast should be pretty well evacuated by then. Given the TV coverage, you'd have to be a grade-A moron to stay by the ocean today."

Reggie stopped at the base of what looked like a World War II–era watchtower at least seventy feet in height. Although it hadn't been used in years, it still looked sturdy enough.

"Should be a little quieter up there," he said.

Kai shrugged and followed him up the stairs. At the top, they were treated to an expansive view that stretched all the way to the shoreline five miles to the south. The fresh breeze felt good on Kai's face, carrying away the stink of his sodden clothes.

"This is going to get worse before it gets better, you know," Kai said. "A lot worse."

"Tell me about it. All the power stations are knocked out. It could take a year to build new ones. They've already estimated at least three hundred thousand homeless on Oahu alone."

"We're two of them."

"Right," Reggie said. "I wonder where we're going to sleep tonight."

Kai wondered *when* he was going to be able to sleep again. All he could think of was Rachel, trying to fix her image in his mind before it faded. The twinkle in her eye when she knew Kai was going to unleash a dreadful pun. Her delightful bray of laughter at Lani's wrestling matches with the dog. The touch of her lips. The smell of her hair when she curled up with him just before they fell asleep. Without her, sleep would be a long time coming.

"Looks like we'll have to bed down in the airport hangars for now," Kai said. "With only one working runway in the entire island chain, any airlift is going to go slowly."

"Hell, I don't know how they're even going to get jet fuel up here to fill up all these planes," Reggie replied. "I heard someone from the government talk about resupplying Hawaii with the biggest ship convoy since World War II. Who knows how long that will take? At least two weeks before it gets here. I bet they move half the population to the mainland—"

"Reggie," Kai interrupted. "Do you mind if we just stand here for a few minutes and not talk?"

Reggie nodded and leaned against the railing. Kai just wanted to have a moment to himself before facing the reality of the hardships to come.

So they stood there silently, reflecting on their losses and contemplating the future, staring at the flat blue ocean serenely shimmering in the distance.

EPILOGUE

KAI SAT BACK FROM his laptop and stared out at Mount Rainier from his new house as he lost his concentration yet again. Even this late in the spring, the lower slopes of the peak were still covered with snow. The cool weather of Seattle didn't bother him nearly as much as he remembered. He actually liked the crisp air now, but that wasn't why he had moved back to Washington.

And it wasn't the fact that Puget Sound was a hundred miles from the Pacific. Despite the move, the ocean was never far from his mind, nor were the images of that terrible day in Honolulu.

It always struck him as odd that, with all the videography available from these kinds of time-stopping events, the most iconic images seemed to come from photos.

The sight of the USS *Arizona*, exposed to the air for the first time in over sixty years after it was sunk on the day that pulled America into World War II, washed inland and coming to rest alongside the USS *Missouri*, the ship on which the Japanese surrender was signed, ending the war.

The photos of Honolulu taken from the lip of Diamond Head the day before and the day after the tsunami hit, one showing a bustling metropolis, the other a landscape laid bare for miles.

The aerial photo of Punchbowl National Cemetery, a memorial to those who have died in the service of their country, teeming with the life of those who were protected and saved from the tsunami by its very location.

It was the Punchbowl image with which Kai identified most, and the one he had framed on his wall. It represented everything he did right on that day. He could honestly say that those people would not be alive if it weren't for him and Reggie. It didn't let his conscience completely off the hook for all the thousands who had died, but it was what let him sleep at night now.

He had come to terms with some of the decisions he made. Not all of them. But enough to let him not just mourn the dead but to celebrate the survivors and remember the sacrifices some made so that others would live.

Survivors like Harold and Gina Franklin, who, when seeing the utter destruction of Christmas Island, improbably sailed with the rest of the *Seabiscuit* passengers all the way to the Hawaiian Islands after they realized no one would be coming to rescue them. They and the nine people with them remained the sole survivors of that lonely atoll.

Max Walsh, the assistant manager responsible for saving the lives of sixty-three veterans and their wives, who couldn't have known that staying for just a few more minutes on the Grand Hawaiian rooftop might have made such a difference in Kai's life.

Sheila Wendel and her mother Doris, who touched down at Tripler Army Medical Center only a few minutes after leaving the Grand Hawaiian. Jerry Wendel—for whom Rachel made the ultimate sacrifice—who survived surgery to relieve a subdural hematoma.

Paige Rogers and her children, who couldn't return to their home in Los Angeles until two weeks after the tsunami hit.

Tom Medlock, who was reunited with his parents after three days of searching.

Others had not been so fortunate.

Darryl and Eunice Gaithers, the elderly couple from Mississippi who Teresa had met on the beach, probably returned to the doomed Hilton and stayed in their room until the hotel collapsed. They were never heard from again.

As Kai suspected, the two videographers who had filmed the collapse of The Seaside never got to sell their tape to the networks.

The body of Jake Ferguson washed up on the beach five days later. His family, who lived in Michigan and had sent Jake on vacation to visit his friend Tom, finally made it to Hawaii to claim his remains six weeks after the disaster, consoling themselves only with the details Kai could tell them about Jake's heroic efforts.

These people's endurance under extraordinary circumstances was a testament to the spirit of humanity, a spirit he saw in his own family.

Rachel and Brad stood proudly in his memory as representatives of the best the human race can offer, as symbols of why people would want to go to such great lengths to protect civilization from harm. He wished he could have understood everything that went through their minds on that day, their last day. But he took pride in their actions, the same kind of selfless deeds so many others performed on that terrible morning.

Kai took the same pride in his team, that their warnings saved countless lives around the Pacific Rim. Even though the effects of the tsunami on the rest of the Pacific weren't as powerful as they were in Hawaii, many island nations were devastated and suffered horribly. Over 125,000 lives lost in total, 36,000 of them on the Hawaiian islands, but far fewer than had died in the South Asian tsunami. And although the structural damage along the coasts of the mainland United States, Australia, and Japan was catastrophic, only fifty-seven people in those locations lost their lives.

The recovery of the Hawaiian economy had been stronger than expected. Construction cranes from all over the world dominated the Honolulu skyline. Not surprisingly, people had short memories and were rebuilding huge new hotels and houses right along the reconfigured Hawaiian shoreline, certain that such a disaster would never again happen in their lifetimes. Kai hoped they were right. But he was hedging his bets, and he knew others were too.

One of them was Reggie Pona. In his new post as assistant director of the Pacific Tsunami Warning Center, Reggie gave Kai a tour of the facility where it was rebuilt inside Diamond Head crater, right next to the Hawaii State Civil Defense bunker. With more foresight and more money, that's where it should have been located all along. Now the money was plentiful, and when the next tsunami comes for Hawaii—and it will come—they will be supremely ready and able to handle it.

After the disaster, Kai felt the pull to teach. There was nothing left for him in Hawaii, and he enjoyed working with students. He had applied for a position in the University of Washington's geology department, and they gladly welcomed him. The job didn't allow him to forget about the past, but it did let him focus on the future.

"Kai," he heard from the doorway, "we're going to be late for the movie. Shut that down and let's go."

"Yeah, come on, Dad."

He turned to see Teresa in the doorway, flanked by Lani and Mia. Teresa had finished her residency and continued on at the University of Washington as an attending physician. Kai and Teresa were good friends, and they saw each other often, especially because of the girls.

The emotions of that day were still too raw for him to date anyone. Someday, maybe, when the time was right, when his grief for Rachel wasn't so sharp, he'd be able to love someone again. But that time still seemed a long way off.

Kai often had doubts about what was right, that what he was doing with his life was worthwhile. He struggled with it every day.

The night before the tsunami, Rachel and Kai had listened to Teresa's stories about her experiences as a doctor with rapt attention. Teresa dealt with death on a daily basis, which had affected her profoundly. Kai would never forget one thing she said about it during that discussion, when she was telling them about a daughter who made it to her elderly mother's bedside in time to say her last good-byes.

"She said she was happy that she was able to talk to her mother one last time," Teresa said. "She said she was happy to see her mother pass away peacefully."

"You sound like you don't believe her," Rachel said.

"Oh, she smiled, and she seemed relieved to be there, but happy? No."

"Why not?"

"Life never has a happy ending," Teresa said. "It always ends in death. Death can be dignified or wretched, agonizing or painless, horrifying or serene, untimely or welcome. But it's always sad. Happiness comes from what you do with the time between the beginning and the end."

Now that Rachel was gone, Kai often wondered what she would want him to do with the rest of his life. As he closed his laptop, he looked at Lani smiling at him, and he thought he knew.

Rachel would want him to be happy.

AFTERWORD

ASTEROIDS ARE A VERY real threat to our planet. The story told in *Rogue Wave* is a dramatization of what would happen if one of them struck Earth, but it is not science fiction. When I visited the Pacific Tsunami Warning Center for my research, I spent three hours with the director, Chip McCreery, who graciously gave me a tour of the facility. The tour took place more than eighteen months before the Asian tsunami devastated Thailand, Sri Lanka, and Indonesia in December 2004. When I told him the plot to my story, he agreed that the scenario was indeed plausible.

The reason is that asteroids are very difficult to detect. As I mentioned in the novel, asteroid 2002 MN wasn't discovered until it had already passed by Earth. If that asteroid had hit the middle of the ocean, we may not have known about it until the first waves hit populated shores.

In the future, one of those asteroids won't miss. It may not be in my lifetime, but someday it *will* happen unless we do something to deflect the asteroid.

Spaceguard is a real entity scanning the skies for dangerous near-earth objects. They've identified Apophis, a near-Earth asteroid almost identical in size to the one in *Rogue Wave*. There is a 1-in-250,000 chance that it will hit Earth in 2036.

The computer models that I referenced in the novel are very real and are an example of extensive research into tsunamis caused by asteroid impact. Those models may not match up exactly with the size and frequency of waves I sent toward Honolulu in my book, but until we actually experience an asteroid impact, we have no real data. The computer models may be wrong.

None of that will stop me from vacationing in Hawaii, but when I'm lying on the beach, I'll keep my eye on the ocean.

Turn the page for a heart-pounding look at

THE ARK

Boyd Morrison

Coming soon in paperback
from Pocket Books

Also available in hardcover from Touchstone

ONE

Dilara Kenner wound her way through the international concourse of LAX, a well-worn canvas backpack her only luggage. It was a Thursday afternoon, and travelers crowded the vast terminal. Her plane from Peru had arrived at one-thirty, but it had taken her forty-five minutes to get through immigration and customs. The wait had seemed ten times that long. She was impatient to meet with Sam Watson, who had begged her to come back to the United States two days early.

Sam was an old friend of her father's and had become a surrogate uncle to her. Dilara had been surprised to get his call. She had stayed in touch with him in the years since her father had gone missing, but in the last six months she had spoken to him only once. When he had reached her on her cell phone in Peru, she had been in the Andes supervising the excavation of an Incan ruin. Sam had sounded unnerved, even scared, but he wouldn't elaborate about what the trouble was no matter how much Dilara prodded him. He insisted that he had to meet with her in person as soon as possible. His urgent pleas finally convinced her to turn the dig over to a subordinate and return before the job had been completed.

Sam also made one more request that Dilara found puzzling. She had to promise him that she wouldn't tell anyone why she was leaving Peru.

Sam was so eager to meet with her that he had asked to rendezvous with her in the airport. Their planned meeting spot was the terminal's second-level food court. She got onto the escalator behind an obese vacationer wearing a Hawaiian shirt and a bad sunburn. He was trailing a roller carry-on and stood blocking her path. His eyes settled on her, then looked her up and down slowly.

Dilara was still in the shorts and tank top she wore at the dig, and she became intensely aware of his attention. She had raven hair down to her shoulders, an olive tan that she didn't have to work for, and an athletic, long-legged frame that caused less discreet men to ogle her inappropriately like this creep was now.

She threw the sunburned guy a look that said *you've got to be kidding me*, then said, "Excuse me" and muscled her way past him. When she reached the top of the escalator, she scanned the massive food court until she spotted Sam sitting at a small table at the balcony railing.

The last time she had seen him, he was seventy-one. Now, a year later, he looked more like eighty-two than seventy-two. Frosty white tufts of hair still clung to his head, but the lines on his face seemed to be etched much more deeply, and he had a pallor that made him look like he hadn't slept in days.

When Sam saw Dilara, he stood and waved to her, a smile temporarily making his face look ten years younger. She returned his smile and made her way to him. Sam clasped her tightly to him.

"You don't know how glad I am to see you," Sam said. He held her at arm's length. "You're still the most beautiful woman I've ever met. Except perhaps for your mother."

Dilara fingered the locket around her neck, the one with the photo of her mother that her father had always carried. For a moment, her grin faltered and her eyes drifted away, lost in the memory of her parents. They quickly cleared and returned to Sam.

"You should see me caked with dirt and knee-deep in mud," Dilara said in her flat, midwestern cadence. "It might change your mind."

"A dusty jewel is still a jewel. How is the world of archaeology?"

They sat. Sam drank from a coffee cup. He had thoughtfully provided a cup for Dilara as well, and she took a sip before speaking.

"Busy as usual," she said. "I'm off to Mexico next. Some interesting disease vectors predating the European colonization."

"That sounds fascinating. Aztec?"

Dilara didn't answer. Her specialty was bio-archaeology, the study of the biological remains of ancient civilizations. Sam was a biochemist, so he had a passing interest in her field, but that wasn't why he was asking. He was stalling.

She leaned forward, took his hand, and gave it a comforting squeeze. "Come on, Sam. What's with the small talk? You didn't ask me to cut my trip short to talk about archaeology, did you?"

Sam glanced nervously at the people around him, his eyes flicking from one to the next, as if checking to see whether they were paying undue attention to him.

She followed his gaze. A Japanese family smiled and laughed as they munched on hamburgers. A lone businesswoman to her right typed on a PDA between bites of a salad. Even though it was early October, the summer vacation season long over, a group of teenagers who were dressed in identical T-shirts that said TEENS 4 JESUS sat at a table behind her, texting on their cell phones.

"Actually," Sam said, "archaeology is precisely what I want to talk to you about."

"You do? When you called, I'd never heard you so upset."

"It's because I have something very important to tell you."

Then his deteriorated condition made sense. Cancer, the same disease that took her mother twenty years ago. A breath caught in her throat. "Oh my God! You're not dying, are you?"

"No, no, dear. I shouldn't have worried you. Except for a little bursitis, I've never been fitter." Dilara felt herself sigh with relief.

"No," Sam continued, "I called you here because you're the only one I can trust. I need your counsel."

The businesswoman next to Sam picked up her salad plate and rose to leave, but the purse slipped off her lap to the floor near her feet, causing her to trip. She stumbled into Sam, who caught her.

"I'm sorry," the woman said with a light Slavic inflection while she retrieved her purse. "I'm so clumsy."

"I'm just glad you didn't take a bigger spill," Sam said.

She frowned when she looked down at Sam. "Oh no, I got salad dressing on your arm. Let me get that for you." She took a handkerchief from her purse, unfolded it, and dabbed his forearm. "At least you weren't wearing long sleeves."

"No harm done."

"Well, sorry again." She smiled at Sam and Dilara and headed for the trash can.

"You're as gallant as ever, Sam," Dilara said. "Now why do you need my counsel?"

Sam looked around again before speaking. He flexed his fingers, like he was working out a cramp. His eyes returned to Dilara. They were creased with worry. He hesitated before the words came out in a rush. "Three days ago, I made a startling discovery at work. It has to do with Hasad."

Dilara's heart jumped at the mention of her father, Hasad Arvadi, and she dug her fingers into her thighs to control the familiar surge of anxiety. He had been missing for three years, during which she had spent every spare moment in a fruitless attempt to find out what had happened to him. As far as she knew, he had never set foot in the pharmaceutical company where Sam worked.

"Sam, what are you talking about? You found something at your work about what happened to my father? I don't understand."

"I spent an entire day trying to decide whether to tell you about this. Whether to get you involved, I mean. I wanted to go to the police, but I don't have the proof yet. They might not believe me before it's too late. But I knew you would, and I need your advice. It's all starting next Friday."

"Eight days from now?"

Sam nodded and massaged his forehead.

"Headache?" she asked. "Do you want some aspirin?"

"I'll be okay. Dilara, what they're planning will kill millions, maybe billions."

"Kill billions?" she said, smiling. Sam was pulling her leg. "You're joking."

He shook his head solemnly. "I wish I were." Dilara searched his face for some hint of a prank, but all she could see was concern. After a moment, her smile vanished. He was serious.

"Okay," she said slowly. "You're not joking. But I'm confused. Proof of what? Who's 'they'? And what does this have to do with my father?"

"He found it, Dilara," Sam said in a lowered voice. "He actually found it."

She knew immediately what "it" was by the way Sam said it. Noah's Ark. The quest her father had dedicated his whole life to. She shook her head in disbelief.

"You mean, the actual boat that . . ." Dilara paused. The remaining color had drained from Sam's face. "Sam, are you sure you're all right? You look a little pale."

Sam clutched his chest, and his face twisted into a mask of agony. He doubled over in his seat and fell to the floor.

"My God! Sam!" Dilara threw her chair back and rushed over to him. She helped him lie flat and yelled at the teenagers with the cell phones. "Call 911!" After a paralyzed moment, one of them frantically dialed.

"Dilara, go!" Watson croaked.

"Sam, don't talk," she said, trying to keep her composure. "You're having a heart attack."

"Not heart attack . . . woman who dropped purse . . . handkerchief had contact poison . . ."

Poison? He was already delirious. "Sam—"

"No!" he yelled feebly. "You have to go . . . or they'll kill you, too. They murdered your father."

She stared at him in shock. Her deepest fear had always been that her father was dead, but she could never allow herself to give up hope. But now—*Sam knew. He knew what had happened to her father!* That's why he had called her here.

She started to speak, but Sam gripped her arm.

"Listen! Tyler Locke. Gordian Engineering. Get . . . his help. He knows . . . Coleman." He swallowed hard every few words. "Your father's research . . . started everything. You must . . . find the Ark." He started rambling. "Hayden . . . Project . . . Oasis . . . Genesis . . . Dawn . . ."

"Sam, please." This couldn't be happening. Not now. Not when she might finally get some answers.

"I'm sorry, Dilara."

"Who are 'they,' Sam?" She saw him fading and grasped his arms. "Who murdered my father?"

He mouthed words, but only air came out. He took one more breath, then went still.

She started CPR and continued the chest compressions until the paramedics arrived and pushed her back. Dilara stood to the side, crying silently. They worked to revive Sam, but it was a futile effort. They pronounced him dead at the scene. She made the obligatory statement to the airport police, including his baffling allegations, but for such an obvious heart attack, they shrugged it off as incoherent babbling. Dilara collected her backpack and walked in a daze toward the shuttle that would drop her off at her car in the long-term parking lot. Sam had been like an uncle to her, the only family she had left, and now he was gone.

As she sat in the shuttle bus, his words continued to ring in her ears. Whether they were the ravings of a demented elderly man or a warning from a close friend, she couldn't be sure. But she could think of only one way to check whether Sam's story had any truth to it.

She had to find Tyler Locke.

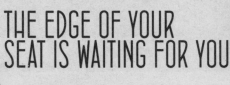